The Tree Trunk

A Story Of Life, Love, Family And Food

E. HAYDEN FREDERICKS JR

The Tree Trunk
Copyright 2025
All Rights Reserved

Disclaimer: This is a work of fiction. All names, places, events, and persons depicted are fictional and are the sole work of the author. Any resemblance to actual names, places, events or persons is purely coincidental and not intentional.

ISBN: 979-8-9999514-0-3

Acknowledgements

A hearty thanks to all who contributed ideas and advice. I would like to single out John and Darlene Borgerding for the many enjoyable evenings spent together, sharing a bottle of wine or a glass of Sambuca and discussing current and future chapters of this story. I couldn't ask for better friends and neighbors.

Prologue

Let's pretend. Let's pretend that somewhere in the southwest of France, there is a region where the land is vast and fertile. The sun warms the land during the day, and at night, moisture-laden breezes from the Atlantic Ocean cool and nourish.

Picture countryside perpetually green, with rolling hills, dotted with forests and streams, teeming with wild game and fish. Picture an area dominated by farms, worked by the same families, using the same methods, for generation after generation. They are hardy souls who believe the quality of a person can be seen in their eyes and felt in their handshake.

Now, imagine there is a small town, nothing much really, just barely enough to call it a town. There's a bank, of course, and a municipal building where the mayor resides, a petrol station and auto mechanic, an apothecary, a dry goods and feed store, and finally, at the far end of town, an inn and bistro.

The town never seems open; only the inn and bistro maintain regular hours. Proprietors of the other establishments open when called for, and most leave keys in convenient locations to save themselves from the trip into town.

The town is named Saint Charles en Liberte, the inn, The Inn at Saint Charles en Liberte, and the bistro have the unusual name *The Tree Trunk Bistro*. The inn and bistro have been owned and operated by the Villeneuve family since their ancestors built it back in the 1500's.

It is present day, and that is where our story begins.

Chapter 1

The bright red, three-car train meandered through the rural landscape as it followed tracks laid down nearly two centuries ago. It curved around large plots of cultivated farmland, idyllic villages, and the many small lakes and streams that dotted the French countryside. The train seemed to take its time, occasionally having to slow to a crawl to allow herds of cattle and sheep to clear the tracks ahead.

Michelle Villeneuve didn't mind. She was comfortable in the old but well-kept coach. The sounds the train made, a soothing hum from the electric motors, and the ever-present clickity-clack from the rails lulled her into a semi-conscious state where her dreams allowed her some reprieve from all her personal conflicts.

Every so often, when the train broke its rhythm, Michelle once more became aware of her surroundings, and the demons that taunted her would come back.

Did I fail? She again pestered herself, letting her insecurities take over. *Why am I returning? I told myself I would never, ever, ever return, yet here I am, after just five, well, if you count grad school, seven years, I'm coming back. I just said forget it and left the civilized world to come back here. Ha! Civilization, if you want to call it that.* She grinned and chastised herself.

And come back here to what? To farm animals, stinking sheep, cows, pigs and chickens? I should have seen a shrink. All my friends in New York and Boston went to shrinks. I should have gone too.

But I'm no quitter. I just felt like it was time to come home, and besides, all my friends went to shrinks because they just wanted to marry doctors. She closed her eyes and pleaded in the darkness, *Leave me be, oh please, leave me be, and let me go home.*

A tear gently formed in the corner of her eye. *Bad pollen this year.* She fumbled through her handbag for a tissue, knowing full well, the tear came from her heart. She felt emotionally drained. *Too many bad decisions, too much deceit, too much conceit, too much nothing, too much, too much, and not enough…something.* She paused for a moment and thought quietly. *Yes, that's really it. If only there was something.*

Michelle thought back to her social life and laughed at the absurdity of it. *How many times did I hear, hey, my roommate's gone this weekend, let's party!* She grimaced as she reminisced, *living in supposedly one of the greatest cities in America, and every guy I met, my glorious peers, just wanted to sit around a four hundred square foot apartment and drink themselves unconscious. How wonderful!*

She thought again about her education and her career. *The years in New York were meaningless and moving to Boston turned out to be pointless still; every day, the same dreary cubicle, the same long hours, and the same fudging of numbers to make it work. And for what reason? So, the deal could move forward?* She became agitated with herself. *Someone got rich, and for sure, it wasn't me.*

Again, she felt her inner self stressing and provoking her. *I have to relax.* She closed her eyes. *I have to let it out. I have to get it out.* On a whim, she opened her eyes and screamed as loud as she could. Not a high-pitched roller coaster scream but a deep guttural scream. A scream you would scream if thrown from the top of the Eiffel Tower.

She screamed until a calm enveloped her. *Oh God,* she thought, *John Lennon was right.* She remembered long ago listening to the Beatles and hearing John Lennon scream at the top of his lungs. In an interview, he attributed it to a type of primal therapy and suggested everyone should try it.

Michelle felt much better but still felt the need to cry. She had her head lowered while letting her tears flow when she felt a gentle tap on her shoulder and heard a deep, confident voice.

"Miss, may I assist you in some way?"

She looked up and saw the train conductor standing by her seat.

"Can I get you a cup of coffee, a beverage of some kind?" he asked politely.

The conductor was in the next car when he heard Michelle scream. Seeing there were only two other passengers on the whole train, and they were in the first coach, he couldn't imagine what the young woman in the last car was screaming about. Reluctantly, he made his way back to where

Michelle was sitting, hoping there was nothing to make this more than just another routine trip.

Michelle looked up, fully aware of the tears on her cheeks, her swollen eyes, and hair falling in every direction. Standing in front of her was this impeccably uniformed man, with shining brass buckles, leather straps, a smart-looking cap, and clean-shaven, except for a perfectly trimmed, big and bushy, dark black, handlebar moustache. She couldn't help herself, and in a slow, steady voice, she replied, "You are a very handsome man. Thank you for your kindness. I am fine, just a bit tired."

The conductor, taken aback for a moment by the young lady's admission, admitted to himself. *It's the uniform; women just love a man in uniform.* He was satisfied the situation was resolved, but before he turned away, he made a mental note to keep an eye on the young lady.

"Thank you for the compliment. I'll be in the next coach. Please don't hesitate to ask for assistance." He nodded, tipped his hat, and walked back to his post.

Michelle chuckled to herself while fixing her hair and smiled as she caught the conductor glancing at her over his shoulder as he exited the car. *Don't be such a flirt.* She scolded herself. *He really was handsome, though.* She wondered why she always found older men so handsome. *It's nice to see someone taking care of himself. His uniform was perfect, almost like in a fairytale. Maybe I am dreaming; maybe I am still back in Boston? Oh, please, no!* She chuckled and thought she would write a letter to the railway company, telling them what a fine employee they have.

As the train continued making its way, Michelle couldn't believe how well she now felt, how invigorated and energetic. *Self-therapy*, she thought, *I wonder if I just invented it?* But then again, she remembered John Lennon.

She gazed out through the large, perfectly clear window and marveled at the countryside passing by. She jokingly concluded, *I'm in a time machine with time traveling backward.*

When the train left Toulouse, it immediately headed out to the countryside. From the train, Michelle could see men with large machines, cutting rows of crops and dumping the produce in container trucks that followed. Cows were lined up with machines dumping their feed into large troughs. She even saw what must have been a poultry farm, with machines spraying grain all over the ground, feeding hundreds of chickens. Michelle watched as her train went by and wondered, *how good can those chickens' taste?*

By noon, the train had wandered far into the rural countryside. The large machines Michelle saw were now replaced by small, single tractors, and she could see men using their hands to spread grain for chickens and ducks.

Now, at almost 3 p.m., Michelle only occasionally saw tractors in the fields. More common were horses or oxen pulling plows. The roads were unpaved, and horse-drawn carts were a common sight, much more common than autos or trucks. *How can people live like this?* She pondered *How much they were supported by the government?*

She recalled a conversation she had with her mother. It was during her studies in Paris, and she was home for the holidays and winter break. Mother had just received word from the bank that subsidy payments for the first quarter were in, and the bank reported subsidies had increased seven percent. Mother was satisfied, but Uncle Pierre was irate. He wanted at least twelve percent. It wasn't easy living as they were, she remembered him saying.

The inn and most of the farmers around Saint Charles were recipients of annual Government Grants given to citizens who maintained historical authenticity in their businesses and daily lives. Michelle never really understood the purpose of the payments, and after her first year at university, thought the government handouts ridiculous. Now she appreciated more the concept of culture and thought it justifiable, the government preserving and fostering an appreciation for the French way of life.

I am proud to be a French citizen, born and raised here. She said to herself in a stern voice. She recalled wanting to be an American, but she remembered waking up one day and realizing, Why *be an American? I don't need to renounce my citizenship just to get away. I am French; I am proud to be French; I am proud of my country and what it has to offer. I am French and will always be French.* She said again to herself, in a defiant tone, daring someone to disagree.

Michelle thought about culture and her family's business. Mother had married into the Villeneuve family, marrying her father, the eldest of three sons. The family could trace their roots back centuries. Her ancestors founded the town, named it Saint Charles en Liberte', called Saint Charles by locals, and built the inn. Later the bistro was added after travelers, seeking refuge, overwhelmed the tiny kitchen the family ran. When building the addition to the inn that was to be the bistro, a large tree trunk was used to support the entranceway, hence the name *Tree Trunk Bistro.*

The inn has been home to the Villeneuve family for generations and the few inn and bistro workers not local to Saint Charles for as long as Michelle could remember. *When she left for studies in Paris, almost ten years ago, there were only four rooms available for travelers, and many times, the rooms were given to local farmers who had overstayed and were now so drunk, mother was afraid to let them drive home.* Even though the inn had a primarily local clientele, the rooms were kept quaint, comfortable, and spotless. There were telephones, but no televisions or internet. Mother liked it that way, and the government, in order to warrant historic subsidies, insisted it stay that way.

No one ever seemed to travel to her village; at least she couldn't remember the last time the inn had other than local guests. Michelle grinned. She couldn't remember a time, ever, when strangers were staying at the inn. *Isn't that ridiculous? 27 years old, and I can't remember a time when visitors from outside the province stayed as guests at the inn! That's absurd. Why are we in business?*

She recalled teachings from her business education in America. *If an investment is inefficient, liquidate it and deploy the capital elsewhere to earn appropriate returns. We are the epitome of inefficiency. We couldn't survive on our own. If it weren't for government subsidies, we'd be broke and out of business,* she said curtly.

Maybe we should shut down? She began contemplating possibilities. *Mother has been managing the business ever since Father went off to be a troubleshooter for the Diplomatic Corps. She should retire. Maybe move to Florida. There are probably French-speaking areas of Florida.* Michelle just let her imagination wander, but she soon stopped herself; *fat chance, Mother wouldn't go to Bordeaux to get her hair done or even shopping in Paris, let alone Florida, USA.* Michelle frowned as she pondered the reasons. *I think she thinks she owes it to Papa. He's been gone, what, sixteen years now, but still, she remains married to him and loyal.*

Michelle began to feel emotional as she remembered her father. She remembered sitting on his lap for the last time and asking why he had to go. She remembered his warm, loving smile and his reply. "Because the people of France need me. I must go and help our country." *He was such a handsome, elegant man,* she thought. *No wonder Mother stood by him; how could a woman not? A man like Papa only comes around once in a lifetime.* She understood her mother; she lowered her head and closed her eyes. She understood.

Michelle went back to staring out the window, not really looking at anything. A bump in the railroad tracks brought her back into focus. *Back to business,* she said to herself. *If we are to stay in business, we must stand on our own. We cannot rely on subsidies or welfare to be solvent.* Michelle practiced what she was going to say when family talk eventually came around to the topic of business. *We either run a business properly, or we retire. I don't want to spend the rest of my life running a country club for dirty, illiterate farmers.* She smiled and thought the last part was a bit more forceful than it needed to be. *Besides,* letting her sense of humor take over, *farmers are not always dirty.*

She smiled and thought a person would have their head removed for voicing that opinion. She continued with her thoughts, *how to get people to visit? How about an art fair? No, we couldn't compete with Paris. Maybe organize a farmer's market? No, who would drive way out here for a sack of potatoes? What can we do?* In a satirical tone, she announced to herself, *I know, we could resort to public executions. We could build a guillotine, and that would keep it historical.* She smirked at her last idea; with her opinions, she would be the first one executed. Staring out the window, she continued her daydreams. *We have to be inventive. We have a good product, with a bit of work, well, a lot of work, it could be a great product. How to get your product known?*

What we need is a real 3-star chef. One of those celebrity chefs. We could have a cooking show every week, filmed right there at the inn. We could call it Inn Cuisine. Brilliant. She complimented herself on her clever double entendre. *We'd make a boatful, what with product endorsements, maybe even our own brand of cookware.*

Michelle's confidence grew by the minute. *We could even close during the week and only open on weekends.* Once again, she recited from her business education, *reducing supply increases demand, and increased demand results in higher prices.* Michelle pulled out her notepad and made a few entries; she didn't want to lose this idea.

She then thought about her Uncle Daniel, who took over the kitchen when Dad left. Daniel is Dad's youngest brother. *Uncle Daniel is such a sweet man, but just, just…crazy,* she lamented.

"Daniel is brilliant in the kitchen; you just have to understand him and learn to control him." She remembered her mother saying.

That's certainly true. She thought back to the time Daniel went missing for the day, finally returning mid-way into dinner service, smiling broadly, and carrying two large hogs' heads under his arms, freshly severed. He announced to the dining room, "Tonight's special, braised pig's cheeks!"

She laughed, remembering the dining room roaring with applause and everyone ordering more wine, appetizers, and pig's cheeks. *They were very good* too! She recalled fondly. *Braised in a young burgundy. But his first course, what a surprise, pig brain consommé with black truffle.* She started to feel a distinct yearning for food. *Very delicate and so delicious, Mother even asked for a second portion, telling him to write down the recipe, which of course, he didn't.* She reminisced with a sigh. *Yes, Uncle Daniel,* being careful with her words, *is a bit loose upstairs. But he is brilliant in the kitchen.*

She erased the entry in her notepad, deciding it would be better to change the inn's name. *Maybe we should change the name to something like, "The Inn at the River Bernadin"* She pondered. She liked the rhythm of her new name, *"The Inn at the River Bernadin".* She said, repeating it over and over, in a singsong manner. *The one problem, of course,* she finally concluded, *there was no River Bernadin.*

If this were America, we'd build a river. People would figure it out and truck in all the water we needed. Then we'd hire a marketing firm to develop a history for it. Even have fake antique pictures of men on rafts with giant poles floating down the river. She smiled at her insight into American culture and contemplated, *I wonder how much it would cost to have a river built?*

The train continued into the late afternoon, giving Michelle enough time to decide that the name "Tree Trunk Bistro" was ultimately the issue. She was confident; once the name was changed, nobility from everywhere would cue up for a table at the bistro and a night or two stay at the inn.

Chapter 2

Maria Villeneuve, Michelle's mother, lay in bed and rolled over again, shielding her eyes, trying to avoid that one pesky ray of morning sunshine. Not quite fully awake, she managed to sit up when she heard the clank, clank, clank of the antique elevator struggling to reach the top floor of the inn. When the horrible noise stopped, she heard the gate open and Pierre Villeneuve's familiar voice, "Hello, Good Morning, Madam. I have coffee and croissants; may I come in?"

Pierre was the second son of the Villeneuve family. He was living in Paris, mostly playing cards and other games of chance, being, as he would say, "A regular scoundrel, up to no good," when news arrived of his older brother's death. He immediately came to the aid of the family and has been remarkably loyal and helpful, especially to Maria. He openly admits that coming back to Saint Charles probably saved his life, given his direction and the company he kept.

"Good morning, Pierre, yes, of course, come, I am decent except for this horrible mess I call a hairdo," she replied as she did many times before when Pierre would bring her breakfast. "So, what is on the schedule for today? Anything exciting?" She tempted Pierre, knowing full well he was as excited as she was that Michelle was coming.

"The day has finally arrived. Your little girl and the second most charming lady in all of France will be arriving this evening." Pierre boasted, giving Maria an obvious wink.

"Pierre, you are as charming as they come. Where does all this goodness and charm come from? Have you found some magic root or pill of some kind?" Maria was amazed at how energetic and full of life he always seemed to be.

Pierre smiled that big smile of his, accented by his thin black Corsican mustache. He adeptly added two spoons of sugar to a cup, poured in the pitch-black elixir, and handed it to Maria.

"Thank you, my kind brother," she responded. "You certainly know what a person needs in the morning to get going. What time will you leave to meet her?" she asked in a casual tone.

Pierre didn't miss a beat. "The train is scheduled to arrive at approximately 7 p.m., so my best guess is it will pull in about 8 p.m. I will depart at about 6 p.m. I don't mind arriving a bit early. Besides, I want to be there when she arrives so I can help her with her luggage."

"Good," Maria replied in between sips of her coffee. "Did you make this coffee? My goodness, it's so good." Maria took another sip.

Pierre smiled again. Maria was always so appreciative of the little things he did for her. "Try a croissant. There's also fresh strawberry jam in the basket."

Maria reached inside the small basket on the coffee tray and pulled out a croissant. "Oh Pierre, they are still warm; how wonderful." Maria sighed with satisfaction. "Thank you, Pierre; you're a good man."

Pierre nodded and made for the rickety elevator. He pulled open the gate, and replied, "Thank you, Madam. I must go now. I must ready the dining room for the lunch crowd."

She smiled and nodded back. *The lunch crowd…hardly a crowd. There will be the mayor, the bank manager and clerk, a couple of municipal workers, and a half-dozen or so farmers. The farmers, as usual, will come in late and stay through dinner.* She made a note to ensure the rooms have been cleaned and beds made with fresh linens. *There will probably be guests tonight,* she concluded.

Maria got herself out of bed, took a quick shower, and put on her work clothes. She had been working on Michelle's room since she called and gave her the news.

Maria had selected her oldest son Roger's old room to be Michelle's. It was a large room on the third floor. It had beautiful views of the countryside and, facing east, received wonderful, warm morning sun. She made sure there was fresh paint, windows cleaned, and had the old wooden plank floors cleaned and polished. She even ordered Michelle a new mattress.

Today, she wanted to work on the washroom. *Give it a good scrubbing,* she thought as she stopped at the third-floor maid's pantry and gathered the required cleaning tools.

The washroom was a good size, the second largest in the Inn, next to Maria's. It was decidedly retro, but not on purpose. It had been installed early on when running water was introduced and renovated later when the large steam boilers in the basement were installed, and hot water pipes were run through the walls. She decided it was a very romantic washroom, with a large antique, claw-foot tub and a very feminine set of pink and yellow curtains that were a nice contrast to the stark black and white tiles.

Maria got down on her hands and knees to scrub the old tiles. *They don't make tiles like this anymore,* she said to herself as she marveled at how brightly they shone after applying a little bleach and elbow grease. She scrubbed everything in sight, then stood and took a step back to admire her work. The tile sparkled, making the room much brighter than she remembered. *Indeed, suitable for a young lady.* She complimented herself on her cleaning prowess and her choice of rooms.

Maria turned around to leave, but not before pausing a moment to survey the bedroom. It once belonged to Roger, Maria's eldest child. It had been kept just as he left it when he went off to university, but then decided to accept a commission in the Army. *He was so much like his father; he couldn't sit for a moment, always on the go and always wanting to be part of something. He needed purpose,* Maria lamented; the full emotional impact of never seeing her son again caused her shoulders to droop and tears to fill her eyes. *Oh no, I've been through this. I must be strong. As a mother, I must accept the fate of my children. Life must go on; we must be content with our memories and the choices our children make,* she once again reminded herself and regained her composure.

After receiving his commission, Roger volunteered for commando school and, a year later, was sent to Africa. He was killed while assisting in the evacuation of citizens from some French colonial province in Africa. Which one, she couldn't remember. He is buried in the military cemetery outside of Paris.

Maria was putting away the cleaning supplies when she heard Daniel's door open.

"Good morning, Maria. Are you finished with Michelle's room?" Daniel popped his head into the room. "Ah! I love the smell of clean," Daniel stated as he took a highly audible sniff of the air. "Clean and fresh paint, and the sun, it feels so good on one's face. This is one of the better rooms. I like that it faces the sunrise. Morning sun is good, motivating. Can I help you with anything?" He walked over to the closet, took the cleaning utensils from Maria, and put them away.

"Thank you, Daniel," Maria offered, "You're up early this morning. Have you something planned?"

Daniel smiled, "I will make a cake for tonight, something unusual. Do you think she still favors strawberries and chocolate?"

"Who doesn't?" Maria smiled, thinking *maybe I'll break for a little snack*.

"Yes, especially covered with buttercream," he added with a big grin. "But first, I have a notion of where I can find truffles."

"Oh really?" Maria said.

Maria, more attentive now, let Daniel continue, "Yes, down by the marsh, near Henri Tremont's place, where he keeps his horses. Do not mention this to anybody, but the conditions there are perfect for truffles. Moist, warm but not too much sun, large oak trees with many roots; I wouldn't be surprised to find some the size of melons." Daniel was visibly excited as he described his hunt for the rare and elusive tasty fungi growing wild in the forest.

"Well, I hope you're successful. Good luck," Maria replied as Daniel turned and walked down the narrow rear staircase. Maria started thinking about how wonderful truffles made any dish, changing her mind and now contemplating having brunch of creamed eggs with just a few small shavings of truffle. *Yes, Daniel will be successful,* she thought to herself. *As crazy as it sounds, digging around in the muck, he'll probably find Solomon's Lost Mine of Truffles.* She smiled at her humor and headed downstairs to the family kitchen.

Maria liked to use the back stairs to travel up and down the three main floors of the Inn. "Much quicker than the lift, plus I get a little exercise," she would always say. The fourth floor was the master suite and was only accessible by elevator. Villeneuve's great-grandfather had the attic converted into a master suite for his son when he married. The suite was passed down to his eldest, Roger, who married Maria. She has called it home since she married Roger forty years ago this spring.

As she came down the winding stairs into the kitchen, she could smell the exotic smells of the Far East. She could smell cumin, curry, cinnamon, and a hint of clove. *How wonderful,* she thought as her hunger pains intensified. "What are you making that smells so marvelous, my dear?" she asked of the young man standing by the stove, hoping he had made enough for two. "And shouldn't you be sitting down?"

"I have the rest of my life to sit down. If I want to be the sous chef, if I someday want to take Daniel's place and be head chef, I need to stand. So, for now, I will stand; just don't ask me to move." The young man smiled as he turned his head to face Maria, one hand holding on to the stove, slowly stirring the pot with his other. Maria could see he was trembling a bit as he used his knee to brace himself.

"Well, don't hurt yourself to make a point," Maria admonished. "You're as stubborn as a Villeneuve and twice as intense. Now, what is it that you have cooked up?" she added playfully to remove the tension from the air. "It smells absolutely delicious."

"Just a little something I learned to fix while in Kathmandu. It's curry gravy. It's typically poured over a fried doughy egg batter called *Pratha*. I don't know what its official name is. Everyone I knew, including locals, called it gravy, mutton gravy, but I didn't add any mutton. I'm going to have it with scrambled eggs." The young man continued. "Can I get you a plate?" he asked Maria.

Maria was happy, he asked. "Yes, of course. You stay by the stove, and I'll grab some plates. Shall I pour us water?" she added, reaching for the plates and grabbing a couple of glasses. "

The young man replied, "No, not necessary; I also made chai, authentic Nepalese chai. Wait until you try it. You'll fall in love with it."

"That good?" Maria quizzed, but she didn't care at this point. She was so hungry.

As they sat and savored the meal, she thought, *how incredibly flavorful yet simple*. She remarked to the young man as if he knew her thoughts, "That's what good food should be all about, simple but full of flavor." Maria looked across at the handsome young man, who didn't respond to her remarks but just kept eating.

He went by the name Rudy. Her husband had brought him home one day when the boy was only nine. His parents were diplomats, killed by a terrorist bomb in Lebanon. He has stayed with the Villeneuve family ever since.

Rudy was a brilliant, talented young man who did well in university. However, when he graduated, he didn't take to the business environment and disliked the confines of office work. He would rather be out backpacking in Kathmandu or scuba diving on the Great Barrier Reef, both of which he had regularly enjoyed.

His recent passion was bicycle racing. But while racing through the Alps in the Swiss Invitational, he had failed to navigate a turn and crashed. He suffered major nerve damage to his legs, and his spinal cord was almost cut. With his spine so fragile now, doctors recommend he not stand or place pressure on it.

"You enjoy cooking and being around people, don't you?" She attempted again to engage the young man.

He looked back at her steadily. "I am fascinated by flavors. Flavors created by the simple chemical composition of ingredients interacting, bringing out new flavors, flavors you never knew existed. It's like abstract math; one and one equals three. I am intrigued by the colors and the textures of ingredients and how they're affected by preparation, but I am also challenged by presentation, how a plate should be arranged, so it's not crowded, not sparse, yet pleasing to the eye. Daniel said to me once, 'People eat with their eyes.' I thought that was particularly good advice." Rudy's facial expression remained stoic, but his eyes flared with intensity.

Maria smiled, wondering if he was really this intense or just used it for show. "I like that; one and one is three. That should be our new family motto. What do you think?" Maria tried to keep the conversation casual.

"Yes, it's good. It means a lot of things, we do more with less, or we take chaos and come out ahead," Rudy said, much more relaxed now.

Maria added, "Much more the latter than the former." Rudy chuckled, "Yes, you are right, this place is chaotic at times, but we always come out alright."

Just then, Daniel came marching through the kitchen, sounding like a Clydesdale horse, wearing large, cumbersome, waist-high boots. Over his shoulder, he carried a rake, a shovel, and a burlap sack. "Well, I'm off," he proudly announced.

"Going truffle hunting again?" Rudy asked more as a statement than a question.

Daniel abruptly stopped. Surprised, he glanced at Rudy, then Maria, and back at Rudy. "How do you know? "He looked back to Maria, "Did you say something?"

Maria returned Daniel's indignant look, obviously offended by his accusation. "Of course not. I would never divulge something said to me in confidence."

Annoyed, Daniel turned to go out the door, "There are no secrets in this place. Please don't follow me. Good day." And out he went, closing the door behind him, rather forcibly.

There was a moment of silence. Maria, unable to hold in her laughter, started with a slight snicker. Rudy joined with a throaty half-gurgle, half-laughing sound. Soon, the contagion spread, and both were openly laughing. Rudy straightened up enough to add, "I bet he is going down to the marsh near Tremont's horse stables."

Hearing this refueled Maria's laughter. In between attempts to catch her breath, she managed to get out, "He is!"

Hearing Maria's reply, Rudy added, "He has been searching that area for months. He swears truffles are there. It's as if a mysterious, magical pig told him where to dig." The vision of Daniel discussing where to dig for truffles with a pig was too much, causing the two of them to roll with laughter. Rudy finally added, "And since he can't find any, he thinks the pig is holding out, not giving him all that he knows."

"The pig should be warned about Daniel's penchant for pig's cheeks," Maria said in between gasps for air.

The two laughed until tears were streaming down their cheeks and their bellies ached. "Oh Daniel, I love him so." Maria finally opined and continued, being more candid than she intended. "Every family needs a Daniel, someone who just doesn't see black and white."

Rudy, looking serious again, said soberly, "If sanity is black and white, Daniel is a whole host of colors. He is our very own rainbow."

Maria laughed again but quickly regained control. "Yes, he is our rainbow; he is a beautiful rainbow." She didn't want to leave the conversation disparaging a family member. "We are all different, we all have our little quirks. It is what gives our family its personality. You must admit, life would not be so, so…". she looked for the right word and satisfied she'd found it, finished her thought, "entertaining if it weren't for Daniel, or Pierre, Michelle, or you."

Rudy, who had gone back to finishing his eggs with gravy, stopped for a moment. "Yes, you are right; I apologize, it would be very boring if we were all perfect."

Chapter 3

I t was almost 8 p.m. by the time Michelle's train pulled into the Saint Germaine station. Michelle was more than ready to debark after spending her entire day on the train. She had been seated on the train for so long; as she climbed down the stairs, she momentarily lost control over her legs. Sensing all was not right with the woman, the conductor caught her and lifted her firmly under her arm, allowing her feet to come down gently on the station platform.

Michelle, always wanting to be clever and sensing an opportunity, regained her balance, quickly turned, and quipped, "Ah terra firma," but to her embarrassment, no one was there. *Such a good line too,* she thought, *oh, well, maybe next time,* shrugging it off.

The conductor reappeared with her luggage, disappeared, and reappeared once again with the rest of it, placing her bags neatly at her feet. "How efficient. You've done this before," she said smartly, trying to engage the conductor in a little banter.

She went to give the man a tip, but he refused, holding up his hand. "It is not necessary and not the policy of the railroad to accept gratuities. Please, Madam, it was my pleasure." With that, the train whistle sounded, and the hum of the train's electric motors grew louder as the train began to move. The conductor stepped onto the metal stairs and waved as the train disappeared into the night.

Now that was a classy man. Michelle thought matter-of-factly, still not fully in command of her legs or her balance. *They don't make them like that anymore. I bet he'd make a great husband and father, too.* She smiled as she bent down to grab her bags. *What am I thinking? Good heavens, Michelle. Get a hold of yourself.* She smiled as she gathered her luggage. *What did my friends use to call it, oh yea, my biological clock. My clock is ticking.* She grinned at the absurdity of the concept. *A woman's biological clock, who thinks of these things?* Then continued with more pleasant thoughts; h*e was indeed a handsome man.*

Michelle looked around and realized she was alone on the barely lit station platform, except for what looked like a man in a long overcoat at the far end of the platform. *How cliché, is he a mugger, a pervert, or what?* She thought, feeling only slightly alarmed. *If this were New York, I'd be on my guard and have my pepper spray out and ready.* She then started to think, looking around at the desolate platform, *I wish I had it with me,* when she heard a familiar voice, a man's voice, coming from far down the platform, "Michelle, is that you, Michelle?"

Pierre had spent the idle moments waiting for the train at the local bistro. He had bumped into some distant friends of friends and enjoyed discussing vintages of wine, approximately where the best sardines originate, and other matters of great importance and national pride. A discussion he enjoyed with more than one glass of cognac, and, to that extent, became completely engrossed in the debate, forgetting about Michelle and her train. It wasn't till the house matron announced the pending departure of the evening train that he remembered.

He reached the station just as the train was departing. *Good lord,* he thought, *I hope she remembered to get off.* Looking down the platform, in the dim light, he could see someone's silhouette, someone standing alone with luggage. He called out.

"Yes, it's me," Michelle answered. "Is that you, Pierre?" She spoke loudly so he would hear.

"Yes, my dear." Pierre quickly walked down the platform and when he was just a few feet from her, he held out his arms. "Welcome home, my darling. Welcome home. It has been too long." He wrapped his arms around his niece and hugged her while kissing her on the cheek, as any Frenchman and Uncle would do.

Michelle giggled from the attention, noted the distinct aroma of cognac mixed with cigarettes, and hugged him back, giving him a brief kiss on the cheek in return and hugging him again. "It's good to be back, Uncle; you don't know how good it is to be back."

Pierre let go and looked her straight in the eye. With a serious look on his face, he scolded her. "You should not be gone for so long. In fact, from now on, you should not go at all, you stay, you stay here with us." He sounded like he was scolding a young child or puppy, "We need you; your mother needs you, more importantly, we want you to be part of the family again, not an infrequent visitor." He winked and smiled a smile that seemed to reach from ear to ear.

That was what Michelle hoped to hear. It was the *something* that was missing from her life ever since she went to America. She slowly put her arms around Pierre and hugged him firmly. Between her soft sobs and tears, she spoke softly and deliberately, "Oh uncle, I saw the world. It is cold and heartless. It is not that exciting. I realize now true happiness is most important; it comes from family, and I missed my family so much. Forgive me, Uncle; I'll never do it again. "

Pierre took a step back and eagerly replied, "Nothing to forgive; everybody needs their opportunity. I'd be disappointed if you didn't run away, and so would you." He reached down and picked up the two largest suitcases. "Come, the auto is in the lot on the other side of the station." Michelle reached down, picked up the two smaller bags, and walked briskly behind Pierre.

The only car in the lot was Pierre's bright yellow 1964 Citroen Coupe. "Oh my god." Michelle laughed sarcastically, "You still have this?" She remembered the problems the car gave him years and years ago. *What must it drive like now?* she wondered.

Pierre managed to get all four suitcases into the car, and after wrangling and pushing, managed to get the passenger door open. Michelle climbed in and marveled at the outdated opulence of the interior of the vehicle. The seats were large, made of leather with switches on the side, allowing a person to make many different adjustments. Michelle tried all the buttons, pushing forward and then backward. She heard a whirring sound but wasn't sure anything happened. "Well, the seats are very comfortable," she said, complimenting Pierre, "and plenty of legroom. Maybe as old as it is, it is worth keeping."

She changed her mind once Pierre backed out of the lot and scooted down an alley to the main road. "A shortcut." He announced.

Michelle had no idea what Pierre felt behind the wheel, but to her, she was pretty sure the car had wheels of gelatin. Every bump in the road forced the car to move a bit sideways at first, then up and down and up and down, in slowly reducing gyrations. As soon as the car seemed to settle down, another bump came along, and the gyrations started all over again.

But Michelle was amused by the car's ride. She looked at Pierre, who winked back at her. "I have the suspension set for comfort. Would you like a sportier ride?" he asked as if trying to impress her.

She playfully replied, as if impressed, "Yes, why not, let's have some real excitement; let's go with a sporty ride."

Pierre flipped a lever, then hit a button. The car immediately settled down, and now every bump in the road became a loud, jarring bang. It reminded Michelle of war movies when large planes would bounce around in the sky when attacked from the ground by cannon fire. Michelle managed to smile but quietly thought, *I will need dental work after this.*

It took some time traveling the old roads leading to Saint Charles en Liberte. Towards 10 p.m., they finally pulled up in front of the Inn. Michelle sat there gazing up at the Inn, with its lovely, time-worn stone façade and what seemed like just the right amount of ivy spilling down from the second floor. A short distance away was the main entrance to the Bistro, with a small tree trunk sitting outside for emphasis.

It's gorgeous, much prettier than I remembered, she thought while getting herself together and using her shoulder to push the car door open.

Pierre had come around the car and helped pull the passenger door open. He gathered Michelle's luggage from the back seat. "Well, what do you think? Some automobile, eh? A classic. No? Citroens are built to last forever. This auto will be here long after I am past," Pierre boasted.

Michelle simply nodded, "Thank you, Uncle, for picking me up and for the sporty ride."

Pierre struggled to open the door to the Inn while carrying Michelle's two large suitcases, and she wasn't quite sure if he heard her. She rushed over and held the door open, allowing Pierre to stumble into the lobby of the Inn. She followed, seeing for the first time in years, her mother, standing behind the Inn's registration desk, Daniel, her other uncle, stood in front of the desk, sipping a large snifter of cognac.

Michelle stood there taking it all in: the lobby, the dining room beyond, the warm smell of home, a smell she remembered fondly. Maria came out from behind the desk. She was dressed in an elegant dark blue dress with a blood-red rose on her lapel. Her bright blue eyes glowed, accenting her sandy grey hair, neatly layered up in a bun. Michele thought she had never seen her mother look so beautiful.

Maria spoke, so happy to see her daughter, "Welcome home, child. We missed you."

Caught up in the moment's emotions, Michelle burst into tears, ran over to her mother, and collapsed into her arms. "Oh, Mother, you don't know how wonderful it feels to be home."

Sensing the emotional needs of her child, she said in a soft, warm, loving voice, "We are so happy you are home. We missed you. You are safe now, my darling, you are safe and with family." She softly stroked the back of Michelle's head, trying to bring comfort to her child.

Hearing her mother's words made Michelle sob even louder, allowing all her pent-up emotion to spill out. Michelle lifted her head, "I'm sorry, Mother. I'm ruining your dress." There was a large, visible wet spot on Maria's shoulder where Michelle had lain her head.

"You need not worry, child," Maria said, smiling and comforting her daughter.

Michelle turned to Daniel, "Uncle Daniel, I'm sorry, I have ignored you." She left Maria's arms and walked over to Daniel with her arms open.

Daniel took her in his arms, gave her a warm hug, and told her, "I know, I am standing here wondering, *what am I, fish stew?*" Daniel, attempting to be clever, inaccurately recalled a scene from an American gangster movie he once watched.

Michelle corrected him, "No, that's chopped liver, the saying is 'What am I, chopped liver?'"

Daniel looked down at her with an inquisitive look on his face, "What is chopped liver? I don't understand chopped liver?"

Michelle tried to clarify the confusion. "Pate', Daniel, chopped liver, think of it as pate."

Daniel, looking even more confused, "Pate? What am I pate'? That doesn't seem correct; I like pate, I would not ignore pate. A good pate is like, like, very satisfying."

Maria, fearing they would be there all night arguing whether pate was a suitable metaphor for chopped liver, quickly cut in. "Well, let's all have some cake and a cognac. Then I'm sure Michelle would enjoy a hot bath and a good night's sleep."

The Villeneuve family moved into the dining room, mother and daughter, arm in arm, and came to a table lit with candles. A stack of plates sat next to a large buttercream cake, adorned with chocolate-covered strawberries.

Daniel's voice could be heard in the background, "Would you prefer pate? I have an excellent pate I made just yesterday, with goose, pork, you know for the fat, cognac, and black truffle. It's excellent on a piece of buttered bread, toasted, of course."

Michelle chuckled and said to no one in particular, "It's good to be home."

The cognac flowed freely, as did the laughter. The family reminisced and told stories, not always complimentary, of years and memories gone by. Michelle couldn't help thinking how lucky she was to have the memories and loved ones to share them with. When fatigue finally set in and Michelle could hardly keep her eyes open, partly because she had been up traveling for what seemed like days, but mostly because Daniel kept filling her glass, Maria announced the party was over.

"Let's adjourn, and everyone get some rest. The hospitality business offers no days of rest and, though Michelle is back, and I am sure eager to participate, we all must wake early and attend to our duties."

The men let the ladies go up first in the small antique elevator. "I have given you Roger's old room, but first, come to my room for a moment," Maria said casually to Michelle.

"Ok," she replied, half asleep.

The elevator groaned from the weight of the two women. "The government will not let us modernize it." Maria spoke of the elevator, "In fact, they remind us they should never have permitted us to install it in the first place." She frowned, "But I have Rudy working on a plan to modernize it while maintaining its antique look. But that's very hush-hush."

"Good idea," Michelle made the obligatory response, trying to keep her eyes open.

Once in the master suite, Maria beckoned Michelle to sit down, which she did obediently on the small settee by Maria's make-up table. Maria began, "Over the next few days, I want you to look around and see where you fit in. By far, we are not a well-oiled machine, but everyone has their niche, everyone has their own little corner. Daniel is brilliant in the kitchen, though he will have you biting your nails frequently; Rudy, darling Rudy, despite his misfortune, wants to be the Sous Chef, and in a way is the perfect complement to Daniel. But it will be a challenge to get them to work together."

Hearing Maria's view of the two men made Michelle chuckle a bit. But she knew it was an accurate observation. Daniel is crazy and has no structure to his thoughts, while Rudy is mathematical and, at times, far too analytical. "That's so true, mother," she said, agreeing with her mother's insight.

Maria continued, "Pierre is the social butterfly; he wants to know everyone and their business, so let him run the dining room, let him stay Maitre'd. I want you to think about this because it will be your responsibility to carry on the family business before too long. So, we must get you ready. You must find a job, while at the same time, you must learn everyone's job, including mine." Seeing Michelle's eyes gloss over, Maria concluded, "Now go to bed. You've had a long day."

"Yes, mother. I am absolutely finished. 'Running on empty,' as they say." Michelle got up, waited for the elevator, gave one last hug to her mother, said goodnight, and descended one floor, stopping at the third floor.

She opened the door to her room, turned on the lights, and went in. It made her happy and sad. It was a beautiful room, large by Inn standards, with a big comfy-looking bed. She could see the bath's sparkling black and white tiles and pretty curtains, but the room also reminded her of Roger, her older brother. *Rest in peace, my wonderful brother. May God's grace be with you,* she said to herself while, for some reason, glancing upwards.

She walked over to the bed, frowning as she remembered her suitcases were still in the lobby. She spotted a lovely, light pink silk nightgown folded at the foot of the bed. *Oh, Mother, you shouldn't have.* After a quick wash, she slipped on the gown and crawled into bed. She fell off to sleep before she could finish her last thought.

Chapter 4

Michelle woke, feeling the pain in her joints, the stiff pain a person gets from sitting for so long. She lay in bed, relaxing, feeling warm and cozy, a thick goose feather comforter pulled up to her chin, not wanting to do much of anything except lie there. She didn't know the time, she didn't care really, when a knock came at her door.

"Hello, my long-lost, adventurous cousin," a young man's voice sang out. "I hope sleeping till noon is not a new habit you picked up while abroad," the voice continued.

Michelle immediately recognized the voice and played along, letting out a loud moan, "Oh, god. Is it noon?"

"May I come in?" the young man's voice called out.

"If you promise to mind your manners and act like a gentleman," Michelle countered in a stern voice, somewhat diluted by a lazy yawn.

"Never!" The door swung open. "That would take all the fun out of life." Rudy came through the door in his wheelchair, a specialized wheelchair that bore a strong resemblance to a unicycle with training wheels. It allowed him to maneuver adeptly and to sit upright. Rudy had it specially made after seeing similar wheelchairs used by athletes in the Special Olympics.

Michelle leaned over and gave him a big hug and a kiss on the cheek. "We missed you last night. We stayed up till the wee hours, telling stories and being silly," Michelle added.

"Yea, sorry. I wanted to wait for you, but I had to take my pills, and they just put me right out. But it's sure good to see you, good to have you back," Rudy replied.

Michelle took the opportunity to ask a few questions, questions she didn't know if she should ask: "Are you in pain?"

Rudy looked at her solemnly. "Only when I think about what I could be doing. Then it hurts. Sometimes I wonder, why me? I was showing promise, chalking up some world-class times. Then this." Rudy gestured to his chair and his semi-responsive legs.

"But I'll recover. Most of the medication I take is simply for swelling. The doctors don't want my back muscles to swell and push against my spinal cord." Rudy continued without emotion. "If I'm not careful, I could lose what little feeling I have left in my legs."

Tears welled up in Michelle's eyes. "Oh, Rudy, I am so sorry."

"Don't be," Rudy chimed in, cutting through Michelle's emotions. "I believe in Karma. I believe we influence our lives in many ways and believe there are forces in the Universe so advanced that we humans can't even comprehend their potency or purpose. So, don't say you're sorry, be positive, say 'I believe in you,' or better yet, say 'my money is on the guy with the wheels." With that, Rudy twirled his wheelchair, stopping after half a dozen spins once again facing Michelle's bed, his arms outstretched and reaching for her.

Michelle was amazed at Rudy's vigor. She couldn't believe how positive and upbeat he was and how positive he made her feel. She reached out and hugged him as hard as she could. As she did, she thought to herself. *What did I expect? He would turn into a recluse, bitter, and mean? No, not Rudy. This is the same Rudy I grew up with, such a passion for life, confident, invincible.* "It's so good to see you," she said while holding on tightly.

As Rudy and Michelle embraced, the silence was broken by a brief knock and an accompanying voice. "Rudy, I hate to interfere with your moment, but we have lunch to serve," Daniel said, standing at the door, holding his apron and feeling as awkward as he had ever felt.

Rudy slowly let go, as did Michelle, but both lingered just a moment too long, Rudy finally saying, "Come down to lunch when you are ready." "Michelle, feeling very flush, could barely talk but managed to whisper, "I will."

Rudy closed Michelle's door as he left, but soon another knock came. "Hello, hello, this is Andre from reception. I have your luggage," an even younger man's voice shouted. Michelle quickly got out of bed and found a robe hanging in the bathroom. The knock came again, "Hello, hello." Michelle opened the door, catching the young man in mid-sentence.

"Hello, Andre. I'm Michelle. Please put the suitcases by the window," Michelle said casually.

Andre placed all four suitcases neatly by the window, then stood straight up, adjusted his waistcoat, and asked, "Is there anything else I can do for you?"

Michelle started to walk into the bathroom, but noticed Andre was still standing there by the suitcases. "No, thank you," she said with a quizzical tone, again noticing Andre was not moving. She chuckled, realizing what she had missed, then grabbed her purse, walked over to Andre, and quietly spoke, "Thank you for your service," and placed two one-euro bills in his hand.

Andre politely replied, "You are very welcome. Please call reception if you have any further needs." He sprinted out of her room. Michelle smiled slyly, "Looking for a tip, even in my own place. We will have to think about that."

Michelle had finished bathing, was dressed, and had just finished combing out her hair when another knock came at her door. "Boy, looks like I am Central Station this morning," she thought. "Come in, please; it's unlocked."

Andre shyly shuffled into the room and held out his hand. In it were two one-euro bills. "My apologies Miss Villeneuve, I did not know. Today is my first day back. I have been helping my grandfather, and today is my first day in over a month. I am sorry I did not know." The young man kept stammering, hoping something he said would prove his innocence.

Michelle smiled at the embarrassed young man. "There is no need for apologies. I understand completely; it is a custom. I spent the last seven years in America, and there, nothing gets done without a little something extra. In America, they say, 'if you want something done, you got to grease the wheels.'" She said with a smile and a wink. "You go ahead and keep it. Let's just say you owe me a favor."

With that, Andre smiled and bashfully said, "Thank you, Miss Villeneuve. Ask me anytime for anything." He walked proudly out the door. Michelle smiled. *Management 101: Look someone in the eye and tell them how it is. Let them have their pride.* She continued her thought; *A little investment today may bring sizeable returns later. Management 101: Invest in your people.*

Maria finished her hair, took one last look in the mirror, thinking she looked casual and comfortable, and took the elevator to the lobby. To Michelle's surprise, Maria was busy registering an elderly couple. She stood silently by her mother as she listened to the exchange.

"Good afternoon, Mr. and Mrs. Ziegler. Yes, I have your reservation. You have reserved accommodation for two weeks. You are starting today, September 7th, and departing the morning of the 21st. As you requested, I have reserved room 201, the Master Suite. Welcome back. I hope you enjoy your stay with us," Maria said in her best business voice.

"It is wonderful to be back at your marvelous establishment, and good to once more visit our family. I hope the past year has treated you and your staff well?" Mr. Ziegler said in decent French but with a distinct German accent.

Maria smiled, "Yes, of course, we are all well. Thank you for asking."

Mrs. Ziegler added, "And how is Daniel? What is he doing in the kitchen these days? Did he ever find his trove of truffles?"

Maria answered her inquiry. "Daniel's imagination is hard at work; I'm sure he will surprise you. I am not sure about his truffles. He keeps that very secret."

Mrs. Ziegler then added, slightly disappointed there wasn't more to Maria's reply, "He does wonders in the kitchen. We look forward to seeing our relatives, but even if we didn't have family here in Saint Charles, we'd come to enjoy Daniel's cooking." She paused for a moment. "And, of course, to enjoy the gracious hospitality of your establishment," she added with just enough sincerity that you believed what she was saying.

Andre appeared, asking the Zieglers to follow him to their room and adding that he would bring the luggage along once they were in their room.

Almost to the elevator, Mr. Ziegler turned abruptly, came back to the desk, and asked quietly, "My apologies, I should have asked…I assume all of the financial details have been taken care of?"

"Yes, of course. Mr. Ziegler, we received your bank wire approximately one week ago," Maria responded to his inquiry.

"Good," Mr. Ziegler answered. "If there are any other charges, please don't hesitate to…" his voice trailed off as he turned.

Maria said again, using her warmest voice, "Everything is taken care of, Mr. Ziegler. You are our guest; we will take care of you. Relax and enjoy your visit and our wonderful fall season."

He turned once more, nodded, and smiled at Maria, "Thank you."

The Ziegler's followed Andre into the elevator. When the sounds of the elevator lifting them to the second floor subsided, Maria turned to Michelle, "Well, good afternoon, child. I trust you slept well."

Michelle smiled and looked at her mother. She was dressed much more casually, in a stylish blouse and long skirt that one would consider perfect for a day in the country. "Mother, I haven't slept that well and that long since my days in Paris."

Maria smiled and organized the papers on the counter. "That's good. A good night's sleep is important to your health." She finished by saying, "I have something very important to discuss with you." Maria focused her attention on sorting the paperwork in front of her.

"Mother?" Michelle started, "What is the Master Suite, and who are the Ziegler's?"

Maria smiled at her daughter and replied, "Yes, we have a lot of catching up to do. Let's sit down and have coffee, maybe a bit of lunch, if we can find a table."

Michelle couldn't help but laugh at her mother's last remark. "If we can find a table? You have to be joking, mother."

As they walked into the dining room, Michelle glanced about. Much to her surprise, all the tables were either occupied or had 'Reserved' signs on them. "My word," Michelle said, astounded by the possibility of a full dining room.

Pierre suddenly appeared, looking very official in a black tuxedo and carrying a clipboard and pen. "Good afternoon, ladies, Madam Villeneuve. It is a treat to see you again. May I find you a table?" Pierre asked as if he were Maitre'd of the most fashionable establishment in Paris.

Maria smiled, keeping up the charade, "Yes, if you would please. If you can find us something close to the fireplace, but not too close. I don't want my hair ruined."

Pierre bowed slightly and brought his heels together, "As you wish, Madam. Please follow me; I have just the table for you."

Pierre led them to a table, marked 'Reserved,' removed the sign, and pulled out the chair for Maria first, then for Michelle.

Michelle couldn't help herself and giggled as she said, "Thank you, Uncle."

Pierre bowed politely, gave Michelle a quick wink, and strolled off.

A short time later, a young man wearing a white dinner jacket with a black tie arrived with a large tray. Michelle had never seen him before. The young man started placing dishes on the table: coffee cups, a large pot of coffee, sugar, cream, a basket of pastries, toasted bread, and a small block of pate. He said nothing until he finished. Then, taking a step back and bowing slightly, he announced, "Compliments of the house, enjoy." Then he walked away.

Maria poured cream into Michelle's cup and poured her coffee, repeating the procedure for her own cup. While sipping her coffee, Maria began speaking, "Rudy has become something of a Master Baker. He found a technique somewhere, a technique where you test the yeast for vibrancy, then once incorporated, you test the dough to see if the yeast has fully evolved, if it has developed enough sugar. Even Daniel says Rudy's baguettes are the best he's ever tasted. On weekdays, Rudy bakes early, and we sell to the public."

Maria continued in a matter-of-fact tone. "Our friends," she corrected, "our customers have asked for pastries as well, but that's Daniel's area, and he has flatly refused. He says he doesn't want to work too hard. After closing the kitchen following dinner, it is impossible to get him up early to bake."

"Hmm, some problem. But are we talking about a lot of revenue?" Michelle stated, thinking like a business manager, "Businesspeople call lost revenue an opportunity cost. It represents income lost while not taking on the business. Say, for example, if I didn't want to make pastries, and instead wanted to swim every morning, what is the opportunity cost of my preference for swimming? It's the lost revenue from not having pastries to sell." Michelle looked at her mother, not sure if she understood.

Maria countered, "You mean the cost of doing one thing is the loss from not making money some other way?"

"Yes, mother, exactly." Michelle was surprised her mother caught on so quickly. She always knew her mother was bright, but Michelle was surprised all the same.

Maria summed it up, "Well, I guess you could look at it that way. It's an odd point of view, though, counter-intuitive if you want my opinion."

"Much of business is odd, mother," Michelle observed.

"Indeed, it is." Maria agreed, and the two women laughed like old friends. Michelle, still curious about the changes to the inn, pressed again. "Mother, what is the master suite, and when did this come about?"

"Ah, yes." Maria took a long sip of coffee, giving herself time to organize her thoughts. "Well, after you left for Paris, we suddenly had an abundance of rooms, what with Roger and Rudy also gone, but we thought the configuration was outdated, with common bathrooms for many of the rooms. That was fine when you children and the bistro staff occupied the floors, but it didn't attract many paying guests. Sure, we had guests when there was a special event at the restaurant, but we did not feel confident promoting the Inn when it resembled more a dormitory or a youth hostel."

Michelle, interested, paid attention and let her mother continue, "We hired an architect from Bordeaux and had him draw up plans utilizing the second floor more efficiently. Meanwhile, Mrs. Dubois, remember Mrs. Dubois?" Maria asked.

"Of course, she owned the old mill behind us. We used to bring her flowers, and she would be so pleased," Michelle recalled.

Maria continued, "Well, she passed, and we were able to purchase the mill from her estate. Because we were already registered with the Antiquities Department, we received permission quickly, allowing the estate to conclude its business. They accepted our offer without countering."

"That's wonderful and very lucky timing," Michelle observed.

"Yes, I agree; our timing was fortunate," Maria chorused, continuing, "We had the architect examine the property. We really didn't know what to do with it, but we decided to create retail space, expand the kitchen, and then use the remaining space for employee rooms. Doing so gave us some flexibility in renovating the inn and allowed us to create six suites on the inn's second floor and six on the third floor. You and Daniel are the only family members staying on the third floor." Maria paused, giving time for Michelle to absorb it all.

"So that's why there is the door in the hallway?" Michelle suggested.

"Yes, when guests are present, we keep it closed and locked. It's a partition between family quarters and guest rooms. When there are guests, we ask Daniel to use the back stairs. He doesn't seem to mind. Anyway, I don't think he likes the elevator," Maria replied.

"I'll do the same. I don't mind using the stairs," Michelle added, but her curiosity was stoked. "Has the retail space been rented out?" Michelle asked.

"Yes and no." Maria continued, "We created three retail spaces. We have rented two. One is a Tailor and Shoe Repair shop. The proprietor is a clever man who goes by the name Charles. He does an excellent job with shoes, but also sharpens knives, fixes small appliances, and repairs jewelry. He is quite handy. "

"Really?" Michelle added more to give her mother the impression she was listening.

"The other is a gift and sweet shop. They sell the most exquisite chocolate and delicious macarons. The proprietor is a middle-aged woman, related in some way to the Legrand family. You recall the Legrand family?" Maria paused to ask.

"Yes, I remember Suzette and Claude. I went to school with them, but they were much older, so we weren't really friends," Michelle recalled.

Maria continued, "She gave Mr. Legrand as a reference. She is an attractive woman and very personable. I think Daniel has his eye on her."

Michelle smiled. "And the third store?"

"We have not rented it out. We use it when we offer bread to the public. I thought we should make it a bakery, but so far, no one except Rudy has expressed interest, and Rudy's interest is not strong," Maria stated with a bit of a frown, which Michelle interpreted as disappointment.

Michelle spoke before she realized what she was saying. "Well, maybe I could get involved. I've always enjoyed baking, and I'd love a chance to meet people and offer them cakes, pastries, bread, maybe even spices, or cooking utensils. Really, Mother, where does a person go if they need a new pan or utensil, or freshly ground cinnamon?" Michelle was excited by the prospects.

"You are right, I always thought people would love a bakery or a casual place for coffee, but a convenience store would work as well. I remember when you were young, and I was tasked with finding you a shoelace," Maria reminisced.

Michelle exclaimed, "I remember that too, Mother. Isn't that a hoot?"

"A what?" Maria looked at Michelle, a puzzled look on her face.

Michelle answered, "A hoot; it means ironic but funnier."

"Oh, ok, a hoot." Maria smiled, shrugged her shoulders, and sipped her coffee.

Michelle asked a third time, "The Zieglers, you seemed familiar with them. Who are they?"

Maria took another sip of her coffee and talked while she refilled Michelle's cup, "Nobody in particular, but very nice people. I think he is a retired Swiss bureaucrat. They have relatives here and visit once, sometimes twice, a year. Mr. Ziegler mentioned that they could stay with their relatives, but they'd be put to work if they did. He said he is too old to be milking cows."

"That's cute," Michelle replied while adding cream and sugar to her coffee.

"Mrs. Ziegler is quite smitten over Daniel. Mr. Ziegler, God bless him, said to me once, 'if he had known she was so fond of food, he would have learned to cook,'" Maria said with a smile.

Michelle thought for a moment, "I would want my husband to cook.

To come home and be surprised by my husband, wearing an apron, having spent the day cooking, and surprising me with a gourmet meal. I think that is so hot."

"You mean a hoot?" Maria asked, wanting to communicate on her daughter's terms.

"No, hot, not a hoot, hot," Michelle clarified.

"Hot, not a hoot?" Maria asked again.

"Yes, hot. A hoot is something else," Michelle stated.

"Can't a hoot be hot?" Maria asked, a little confused.

Michelle pondered for a second, "A hoot can be hot, but most likely hot is not a hoot."

Maria looked at her daughter, "If a hoot can be hot, but hot isn't a hoot, then what is it?"

"Cool," Michelle answered without hesitation.

"Cold?" Maria replied.

"No, cool is not cold; cool is hot," Michelle once again tried to clarify.

Beginning to feel frustrated, Maria tried one more time, "Ok, a hoot is hot, but hot isn't a hoot, it's cool, but cool is not cold, it's hot, so being cool must be a hoot?"

"It can be, but most likely if you are cool, you're chilling," Michelle said, thinking her mother was getting it.

"Oh, my word," Maria stared at her daughter with a look of resignation while saying slowly and sternly, "I think you've spent entirely too much time in the States."

"Oh, Mother, you are such a hoot," Michelle laughed.

Maria laughed along, "I think I'd rather be cold."

Michelle corrected, "Cool, Mother, not cold; you'd rather be cool."

Maria answered in a patronizing tone, "If you say so, dear."

Chapter 5

Michelle placed the key in the old lock and jiggled it every way she could. Finally, she just put her shoulder into the door and pushed. The door popped open, leaving Michelle off-balance, stumbling, barely able to stay on her feet. Standing inside the doorway, she surveyed the space in front of her. It was a good-sized room for a retail space, bright with the remnants of morning light. To her left were rows and rows of shelves, floor to ceiling. To her right, there were more shelves. Separating her from the shelves on the right was a counter. It looked well built, with a glass front and top. She could see doors in the rear enclosing the case. The space smelled strongly of various household chemicals. *Cleaned and freshly painted,* she concluded.

Another counter was straight ahead, against the far wall, with a few shelves and an aisle behind it. A large double doorway led, Michelle guessed, to a back room. The far case had some type of indent cut out. *Probably for a cash register*, she thought as she found the light switch and turned on the large overhead lights.

"Nice space," she said out loud. "Very nice space," she repeated as she looked more closely at the shelves and the cases. "This is not a convenience store or a general store. This is a specialty shop." Michelle said under her breath. "Mother was right; this would be perfect for a bakery. The space is too small for a coffee shop unless you offer to-go only. Maybe we could fit three or four small tables…No, let's not do that." She talked out loud to no one in particular, "The last thing I want to do is be a Starbucks."

Michelle wandered about, looking in the back room, concluding there was plenty of space for ovens and sacks of flour, finally walking back outside and across the street to get a sense of what the public would see. "I think Mother is right. I think a bakery would work well in the space." Michelle once again said aloud, picturing baskets of baguettes sitting in the front window, a sign above saying, "Tree Trunk Bakery." *No,* she thought, *this is an excellent time to remove the Tree Trunk name. It's a new venture; start with a new name, a new image.* She easily persuaded herself while wondering *what rhymes with boulangerie.*

Michelle stood across from the space for some time, watching the cars go by, watching and counting. *Not a heck of a lot of traffic,* she mused, *but better than I thought it would be. Maybe it will improve once the bakery is opened?* She sat on a small bench, meant for the public waiting to take public transportation, but there were no buses. The town only had two taxis.

I don't know if traffic justifies a bakery to be open all day or every day. Don't most people shop in the morning? she pondered. *I think we should try a bakery, but start with reduced hours, open maybe 7 a.m. to 12 or maybe 1 p.m. Then I could close, make dough for the following day, let it proof overnight, and still have time to join the family for lunch.* Michelle thought the idea was brilliant and couldn't wait to present it to her mother.

There is so much shelf space; what else should I offer? Well, I must have bread and croissants, but those will go in the case. She made a mental note to figure out somehow how to make Daniel's croissants. *Jams and homemade preserves would be wonderful and would certainly complement the croissants. Maybe butter as well. Most people churn themselves, but who has the time? People would buy if it saved a little time. Perhaps I could flavor it? That would be a selling point. I could even have a flavor of the month. That's clever.* She made a mental note to talk with Daniel about how to flavor butter and what flavors he would recommend.

Michelle sat observing the storefront for quite some time, debating with herself over various points, such as what the shop's name should be and how broad a product line to offer. She concluded that the broader the product line, the greater the inventory, which means a greater investment in working capital, as well as time and effort. *Gees, this is turning out to be a real business,* she lamented, not realizing until then that she had a more romantic notion of running a bakery.

Some sort of software would make this so much more efficient, something other than just a spreadsheet, she surmised. *I have my laptop. I can look online. I need to also order a printer.*

She sat thinking about software and software specifications when a man's voice spoke out, "Michelle Villeneuve, is it not?"

Startled, Michelle spun around and found herself looking into the belly of an older, rotund stranger. Glancing up, she at first could only manage, "Hi." But she quickly composed herself, stood up, smiled, and offered her hand. "Yes, I am Michelle Villeneuve. Who might you be?"

The man shook her hand, smiled back at her, and introduced himself. "I am Arnaud Martin, the Mayor of Saint Charles. It is a pleasure to meet you, finally. You may call me Arnaud; most people just call me Mayor." He ended with a strange squeal of a laugh.

"Thank you," Michelle replied, rather uncomfortably, not receiving a good first impression.

Michelle took stock of the mayor. Not fat she decided, more like portly. His clothes seemed of good quality but needed pressing. His unshaven face, along with the wrinkles in his suit, gave the mayor an overall unkempt, slovenly look, and there was something else, something about him that made her feel uneasy and distrustful. *His eyes,* she told herself. *Yes, that was it.* The mayor had beady little eyes that darted left and right as if he were a spy, passing on important military secrets.

"May I sit with you a moment?" the mayor announced, not really asking and taking a seat on the bench next to Michelle.

Michelle stumbled on her words, unsuccessfully searching for a polite way to say no.

"Thank you," he replied cordially. A moment later, he began to speak, "So you went abroad and studied Business, earning an MBA?"

Michelle was startled at first by the mayor's questioning. "I did," she replied, hesitant with her guard up.

He sensed she was uneasy, and so he relaxed his approach, "That must have been a wonderful experience. Certainly, a great opportunity for personal growth and accomplishment."

Michelle went along with it, "I guess so." The mayor's line of conversation was suspicious, and he failed at his first attempt at putting her at ease.

"Did you study economics? Investments?" he queried.

"Of course, I was a Finance major."

"Oh, a Finance major, very good. How long did your studies take?" He was picking up the pace of his questioning.

"Two years, my course of study was two years. Then I worked in

Investment Banking for five years. Why do you ask?" Michelle replied, growing irritated and wanting to know why she was being interrogated.

The mayor continued, ignoring her question. "And who was your employer?"

She sighed loudly, annoyed of his probing, and offering him an obvious hint to stop, "I was recruited out of school by the firm Harrison, Brown, and Kemper," she said with more than a hint of attitude.

"A very good name indeed," The Mayor added, but he still went on. "You must have learned quite a bit."

"I worked in the Corporate Restructuring Department. I assisted in structuring deals, mostly in the energy sector. I did a lot of 'what-if' analysis, looking at the potential upside and downside," she replied, using as much industry jargon as she could, hoping he wouldn't understand and would change the subject.

"What kind of deals?" the mayor asked.

Gees. She thought, *this guy just won't quit.* "We did a lot of carve-outs, created Limited Partnerships, which were referred to as value enhancement deals."

The mayor replied like he was talking with an old friend from school, "When I was in banking, we used different terms, but the concepts were the same, similar rationale, get the market to recognize hidden values within a company."

Michelle simply added, "Exactly." Michelle had the feeling there was more on the mayor's mind, but his interrogation-like questioning had put her off. She wasn't feeling very social to begin with, and he had left her feeling annoyed and irritated.

The mayor paused to light a cigar. "You don't mind if I smoke? I find a good cigar helps me focus and articulate."

It didn't matter what Michelle thought; he only asked out of habit. He took a few puffs of his cigar to ensure it was lit and began talking, finally getting to what was really on his mind.

"I am glad you have arrived. With your education and experience, you should not only understand my position but agree with it, and I am hoping, help persuade key decision-makers to go along with my plan," he said without emotion.

"Your plan?" she replied, her curiosity aroused, but every warning sign in her head was flashing.

"Yes, now listen, let me talk," he admonished. "I believe, and many others agree, the inn and bistro are, how would we say, diamonds in the rough, or what we bankers would call 'underutilized assets'. Again, I, along with others, firmly believe the Villeneuve family has mismanaged this gem for too long and that new management is needed to realize value and earn attractive returns on investment. You might not realize this, but the government has funds available for the purchase of mismanaged and underutilized historical assets. The fact that the inn and bistro have subsisted on grants and historical awards for years is proof of the inefficiency of current ownership and the need to bring in fresh thinking."

In shock, Michelle blurted out, "What are you suggesting?"

"Yes, please let me finish," the mayor said, taking the opportunity to re-light his cigar.

"I have several friends and associates in key positions within the Ministry of Antiquities. They have given me assurances; my application for government funding will be accepted, in fact, welcomed," the mayor said confidently.

"Funding for what?" Michelle said, showing a great deal of contempt.

The mayor looked at Michelle with an incredulous look on his face, "To buy out your family's interest in the Inn at Saint Charles and The Tree Trunk Bistro." He continued looking directly at her to gauge her reaction. Seeing nothing he didn't anticipate, he continued, "If your family doesn't accept my very reasonable offer, I will petition the Ministry to halt any future payments, essentially driving your family into insolvency. My associates at the Ministry will then take control and will sell me the property. In either case, I will end up owning these assets. I hope you will be reasonable and convince your family to negotiate with me so the matter can be quickly settled," he stated as if Michelle should be in complete agreement.

She sat there quietly, silently, trying to comprehend all that was said, a feeling of disgust growing inside of her. She was having a hard time controlling herself and didn't know whether to spit in the man's face, kick him in the groin or break down and cry. But she remembered something her boss used to tell her, "Never let them see you panic, never, in front of clients or adversaries, lose it. Always be in control."

As Michelle sat there silently, trying to compose herself, the mayor once more started talking, this time with a very soft, comforting voice, "As a young woman, wouldn't you rather live in Paris? You would have enough funds to buy an excellent apartment and live very comfortably. Meet people, travel first class, do what suits you. I'm sure out here you can see you are far from civilization and anything of interest. "

The mayor finished his presentation and was confident he had done a good job of presenting the facts. He thought that there was a good chance Michelle would be an ally in his attempt to complete the transaction. He looked at Michelle, who sat quietly, carefully hiding her outrage.

After a few moments of silence, finally getting her emotions under control, and repulsed by the mayor's confidence, she stood up, faced the mayor, and spoke, slowly and clearly, "Mayor Martin, I will take your position under advisement, but not without first verifying the facts. What I can say with certainty, though, is my family has owned the Inn at Saint Charles and The Tree Trunk Bistro for many, many years, centuries even. I see no obstacles or reasons why we wouldn't continue to own it for many centuries to come. Good day, sir." With that, she spun around and walked away, satisfied with what she had said and not looking back.

The mayor, surprised by her reply and sensing his expected ally and a quick closing was slipping through his fingers, spat out, "Perhaps we can be partners? We are flexible in our terms. Let's not be so abrupt. Let's think about this. There are benefits to a deal." But Michelle kept walking, without acknowledging any of it.

Michelle walked defiantly down the street and turned the corner. Once she was sure of being *out* of the mayor's sight, she broke down, doubling over with fear and a dreadful sense of confusion and doom. Oh God, she thought, *I let my guard down, and I let some cheap hoodlum, masquerading as a government official, get to me.* "

She regained her composure and started walking back to the inn. As she walked, she thought back to her experiences in New York and Boston. She remembered another lesson she learned from her boss. *If you are dealing with a real bastard, the only way to counter is to be a bigger bastard. But* he always would say, *Protect yourself, keep it legal.* She grimaced. *Good advice. I'll show them who's the bigger bastard.*

She picked up her pace and almost ran into the inn's lobby, looking for her mother. Andre was standing behind the desk. "Where's my mother, Andre?" she quickly blurted out, telling herself to keep cool, calm down.

"Hello, Miss Villeneuve," he replied, picking up on her urgency. "She had a call from Paris, and she wanted privacy, so she went upstairs."

Maria had a phone installed in her bedroom after many calls went unanswered, as the only family phone was in the lobby. Michelle rang for the elevator. After what seemed an endless wait, she took the elevator to the fourth floor and the master bedroom. Bounding out of the elevator, she came upon her mother, sitting on the bed, engaged in what must have been an excruciating conversation. Tears had welled up in her mother's eyes, and she was trying her best to keep them from cascading down her cheeks.

Oh, dear God, this is a nightmare, was all Michelle could think. She couldn't sit still and started pacing alongside her mother's bed, waiting for her mother's call to end. As her mother's call ended, Michelle couldn't contain herself and pleaded with her mother. "Mother, what is going on? Please tell me; I've got to know?"

Maria remained calm, stood up, and grasped Michelle in her arms and hugged her tightly. "Nothing is happening that we can't remedy. I don't know how much you know or what your source of information is, but there is an element here in Saint Charles that wants to take Tree Trunk away from us. After nearly 500 years of ownership, a petition has been submitted requesting funding for the purchase of Tree Trunk. I just got off the phone with our lawyer in Paris. He has a copy of the petition. It was filed by an organization named 'The Gold Development Group.' It has already received preliminary approval from the Ministry. The lawyers are sending a copy of the petition to us by courier. We will have it tomorrow morning."

Michelle, from her experiences in New York, knew what was happening. But she never expected something like this to happen to the family business. "Forgive me, Mother, I am much stronger than I act; it's just that I never expected this kind of action way out here. It's so peaceful and quiet, and people are simple and honest. I never expected thieves or an unfriendly takeover of our own business."

"These people are not from here." Maria sat down on the bed and began telling Michelle what she had just heard from the lawyers. "There is a clause in the doctrine that grants funds to historical places. The clause permits the Ministry to withhold or even halt payments if the receiving party is not sincere in maintaining historical accuracy. It's hardly ever invoked, but the terms are so vague that people don't have a chance to defend themselves if it is invoked. Anyone can bring a violation to the Ministry's attention." She paused and looked at Michelle, who sat quietly next to her mother. "The petition filed with the Ministry by the Gold Group includes a violation. It is the basis of the petition," Maria finished.

"Mother," Michelle questioned, "so the Gold Group claims we are not doing a good job, so they want funding to buy us out?"

Maria, sadly, looked at her child, slowly nodded her head, and simply answered. "Precisely."

* * *

John DeHaven, Deputy Administrator of the Ministry of Antiquities, sat back in his chair, put his hands behind his head, and looked up at the blank white ceiling. *Ah, in just a matter of months, I will be out of this bureaucratic morass of a job; ugh, I can hardly wait.* He then thought about his new position, *Senior Vice President of Development, Gold Development Group Ltd. Has a nice sound to it.* He amused himself further, *I hope I can get it all to fit on a business card.*

The ring of the phone jolted him out of his daydream, and looking at the phone, he recognized the number. Pressing the speaker button, he answered with the friendliest of voices, "Hello, Mr. Miller, what can I do for you today?"

The voice on the phone was deep and official, as if the person it belonged to was used to giving orders. "Hello, John, just calling to get an update and to see if you had any questions concerning the contracts I sent over."

"Well, I'm sure there is an issue or two that we would like changed or added, but we are focusing on property acquisition and the identification of other opportunities at the moment," John replied with the same answer he gave to Miller two days ago.

"I see," he answered with a bit of concern. "You know, we would like to wrap this up quickly and move to the next phase. Corporate is very keen on launching the Boutique brand. We want to start taking summer season reservations by the end of the fourth quarter."

John hid his disdain for the pressure Miller was applying. "We have approvals at all levels from the Ministry. My man on-site is negotiating with the family and is looking to finalize terms in a matter of days. I think we will need at least a couple of weeks to get all the paperwork signed and processed. Unfortunately, the French Government is no different from any other government. Time is not measured in hours and days but in weeks and months. I appreciate your position; we will strive to progress and meet your schedule."

Years of service with the Ministry had given DeHaven the ability to pay lip service as good as anyone. Miller knew that's what he was getting and cursed under his breath. As the new Chief of Acquisitions and Special

Projects for Benelux International Ltd, a global operator of luxury accommodations, he was hoping for something a little less strenuous as his first project. He didn't want to do business with the Gold Group, an entity with no track record, but politics got in the way. A relative of the Chairman put Gold Group together, so Gold Group was put on the list of approved subcontractors. It was even simpler; Miller received a phone call from the Chairman's Office, the message was *do the deal.*

Later, more pressure came from Corporate with the creation of the Benelux Boutique brand, a collection of smaller, intimate, and architecturally interesting accommodations. Corporate liked The Tree Trunk and drew up plans to re-develop the property into a modern mini resort with historical relevance and launch it as the first Benelux Boutique. The plan called for Gold to acquire the property and lease it to Benelux for 100 years. Gold and Benelux would share the cost of developing and modernizing the property.

"Well, look over the architectural plans and the artist's rendition. At least sign off on those so I can give Corporate something," Miller stated, sidestepping the bull he had just been given.

"Will do." DeHaven replied, concluding the call.

Chapter 6

I t was late. The bistro had closed, the doors were locked, and the inn's front desk had a sign on it that said: "Back at 7 a.m.". The streets of Saint Charles were deserted and dark, lit only by dim lights, mounted high up on lamp posts, and spaced meters apart. The four Villeneuves and Rudy sat quietly around the large rustic table in the family kitchen. Maria had just finished telling everyone what she knew about the Gold Development Group's offer, and Michelle spoke of her conversation with the mayor.

Daniel was the first to speak. "I don't want to sell. Where would I go? What would I do? I would probably just sit around and cook. I'd rather do that here. It's the only thing I know. And the money, I have money in the bank. What do I need more money for? I have a brand-new pair of boots. I don't need the money."

Maria smiled when Daniel mentioned his boots. "I agree, Daniel. I have all the possessions I want or need; I really want for nothing, well, almost." She stopped there, not wanting to get overly emotional.

Michelle spoke up. "In the states, I worked all the time and never really had time to spend any money, so I saved quite a bit. I could live for a few years on my savings. This is my home. I came home to live, not to watch it taken away or sold. I cannot even begin to think about life without Saint Charles and the inn and bistro. We can't let this happen. If anybody needs money, I will give all I have. "

Maria smiled again, a warm embracing smile, as tears welled up in her eyes. "Thank you, daughter."

Pierre spoke next, "One benefit of living in Saint Charles, there are no vices or places that are known to separate people from their savings. Even I have saved up a bit of money, and agree, I want for nothing except a dining room full of happy patrons. Well, Maria, my apologies, there is something."

"Yes, what is that?"

"Well, I do need a new tuxedo; wearing the same one every day has caused the fabric to weaken. Perhaps we can discuss this at a better time?"

She smiled. "Of course, Pierre, please, whatever you think is suitable. I think you should have several jackets for different occasions. A white jacket for weekends, black for weekdays, and perhaps a maroon jacket for holidays and special occasions."

Pierre smiled, liking what he was hearing. "A wonderful idea, Maria. If I could add, I hear yellow dinner jackets are the fashion on the Riviera and Monte Carlo this year. I think a dark red jacket is a must for the winter holidays, but yellow is perfect for summer."

Maria smiled again, "I think you know best how to present yourself and the bistro. I leave this decision up to you."

"Thank you, Madam Villeneuve." Pierre always addressed Maria formally when conducting business.

Rudy sat silently, listening to the conversation. When it was his turn, he decided someone needed to be rational. "Well, we are all in agreement not to sell. But suppose we must? If their plan works, we lose, and we lose big. Maybe our best option is to go out on top?"

Michelle quickly added, "In banking, when a firm is faced with an unfriendly takeover, the firm will seek a friendly third party to sell to; this is called 'a white knight.' A white knight pays a fair market price but is friendly to current management. If we must sell, maybe we can find a white knight. Why don't we be our own white knight? We all said we have savings. Perhaps we can form a corporation, capitalize it with our savings, purchase the property, and then pay ourselves a big payout. Maybe we can even finance the purchase with a loan from the government?"

Michelle was on a roll now, but only Rudy followed what she was saying. It was Maria who finally cut her off, "Michelle, darling, I'm afraid you've lost us."

"Yes," Daniel added, "what is capitalize? I have never heard this word used in this context, and a payout? What is a payout? If we need to put money in, why do we need to pay out?"

Rudy was quick to interject, "Capitalize is putting money in as equity, so a business has the liquidity to operate. If you capitalize with one million euros, the company has a net worth of one million euros. A payout is withdrawing capital, a dividend."

Michelle smiled. "That's correct."

"Ok," Daniel continued, "I still don't know why we put money in, then take money out? It sounds like a game of shuffle."

Michelle answered, "I agree; the concept is a bit abstract. Let's just say we put money in to show we are serious; we then add to our money with borrowed money. Since the company has too much money now, we pay out the extra money. But to whom?" She paused for a minute to look at everyone's face and was satisfied everyone was following along. "To the owners, us." She smiled like she had just been awarded the grand prize.

Pierre, who had been silent, lit his third cigarette and finished his espresso. "I think I follow along. I see it as a gamble. Money doesn't magically appear. We will need to pay it back. We need to talk about who, how, when and, most importantly, how much?"

Again, Rudy jumped in, "That's right, we have been talking in very broad terms. we need to start talking specifics and come up with a plan."

Rudy then looked directly at Michelle, "Cousin, I hate to throw this at you, but with your education, knowledge, and experience, you need to take the lead."

Maria looked at Michelle and placed her hand on her hand, "Yes, daughter, I ask you, will you represent the family in this matter?" All eyes were on Michelle as if her answer could go either way.

Michelle looked around, feeling at first scared, but then very proud, "I am a Villeneuve; you are my family. While I have a breath in my body, a penny to my name, I will not let any harm come to you or the family business. I belong here with you; we all belong together. Let's get these bastards."

One at a time, she stared each one in the eye, showing her sincerity and her defiance. When she looked at her mother, she held out her arms, and the two women embraced. Maria could be heard softly saying, "Thank you, daughter, I am so proud of you."

Meanwhile, Daniel pounded the table, agreeing with Michelle's sentiment. "Yes, let's get these guys."

Pierre smiled for the first time, lighting another cigarette and adding, "I wouldn't want to be wearing their shoes."

Rudy smiled as well and simply said, "Go get them, Cuz."

The meeting was adjourned. Daniel asked if anyone wanted to join him for a nightcap. Pierre and Rudy agreed and followed Daniel to the bar. Maria quietly asked Michelle to come to her room. The two women took the elevator to the fourth floor.

Maria beckoned for Michelle to sit down while she poured two cognacs. Handing one to Michelle, she spoke. "My darling daughter, I need to talk to you, but what I have to say cannot leave this room. You must promise me to keep what I tell you secret until I determine when it is appropriate to inform the others. Michelle, do you promise?"

Michelle, looking very serious, replied, "Of course, Mother, I promise." Maria continued, "If you break this promise, I will never speak to you again, and you will be asked to leave Saint Charles." Maria looked Michelle dead in the eye.

"Oh my God, Mother, I don't know if I want to know?" Michelle cried out.

Maria tried to comfort her, realizing she might have been a little too harsh, "But child, you must know, I told you when you first arrived, that you must be prepared to assume my responsibilities."

Michelle openly fretted, "Mother, are you alright? Are you ill?" She gulped her cognac and held out her glass for a refill, trying to prepare herself for what she wasn't sure she wanted to hear.

"I am fine, sweetheart; it is nothing like that. It is about your father," Maria said in a soothing voice that, along with a generous pour and another large gulp of cognac, allowed Michelle to relax. "How much do you know about your father and the circumstances surrounding his death?" Maria started to get serious and emotional while also feeling the effects of her drink.

"Not much, Mother; I was young. I just know he was government security and was killed doing his job."

After once more refilling both glasses, Maria sat on the settee, exhaled as she got comfortable, and brought back memories she had tried for so long to repress. She started, "There is more, much more. Your father had special skills that he learned while in the military. When he left the military, he was asked by the Foreign Ministry to start a special security service to protect dignitaries, diplomats, and their families as they travel abroad on official government business."

Michelle listened intently. She was having difficulty picturing the gentle, wonderful man she knew as her father as the kind of man who would head up a government security organization.

Maria continued, feeling very relaxed, honest, and content to be finally sharing the memories that she had kept to herself all these years.

"The security organization was very successful, stopping a number of kidnapping and bombing attempts by extremists and terrorists. The French government was involved in a North African country. To forge friendly ties between the French and African people, they built a large bridge over what was assumed to be an impassable gorge. This was intended to increase commerce and make life easier for the locals."

"The government was proud of its accomplishment and wanted to make a show of opening the bridge to traffic. The Foreign Minister himself traveled there to cut the ribbon and be the first to cross the bridge, officially opening the bridge. Your Father did not want to take any chances and put himself in charge of security. There were numerous rumors that terrorists wanted to blow up the bridge. Your father tried to warn the Minister not to go, but he wouldn't have any of it."

Michelle thought she knew where this was going. "But, Mother, the bridge is still there. Some consider it a miracle of engineering."

"Yes, I know child, there is more. On the day of the ceremony, the Minister cut the ribbon and proceeded by car across the bridge, followed by the ambassador and other dignitaries. Reports are that two men approached from the opposite direction on motorcycles. They were wearing the uniforms of the National Police."

Maria began to weep as she continued, "Your father pulled out his handgun and shouted for them to stop. They kept coming. Correctly surmising they were suicide bombers, he shot the first one, ran to the body, picked it up, and threw it over the side of the bridge. The body blew up in mid-air. By this time, the second man was on top of your father, they wrestled and then…"

Maria had tears cascading down her cheeks, "and then, fearing a bomb and not being able to subdue the man, he grabbed the bomber and jumped off the bridge. The bomb went off before they hit the ground. The bombs were big enough to take down the bridge but exploded harmlessly in midair. Your father gave his life for the Minister, for the Ambassador, for all the dignitaries. Still, the force of the bomb…" Maria could hardly contain herself, "but the force of the bomb disintegrated your Father. His body was gone in the blast. He never came home. I didn't even have his body to bury. Oh God, help me." Maria bent over as the painful memories of her loss returned.

The agony that came back to Maria was severe. The memories of her life before, and then how her life had changed, were vivid and traumatic. She had met the most wonderful man, married him, and lost him to some radical idealists who hated the world. This beautiful man lost to ignorance and hatred. She recouped her composure. "I am sorry, my child, I will never recover from what I have gone through, from what we lost. My memories are all too vivid. I try not to remember, but at times, it just comes back."

Michelle also had tears in her eyes as she listened. This was the first time she had heard the details of her father's last moments. "But why the secrecy? Everyone should know how Father unselfishly gave his life and saved the lives of others. Why must this be kept secret?"

"There is more." Maria once more regained her composure, drying her tears with a tissue. "It became apparent that the Minister had been warned but still went, imperiling the lives of others. When this became known, the President forced him to resign. In secret, the President traveled here, thanked me and apologized for the error in judgment shown by the Minister. "

Michelle was shocked. "The President came here?"

Maria answered, "Yes, it was a lovely day. We had lunch, and then we strolled through the streets of Saint Charles."

"Did anyone recognize him? Who was in the kitchen? Who made lunch?" Michelle asked, now wide-awake.

"Daniel made lunch, a wonderful chicken in red wine. The bread was freshly baked and was hot as it reached the table. It was, it was," Maria did not know if it was the proper thing to say, but she said it anyway, "It was very romantic."

"You are joking, Mother; tell me this is not true." Michelle laughed as if this was one big joke.

"Of course, it is true. Ask Daniel, he'll tell you, though, he thinks it was just my lawyer visiting from Paris." Maria said.

Michelle was flabbergasted and curious. She acted like her best friend had just returned home from her first date. "What's he like, Mother? What did you talk about?"

Maria was honest with her daughter, "He is an elegant man, much like your father, with strong traits of purpose and sacrifice in his personality. He keeps in touch and has asked me to come to Paris on several occasions." Maria confessed.

"Did you sleep with him?" Michelle asked as if she were asking the time.

Maria replied with an unapologetic tone, raising her head, "I was weak, he was strong. I needed something. He kept me alive. To this day, I thank him for his kindness, his passion, and his strength. I am not ashamed."

Michelle recognized how truly incredible a woman her mother was and how much she admired her, but feeling the effects of three cognacs, she loudly blurted out, "Mother, you are unbelievable. Dad passes, and to ease the pain, you have an affair with the President of France?"

"Yes, but remember, you promised." Maria countered.

"Is that your secret?" Michelle asked, while looking to see if enough was left in the bottle for one more round of drinks. "Here, let's split this," she said as she emptied the contents of the bottle.

"Well, there's more. The important part," Maria replied, taking a sip.

"The important part?" Michelle laughed nervously, inebriated and having difficulty with her balance. She teased, "Oh no, you're not going to tell me the President of France is my real father or, better yet, tell me I have a twin sister, and she's like the Queen of Egypt, are you?"

Maria laughed at her daughter's imagination. "No darling, you've had too much. Perhaps we should continue this tomorrow?"

"No, Mother, if it's important, tell me now. I promise, I will be serious," Michelle said slowly.

"Can you read?" Maria asked, losing a bit of patience with her inebriated daughter.

"Of course, I can."

"Then read this; this is the secret. We can discuss this later, but it must be kept secret," Maria spoke sternly, herself feeling a bit tipsy from the cognac, she handed an envelope to her daughter.

Inside the envelope was a letter, folded properly. Michelle unfolded it and the seal of the Office of the President, Republic of France, became visible. The letter was handwritten. It began "My Dear Madam Villeneuve" and went on to express the grief felt by the whole world at the loss of Roger Villeneuve. It then explained how Roger was a protector of France, not just of its property but of its people and their ideals. How he couldn't do his duty, he couldn't make the sacrifices necessary to do his job unless he knew his family would be taken care of. "Wow, this is incredible," Michelle stated as she kept reading.

The letter detailed how Mr. Villeneuve gave his life for France. "It is now France's responsibility to take care of his family. It is the country's solemn responsibility to ensure the family wants for nothing so that Roger can rest in peace." The letter was signed by the President of France.

Michelle, drunk and now with her head spinning, asked, "So what does that mean, wants for nothing? I want the Eiffel Tower moved to Saint Charles. Now." Michelle laughed, then, with a belligerent tone, said, "More importantly, I want my father back. May I have him back, please, Mr. President?"

Maria folded up the letter and offered Michelle another. This envelope had the emblem of the United States on it. Michelle opened it and found a letter written by the US Ambassador to France. Michelle began to cry as she read how the whole world admired her father.

Finally, Maria handed her a letter from a Swiss Bank she had never heard of. It simply said that the sum of $28 million in US dollars had been deposited in an account under the name Villeneuve. Michelle looked at the letter. It was dated sixteen years ago, a year after Father died.

"What was the date on those letters, Mother?" Michelle got her mother to reopen the letters. They were dated one month before the Bank's letter. Michelle announced sarcastically, "So that's the price of a citizen. It's disgusting; it's blood money."

"No, Michelle, it is not. It is money to ensure we can continue as a family." Maria counseled her daughter. "No one can reverse what has happened. They can only make sure our pain does not grow. Our sorrow does not spread. Try and understand. The generosity of these people is because of the generosity of your Father."

"Where is the money now, Mother? Did they take it back, tax the hell out of us?" Michelle asked bitterly.

"It is still there. It is in a Swiss account so that we wouldn't be taxed. I have invested some of it. I worked with a gentleman, a bank officer named Henri Salazar. He has directed my investment. I get a statement every quarter. It comes in an unmarked envelope, so it doesn't arouse suspicion," Maria informed her daughter.

"Here is the latest quarter; it should be dated June 30th."

Michelle took the thick envelope, not yet opened, "Why haven't you opened it, Mother? It's important." Michelle admonished her mother.

"I know." Maria replied, "But after a while, it doesn't mean anything; it's just numbers written on paper."

"Well, it could definitely save the day if there is a significant sum…"

Michelle's words trailed off as she examined the contents of the envelope. It took her a minute to catch her breath. "Mother, do you know how much is in the account? Do you have any idea?"

Maria looked puzzled; she really couldn't remember the balance, but she hoped it was sufficient. "Well, I withdrew some for your and your brother's education. I also helped Rudy with his medical bills. I am not sure, perhaps $10 million or so?"

Michelle looked at her mother, holding up the statement so her mother could see. "See that line, that's the value. See it, Mother? Now read it."

Maria had to squint without her glasses, but silently read it and replied, "Oh my word…is that correct? It can't be."

Michelle answered back slowly, deliberately, "In US dollars, $67,839,762.37. We are rich, Mother; we are rich." Michelle started looking through the statement, looking for any catches, ifs, or buts.

"No, darling, "Maria tutored her daughter, "that is not the way to understand this. We simply have resources; think of it as having choices."

Chapter 1

It was early when Michelle woke up. She knew it was early from the sky outside her bedroom window. She could see lingering darkness and just the beginnings of a sunrise. *Days are getting shorter,* she thought. *Soon it'll be winter and then the Christmas season.* The thought of Christmas made her smile through the pain she was suffering from too much cognac the night before.

She became ill and rushed to the toilet, making it just in time. Once the sickness was over, she felt drained. She washed her face, brushed her teeth, and went back to bed. Lying there, feeling much better, she began to think about the conversation she had had last night with her mother.

I must have been dreaming. The President of France, here? No, I don't believe it. But why would she tell me that if it wasn't true? She pondered the possible reasons her mother might have misled her. *The money,* she quickly thought. *Close to $68 million, and she had statements. The statement was indeed real; I opened it. Wait, why did Mother have me open it? Why was she ignoring $68 million? Wait a minute.*

Michelle jumped out of bed, threw on her robe, and ran to the elevator. She quickly went to the fourth floor, where she found her mother, fully clothed, curled up in a ball, asleep on top of the covers. Michelle quietly went to the closet and retrieved a spare blanket to cover her mother. As she was covering her, she spotted the plain brown envelope containing the statement from the bank. She carefully withdrew the document and again perused its contents.

"Well, it sure looks real," she said out loud, going through it line by line, not thinking of her sleeping mother.

"It is authentic," Her mother interrupted, slurring her words as a newly woken person would. "I need to introduce you to Mr. Salazar. It is your responsibility from here. I will maintain oversight until I am confident you are mature enough to administer the portfolio."

"Mother, I am 27 years old; I have been abroad, on my own mind you. I have been instrumental in raising millions of dollars of capital in the Global financial markets. I think I am quite mature enough to manage the family portfolio," Michelle countered, arrogantly and abruptly, still feeling the sickly effects of too much cognac.

"Yes, Michelle, you are accomplished. But you show your emotions very quickly, perhaps capriciously. It is not a sign of immaturity; I apologize, I used the wrong word, but it is a sign you need more experience. You need more experience being responsible. If word ever got out that you are responsible for a sizable amount of funds, every jackal in the forest would come hunting for you." Maria looked directly at her daughter.

Michelle looked back with a solemn look and a frown, knowing her mother was probably right, on all accounts. "I accept your decision, Mother. You are undoubtedly the most grounded person I know, and I hope…"

Maria cut her off in mid-sentence as she climbed from under the blanket, "Thank you dear, but no time for pats on the back. I have a plan I want to discuss with you. Go take your bath and freshen up; I will meet you downstairs in the kitchen in an hour. We'll talk over coffee."

Michelle jumped up, giving her mother room. "But just one thing, Mother…"

"Yes?"

"Did you really have a fling with the President?"

"Shush, daughter, that's not important." Pausing while straightening up her bed. "Please go, get yourself cleaned up," she replied, trying to hide her smile and giving Michelle a wink.

"Mother, that's so romantic." Michelle smiled broadly, twirling around like a waltzing ballroom dancer, maneuvering to the waiting elevator.

Michelle was ready with plenty of time to spare. As she was leaving her room, Daniel was coming up the backstairs, looking very solemn and carrying a large cup of coffee. "Good morning, Chef," She smiled at Daniel, having shaken off the effects of the previous night and feeling back to normal.

Daniel tried to smile back, but the pain was too much. "I'm going back to bed. I think lunch will be late today. I don't feel so good." He shuffled down the hallway past Michelle and into his room.

Wow, I wonder what happened last night? The guys must have stayed up late, she surmised as she navigated down the narrow, winding rear stairway, finally reaching the family kitchen. She took a spot at the table, grabbed two cups off the shelf, collected the sugar bowl, and proceeded to make coffee. She poured spoons of sugar into the cups and, thinking her mother was on the way, poured in the coffee.

As she sipped her coffee, she opened her laptop and started thinking about a plan. *Let's see, what do we want to accomplish? We first need goals. Well, the first goal is to get rid of these people; what were they called, The Gold Development Group? I think we need a hit man rather than lawyers.*

Michelle's thoughts were interrupted by hearing her mother's footsteps as she descended the stairs. Her mother smiled as she entered the kitchen, "Good morning, Daughter."

Michelle answered back, "Good morning, Mother; I made you coffee."

"Oh, thank you, dear. I don't mean to be abrupt, but I want to talk before we are interrupted by others."

Michelle understood.

"I have given it much thought, and I believe what has happened is good for our family." Hearing this, Michelle could only look at her mother quizzically.

"Think about this, we have sizable funds in the bank, yet we run a business that needs support from the French people to continue. I don't think it's right. I don't want the business or the property taken away from us, but the French people have already done enough for us. If we can't make this work, then perhaps we need to make changes."

"Here's what I propose. I want you to determine how much it will cost to run the inn and bistro, our business, including any new ventures we might attempt. Salaries, fees we need to pay, supplies, everything we will require for the next five years."

"Ok, you want me to develop a budget for the next five years," Michelle agreed, then added, "and you want me to include everything?"

"Yes, absolutely," Maria responded, then went on with her plan. "I have a meeting today at 11 a.m. with the mayor, or as he is now known, the representative of the Gold Development Group. I will call his bluff. I will refuse his offer and any counter-offer he may make. I anticipate he will then tell his friends at the Ministry to move forward with the violation if indeed he does have friends there."

"I follow so far," Michelle was typing notes as Maria spoke.

"You tell me how much we need to fund the business, and I will transfer a single lump sum into the local bank. We will draw on it as we need. In five years' time, if we cannot run this business properly, we will be broke and need to make changes. "

"You are giving us, the family, five years to make the necessary changes to put us on a sound financial footing. Ok, five years sounds reasonable," Michelle said with a shrug, then added, "That should also leave plenty in the bank to fall back on, in case."

"Yes, the thought has crossed my mind that in five years, if not sooner, I will want to enjoy life. I may want to travel, I may want to be the guest for a change," Maria said easily, as if she had given it more than just a passing thought.

"So, in my budget, you want me to include every possible revenue, expenditures, and other amounts we might need in the event we are successful, such as additional staff?" Michelle asked again while typing away. Maria replied, "Yes, please include everything, and try to be as accurate and realistic as possible. I don't know what the amount will be. I have an idea, but I want to see your calculations. I want a good, informed second opinion."

"Now, while you do that, I need to travel to Paris. I am going to find out who these people are and what I can do to make sure they never cause us, or any others, trouble again." Maria continued.

Michelle paused her typing, "Are you going to see him?"

Maria knew the question was coming, "I might, perhaps, I might need to ask a favor or two of an old friend. I will be gone a few days. I will leave you in charge. I will inform everyone that they answer to you," Maria stated.

"I will tell the others I am going to Paris to arrange funding from; what term did you use? A knight?"

Maria asked her daughter, who replied, "A white knight."

"Yes, a white knight. I will tell them I am going to meet a white knight. Meanwhile, before I leave, I will show you all the forms and records we keep. You can go to the bank for additional information. I will inform them that you are now the Business Manager for the Inn and Bistro and, as such, are entitled to see all the financial and business-related records. I will tell them that you will be performing a comprehensive review of the family business in the next few days and will be making many requests for information. I will ask them to expedite any requests you make. We are the bank's biggest client, and they are also outstanding clients of ours, so I don't anticipate any problems. I will leave you the phone number of a contact there. Her name is Christina. She is the wife of the bank president and is the real person in charge," Maria stated, finishing with a wink.

Michelle was impressed with her mother's focus and confidence. "When are you leaving, when will you return, and when do you want this?" Michelle asked in a serious tone, identical to her mother's and referring to the requested budget.

"I am leaving tomorrow. I believe I can conclude my business in two, maybe three days. I have made reservations at *The Royal*, on the *Rue de Adroismont* for three nights."

Michelle stopped typing for a minute and looked at her mother. "You are impressive. I have seen many people take charge and get things done, and you are as good as they come. I will have the analysis ready by the time you return."

"Thank you, daughter. That's very nice of you to say. Take your time with the analysis, the budget. I want it as detailed and real as possible."

Maria looked at the time. "I have time for another cup; then, I must get ready for my meeting with the mayor."

"Ok, let me save my notes; then I'll make us another cup." Michelle got up and started to prepare the coffee. As she waited for the water, she spoke. "When businesses budget, they usually use either a three-year or a five-year cycle. So you were smart to use five years. But in terms of accuracy, by definition, a budget is a forecast, and no one can predict the future. Ever since the terrorist attacks on the United States, investors and businesspeople have focused on what they call Event Risk. The risk or probability of something out of the ordinary; something completely unanticipated happening."

"Like someone insisting on buying your business," Maria added.

Michelle laughed at her mother's sense of humor. "Yes, I would call that event risk, but others may say an unfriendly takeover is not so unanticipated. In fact, you can say the purpose of a market is to price an asset correctly. If an asset is underpriced, the market will see to it that a buyer comes forward and makes the purchase."

Maria countered, "Even if the asset is not for sale?"

Michelle was quick to reply. She had had this argument with her co-workers over many a bottle of wine, "Mother, every asset is for sale, every asset, no matter how precious, no matter how symbolic, has a price." She cut her mother off as she tried to speak, "I bet I could buy the Eiffel Tower if I had enough money. Just make the argument, sell the old one and build a new, better one. If I was willing to pay a sum that allowed the government to pay every citizen of France 10,000 euro and still have enough to build another tower, I bet the citizens would say 'Take It!'"

Michelle continued, "Whatever that number is, that's the price." Maria thought the argument was absurd but allowed Michelle to make it. She was glad when Michelle changed the subject. "How will you travel to Paris?"

Maria had already made her arrangements. "I thought I would catch the morning train to Bordeaux then take the High-Speed train to Paris. The morning train leaves at 8 a.m. and gets to Bordeaux around 10. I should have time to make the noon express. It arrives in Paris around 2:10."

"Will Pierre take you to the station?" Michelle asked, trying to picture her mother riding in Pierre's Citroen.

"It's the only option. I could ask Christina at the bank, but she will have enough on her plate, dealing with you," Maria replied. "Besides, I don't like to ask favors of others. I have my own family to rely upon."

"Maybe, the Inn should purchase a Van. In the states, most Hotels, Resorts, Inns have van service. They use the van to pick up and drop off guests. Maybe we can even save some money by leasing one?" Michelle took a minute to add a note to her computer file to obtain a van for the Inn. She went back to preparing the coffee. "We can also use it to take some of the locals home after a long day at the bar," Michelle added, her mother nodding in agreement as Michelle poured sugar and then deep black coffee into their cups.

* * *

John Léger, the ex-president of France, sat in his study, sipping a glass of red wine and listening to the muted patter of light rain, typical for this time of year in the eastern French region of Burgundy. He sliced open the package dropped off by the courier earlier in the day. Experiencing a hectic day, he had waited until the evening to open the package, when it was quiet, and he could look through it without being disturbed.

The contents consisted of a bound presentation, very professional looking, with an executive summary, a description of the property, and a dozen pictures, taken at various times of the year. He recognized the inn and bistro from the pictures. *Hasn't changed in all these years*, he thought with a smile.

The Executive Summary laid out the plan to acquire the inn and bistro. The narrative detailed the rationale behind the plan, stating how the Villeneuve family had defrauded the French Government, had not taken the necessary steps to maintain historical authenticity, and portrayed the bistro as simply a saloon for locals to get away from their families, implying acts of infidelity after hours were a common occurrence. The presentation recommended that no further financial support be provided to the family and requested funding to buy out the family's interest in the property. The declaration further outlined how the property would be developed as a luxury mini resort with historical relevance, attracting affluent global travelers. This would improve the local economy by providing employment opportunities, encouraging tourism and discretionary spending, and generating tax revenue. *These guys know all the right buttons to push.* The president concluded, trying to quell the queasy feeling rising in his stomach.

He tossed it carelessly onto his desk when he finished reviewing the document and stared out the window. *This is outrageous and sad*, he thought. *How could people, in all seriousness, create such a tasteless fabrication? Is this what we all worked and sacrificed for, a government that acts in this underhanded manner?* He wondered, becoming more and more agitated as he recalled certain parts of the document from memory. *This will not stand. I won't have it. Not in my France and not to my friends.*

Leger bit his lip and picked up the phone. Even though it was 8 p.m., his call was answered on the second ring. "Yes, sir?" a very business-like woman's voice spoke. "Hello Suzette, I am glad you are still at your desk," Leger said, knowing full well his personal secretary would stay until 10 p.m. unless he said differently.

"Whom do we know over at the Ministry of Antiquities?" he asked. The reply was quick and efficient, "No one comes to mind, sir, but I do know the Minister is not considered a cabinet post, and the office is typically run by career bureaucrats. The Ministry itself belongs under the Department of Interior, headed by Bertrand DeHavre."

"Ah, my old friend Bertrand. Please call him and ask if he will join me for lunch tomorrow, 1 p.m., in the main dining room of the Royal Hotel; they serve a very nice lunch. Make reservations for two, please, out on the terrace if the weather's nice." "Yes, sir," the woman's voice said obediently.

Léger continued, "Please arrange for a car to take me to Paris. I will need it for at least three days. Call my wife and tell her I need to travel to Paris and will leave tomorrow at 9 a.m. I will be away for the next three days and will be staying at the apartment if she needs me for anything." He finished but had an afterthought, "If she asks, tell her I am going to Paris to right a wrong."

"Yes, sir," the woman on the phone complied and hung up.

A short time later, the phone rang. Léger picked it up.

"Yes?" On cue, the same woman's voice began speaking, "Your car, driver, and security detail will be downstairs at 8:45 a.m. The Honorable Minister DeHavre said it would be his pleasure to meet you for lunch at 1 p.m. at the Royal. He also wanted me to relay to you that he won't be bringing his Rugby shoes."

Léger chuckled and added, "Neither will I."

Suzette continued, "The Royal said it will be wonderful to see you again, and they will have a table for you at 1 p.m. on the terrace, weather permitting."

"Very good, Suzette," Leger concluded.

"Oh, one last item, your wife says there are no events planned, but to be safe and hurry home for the nights are getting longer and the weather colder."

Leger chuckled. "Indeed, that is so. Send my wife a dozen red roses. Write on the card, 'To my loving wife, I will be home soon. Sign it 'with loving adoration, your husband.'"

The ex-president thanked his secretary and gave her one last instruction. "Please call the Reception at the Royal and ask them to give Madam Villeneuve room #309. Ask them to place fresh flowers, pink and yellow roses if possible, in the room, with a bottle of their best champagne, two ounces of caviar, and two glasses. She should be arriving approximately 3 p.m. And of course, place the charges on my personal account."

"Yes, sir," Suzette said crisply.

"Thank you and good night," Léger replied.

"Good night, sir," Suzette added before hanging up the phone.

Chapter 8

As the Villeneuve family sat at their table and strategized, the mayor held a 'by invitation only' town meeting. Town meetings were usually held at the Bistro over lunch or dinner, but this meeting was being held in the community room located in the basement of the Municipal Building. Only a select group of prominent locals were notified and invited to attend. The mayor preferred small groups, *easier to control,* he would admit.

The mayor invited ten, and as he sat in the front of the seated group, he counted nine. *Good.* He thought, *all but one.* He stood up and spoke loudly, "Okay, let's come to order. Everyone knows me, Mayor Arnaud Martin, and of course, my secretary Claire. She will be taking the minutes. We will start with taking roll call."

After attendance was recorded, the mayor got down to business. "I called you here to regretfully inform you that ownership of the Inn at Saint Charles and The Tree Trunk Bistro will soon change." A murmur went through the crowd. The mayor continued, "Please don't be alarmed; I promise you, in terms of appearance, nothing will change. The reason for this is due to Madam Villeneuve's health. She has a condition and wishes to seek treatment. She needs time and, of course, funds to procure the very best care."

A voice from the audience spoke out, "We have known Maria for years and the Villeneuve family for generations; why isn't she talking to us?"

The mayor was ready for this line of questioning. "Madam Villeneuve is a very private person. She feels uncomfortable having her health discussed in a public venue. Suffice it to say she is in declining health. She knew I had a background in banking, so she asked me to find a suitable buyer. This was done some time ago and is now just being finalized. Of course, being the mayor, it is my duty to keep the population informed." The mayor thought his answer was particularly clever.

"Who is the buyer?" came from another attendee.

The mayor was also ready for this question. "After lengthy and involved negotiations, Madam is going to move forward with an organization called The Gold Development Group, Ltd."

This caused the murmuring to start again. "Please, please, please settle down," came from the mayor, who then added, "I think it's the right decision; the Gold Group has been around for some time and has a very extensive track record of managing properties in the hospitality industry. They are willing to pay top dollar, so that bodes well for Madam Villeneuve and her family. A spokesperson for the organization has assured all parties, nothing will change. I heard that directly from them. There will be a lengthy review as they get to know the town, the people, and the operation; you will see little difference while this is being accomplished. The changes they will make will be done carefully to maintain the local charm of the inn and bistro as well as the town itself. Perhaps one change they will make will be an expanded menu or new dining furniture. I have been here in Saint Charles for five years, and I believe I am eating off the same table, chair, and tablecloth."

A chuckle came from the small audience, with someone adding, "And utilizing the same silverware."

A few more questions were asked, and then the meeting was adjourned. Once the room was empty, the mayor turned to his secretary, "Well, that went well. I think everyone will cooperate. What do you think?"

Claire looked at her boss. "None of it was true. These people elected you the mayor, and you stood in front of them and lied. I am appalled."

With a grin on his face and feeling close to successfully completing the deal and earning himself a sizable finder's fee, the mayor replied without any remorse, "Claire, I am the mayor. My job is to promote growth and progress for our little village. Nobody is comfortable with change. If I must tell half-truths to sway public opinion, if I have to lie to get people to agree with the plan, then I must. It's my duty."

Claire responded, "I cannot believe…"

The mayor interrupted her, "It's late, but please stay and type up the minutes. Have them on my desk by morning. Do not enter them into the record, understand?"

Claire simply nodded her head. She was feeling very despondent.

The mayor walked off with a grin on his face, thinking, *She's appalled, huh, calling me a liar? Well, my dear, I hope it takes you all night.* "Lock up when you finish," he said over his shoulder, smiling while he exited the building.

* * *

Maria changed into a plain, casual business outfit for her meeting and was ready with time to spare. She felt uneasy, not having slept well the night before and drinking too much coffee that morning with Michelle. Adding to her stress level, she knew her meeting with the mayor would be antagonistic and combative. She knew what she wanted to say but could she say it? Would she find the words? She had an idea how the mayor would take it. *I know he has something at stake in this; he'll blow his top*; she just knew.

On her way out, she stopped at the front desk to get the folder she had prepared for the meeting and let the bellboy know she would be at the mayor's office. She checked the contents of her folder. Inside was a detailed list of the mayor's visits to the bistro, and his outstanding balance, having put every one of his meals on his official business account. Not only was she going to refuse his offer, but also demand payment for his meals, a sizable sum for a man with limited means. *Let him feel the heat for a change.* She smirked.

In the corner sat a large bouquet of flowers. *Isn't that lovely?* she thought and asked Andre who the flowers were for? He didn't know, so she took a quick look at the card. She read it quietly, "Maria, we hope you are feeling well and wish you a long and healthy life." It was signed "The Villagrosa Family." "*What in heaven's name?*" she thought.

She didn't have the time to worry about flowers and odd commiserations, so she put the card back and left, heading off to her appointment.

Maria walked into the mayor's office a few minutes early; it was empty and quiet and, not surprisingly, a bit dusty.

Claire stood up from her desk to welcome the visitor. "Good morning, Madam Villeneuve; it's wonderful to see you."

Maria looked at Claire, noticing she seemed particularly happy. "Good morning, Claire, it's a pleasure to see you. How is your family?" Maria inquired.

"Well, thank you. You look lovely today, Madam Villeneuve. Well, I apologize; you look lovely every day."

Maria smiled, "Thank you, Claire. Nice of you to say. You don't need to stand; please sit and do call me Maria."

"Thank you, Maria." Claire's face bloomed as she thanked her.

Claire sat and immediately buzzed the mayor to inform him his appointment had arrived, but she also pressed the speaker button unbeknownst to the mayor.

Maria thought it odd until the mayor answered. "Yes, Claire?"

"Sir, Madam Villeneuve is here for the 11 a.m. meeting," she said efficiently.

"Good," the mayor replied. "Have her wait; tell her I am in a meeting. At 11:20, bring her to my office, do not talk to her or offer her refreshment, I want her to sit and stew, I want her to be a little flustered."

Claire replied, "Yes, sir," and hung up. Claire smiled at Maria, that smile you give when you find yourself privy to someone's secret, and as she smiled, she pushed a folder across her desk towards Maria. Maria picked it up and looked inside. Inside were the minutes from the previous evening's Town Meeting, neatly typed on the mayor's letterhead, along with the mayor's signature. Claire had made sure to have the mayor sign the minutes, arguing that, eventually, they will have to be entered into the record.

Maria read the first page, slowly shook her head, and looked at Claire in disbelief before continuing to read. Finally, she spoke softly and slowly, "The audacity of this man."

Claire moved from her chair, went around to the front of her desk, and gave Maria a warm, generous hug. While they embraced, Claire whispered, "Do not fear this man, he is evil, yes, but he is a weakling. He is afraid of you."

Claire went back to her desk checking the time, saying to Maria, "The powder room is outside and just down the hall." Maria thanked her and went to the ladies' room to get herself together.

Returning to the mayor's office, she found him waiting for her in the reception area. "I'm so sorry, Mayor Martin. I thought I had enough time to freshen up," she said pleasantly.

"No problem, my meeting concluded just a few minutes ago; please come in. Claire, please, no calls."

"Yes, sir." Claire smiled and winked at Maria as the mayor led her into his office.

As they positioned themselves, the mayor did not offer any comfort to Maria. He had her sit in a cushion-less wooden chair, not at all comfortable, while he sat in an oversized leather executive chair. It made a swooshing sound as he sat.

The mayor began, "Madam Villeneuve, may I call you Maria?"

Maria looked straight at the mayor, revealing no emotion, and simply answered, "No".

"So be it then." The mayor toughened his demeanor. "We have known each other for many years, so that we can dispense with the pleasantries. My investors are getting impatient. Please tell me yes or no to the question, will you accept our offer, subject to contingencies and other adjustments?"

Maria shifted in her chair, more for effect than any other reason, though it was an uncomfortable chair. Again, not showing any emotion, she replied, "No."

The mayor sighed, "Do you want more money? This does not have to be difficult. As I mentioned to you and your daughter, either way, I will own the inn, and I will own The Tree Trunk. Now be serious, give me a number, give me your terms, just tell me, what do you want?" The mayor emphasized his last points by pounding on his desk.

Maria smiled at the mayor's bravado; it was all for show; he was trying to intimidate her. She stood up, took a step towards the mayor's desk, looking down at this unattractive, pitiful man. With a steady voice, she spoke clearly, "I want you to go to hell."

She turned towards the door, took a step, and turned back to face the speechless mayor. "We have implemented new policies; your bill is due in full." She tossed the folder containing his expenses onto his desk, turned, and walked out.

She left the mayor's office, closing the door behind her while the mayor swore and pounded his desk.

As she walked past Claire's desk, the mayor cried out, in a somewhat pleading voice, "Wait, please, wait for a moment." He came quickly out of his office and stood close to his secretary, hoping the sight of Claire would create some empathy. "Madam Villeneuve, we need not be so unfriendly to each other. Please, let's sit down again and determine how we can help each other. I am sure there is some accommodation we could make that would satisfy you. Why drag this out? Please come and sit down, would you like coffee?" The mayor was trying his best to get Maria to sit down and negotiate.

Maria turned to the mayor, clearly losing patience and no longer willing to put up a front, "Sir, I have given you my answer. Our business is therefore concluded. I find your presence repugnant, and I can hardly contain myself. I must leave before I say something not fitting for a woman to say."

"Okay," the mayor reluctantly concluded, "we will accomplish this with some difficulty, but I will give you advice; your refusal to negotiate, your little schoolgirl tantrum, will not change the outcome. Do you understand? Nothing has changed. I will own the Inn and The Tree Trunk, and I look forward to throwing you and your family out on the street."

The mayor looked at Maria, who just stared back, giving him the most disdainful of looks. The two looked silently at each other; finally, the mayor broke the silence. "Claire, give Madam Villeneuve the envelope."

"Which envelope, sir?" She replied.

The mayor, clearly agitated, replied, "From the Ministry, the one I gave you this morning. "

"Oh, let's see, where did I put that?" Claire searched through nearly every drawer in her desk, taking her time, further infuriating the mayor. She finally reached into one of her bottom drawers and pulled out an envelope. She sheepishly handed it to Maria, again, giving her a wink.

Maria took the envelope, turned, and left the Mayor's Office.

Claire started to speak, "Sir, I…"

The mayor cut her off, "Shut up," and stormed into his office, slamming the door.

Claire jumped up from her desk, ran outside, and caught up with Maria, standing on the corner, with her head down, seemingly upset.

"Madam Villeneuve, I must apologize." Maria turned around, catching Claire in mid-sentence. As Maria looked at Claire, Claire could see Maria wasn't crying; she was grinning; her eyes were bright and clear.

Maria gave Claire a warm hug. "Claire, I might not have said what I wanted to say, but I accomplished what I wanted to accomplish," Maria stated as the two started walking arm and arm down the lane to the Inn.

"What was that?" Claire asked innocently.

"Giving the mayor a stroke," Maria replied.

"Yes, I agree; I think you accomplished just that," Claire answered, and the two women laughed as they strolled along.

As they got closer to the inn, Maria stopped and looked at Claire. "Thank you for your assistance. You are a clever woman. I think you are wasting your time working as a secretary for a man as worthless as the mayor."

"I know." Claire admitted, "It's just a job, but this is my home. I want to stay in Saint Charles, I love this place, but there are not many opportunities."

"I want you to come work for me. We are making changes at the Inn. Michelle has brought new energy and new skills. We need bright people like you to be involved. But you need to recognize that there is little structure at the Inn. You will be called upon to do many tasks, some of them, perhaps, not so pleasant," Maria counseled.

Claire smiled eagerly, "Madam Villeneuve, I'm a farmer's daughter. We were raised with the idea that it's more important to get the work done than to wonder whose job it is or who gets the credit. Father always told me the most important thing is to get it done. When would you like me to start? "

Maria smiled, "Tell your father, I said you were raised well. How does right now sound?"

Claire smiled back and replied, "Wonderful. Give me about 30 minutes to resign and clean out my desk, and I'll be over."

Claire ran back to the mayor's office. He was standing over her desk, looking through her papers, searching for something. "Where have you been? I am looking for the Gold folder; what have you done with the Gold folder?" scolding her, still agitated from the meeting with Madam Villeneuve.

"Look on your desk. I saw it there this morning," Claire answered him, not knowing where the folder was but wanting the mayor to leave her alone.

When the mayor had gone back to his office, she placed a piece of paper in her typewriter and quickly typed, "As of this moment, I resign." She ripped out the paper, signed it, placed it in an envelope, placed the few personal items she had on her desk into her valise, and walked into the mayor's office without knocking. She threw the envelope containing her resignation on his desk and walked out.

Behind her, she could hear the mayor, "Fine, go, quit, but don't ask me for a recommendation; you won't get it. And where's the Gold folder? Before you go, get me the Gold folder. Claire? Claire? Claire!"

The mayor sat back in his chair, lit a cigar, and said out loud, "Good heavens, what a mess."

Reaching the inn, Maria closed the door behind her, leaned back against it, exhaled, and thought, *Ah, the peace and serenity of home….* No sooner had she finished her thought when the banging of pots and pans and shouting came from the Bistro's kitchen.

"No, never, the acidity would destroy the flavor. Seafood is delicate, it must be carefully prepared."

Daniel's heated voice could be heard, with Rudy's following along, "But it would add depth and act as a thickener; we could serve a small bowl as a starter, and a larger bowl as a main course."

Then, following Rudy was more of Daniel's shouting, "Fat, fat is what we want. Fat to caress, to massage the salty flesh of the fish. We want butter, cream, perhaps a touch of garlic, fresh pepper, mustard, or lemon to enliven the palette. Nothing else, no potato."

As Maria entered the kitchen, Michelle entered through the back entrance. She also had heard the commotion and came quickly.

Rudy saw the two women, smiled at Michelle, and then turned to Daniel, "Potato, who said anything about potato?"

Daniel, looking a bit confused, thought for a minute, "Tomato, I meant tomato, but we also have to be careful with the starch. Otherwise, our broth turns into something like porridge. Terrible. Ugh, like an English chowder."

Both men paused for a moment, not sure who had won the argument. Maria calmly spoke, "Gentlemen, we have a restaurant to run, and can I please remind you, we are currently serving lunch. I don't think our diners will enjoy their meals with a cacophony emanating from the kitchen. Now you two have to work out your differences. But I will say this: in the kitchen, in all matters, Daniel is in charge. I am sorry, Rudy, but that is the way it must be. You work for the Chef, and Daniel is the Chef. Now, please, gentlemen, behave."

Just then, Pierre, entered the kitchen. "Is everything alright? I was in the bar, and someone told me there was a fight in the kitchen." Maria looked at Pierre, gave him a look of displeasure, and said just loud enough for Pierre to hear, "So you finished your drink and came to investigate? I need to see you immediately." As she turned, she shouted, "Michelle, would you please watch the dining room?"

"Yes, mother," she replied.

Maria turned to leave, pushing open both swinging doors to the dining room.

Daniel, in the background, could be heard, "Ca co what? Is that an actual word? She always finds these odd words, cacophony? What does it mean?"

Michelle walked over to where her mother was standing, pushed open the doors just like her mother did, and said over her shoulder, "It means noise, Daniel, noise."

Daniel said to Rudy, "I know it means noise, but there are different types of noises, pleasant noises, and bad noises. Why doesn't she speak plainly? That's why you and I get along. We have our differences, but I like you; you speak plainly. I understand you. When you speak, I understand you."

Rudy smiled, "You know, Daniel, I like you too. I think you have more going for you than people give you credit for. I think you are brilliant, and there is no one more talented in the kitchen. My apologies. I will continue to make suggestions but follow your advice and instruction."

"Very good, thank you, I accept your apology, but what do you mean, 'You have more going for you? I don't understand; who gives me credit and for what?"

Chapter 1

Maria led Pierre into the small office behind the Inn's reception desk, taking a seat behind the desk, she asked Pierre to close the door, and then offered him a seat.

She started calmly, "Pierre, you are family, and I love you dearly, so I am going to be frank and straightforward. Have you been drinking? Why were you in the bar and not at your post? Daniel and Rudy shouting at each other was an embarrassment. If we want to be recognized, we must be professional at all times. We can't scoot off for a glass at the bar in the middle of service." She finished and looked sadly at Pierre, wishing she didn't have to have this conversation.

Pierre lit his cigarette, slowly inhaled, exhaled, and spoke, "Maria, you need not worry. I haven't had a drink in days. I don't need to drink. I was at the bar because Paul Stephenson brought his nephew around and wanted us to meet him. We talked; I sipped mineral water. I didn't know anything until one of the waiters came for me."

Maria almost cried, being so relieved. "Oh, Pierre, please accept my apologies. I am so sorry for my accusations; I am sorry for not having faith in you."

Pierre added quickly while still on the subject, "You need to meet this young man. He's very impressive. He would make a perfect mayor, if he wanted the job. We will need someone. The current mayor won't be around long once word gets out of his little scheme."

Maria looked at Pierre with the look of someone who had just been given proof that the Earth was round. She took a tissue to her eyes and continued, "I forget how smart and clever you are. You go about your duties in such an unassuming manner. It's easy to underestimate you."

Pierre smiled, "To be underestimated is like being dealt an extra card."

Maria smiled back, not sure if she was comfortable with Pierre's metaphor. "I have been too busy dealing with our current mayor, the Ministry, and the Gold Group to think about what or who's next. You are right, though; we need to rid ourselves of the mayor; better yet, the town needs to get rid of him. Vote him out of office. We need to start a recall." She paused then asked with a half-serious smile, "Tell me more about the new mayor."

Pierre chuckled at Maria's reference to the new mayor and then described the man he had just met in the bar. "His nephew is a fine-looking gentleman, an American. He just left the military. He was an officer, a Marine fighter pilot, shot down over Lebanon. He said it happened so fast, he didn't have time to be scared. But the episode gave him religion, so to speak. He figured he had cheated death once and didn't want to give it another chance, so he resigned his commission. He's looking to settle down here in Saint Charles. I think he would make a fine Mayor. "

"He sounds like an excellent candidate; I'd like to meet him. Let's welcome him to Saint Charles," she said with a wink.

Pierre nodded, "Good idea."

Maria then asked, "I meant to ask you earlier, can you take me to the train station tomorrow morning? I need to catch the 8 a.m. train to Bordeaux."

"Certainly. We will need to leave early, perhaps 6 a.m.," Pierre replied.

"I'll be ready. I will meet you out front at 6 a.m." Maria smiled, "Thank you, Pierre, let's go back to work, and let's hope there's no further bloodshed in the kitchen."

As they were getting up, Pierre suggested, speaking softly, "Of course, if we had a guillotine, we could dispense with the mayor once and for all. We could invite everyone; have quite the time of it."

Maria laughed at such an absurd suggestion. "Don't talk like that, Pierre. For all we know, one of the local farmers has an old one hidden away in his barn."

Pierre chuckled at the notion and added, "and is just waiting for such an opportunity to use it."

They came out of the office and were immediately met by a deliveryman carrying a large bouquet of fresh flowers. "Oh no, not another," Maria exclaimed.

The delivery man smiled and said, "For Madam Villeneuve."

"I am Madam Villeneuve." Maria accepted the bouquet, took the card out of the small envelope, and read it out loud, "Dear Maria, life is full of adversity. Our family's prayers are with you for your continued good health and happiness. The Tremont Family."

Pierre looked quizzically at Maria, "Maria, what do they know that we don't know? Is there something you need to tell us?"

* * *

That evening, Maria closed the bistro early so the family could meet. Only the Zieglers remained as guests, the other two parties having checked out that morning. Maria made sure they had an opportunity to dine before closing.

Even though the bistro had closed early, it was after 8 p.m. by the time the family sat down together. Maria informed everyone of the outcome of her meeting with the mayor. She announced her decision to decline the mayor's offer and her intention of going to Paris to meet with a white knight.

She then described the task she gave to Michelle and the five-year plan. "Michelle?" Maria asked, "Have you made any progress on the budget?"

Michelle flipped open her laptop, pressed a few keys, and intently focused on the computer's screen. "Well, yes and no," she replied. "The problem is, so much is done on a bartering basis, and prices charged for meals fluctuate, not only day-to-day but also within the course of a single service, making it difficult to pin down historical revenue and costs. Without historical numbers, I have nowhere to start the forecast. We might as well just come up with some margin assumptions and go from there."

"Ok, dear, try your best," Maria said simply and then asked, "Has Claire been helpful?"

"Yes, very, thank you." Michelle replied, "She's been great at collecting data and sorting it out. I ordered her a laptop; she's eager to learn. I hope that's ok?"

Maria shrugged, "You're the business manager, just make sure it's in the budget." Maria continued, "Do I also understand that you are recommending consistency with our pricing?"

Michelle was surprised. Her mother seemed to know where she wanted to take the conversation and quickly agreed, "Yes, consistency across the board. Consistency in pricing our product, consistency in our menu selections, consistency in our presentations, and most importantly, consistency in the quality of our offerings."

It was Daniel's turn to speak, "How do we obtain so much consistency? Sometimes we don't know what we will serve until Stephenson or Tremont drive up in their trucks and show us what they have, and they don't know what they will have until they return from the market. If they have chicken leftover, which they usually do, they offer us chicken, and sometimes it's beef or pork."

Pierre entered the discussion, "What we need to do is tell Tremont, Stephenson, and all the other Farmers, tell them to see us before going to market. Tell them we will give them a fair price, and we also need to start telling them what we want. They are our suppliers; we are not orphans deserving only of the leftovers."

Daniel replied, "Fine, yes, I agree, but how do we know what price to pay, what is fair? Plus, they leave for the market at 4 a.m. Do you want to get up at 4 a.m. to negotiate pork or chicken prices? I don't. I work late. I cannot be in the kitchen 24 hours a day."

Michelle said to herself, *Well, here goes*, then spoke, "I want to start the retail bakery. I will need to be up to get the ovens on, finish proofing the dough and get the bread into the ovens. 4 a.m. sounds about right; I'll be up; I'll purchase the supplies if you tell me what to buy. But we still need to solve the pricing question."

Rudy offered his help, "I'll get up with you, at least temporarily, until you know what you are doing, rather until we know what we are doing. Daniel and I will work on setting a menu. We need to agree on the structure of the menu. We'll limit it to three or four regular items, then maybe a seasonal special or two. Maybe Daniel finds his truffles, and so in the fall, we offer a special truffle entrée."

Daniel quickly cut in, "Shhhh, you must not speak of truffles, please, everyone. You never heard me speak of truffles."

Rudy laughed, "When the menu is set, we will know what supplies to buy, but two problems remain; how much to buy and how much to pay? We never know if we will have five or fifteen for dinner."

Daniel added, "Yes, on Thursday it could be fifteen, but Wednesday only five, Friday and Saturday, it depends. If it's spring, farmers are busy planting and are tired, and they don't want to go out. But in winter, we are busy. The locals are finished for the season, and they want to get out, see friends, enjoy life."

"Michelle?" Maria spoke, "Could you also do a study of customer habits, starting with how many visitors per day, per month. Is that possible?"

Michelle was typing away, taking notes, speaking as she typed, "Customer trends, if the data is there, we'll put it together."

"Good," Maria replied. "Could you then look at the money spent, the revenue? I know you said earlier that it varied, but let's see what the data shows."

Michelle was impressed, "Mother, what you are asking me to do is called data mining. You have an idea, but you want the data to reveal itself. You want the answers to verify the questions."

Maria, looking a bit unsure, replied, "Yes, I think so."

Daniel laughed, "That's what it sounds like; you want the data to come alive."

Pierre supported the notion, "How many times have you heard the phrase 'it's a data-driven world?' Well, here we are, looking for the data to give us answers to questions we haven't even asked."

Michelle looked at Pierre and said, "That's brilliant, Uncle; my Marketing Professor said those exact same words. Brilliant."

"Let's talk to Claire and see if she knows what her family does. They've been delivering produce and meat to the market for generations. If anyone's plugged in, they are," Rudy added.

"Ok, good. It feels like we are all together on this and making progress. That makes me very happy. I am proud of everyone, very proud. "

Everyone seemed happy and content. Maria then took on a more serious tone, "Everyone recalls, I'll be in Paris till Friday, possibly Saturday?" she stated, looking them in the eye, making sure they all understood. "Ok, good, Michelle is in charge while I am away." Again, she looked at everyone to get acknowledgment. Satisfied, she ended the meeting.

* * *

Everybody was up and going about their business by the time Pierre returned from dropping Maria off. As he entered the Inn, he looked at his watch, "Ah, 10 a.m., still time for a cup of coffee before I have to prepare for lunch," and headed to the family kitchen.

Rudy and Daniel were up and working, sitting at the table. In front of them were a stack of blank paper, pencils, and a couple of half-empty coffee cups. Crumbled pieces of paper, each symbolizing a failed attempt at accomplishing something, were everywhere, on the floor, across the table, on the empty chairs, filling the trash bin, everywhere.

The two were working on the dinner menu, and as Pierre walked by on his way to the stove, he glanced over Rudy's shoulder. He could see the notes and thus the progress the two had made. At the top of the page, the word 'Menu', then farther down the page, was the number one, and the word chicken. The remainder of the sheet had various doodles and scribbles down the margins but otherwise was blank.

"How long have you two been working on this?" Pierre inquired as he sat down with his coffee. Daniel replied, "Only about, since 7:30 a.m."

Pierre looked at him. "Are you serious? Its 10 a.m., 2 ½ hours? You've been at this for 2 ½ hours?" Rudy looked up from his recent scribbling and, with a look of defeat, simply nodded.

"Look, let me help. Sometimes it's better to have three; that way, the vote goes either way." Pierre advised, "And besides, I've eaten in enough establishments to know what a menu should look like."

Rudy fired back, "Ok, Uncle, give it your best."

Pierre lit a cigarette and began, "Ok, Daniel, the first item, chicken, we'll offer a roast chicken, with of course pan gravy, potatoes, a green vegetable. It'll make for a very nice presentation."

Daniel answered with a concerned look on his face, "Roast, why call it roast? Sometimes I like to braise it with red wine, sometimes I grill it or sauté. I don't always roast. It depends on the chicken, the weather, many things."

Rudy was first with his thoughts, "Weather? What does the weather have to do with how we prepare chicken?"

Daniel simply shrugged his shoulders, "The weather changes your emotion. It changes your appetite. It affects how food should be prepared."

Pierre quickly stepped in, "We need consistency, remember?"

Daniel replied in a serious voice, "It's chicken, that's consistent." Pierre was about to speak when Daniel spoke again, "People order my chicken because they like it, and they know I will make it entertaining."

Pierre gave Daniel an odd look. "Entertaining?"

Daniel replied, "Yes, entertaining, you know, fun."

Rudy said softly to Pierre, "He wants us to put Fun Chicken on the menu."

Pierre didn't know if the two were truly serious. Instead, looking bewildered, he said, "Well, let's move on, pork, shall we offer a grilled pork chop or loin roast, perhaps with figs, plums, or other stone fruit? It would be a simple dish, easy to prepare, and not burden the kitchen."

Daniel again spoke, "Maybe not grill, well, yes, sometimes, but you see, pork tells me; it lets me know, it's friendly, it tells me, 'Make me taste good,' I ask how, and it tells me. Pork is very friendly, very helpful in that way. You know, it has lots of fat. Fat means flavor. If you don't use it, it is not happy."

Pierre looked at his brother, looked at Rudy, then back to Daniel. "Are you serious?" he asked in a soft, muted tone.

Daniel replied without expression, "Of course, I never joke about food, especially protein. Protein is very important."

"And it knows it." Rudy added with a sarcastic nod.

"Exactly," Daniel exclaimed, thrilled, finally someone understood his point of view. He continued, "That is what I am trying to say. Exactly." Daniel was now quite happy, happy they were making progress.

Pierre gave each a glance, finally saying slowly, softly, and deliberately, "We need to be serious."

Daniel nodded in agreement.

"I am sorry, but we cannot put 'Fun Chicken and Friendly Pork' on the menu." Pierre insisted.

Rudy, who had been listening to the exchange, started slowly snickering and exhaling out his nose, trying to control his laughter.

Pierre knew he shouldn't ask but was just too curious, "Beef? What can we offer?"

Daniel thought for a moment, finally telling Pierre, "Beef? Beef is a snob. It knows it tastes good. You must respect beef when you prepare it. When I'm about to prepare beef, it tells me, 'Hey, don't mess up. Make no mistakes, or I'll be tough and tasteless.'"

Pierre was beside himself, "We've got Fun Chicken, Friendly Pork, and Snobby Beef? That's our menu? It sounds like a Chinese restaurant."

Rudy erupted in laughter. Daniel replied, "Well, maybe snobby is too harsh a word, call it, say, call it egotistical. Yes, egotistical. No one would argue if you called beef egotistical. I'm sure everyone would agree."

Pierre folded his arms and put his head down on the table, and though it was muffled, he could be heard moaning, "No, oh god no, why me, no, no."

Daniel got up and asked, "I will make more coffee; does anybody want another coffee?"

"Sure, I'll take another cup," came from Rudy.

Pierre kept his head on his hands, finally lifting his head, "Daniel, lunch will start soon. "

"I know, look, this is what I think; even if raw chicken were on the menu, I would not prepare it exactly the same. We need consistency, but that's from Michelle's point of view, a business point of view. So, our menu is chicken, and we charge, for example, 22 euros, pork 32 euros, and beef 45. We tell people what ingredients we have, and I will cook for them."

"Well, we can't seem to decide on a menu. Maybe it's the approach we have to take. You have to admit, it allows us the flexibility to use whatever ingredients are available," Rudy said as he finished his coffee, then added, "Time to hit the trenches."

Daniel finished his cup and added, "Yes, it is time, time to see all my friends. But we did not discuss one important ingredient."

Rudy, curious, asked, "What, seafood?"

"No, but that too." Daniel replied, "What I was thinking of was lamb."

Rudy took the bait, "What about lamb? What do you say to lamb?"

With a big grin, Daniel replied, "Well, you see, lamb, lamb is very sheepish."

* * *

Maria's train to Bordeaux was on time, leaving her plenty of room to catch the noon high-speed train to Paris. But some technical difficulty delayed the train's departure by 30 minutes. The delay and the two-and-a-half-hour train ride gave her ample time to contemplate right and wrong.

She wondered what to say to a man she hadn't seen in years. How inconsiderate was it of her to contact him and ask for help out of the blue? Would the feelings she had for him years ago come back? How would he feel about her after all these years? She gazed at the landscape as it went flashing by. *Why didn't I just use the money and pay these men to go away? But I would be paying for extortion. It is wrong, and what happens the next time, and then the next time? Pretty soon, the money is gone, but not the trouble. No, the correct way to deal with these people is to squash them like cockroaches. John is just the man to do that, and if he can't or won't, he'll know people who will.*

She drifted off to sleep, lured by the even hum of the train and the occasional slight bump that reminded her of movement.

Chapter 10

It was a pleasant autumn day in Paris, slightly overcast, but with temperatures in the low 20s C, making it comfortable for those wearing business attire. Leger's two-person security detail was first to enter the main dining room of the Royal Hotel and was immediately directed to the rear terrace. A few patrons were already having lunch, and a table was set off to the side, held in reserve for Leger. The security detail surveyed the situation, signaled the go-ahead to Leger, and took positions inconspicuously on either side of the wide terrace. John Leger entered and was led to his table by the Maitre'd. His table was situated well away from prying eyes and ears.

A waiter appeared and pulled back the chair, helping Leger sit. "Good afternoon, Monsieur Leger. As always, it is a pleasure to have you visit us." The waiter, looking impeccable in a black tuxedo, asked respectfully as he cleared the table of unnecessary dishes and cutlery, "Sir, will you be expecting company?"

"Yes, an associate will be joining me shortly," Leger replied as he was handed a menu. He briefly examined the menu and handed it back to the waiter. "Is Charles Dupre in the kitchen today?" Leger asked.

"Yes, sir, he is," the waiter replied.

"Please send him my regards, and ask if he would do me the honor of cooking for my associate and myself?" Anticipating he would, as he always did, Leger added, "Three courses would be fine."

The waiter nodded and was back before Leger could sip his water. "Chef Dupre said it would be his pleasure. He asks that you accept this bottle of L'Hermitage White Burgundy as he prepares your first course," The waiter commented as he started to uncork the bottle."

Leger smiled, "I know this Chateau well." then glancing at the label, "1995 was an excellent year, a perfect vintage. My compliments to the Chef, his taste, his judgment as always, are impeccable."

As the waiter nodded and poured a taste for Leger to sample, a voice came from a short distance away, "I hope that's not some overly sweet fabrication from California that you're going to force me to drink?" Bertrand DeHavre, Minister of the Interior and the third most powerful man in France stated in a smart tone but with a large smile, demonstrating he wasn't to be taken seriously.

"Ah, Bertrand," Leger stood up and extended his hand, "so good to see you. It's been a while, old friend, it's been too long."

Bertrand took his friend's hand, and with the other, hugged Leger, as only a close friend would. "Good to see you. Thank you for the invite. I am embarrassed that I have not kept in touch with you. Forgive me." Bertrand added as the waiter assisted him with his chair.

Leger sat and smiled, "No problem, I fully understand; you have a country to run. I am sure the incompetence of your associates is providing you with plenty of opportunity for extra effort."

Bertrand smiled, "There's good, and there's bad. Yes, extra work, but their incompetence leaves plenty of openings for political maneuvers. But I tell you in all seriousness, everyone has their hand out, everyone. If we are not careful, we will soon become Italy."

Bertrand sipped his wine, "Lovely, hmmm, what flavor, excellent." Checking the label on the bottle, he added, "1995, no wonder. I didn't think there were any left; this is indeed a special occasion." Bertrand sipped again and smiled.

Chef Dupre served a marinated chilled seafood salad with sardines, octopus, and prawns. The saltiness of the fish was enlivened by a touch of vinegar and tart lemon juice. The dish nicely complemented the buttery texture and oak flavors of the wine. Both men agreed; the first course was perfect.

The two men had finished reminiscing by the time the second course was served. The waiter brought another bottle, this time a red from the Rhone Valley region, lighter than a Bordeaux or Burgundy but flavorful and a refreshing accompaniment to the heavier beef dish served as a second course. Neither man could find fault with the second course.

Leger stated his business, "Bertrand, I have a problem I am asking for your help in solving."

Bertrand was quick to offer his assistance, "How can I help? You know I will do what I can."

"Yes, I know, and thank you," Leger replied and continued, "Tell me what you know about the Ministry of Antiquities?'

Bertrand laughed briefly and shrugged his shoulders, "The Ministry, if you want to call it that, is my responsibility. It is a quagmire of innuendo and backstabbing, fueled by career bureaucrats with nothing going for them except a steady paycheck. We joke that the men there would rather go to fashion shows than a rugby match and the women to rugby matches rather than fashion shows."

Leger chuckled at Bertrand's humor, not because it was funny, but more so because he had heard similar from other sources. Leger handed Bertrand the presentation prepared by Gold Development Group. "Here, please review this. It is the problem. There is a man inside, at the Ministry, who is enabling this to go forward. I believe he might be the catalyst."

After a few minutes, Bertrand handed the presentation back to Leger. "It's a travesty. Situations like this should not happen. We consider ourselves civilized, ruled by laws. The law is not working if situations such as this are allowed, are permitted to take place. Knowing you as I do, I presume it is your goal to stop this. What is your plan? What do you propose, and how can I assist?"

"I would like to visit this man. I believe his name is John DeHaven." Leger laid out his plan with Bertrand listening intently, adding a few points, and agreeing to be Leger's accomplice. The two decided that Friday evening, towards the closure of business, would be the perfect time to pay a visit.

Bertrand summed it up, "I like this plan. Sometimes a man must get his hands dirty. I will do my part and be ready by Friday. I am more than happy to participate. Together, my old friend, we will preserve justice. Viva la France."

Leger smiled and saluted back, as they did years ago, back in their university days, "Viva la Liberte."

The meal concluded with a dessert of crème brûlée served with a hazelnut madeleine and followed by double espresso. The two men departed after agreeing to a time and place to meet on Friday. Bertrand went out the back way, through the kitchen, followed by his security detail, while Leger settled the bill, thanked Chef Dupree and the dining room staff, and headed for the front desk. "Has Madame Villeneuve arrived?" he asked the concierge.

"Yes, she arrived 20 minutes ago. She is assigned room #309 as requested. Flowers were placed in her room 30 minutes ago, anticipating her arrival, and champagne and caviar were delivered approximately three minutes ago."

Leger smiled, thanked the young man, and then turned to his security team. "I will not need you any longer today. Please, if you could meet me at 7:00 a.m., here in the Lobby. I will have my phone if there is any need to contact me; I will be in room 309."

Leger took the elevator to the third floor and walked slowly down the hallway, knowing all along where room 309 was located, but feeling unable to shake his schoolboy hesitation. He had butterflies in his stomach, such as he hadn't had in years. He was eager to see Maria, but meeting after so long was giving him butterflies. *Perhaps*, he thought, *it would be easier if their first meeting weren't so perfect.*

He got to the room and stood for a moment, adjusting his tie, telling himself to remain calm. Finally, he tapped lightly, and after a short time, the door slowly opened. Maria stood there in her robe, her hair down, make-up off, eyes gleaming a bright, iridescent blue, her natural beauty fully on display. To John Leger, she was the most beautiful woman he had ever laid eyes on. He stepped into the room. They embraced. Leger softly spoke into her ear, "I must tell you, my only regret in life is that I did not meet you before you became obligated to another."

She replied softly, feeling safe and comfortable in his arms, enjoying his warmth, his masculinity, "Tragedy and a great loss, my loss, brought us together. Please understand when I say I wish we had never had reason to meet yet meeting you has brought passion and meaning back into my life. You are strong, and I am so very weak. Forgive me."

Leger held her tightly, "I understand. Always remember I am here for you. You need not fear." He gently closed the door behind him.

* * *

Michelle gave Claire the new laptop when it arrived while offering her the same advice she had received years ago, "This is the most important tool you'll ever have, besides your own brain. Always remember, it is a tool, a beneficial tool, nothing else. If ever there is a decision to be made, and you don't trust the numbers, trust your gut."

"My gut?" Claire asked, "What kind of word is this? Gut?"

Michelle laughed and explained the uniquely American word.

"Oh, I see," was Claire's response.

The two got down to business, with Claire an eager and intelligent pupil. She picked up the basic computer skills needed and was quick with her understanding of business terms. Claire easily followed Michelle as she moved along quickly, explaining basic business concepts such as assets and liabilities and then various advanced business concepts such as working capital, liquidity, depreciation, cash flow, and operating leverage.

Michelle marveled at Claire's ability to absorb and comprehend, jokingly saying to her at one point, "Good heavens, I paid 100,000 US dollars in tuition and spent two years studying for an education that you are picking up in an afternoon. Either I've been hoodwinked, or I am the best teacher the world has ever seen!"

She stopped suddenly, caught herself, and added, "More likely, you are the brightest and best student any teacher could ever hope for. We are lucky to have you with us."

Claire blushed and smiled, "You are an excellent instructor. Thank you for spending the time to teach me. I have been debating whether to attend University. I don't want to leave Saint Charles, but I want to learn. I think what you are teaching me is wonderful and very useful."

The two women worked diligently, trying to capture the operating financial characteristics of the inn and bistro. It was confusing work, with one change in assumptions seemingly having a magnifying effect across the whole analysis and prompting changes everywhere. More than once, Michelle threw up her hands and insisted they start over. But every change, edit, or do-over brought them that much closer to having a solid model, one they were confident in and one that yielded valuable information.

While taking a coffee break, Michelle noticed Claire had a copy of the latest issue of a popular woman's magazine. She mentioned casually to Claire that she was also a reader of the magazine and especially liked the "Away for The Weekend" travel section. The section highlighted various places around France that a woman might find interesting and entertaining and enjoy with a spouse, friend or lover, as a quick weekend trip. In the past, Michelle had enjoyed reading articles written on the Pyrenees Mountains, Bordeaux and the countryside, the Italian Riviera, and of course, the popular ski and spa adventures to the Alps.

Claire nonchalantly commented, "We should write a letter inviting the magazine to spend the weekend here in Saint Charles. We could say the hiking is spectacular, the food, fresh and natural, and a person could sleep because there are no cinemas, or clubs, or even television for that matter."

Michelle laughed, "Yes, we could offer it for travelers who want to go back in time."

The two girls laughed at the notion, but the more Michelle thought about it, the more she liked the idea. Finally, towards the end of the day, she confided in Claire, "I want to do it."

Claire replied, puzzled, "Ok, but what is it you want to do?"

"Invite the magazine to Saint Charles for the weekend," Michelle replied with a mischievous smile.

* * *

Rudy woke at his usual time; shortly after sunrise, he got himself out of bed, made his way to his small kitchenette, and started to prepare coffee. He felt stiff and uncoordinated and thought he needed to put himself through a solid, strenuous workout to get back to normal. As he waited for the water to boil, he heard keys being fumbled and the pronounced click of a padlock being unlocked. Looking out the window, he saw Daniel, all muddied in his overalls and boots, with a large wicker basket covered with burlap, not full, but obviously holding some contents.

Daniel unlocked the old root cellar door and started down the half-dozen or so steps to the cellar. Before entering, he looked back and carefully surveyed the scene around him as if he were a commando on a mission, deep inside the enemy-controlled territory. He did not notice Rudy peering through his kitchen window.

I wonder what he's up to. I didn't think anyone went down there anymore, Rudy thought, though there was talk that Daniel would use the cellar to cure hams and sausages to offer in the restaurant. *Has he started already? Where did he get the hams? Maybe he's doing some sausage or something easy? I think it's best to try something simple; I don't know if the root cellar is suitable for curing. It could be too wet, too moldy, and ultimately toxic. I should do some research just to make sure.* Rudy smirked. *That would sure make us famous. Historical Inn poisons its patrons.* Rudy, picturing the headlines, shrugged his shoulders, poured a cup of strong coffee, and started to loosen up for the challenging workout he planned for himself, not giving the root cellar another thought. As he was loosening up, he started to think, *That new girl, Claire, she's a cute one, and I hear brilliant too. I think I will have to take a closer look.*

* * *

Daniel returned from foraging in the woods and meadows, visiting a few of his favorite spots and not being disappointed with his bounty. He found a small patch of Morels, standing tall and healthy. He found delicate, buttery Girolles, bright yellow with a hint of orange. Amazingly, one of his favorite spots, because of the apparent potential, had Cepes growing everywhere. *Wonderful,* he thought as he carefully picked a dozen of the larger fungi and noted where the smaller ones were, estimating they would be ready in another month, weather permitting.

Finally, as he was walking along, visually scouring the ground around him, he had a hunch. In a dimly lit area of the forest amongst a cluster of mature oak trees and just on the edge of a swamp, where the earth was still solid, but just barely so, he got down on his hands and knees. He put his face to the ground and slowly inhaled the earthy, decaying smell of the swamp as if determining the quality of a newly opened bottle of wine. But Daniel, like many others, suffered from the late allergy season, and as he inhaled, his congestion caused him to grunt, almost like a pig.

Not smelling what he hoped for, he crawled slightly forward, smelled again, grunted two or three times, moved slightly forward, and smelled once again. This time, he noticed something. He took out his handkerchief and tried to clear his sinuses as best he could, then put his face back into the dirt and took another prolonged inhalation.

Daniel's eyes lit up. He stood, grabbed his shovel, and stomped the shovel into the ground using his foot and all his weight. Then with all his strength, he pulled up a large clump of muddy earth; the swampy water and roots cascaded off his shovel. He quickly got on his knees and used his fingers to carefully sort through the pile of thick mud and forest debris, finally finding his prize. "Hello, my little babies. Did you think you could hide from me?" Daniel whispered as he held up a cluster of oddly shaped black truffles.

Chapter II

Pierre woke up feeling anxious. He didn't feel he was carrying his weight, doing his part. Daniel always seemed busy. Rudy was always involved with something. Maria, Michelle, who just arrived, and even the young boys hired as bellhops, were always scurrying about. Yet he, at many times during the day, had to think of something to keep busy and many times couldn't think of anything. He could ask Maria for something to do, but he had his pride and, heaven forbid, she might assign him to work for Rudy or, worse yet, Daniel.

So, when the opportunity came, he was ready to take the initiative. After consulting with family members, everyone agreed to let him lead the negotiations with the local farmers.

Pierre invited the six most prominent and active farmers to an end-of-the- week, early dinner meeting. He knew the farmers got up early, worked hard throughout each day, liked to eat an early dinner, and then relax with more than a glass of wine. He wanted the farmers to be comfortable, calm, and candid when answering his questions and agreeable to his proposals. He preferred the end of the day. Negotiations would be relaxed, and Daniel, Rudy, and Michelle would be able to attend.

Pierre started the discussion as Daniel poured cognac all around. Michele sat quietly while Daniel filled her glass. *Oh no, not again.* She remembered the last episode with cognac and the resulting pain. *Pace yourself, don't try to keep up.*

"Gentlemen, we here at the Tree Trunk are changing; call it maturing. We no longer want just to exist; we want to be noticed. We want to offer world-class regional cuisine. We can only do it if we have the finest, world-class ingredients. We can only do it with your help," Pierre stated loudly to ensure everyone took him seriously. He paused for a moment to look each one in the eyes. In his mind, he was dramatic.

"We no longer want to be just a drop-off, an orphanage, a place to rid yourself of whatever didn't sell in the market, only worthy of your day-old bread and your charity." Pierre continued speaking metaphorically, feeling confident he was making his point.

"Let us have your best, and not only will we pay your price, but we will tell the world where we sourced our ingredients. We will use only locally grown and harvested and promote locally grown and harvested." Pierre stopped to take a sip of his cognac.

It was almost like begging the question to be asked. "We all produce excellent wine, but what about beer and liquor, cognac? I don't know anyone who distills gin or scotch. I don't drink the stuff, but I know it can be very popular with tourists, especially the Brits," a farmer asked. A few others murmured in agreement.

Pierre nodded his head in agreement and took his time answering an obviously difficult question. "I don't have all the answers; some issues still need to be worked out. But I will say this. I feel very strongly about the regional theme. I would rather stay true to the regional theme than violate it. We don't have a policy yet as to what defines local, but I would say if we can't source it within 200 or 300 kilometers in any direction, we're not going to offer it. Besides, Brits will drink anything you put in front of them." Pierre smiled at his humor, as did the farmers who seemed to agree with his conclusion. Pierre used the opportunity to rest and allow his point to sink in before continuing, "But in order to have a policy, we must discuss and have an agreement. I only meant to demonstrate to everyone what we mean as 'local.'"

Michelle motioned to Pierre, asking if she could have the floor. Pierre bowed and stood aside as Michelle stood up and faced the crowd.

"Hello everyone," she started slowly, "my name is Michelle Villeneuve. Some of you may recognize me. I have been away for the last ten years and only recently returned. I was away in America, where I earned a business degree and worked on Wall Street. I like to think I know something about business, a lot of book knowledge for sure. But I must confess, I am just starting to understand how to run a business. With that in mind and understanding my background, perhaps you can educate me, help me understand how we can be successful together, let's be partners. How can we be successful in procuring the very best you have to offer and motivate you to produce goods you don't currently offer? Thank you." Finished, Michelle sat down, giving the floor back to Pierre.

The farmers looked at each other, whispered, gestured, shrugged, smiled, winked, finished their drinks, whispered some more, and asked for another pour. Daniel happily refilled each glass, including his own. Pierre, Rudy, and Michelle wisely declined.

Finally, one of the farmers stood up. It was Peter Tremont. "First of all, we want to say thank you for inviting us here this evening. We are a small community. Our families have known each other for generations. It is good we take opportunities like this to talk, to share, perhaps even plan. Second, our prayers are with Maria. We hope she is well, and if there is anything we can do to support her in her struggles, let us know." Pierre nodded his head and looked at Rudy and Michelle, who simply nodded in recognition. Before she left for Paris, she asked everyone to be mum about the situation, not knowing what would occur there.

Tremont continued, "Lastly, we liked what we heard. Like you, we want to be recognized for our work, and many of us are not entirely satisfied with our relationship with the markets. Many times, we have brought our best, what we consider exceptional quality, but we are treated like ordinary pig farmers, offered less than fair, and told to take it or leave it." The farmers stomped their feet and vocalized their support for Tremont's position. When the group had quieted down a bit, he added, "That is not the way we do business here in Saint Charles, and that is not how we manage our relationships."

Jacques Faucher, ever a quiet man, stood up, allowing Tremont to sit, "We have been waiting patiently for exactly what you propose, a showcase where we provide our best and get recognized for the quality of our product. We have been farmers for generations; we know the land, we know the climate, what the clouds mean. We know how to coax the best from the earth. You tell us what you want, what you need, and we will bring it to you." Again, the farmers stomped their feet.

This time Pierre and Daniel were so taken by the sincerity and outpouring of friendship that they too stomped their feet and clapped. Michelle was amazed at the willingness and generosity of the Farmers. *I guess this has been a long time coming,* she thought as she began clapping her hands, not wanting to be left out.

A third farmer stood, looking humble while the glow emanating from his face showed he was feeling no pain. He started, "I'm just a simple farmer. I agree with everything said and will support as humanly possible, but it seems to me, we are missing one important ingredient...."

Rudy quickly cut in, "Customers."

Everyone was suddenly quiet, wondering why Rudy had to be so rude in stifling their very humble friend. The man standing looked at Rudy, nodded in agreement, and said softly, "Yes, customers." Then he sat down amidst a sudden wave of murmuring and whispers.

Rudy slowly, unsteadily, stood up, placing his hand on Michelle's shoulder for support. "My apologies for talking out of turn and interrupting, but I had been wondering the exact same thing. We cannot just flip a switch and suddenly be a popular destination." Rudy had impressive speaking skills and had everyone's attention, even Daniel's. Out of the corner of his eye, Rudy could see Daniel was fully engrossed and was nodding or shaking his head in agreement with every word he said.

Rudy went on, "I have been fortunate to attend University, and in my business studies, we discussed strategic plans, marketing plans, the analysis of sales channels, and product placement." Michelle watched Rudy closely, amazed at how he really looked and sounded the part. *He would have fit in perfectly on Wall Street*, she thought to herself.

"And based on what I know, and I'm sure Michelle would agree, there are opportunities. But we must work to build a foundation, a good solid foundation, because...." Rudy paused, then continued, with a slower, but even cadence, "all it will take is the right circumstances, reaching the right decision-makers, performing at our best, at the right time, for the right people, and our popularity will explode." Rudy paused again, giving clues that there was more to come, but waiting for everyone, everyone waiting for his final words, "And we had better be ready because we might not get a second chance."

With that, the room burst into cheers, with Daniel screaming, "Are we ready? Let's get ready."

Michelle, taken by the wave of enthusiasm, stood up, clapped furiously, and repeatedly shouted, "We can do it. Let's do it."

Pierre, standing off to the side, stood and clapped along. He looked over at Rudy and signaled silently, "Brilliant, well done."

After a short time, Tremont stood again, and when the room had quieted down, he spoke, "So tell us, where do we start, what do you want us to do?"

Michelle looked at Pierre, with Pierre nodding back, giving her the floor. "My title is Business Manager. I am working to understand and control costs and revenues. I will work with Daniel and Rudy to define an order system. We will list the item and the amount we need. We will deliver the list to you, and you tell us when you will deliver and at what cost. Basically, we ask that you provide an invoice. We will pay the invoice within 30 days. Unfortunately, we must discontinue the bartering that we have done in the past. It is too difficult to manage."

Tremont, still standing, replied, "My boys start loading the trucks at 1 a.m. If you get us the list by 5 p.m. the day before, we will deliver by 6 a.m., any day except Sunday and holidays.

Daniel spoke, "That's a good time; I can handle that. I cannot do 4 a.m., but 6 a.m., no problem."

Tremont spoke again, "Would you rather have 7 a.m.? You tell me the time, and I will make it happen." All the farmers nodded in agreement.

Daniel looked around, a look of bewilderment on his face, not used to public speaking or decision-making. "7 a.m. is perfect; that would give us four hours to prepare for lunch. Yes, if it is not too much trouble, 7 a.m. is preferable. Thank you," he said, smiling as if Santa Claus had promised him a new sleigh for Christmas.

"Before we adjourn, I'd like to say one more thing." Pierre announced. "If we want to be a showcase for regional and seasonal ingredients, we ask that you work with us. Tell us what crops are looking favorable, if your melons are extra sweet, if a late summer made your tomatoes fat and juicy. Tell us what we need to know about your crops so we can plan and order accordingly."

"Yes, good, excellent point." Daniel agreed.

The farmers, happy and all smiles, agreed and took turns shaking hands.

The meeting adjourned with Daniel pouring one more glass of cognac for everyone, shaking hands once more, and accepting compliments as if this whole thing was his doing. Michelle stayed behind to help clear the tables and to talk with Pierre and Rudy about Marketing.

Daniel finished his glass and announced he was turning in, saying something about "the morning worm flies like an eagle."

Michelle chuckled and wished him goodnight, as did Rudy and Pierre. Michelle made cappuccinos for everyone and described her letter to the magazine.

Rudy and Pierre shrugged, "Why not."

"Of course, if they accept, don't surprise us; give us plenty of warning." Rudy continued.

Pierre agreed, smiling like a Cheshire cat, saying, "I'll want to be wearing my new tuxedo."

"No problem," Michelle replied. "To tell you the truth, I would be surprised if we got a response. I just don't think we're exciting enough."

Pierre was more sanguine about it, "You never know until you try. At this point, I don't think we should leave any stone unturned."

Rudy added, "He's right; let's just keep trying. I've seen you reading the travel column; I think you're our target audience. Don't you think?"

Michelle thought about it for a minute and agreed. "You're right, Rudy. You are absolutely correct."

Michelle took out her laptop, turned it on, and said, "I know it's late, but I wanted to give you some numbers to think about." She waited a moment as her computer came on, then started to speak while reading from her computer screen, "It's been very difficult getting viable numbers; the bartering and resulting numbers have been bordering on the ridiculous. Do you realize that at numerous times, and based on market prices for alternative goods, we have essentially paid people to eat at the bistro?"

Rudy smiled, as did Pierre.

"I am serious. Here's one example: a farmer brings in a palette of strawberries and a half dozen chickens. In exchange, we wine and dine him all night; then, he's too drunk to go home, so we give him a room. Given the wine and the number of after-dinner cognacs, plus the room, those chickens cost us roughly 30 euros apiece. I hope they were good."

Rudy smirked and said sedately, "Sis, you are preaching to the choir. At the last family meeting, you mentioned a van. That's a great idea. With a van, we can stop the uninvited guests and probably garner some respect in doing so. I bet every woman in the area would rather see their drunken spouse dropped off by responsible individuals than have to worry about when or if he is ever coming home."

Pierre sipped his cappuccino and added, "Undoubtedly. Goodwill aside, in a way, it's our responsibility. We put him in that condition. We should take it upon ourselves to either prevent it from happening or put procedures in place to get the man home safely. The van is a good idea, but so is putting an end to our over-generous hospitality."

"Well, here's my analysis. I looked at the number of tables, the number of guests per table, a fixed-price three-course meal, with drinks and wine. I assumed fifteen tables with four guests per table, a 45 euro fixed price, 20 euros in drinks, and 50 euros for wine. It comes out to 310 euros a table, or exactly 77.5 euros a person. I checked with various sources, and for the quality we're aiming for, it's a bargain."

Pierre looked at her and commented, "This is incredible. I like this very much."

Michelle replied, "But this is only the beginning; there's lots more. I also assumed we could fill our dining room one and one-half times, making that 90 plates." Rudy added, "Makes sense, fifteen tables, four people per table, that's 60 plates, you fill the room up one and a half times, you get 90."

Michelle paused, checking to see if Rudy wanted to add more. Not getting any indication, she continued, "So what we get is roughly revenue of 7,000 euros a night, 28,000 euros a week, 112,000 euros a month, and 1.34 million euros a year."

Pierre whistled under his breath, "Very clever."

Michelle wondered if either of the two saw the obvious discrepancy in her analysis when Rudy spoke up.

"Wait a minute, 7,000 a night, 28,000 a week. Forgive me if I am wrong on this, but we are open more than four nights a week?"

Rudy looked at Pierre, who was quick to respond, "Don't look at me. If I were any good with numbers, I'd be playing blackjack in Monte Carlo."

Michelle smiled, "You are too smart, Rudy; yes, you are correct, we are open more than just four nights, and we are open for lunch too. What I did is I broke out Sunday. On Sunday, I assume we turn over the dining room two and one-half times since we are open 11 a.m. to 7 p.m. That generates roughly 12,000 euros. Four Sundays a month generates 48,000 euros revenue and 550,000 euros revenue a year. Altogether, Sundays included, the Bistro is capable of generating 1.9 million euros a year, and that does not include lunch or even the possibility for catering or special events."

Rudy once more was quick to pounce, "Fine, now where do we get the customers? What was it, 90 a day, and 150 on Sunday?"

Michelle looked at Rudy and simply replied, "Hey, don't shoot the messenger."

Chapter 12

I t was the end of the working day and the end of the week for John DeHaven. His secretary had switched off her computer and was in the midst of her 'end-of-day routine' while John just sat and stared out his eighth-floor window at the gray, dismal, rainy day. It had rained all day. He'd hoped the weather would clear by the afternoon, making his commute home stress-free and uneventful. *There's always some idiot who is in a hurry, doesn't consider road conditions, and causes accidents.* He pictured himself sitting in his car, engine idling, and waiting for the police to clear a couple of banged-up cars off the expressway.

Without warning or a sound, the lights went out. The sudden darkness and silence were punctuated only by the clicking sound of emergency exit lights coming on. The sparse, dim lights created an eerie glow in the office around him. They cast odd shadows about, and he could just barely make out the detail of his door, only three or four meters away.

This is unusual. It must be the weather. They'll come back on at any moment. He glanced outside and saw lights all around. *It must be just this building.* He shrugged and thought, *Oh well, nothing I can do about it.* DeHaven called out to his secretary but received no answer. *Hmm, I wonder where she's off to?*

A knock sounded at his door, a forceful, aggressive knock, not polite and casual, but hard and loud. "Who in heaven's name is banging on my door?" he shouted. The knock came again. "Come in, please, come in before you break the glass," he added. From the sound of his voice, he was clearly perturbed by whoever was being so arrogant.

E. Hayden Fredericks Jr

Two men walked into the room. One asked politely, "Monsieur DeHaven, Deputy Administrator for the Ministry of Antiquities?"

DeHaven thought it was a rather stupid thing to ask, "Well, we are in the Ministry building, and yes, that is the name on the door."

The same gentleman asked, "May we sit? We need to discuss a very important matter with you."

DeHaven was surprised. "Well, it's considered polite to ask for an appointment, not just come to someone's office at the end of the day, especially in the middle of a power failure. But sit if you must. What could be so important?"

The two men grabbed chairs and sat. The same one spoke again. "Your life, your future, perhaps your soul."

John was not in the mood for such silliness and was quick to reply, "Look, gentlemen, if this is a joke, ok, ha-ha, you have me. If you are here for other matters, then state your business and leave. In fact, just leave - I am not interested in what you have to say. I am not in the mood for silly pranks. If it's important, then make an appointment. Please leave now. If you don't leave immediately, I will call security." John reached for the phone, but much to his annoyance, it was dead. Frustrated, he shouted for his secretary, but again, there was no reply.

One of the men began talking, "Do you recognize me?"

John squinted, trying unsuccessfully to make out the man's features and finally answering, "No."

Again, the man asked, "Do you recognize my associate?"

DeHaven tried to make out the other man's details but couldn't. "No. What's this all about? Who are you?" he demanded, interrupting the man asking the questions. He was clearly irritated and not inclined to cooperate.

He looked at the two men and thought, *This is silly; I'm an officer of the Ministry.* He stood up and was about to say something when the second man ordered, "Sit down and shut up," in a voice that implied consequences if he didn't comply.

DeHaven looked at the man and slowly sat down.

The first man continued in a calm, even tone, "I have reviewed your personal folder, school records, and your bank records. I know your history, everything about you, even your password for your computer. You are an unremarkable man. You have worked at the Ministry since graduating from university. Your academic performance was lackluster at best, and here at the

89

Ministry, your only achievement has been arriving on time. Everything you have obtained at the Ministry you earned by just existing. Even your wife thinks you are nothing. She says she plays cards with the girls on Tuesday afternoons, but instead, she meets a man. They usually get a room at the Martinique Hotel. So tell me, what are your ambitions? What do you stand for?"

"How dare you?" DeHaven answered. "You come through my door like a hoodlum and insult me. You insult my wife. I won't have this." He stood, trying to move around the desk, but the other man stood up, grabbed him by the neck, pushed him back in the chair, and whispered loudly in his ear.

"You little rodent, I can snap you in two without breaking a sweat. Now you sit and give this man your full attention."

The other man continued, "So we have established you are nothing, inconsequential, and based on your past, probably will continue to be inconsequential. Does the name Tree Trunk Bistro or The Inn at Saint Charles en Liberte' mean anything to you? How about Maria Villeneuve?"

DeHaven, feeling uneasy, a slight trickle of sweat dripping down his back, squirmed in his seat and answered, "No, never heard of them."

The man asking the questions quickly rebuffed DeHaven, "Don't lie to me. Lying to me has consequences. You don't want to lie to me."

After a moment or two of silence, DeHaven spoke. "Ok, ok, yes, I know them. It's a little project I'm involved in."

"With the Gold Development Group?" the man asked.

Surprised, DeHaven answered, "That's correct."

The man continued, "I need to know, why did the Gold Group select this property to file a violation? How did you help them? How are they helping you?"

DeHaven answered, "I used the Ministry's database to search for properties with owners who are beyond a certain age. Ideally, single owners. Owners who might easily be persuaded to sell. I passed the information on to Gold Group. They have a contact in Saint Charles who examined the situation and recommended we move forward. We figured... "

"Who are *we?*" The man interrupted.

"The Gold Group and myself," DeHaven replied. "We figured, based on what we heard about current management, the owner would be easy to convince. "

The man said softly, "You mean easy to intimidate."

John, still feeling uncomfortable, was beginning to regain his confidence. He replied with a bit of a swagger, "Well, it was never said in those words, but that's the idea, intimidate these people into giving up their properties. "

The same man asked again, "In return for what?"

DeHaven, now feeling in the right, said smartly, "That's the brilliant part, we've intimidated these people into selling, so why give them a fair price? We offer pennies and tell them to take it or be declared insolvent. I represent the government. I tell the sellers to take the money, it's the most they'll get and the last offer we'll make." He moved his chair around, leaned back, and said to the two men, "It's a tough world out there, you got to protect yourself, or you lose. "

"Have you identified other properties that fit into your business strategy?" the voice said once more.

DeHaven could detect a bit of wavering in the man's voice, as if his rage was subsiding, "Yes, we have identified five properties altogether, five properties across southern France. We are currently in the process of acquiring them, all similar situations as the Saint Charles property."

The man asked again, "Acquiring them in the same manner?"

"Correct," was DeHaven's reply.

"What about Maria Villeneuve? Do you recognize the name?"

"Vaguely," he replied. "Is she one of the sellers?"

The voice corrected DeHaven, "No, she is one of the owners."

DeHaven chuckled, "Well, we consider her a seller. She has decided to sell, hasn't she?" he inquired. "All the reports I've received have been that we are on track." He paused for a minute, then decided to state his case, "Look, you asked me to identify my ambitions; well, my ambition is to take old, decrepit, but potentially interesting properties that are underutilized and a drain on society and develop them into attractive destinations. Attractive, profitable destinations, I might add."

The man sat quietly for a moment and then asked, "What gives you the right?"

"Excuse me?" DeHaven wasn't sure if he had heard the man correctly.

"What gives you the right? You, who have accomplished nothing, dare to take from people who have tried all their lives, who have sacrificed, who have given their lives, or the lives of their sons and daughters. What gives you the right to take away their livelihood? You realize what you are doing is wrong, don't you? You realize it's a terrible thing what you are doing."

Surprised by the man's emotion and mounting anger, DeHaven answered meekly, "Yes, but that's the law of economics. It's not personal; it's just business."

The man, angry at DeHaven's response, replied with controlled hostility and disgust. "Don't justify your actions with economics, some type of efficiency or rational market nonsense. Talk to me about morality, about respect for your fellow man. Talk to me as if it were your family that was being thrown out into the street."

The man stopped speaking, lowered his head, and rubbed his temple as if faced with a stubborn, recurring pain, one that just wouldn't go away. He exhaled as he lifted his head, opened a folder, took out a single piece of paper, and handed it to the man sitting on the other side of the desk.

"What's this?" DeHaven asked.

The man spoke softly but with authority, "It's your resignation. Effective immediately. Sign it."

DeHaven was stunned and laughed nervously, "That's ridiculous, I will not. In fact, this conversation is over. I want you out of my office, now, both of you, go, I demand you leave!" With that, DeHaven stood up and pointed to the door in a show of bravado, attempting to gain control of the situation.

The two men sat silently, calmly. The second man slowly stood up and adjusted his lapels. He was intimidating in size, clearly the larger of the two men. The first man spoke again, "My friend here is a teacher; he wants to teach you to fly. I wonder how quickly you will learn." At that, the second man went over and opened the window.

DeHaven slowly sat down, his courage completely wiped away, now looking visibly upset. The first man took another piece of paper from his folder and slid it across the desk.

"And this?" DeHaven asked, picking up the paper.

"It's the press release from the Ministry, announcing your apparent suicide." The man answered without emotion.

DeHaven laughed nervously, "This can't be happening," he said under his breath.

"If I were you, I'd sign where he told you to sign," the second man said softly, still standing by the open window.

The first man handed DeHaven a pen.

He took it and signed his resignation, thinking, *this is absurd; first thing Monday, I'll go see Human Resources and file a complaint.*

DeHaven slid the paper and the pen back to the man. The man handed DeHaven a package. "This is your severance package; all the forms are here ending your employment." The man then pulled a large stack of currency out of his pocket. "This is your severance pay. It's 5,000 euros. Take it. Use it to start a new life. Leave your wife; she doesn't love you. Go someplace, start over, find purpose in your life. Accomplish something, something positive, something that progresses society, not sucks the life out of it."

The two men got up and started for the door. The first man turned and looked at DeHaven sitting at his desk. There was a look of confusion and self-pity on DeHaven's face as he looked back at the two men, still unable to recognize any details of their faces.

The man spoke once more, "I will remember your name. If I ever hear of your involvement in such activity again, I will make sure you suffer before killing you with my own two hands. Good night."

At that, the two men left. It was quiet in DeHaven's office except for the sound of water dripping onto the windowsill. He could hear the two men as they walked down the corridor, through the double-doors, and down the stairs. A few minutes after the men's footsteps had faded away, the lights came on.

The window was open, and the rain continued outside. The constant drumming of the rain and the dripping of water off the building seemed amplified and felt like a hammer going against DeHaven's temple. The air was cold, and DeHaven's office grew chilly as the wind blew in.

The phone rang, and DeHaven could hear his secretary pick it up. Her voice was subdued as she responded to the call, "Yes, Oh, really? I see. Ok, Ok, Ok, yes, thank you."

She hung up and walked into John's office. "Why didn't you tell me you were going to resign, and why is this window open?"

DeHaven watched her with a blank stare as she walked to the window to close it. Finally, he asked, "Where were you for the last 20 minutes?"

She replied, "I went to the ladies' room before leaving, like I always do. The lights went out while I was there. There are no emergency lights in there, so I was stranded. They need to change that."

He sat quietly then asked again, "Did you hear anyone coming or going, walking in the corridor?"

"No," she replied, "the lavatory door is very thick. A good thing too. You don't want those sounds getting out in the hallway."

DeHaven's secretary went back to her desk after offering to stay late to help him pack. A short time later, DeHaven came out of his office and handed a large stack of bills to his secretary. "Here this is a little present for you. Thank you for your service." Then he turned around and went back into his office, closing the door behind him.

Dumbstruck, she looked at the stack of bills. She counted the money before going back into DeHaven's office. She got as far as saying, "Do you realize this is 5,000 euro..." then abruptly stopped. "Sir?" DeHaven's office was empty, and the window was again open.

Chapter 13

Michael Goldman, President of the Gold Development Group, sat back in his leather chair, put his feet up on his desk, and gazed out through the wall of windows that comprised the exterior of his corner office. He could see clearly, the busy Paris streets, five floors below. He still had a squash ball from the matches he played at lunchtime. He occasionally tossed it in the air, catching then squeezing it, intending to strengthen his grip but mostly out of boredom.

The office was quiet as usual, only the occasional call from someone selling copier supplies. Michael's secretary seemed busy, and she was, researching her upcoming honeymoon, trying to determine if she and her fiancé could afford two weeks in the Seychelles. *If Mikey* (she called her boss Mikey) *comes through with that bonus he promised, not only can we do two weeks, but we could probably fly first-class round trip as well.* She looked up to check what her boss was doing and saw his feet were still up; he hadn't changed position in the last 20 minutes.

Michael was feeling successful, living large as the music videos he watched would say. All five properties had contracts written on them; they were sent out and ready to be signed. Sellers just needed a little more persuasion. He was thinking, *By this time next week, we'll have them signed, filed, and I'll be a millionaire, at least on paper. Ah, but that's how real estate works. People don't understand; it's an asset, illiquid, yes, but still an asset, plain and simple.* He smiled at his apparent genius, that would earn him his anticipated fortune, and continued pampering his ego, *Let's see, Ferrari or Maserati? Ferrari is sportier, Maserati, classier. Which one?*

The phone rang with Michael's secretary picking it up. Seconds later, her voice came over the intercom. "Mikey, it's your uncle," she announced in a soft, purring voice that she knew, in a good way, drove her boss crazy.

"Got it, sweetheart," was his reply.

"Hello, uncle, how's the weather in merry old England?" he asked after pressing the speakerphone button.

"Just fine. Listen, Michael, what are you doing over there?" Michael's uncle's voice was loud and deliberate as it came out of the speaker.

Michael, puzzled by the question, quickly answered, "You know the plan. We've made progress, identified properties, and are now in the process of acquiring said properties. You know that. I went over it Wednesday in the conference call with your Special Projects guy."

"Yes, I remember. Well, look, I was paid a visit this morning by two gentlemen from the French Embassy. It seems you have ruffled some feathers. To put it bluntly, people do not appreciate your tactics." Michael's uncle spoke plainly.

Michael replied, smiling, "Good, I like that. I want to ruffle feathers and then roll right over them. Really, Uncle, no big deal, so what? This is the big league; there's no room for amateurs. I hope you told them to suck it up?"

The uncle's voice turned deadly serious, and his tone changed to flat, deliberate as if there was absolutely no room for discussion. "Michael, you need to close down and return to the states. My secretary has booked you a flight for New York leaving at 8 a.m. Monday morning. Get your affairs in order this weekend and come Monday, be on that flight. That's an order."

Michael was shocked. "What? Is this a joke? Uncle, since when do we..."

Michael's uncle cut in, "Look, Michael, if you are not on that plane Monday, I can no longer support you, nor can I guarantee your safety. Do you understand what I am saying? I can no longer guarantee your safety. Chalk it up to a lesson in cultural differences. "

Michael tried one more time, "Uncle, who did you talk to? Let's sit down and make sure we understand our options. I mean, we've got a lot invested here, and we're almost there, almost at the finish line."

The uncle, disgusted it had come to this, flabbergasted that his nephew did not fully grasp the seriousness of the situation, stated bluntly, "Look, Michael, you are not hearing me, so I will state it as straightforward as possible. Shut down. Close your office. I'll send people over to clean up. Be on that flight Monday, or you're a dead man. Got that, a dead man. That's all I will say on the matter. Your ticket will be waiting for you at the airport. See you at Christmas. My best to the family, goodbye."

The call concluded. Michael's secretary came into his office, thinking it was the perfect time to discuss her bonus; talking to his uncle always left Michael in a good mood. She started in a casual tone, "Excuse me, Mikey, you know the bonus you promised me…."

Michael cut her off, "Sorry, sweetheart, I'm out of business, closing down. I've been ordered to shut the doors. As of now -- you're fired. You have ten minutes to collect your personal belongings and get out."

* * *

Maria's train was scheduled to arrive at 1 p.m. She took an early morning high-speed train from Paris and arrived in Bordeaux just in time to catch the 10 a.m. local. Even though her train was expected to arrive during lunch service, Saturday lunch service was usually light, allowing Pierre the time off to make the drive to meet her. Michelle willingly agreed to stand in for Pierre, allowing her to gain experience as Maitre'd.

For her first day as Maitre'd, Michelle wore her best business suit, a navy blue LaFleur she splurged on after graduation, with an underlying white blouse and pearls. She placed her hair in a bun on top of her head like her mother always did. Looking in the mirror, she said to herself, *Yea, I look the part, I can talk the talk; just watch me now, walk the walk.* She laughed; *I can be so corny.*

She slipped on black shoes with petite heels, never really liking the tall, high heels that many of her friends wore. Besides, she was naturally tall, about 5' 9" last time she measured; she didn't think she needed more height.

She thought she looked impressive, even intimidating, standing at the front door of the bistro. Clipboard in hand, a pleasant, business-oriented smile on her face, she felt efficient and ready, waiting for 11 a.m. to unlock the door.

Michelle immediately started to see spillover traffic from construction on the nearby expressway as soon as she unlocked the doors, officially opening the bistro for lunch service. As she was unlocking the doors, she looked through the glass at the small but growing crowd of people. Never having done this before, she did what she had always experienced when visiting a restaurant; she welcomed everyone and then took their names and number of guests. Most were parties of two or three, and though everybody could see the dining room was empty, went along pleasantly with the formality.

The patrons seemed to all voice the same opinion, "We just wanted off that terrible road and away from the traffic. We are glad to finally find a place to relax and hopefully get something to eat."

The next thing she did was seat the parties and introduce their waiter. The Tree Trunk typically was staffed with only one waiter on Saturdays but seeing the crowd gathering, word was passed to the second waiter, named Thomas, who lived in one of the apartments out back. He came quickly.

Once all the patrons were seated, seven tables were occupied, about half of the dining room. Michelle surveyed the scene and was quite pleased with her organizational skills. Her moment was interrupted by one of the waiters, "Madam, you are urgently needed in the kitchen." She thanked the waiter, who went back to taking drink orders.

Walking into the kitchen, she was immediately confronted by the spectacle of Daniel and Rudy energetically disagreeing. "Hold it, you two." was the first thing out of her mouth, and it seemed to have made an impression. Both stopped and looked at her like two schoolboys caught sneaking a cigarette. Between them was a sizeable antique chalkboard used to list the day's menu. The board was blank.

"What happened to the menu?" She asked.

"What menu? There never was a menu." Rudy replied.

Michelle went from looking puzzled to looking quite perturbed. "Look, it's 11:15 a.m. We are open; we have seven parties seated and more pulling up. This is a restaurant. We serve food. People come here to have our food. What are we serving? Where is the menu?"

Daniel just shook his head, "I don't know. Look, the menu is not my idea; it confines me. I cannot create if there is a list I must follow."

"But Daniel," Michelle pleaded, "people want to know what they are being served; people have preferences. Look, we need to decide right now," Michelle stated with authority.

Just then, a waiter came through the swinging double doors that connect the dining room and the kitchen, "Madam Villeneuve, the customers are all asking for menus. What shall I tell them?"

Michelle turned and looked at Daniel, with venom in her eyes and a snarl on her face. She said, "Daniel, if you ever do this to me again, I will mount your head on a stick. Rudy, go place ten baguettes on the fire; are there croissants in the oven?"

Rudy replied, "Yes, a good dozen or so, they'll be out in five minutes."

"Good, get the bread, and I'll work with Daniel to finish the menu."

Michelle was hitting her stride; she felt engaged, alive, in control. To the waiter, she ordered, "Fetch the other waiter, what's his name, and, hey, what's your name?"

"I'm Paul, and he's my cousin, Thomas. He's taken a few years off from studies to work…"

Michelle cut the young man off. "Fine, good. Will you fetch him, please?" Paul went quickly back through the swinging doors.

"Ok, Daniel." She looked at Daniel with a somber, serious face. "We must do this. Here's what we are going to offer. It's early, so many will want to eat light. We will offer croissants, jam, fresh fruit, and coffee." She wrote that down as the first item; then, she wrote "Eggs" as a category. "Ok, two egg dishes. Let's offer a wild mushroom omelet, served with potatoes and fresh fruit, and what else?"

Daniel started to show some interest. "I could do Creamed Eggs?" then, with a wink added, "with truffles?"

"Yes, that's perfect. We'll serve it with potatoes and fruit." She was writing this as they went along, using a very ornate, flowery script appropriate for a Bistro's menu.

She asked Daniel again, "Do we have steaks?"

Daniel replied, "I have beef. I would have to cut the steaks."

"Is it time-consuming, difficult?" she asked.

"No, not at all," Daniel replied nonchalantly.

Michelle added Steak Frites to the menu and kept at it, asking Daniel, "Can we offer another beef dish?"

Daniel shrugged, answering, "I have short ribs in the oven, but they won't be done for another two hours. I can do a Tournedos with red wine sauce or Tournedos Rossini. I use my duck pate instead of foie gras and fresh black truffle. I personally think it's better than the classic. The duck makes for a more, more," Daniel searched for the right word, finally finding it, "assertive flavor."

"Fine, that's good," Michelle said. Then checking the time and seeing it was 11:30, she increased the tempo, "How about Onion Soup?"

Daniel said, "Of course."

Michelle asked again, "A plate of pate and cheese?"

Daniel again was agreeable, "Of course, with freshly baked bread; I have three pates to plate. I have a country pate, made with pork, very rustic; I have a duck and goose pate made with cognac, very smooth, sophisticated; and a wild mushroom, vegetarian, made with chicken."

Michelle looked at Daniel to see if he was joking, but Daniel just looked back with his usual blank look.

"Daniel," Michelle began, slightly annoyed. "How can it be vegetarian if it's made with chicken?" Daniel shifted his body, now leaning to the other side, looking for the correct answer, not fully recognizing the contradiction he had created. "Well, you know it's mostly mushroom, wine, cream and egg, very little liver, chicken liver, so I consider it vegetarian."

"Daniel," Michelle countered while writing 'Plate of 3 Pates' on the menu, "you sure play by your own rules. "

She continued, "Ok, almost done, chicken, what can we offer?" He started, with his eyes focused on the ceiling, "I can do a pan-seared chicken with mustard and morels, coq au vin. I can also do a chicken chasseur or with wild mushrooms. I have wonderful fresh mushrooms I just picked yesterday. I can make chicken or pork with white wine and sherry or chicken with garlic and lemon; whatever you like, I can do. We should recommend Phillip Blanchard's Pinot Noir. I have ten cases sitting in the cellar. It's drinking very well; it is time we serve it," Daniel stated, seemingly a little bored, checking his fingernails.

Michelle quickly added the chicken dishes and then added "Chocolate Torte, Crème Brule, and Macarons, to the bottom of the menu, along with the Pinot Noir and a Chardonnay. She placed some numbers, representing prices, next to the items and hustled through the swinging doors, the blackboard in hand.

Rudy had just finished retrieving the bread, hot from the fire, and was on his way back to the kitchen. The whole dining room had this wonderful aroma of bread, freshly baked, with a tinge of cheese, when Michelle came through the door with the blackboard menu. She had to quickly dodge and duck to avoid Rudy with his large cages of bread. Michelle just barely missed being branded across the forehead, like a steer from an old American cowboy movie. As he passed, he quickly blurted out, "Sis, could you throw a log or two on the fire?"

She handed the board over to one of the waiters, who brought it close to the first table, briefly explained the items, and proceeded to take their order. Once the table finished ordering, the other waiter took the menu and presented it to the second table. He was soon taking the second table's order. After submitting the second table's order, the first waiter took the menu and presented it to the third table, and so on. Neither waiter could describe what was being offered, but both had worked with the kitchen for quite some time; hence, each knew Daniel's cooking style and was able to inform patrons what to expect.

Michelle headed towards the fireplace and saw a stack of weathered logs beside the hearth. She threw a couple on the fire, stepping back from the intensity of the fire.

The dining room became quite lively with laughter, discussions, bottles of wine, and baskets of bread and plates of food being delivered by the two juggling, hustling waiters. Michelle watched and marveled at the activity and quite proudly said under her breath, *We did it; we pulled it off.* Then she laughed as she countered, *Well, not really, all we accomplished was getting the doors open. We've a long day ahead of us.*

In the background, she could hear the main door open and close repeatedly. She looked in that direction and saw at least half a dozen people waiting to be seated and three more coming through the door. She quickly walked to the kitchen and asked Rudy to place more loaves in the fireplace.

Rudy, busy creating plates of pate and terrine, repeated the order to one of the busboys, who then started placing dough on the specially fabricated grates that fit on the front of the fireplace.

Baking the bread in the fireplace was Rudy's idea. The Bistro kept the fire going whenever they were open, prompting Rudy to voice the opinion it was a terrible waste of energy. Arguing for greater efficiency, he devised a way to bake bread as the fire blazed by suspending the bread dough in cages in front of the fire, utilizing the heat created and adding a smoky flavor to the bread. An added benefit was the unique ambiance warm, cheesy bread gave to the room. Rudy was quite happy with the outcome, calling it a trifecta, a "win-win-win" for the bistro.

But Rudy would also admit he cheated just a bit. To get an evenly baked baguette from the fireplace, the fire had to be very hot, and the bread had to be turned. Given the average temperature of the fire, he concluded the bread needed to be turned in approximately seven minutes. But right before turning the bread, Rudy brushed on a mixture of grated Gruyere cheese and garlic mayonnaise. This created a delicious, golden-brown crust on the bread, making it worthy of being a meal unto itself.

Michelle left Rudy and went over to meet the new visitors with the best smile she could muster, trying hard not to be too obsequious. "Good afternoon and welcome," she greeted whimsically, the best whimsical she could do under the circumstances. "How may I help you?"

She seated the parties at the remaining empty tables, careful to keep the dining room divided between the two waiters. The two busboys were happy to be busy, taking turns between cleaning and resetting the tables and washing dishes. A few guests had to be satisfied with waiting at the bar until a table became available. Now Michelle understood why a maître d' would take the names of parties. So much more civilized to address a party by their names, rather than the generic "you." But having a waiting list for a table was entirely new to the Tree Trunk.

Shortly after the first dishes came out of the kitchen, Michelle could hear the cash register ring and the drawer open, ring and open, ring and open, and ring. She liked the sound, calling it "the sound of another happy patron."

She stood by the entrance, taking a breather, thinking, *nothing to it* as she once again surveyed the dining room. She spotted Rudy brushing his finishing glaze, as he liked to call his mayonnaise/gruyere mixture, on the half-baked loaves of bread before turning them. She went over and stood next to him, "That was a stroke of genius if ever I saw one." She intended to give a sincere compliment to Rudy.

He turned and smiled at her, "Which one?"

Her facial expression quickly changed to one of mischievous loathing, "Oh please, don't get too full of yourself, my dear brother; the higher you fly, the farther you fall."

"Ouch! Consider me brought back to earth. But kidding aside and speaking of genius, that was a masterful job you did with Daniel. For some reason, I can't get through to him. It's like he thinks of me as competition or something, so he fights me every step of the way," Rudy confided to Michelle.

Michelle, watching the activity on the floor, replied, "I understand; I am beginning to sense it."

* * *

Maria's train from Bordeaux was only 15 minutes late from the scheduled arrival time, which prompted some old-timers and regulars to comment, "The first time in years the train's been early." Pierre had just pulled up, switched off the car, opened the paper, and read through the first section when he spotted the train pulling into the station. Surprised as everyone else, he uttered, "My word," climbed out of his car and onto the platform, looking for Maria to disembark.

Having gathered Maria and her luggage and somehow getting it all to fit in his Citroen, the two headed home. On the way back to the Inn, Maria and Pierre discussed the meeting with the farmers. Maria thought it was progressing but acknowledged the work that would have to be done to maintain the relationship and keep the system working smoothly. Nonetheless, she was proud of Pierre for taking the initiative.

On the highway close by, construction caused all traffic to be diverted to the surrounding small, narrow country roads, the same roads Pierre and Maria were traveling on. Ill-suited to handle so much traffic, let alone the large buses and lorries the highways typically handled, the roads quickly became snarled, causing traffic to come to a dead stop. Even the police, called to disentangle the situation, had a hard time getting through.

Pierre decided to pull over and turn the car off rather than sit in traffic with the engine idling. After an hour of sitting quietly, watching the traffic as it barely moved, Pierre suddenly blurted out. "Doesn't this seem a little odd to you? I mean, what in heaven's name are they constructing?"

Maria agreed, adding, "Too bad there isn't a shortcut to our shortcut."

Pierre smiled, then seemed to be figuring something out, finally said to Maria, "You know, I have adjustable suspension; I wonder how firm the ground is in the meadow there." He nodded his head as if to point to the grassy field just to the side of the car.

Maria looked at him to see if he was serious, then egged him on, "Probably firm enough; anyway, you have front-wheel drive!" She remembered Pierre bragging about his traction one blustery winter day.

Pierre started his engine, swung the wheel hard right, said, "Yes, I do," and stepped on the gas. The car hopped over the curb and sped down the embankment. It started bouncing its way across the meadow, finally rolling up a small knoll. At the top of the hill, Pierre slammed on his brakes, his face going completely white. In front, in the distance, was a dirt road leading down to a paved road. A car occasionally sped down the paved road, demonstrating its viability. This would normally be their goal.

But keeping them from their goal, in front of them and all around was the largest herd of cattle either of them had ever seen.

"How are we going to get through that?" Maria asked.

"Through? I was thinking a round; how are we going to get around that?" Pierre responded.

Maria looked at Pierre and replied quietly, "You're the driver. Through, around, over, under, whichever you prefer."

* * *

Michelle marveled at how smoothly the business was running, having just seated the last party on her waiting list. She hadn't kept count, but she guessed they had served at least 200 plates and looking at the clock, they still had another three hours till closing at 8 p.m. She very proudly thought to herself, *that's pretty darn good for a Saturday, and a spectacular performance by the kitchen and wait staff.*

Rather than just standing at the entrance, she decided to take a stroll through the dining room, occasionally stopping at a table to ask how people were enjoying the food. To say people loved the food was an understatement. In the back of her mind, she thought, *Daniel and Rudy are phenomenal. We may have something here. We might really have a world-class product.*

Michelle's enjoyment of listening to the murmur of a full dining room was interrupted by another summons to the kitchen. There, Rudy and Daniel were standing in front of a cutting board with two loaves of bread. The bread, obviously fully baked, with an appealing golden-brown hue, seemed larger and fatter than the typical baguettes the Tree Top served. Both loaves of bread had been sampled, a knife on the cutting board attested to that, and both men were enjoying slices. Busboys darted in and out of the kitchen, making deliberate detours to grab another slice of bread.

Seeing Michelle come through the doors, Rudy smiled and immediately invited her to join, "Cousin, you have to try this."

Daniel smiled and added, "Yes, you must, but butter it first; butter lifts the flavor. It makes the flavors more pronounced."

Rudy countered, "Try this one buttered, this one plain."

Michelle took a piece of the one she was instructed to eat plain. It looked like any slice of bread, but in the middle of the slice, the center was missing, instead replaced by soft brown core, still warm, Michelle guessed, from baking. As she bit into the bread, the core seemed to dissolve, giving its earthy flavor to the bread. It was delicious. She immediately wanted more.

"Wow," was all she could say, then asked, "Can I have another piece?"

Daniel and Rudy both laughed, insisting she now try the other, but this time with butter. Before she could bite into her sample, Daniel stopped her.

"Wait, you must have this; it will complete your fantasy." He handed her a small glass of white wine.

She looked at the slice handed to her. The slice had its center missing, like the other, but instead of brown, the core was a yellowish tan. She bit, and immediately, the complex flavors of aged cheese and rich butter filled her mouth. She closed her eyes and drifted away, the world around her silent; she made the most unflattering moaning sound as she savored the pungent and savory, salty flavors.

From what seemed like a far distance away, she heard Daniel whisper, "Now, take a sip of wine."

She did as instructed. The flavor of the wine spilled over and combined with the butter and the cheese, but then an earthy flavor crept in, countering the richness, creating the most luxurious flavor and velveteen texture she had ever experienced. She opened her eyes, looked at Daniel and Rudy, and said weakly, "Was I dreaming, or did I really taste that?" Her voice steadily became stronger. "It was, was, like a dream, a fantastic dream."

Daniel said with a big smile, "See, I told you. Fantasy bread."

Michelle had the look of wonderment mixed with confusion. "Fantasy bread? Is there more? Can I have another piece? Will it happen again?"

Both men laughed as Rudy cut slices off both loaves for everyone to enjoy. Michelle had just finished her fifth piece when one of the waiters summoned her to the front.

Reluctantly, she left the kitchen and headed to the front door. There she met a very polite Asian woman, standing alone by the front door. She was wearing casual clothes with a silver-white, shiny satin jacket of the type worn by athletes. Over the left breast was a South Korean Flag with "South Korea National Women's Team Volleyball" stitched into the jacket.

Chapter 14

Maria and Pierre sat and watched the cattle graze, contemplating their options. From behind them came a symphony of horn honking, engine noise, and gunfire. Looking in his rearview mirror, Pierre could see a lorry's radiator getting larger and larger. He started his engine, not sure what to do, but just as he did, the lorry sped past, horn blasting, one man behind the wheel, another man hanging out the passenger side window screaming at the top of his lungs and shooting a pistol into the air.

The cattle began to move. The lorry began pushing the cattle out of the way, not slowing by much while leaving a large pathway behind them. The cattle brayed and kicked but were moving. Pierre, not wasting any time, swung his car in behind the lorry and started blasting his horn, not knowing if he was helping or not.

As they gained speed and approached the end of the herd, Pierre let out a cry, "Yahoooooo!" He smiled at Maria, who seemed in shock, not sure what she had just witnessed. Before long, they were on the paved road, leaving the cattle behind. The lorry turned to go south while Pierre turned north. Before turning, Pierre honked his horn twice in salute and gave the lorry the thumbs up. The lorry returned his salute and sped off.

* * *

Michelle met the Asian woman at the Bistro's reception area right inside the main doors and politely introduced herself. In return, the South Korean woman introduced herself as the head coach of the South Korean National

Women's Volleyball Team. The Coach described how the team was traveling to Toulouse to play a match when expressway construction interrupted their trip. Their bus was too large to navigate the narrow country lanes that provided a way around the construction, so they were stranded. Authorities have told her the expressway would reopen later that evening.

Meanwhile, the Team has not had any food since 7 a.m. Thinking the trip would not take too long, they had arranged for lunch to be served after arriving in Toulouse. Their expected arrival was hours ago.

The Coach asked Michelle with pleading eyes, "Could you please feed us? We are very hungry and would welcome any preparation."

Michelle, in return, asked, "Well, how many people in total?"

"We are 23," The coach replied, then counting out loud, "Three coaches, 18 players, one trainer, and an equipment technician, oh, and we must feed the driver. My correction, we have 24 to feed. Can you prepare rice?"

"Yes, but let me first check with the kitchen." Michelle managed to stammer out a reply, not fully ready for the prospect of trying to seat a party of 24, especially so late in the day. She knew the discussion she was about to have with the kitchen would be interesting.

Michelle walked into the kitchen, saw Daniel in front of the stoves, half a dozen frying pans engaged, various concoctions bubbling away, shaking one, and throwing a pinch of seasoning into another. Rudy was preparing plates, adding small amounts of puree, checking the order slips, and ensuring nothing was overlooked. One of the busboys was washing pots, while the other entered the kitchen with a full tray of dirty dishes. Everybody seemed to be in their place, doing their job.

I hate to mess this up she thought, *but here goes,* "Excuse me, everyone."

Daniel, focusing on his cooking, replied, "Not now. Give me five minutes."

Michelle thought, *Fair enough, I shouldn't interrupt when dishes are being prepared.*

Daniel took the pans off the stove, stirred and plated the food, added a further pinch of seasoning, garnish, and cleaned the rim of the plates. He asked Rudy to correct one of his setups. Satisfied, he called for the waiters to pick up.

Once the plates were picked up and out the door, Daniel walked over to Michelle, wiping his hands on his apron, "What is it? What's the issue?"

Michelle really didn't know how to put this, so she just started talking.

"The Korean National Women's Volleyball Team is outside, stuck in traffic. They haven't eaten all day, they're starving, and we are their only hope. There are 24 to feed. Can we do it?"

Daniel, very nonchalantly took a sip of cognac from a snifter handed to him by a waiter, said, "The National Team? I like Korean people. They are very well-behaved and civilized. I can cook their food. If you can seat them, I'll feed them."

Michelle was shocked, happy, but shocked.

Rudy standing off to the side, added, "Feed them what? Don't we need seaweed and fermented cabbage?"

Daniel smiled, "Let's start with rice; we'll bread and deep fry some strips of chicken and serve it with garlic mayonnaise mixed with a little chili. I'll make a soup of chicken stock, hard-boiled egg, spinach, and mushroom, with a bit of garlic and sesame oil. We can simmer beef rib in stock and add sugar, hot pepper, anchovies, wild mushroom and soy sauce, then reduce it, maybe add some truffle. Let's sauté cabbage with garlic and chilies, and finally, let's do a quick pickling of some small mushrooms and onion. I can add a pork dish, too, maybe a breaded fried pork cutlet with a spicy fruit sauce. I think we even have a couple of pounds of green tea in the basement; it's vacuum-sealed, so it should still be good." Daniel sent one of the busboys to fetch the green tea.

Rudy, tired from the long and busy lunch service, became excited and energized listening to Daniel. When Daniel paused, Rudy added, "Let's get the banquet dishes out. Each setting comes with a large bowl. We can use it for rice, and we can use all the smaller plates for the cabbage, chicken, and other side dishes."

Daniel gulped down the rest of his cognac and said to Rudy, "That's an excellent idea, better than excellent, it's a perfect idea."

Rudy smiled, "I can come up with one occasionally."

Daniel smiled back, nodded, and said, "Ok, then, let's get to work."

Michelle was smiling as she walked back to the Korean woman. "We'd be happy to feed you." She said gregariously, "It will be a moment while we set up the tables."

The Korean coach smiled, "Wonderful. Will we have rice?"

Michelle smiled back, "Yes, rice, soup, crispy chicken, beef rib, pork cutlet, vegetables, and more."

The woman was absolutely beaming, "Very good, happy, maybe green tea?" she said, then hesitated for a moment, shyly asking, "How much?"

Michelle wasn't sure, so she just gave a number, "30 euros each person." The woman took out a small pocket calculator and asked again, "30?" Michelle nodded. The woman punched a few numbers, looked at the display, and smiled, "Very good, very happy. When, please?"

Michelle looked at the dining room, saw the busboys moving tables around, making a head table of five then creating a U shape in front of the head table. The busboys were busy placing 18 chairs around the tables and adding table clothes. "Not long, maybe 10 minutes?" she answered.

The South Korean woman watched the busboys, now joined by the waiters, set the silverware, small dishes, water glasses, and cups in front of each setting. She glanced at her watch and left. She returned a moment later, followed by the entire South Korean National Women's Volleyball Team walking in single-file, almost marching.

* * *

As Pierre and Maria pulled up to the Tree Trunk, they were unsure if they had the correct location. A small crowd of people milled around the entrance, smoking and enjoying the fall day's cool temperature. Most seemed to have cocktail glasses and appeared content sipping the contents while smoking their cigarettes.

Cars were parked haphazardly about, and a large tour bus, with "South Korean National Team" written on the side, was parked in the lane on the side of the building, blocking the rear entrance to the Tree Trunk. They could see people inside the bus. A driver was behind the wheel, the engine was humming, and all the trim lights were on, making the bus look very ornate as if it belonged to an entertainer of significant stature.

As the two sat and took in the spectacle of the Tree Trunk's parking lot, a figure wearing a shiny white coat came running out of the Tree Trunk and entered the bus. She soon exited, followed by more individuals wearing similar shiny white sport outfits. In perfect, disciplined unison, they marched single file into the Tree Trunk.

Maria was mesmerized; Pierre sat there, whispering under his breath, "...21, 22, and 23." Pierre turned to Maria and asked, "Should we go in?"

Maria replied with a smile, "No, let them learn. The best lesson is the lesson you learn from actually doing."

"Isn't that also referred to as 'in the line of fire'?" Pierre added with a mischievous grin.

"Let's give them, say, an hour?" Maria insisted.

"Ok, You want to sit here for an hour?"

"Well, we can take a stroll?" Maria suggested.

"Yes, let's do that. I haven't taken a stroll through town in ages, and with such a beautiful and classy woman on my arm. Won't people talk!"

Maria chuckled, replying, "Such a debonair and entertaining escort, yes, won't people talk!"

They walked, arm-in-arm, down the lane leading to the main entrance to the parking area in front of the Inn and Tree Trunk. They turned at Main Street and walked past the apothecary shop, the bank, and the municipal building, referred to as the Town Hall, crossed the street, and walked the other way, passing the Feed Store, petrol station, and the professional building, where a doctor and dentist had offices that were only open two or three days a week. A little farther along, they could see the back of the Tree Trunk and the retail storefronts that were recently added to their building.

Maria commented, "You should be the town's mayor."

Pierre laughed, "Why me? Besides, I don't have time given my duties at the Tree Trunk."

Maria continued, "You are underutilized at the Tree Trunk. I get the sense you are bored and wishing for a challenge."

Pierre confided in Maria; she always knew how to get him to talk. "Perhaps you're right. Many times, I worry I don't have enough to offer. I don't have Daniel's skill, Rudy's intelligence, or even Michelle's energy."

Maria stopped him, "What's important is you have been there for me and I am deeply grateful. "

Pierre replied, "It's what family should do."

Maria went on, "But you are a leader, you have natural leadership talents, you can enter a room full of people and quickly grasp what's going on. You influence people, and you are very brave. You say what others are afraid to say."

Pierre gave a half-hearted chuckle, "You mean very stupid."

Maria offered some advice, "If you just smooth out your style and tone down the sarcasm, with your insight into human nature, you could become a very influential person."

Pierre listened, and for the first time in years, he blushed.

* * *

As the line of South Koreans marched into the dining room of the Tree Trunk, the coach barked instructions to the women. They filed around the

U-shaped table, each team member stopping by a seat. Then, on the coach's command, they all sat.

Rudy, watching from the kitchen, called over to Daniel, "Daniel, you've got to see this."

Daniel stopped what he was doing and came over to peek at the grand entrance made by the South Koreans. He gasped, "My God, they're beautiful, perfect, each one. I have never seen such beauty, such discipline. Paul? Get me a clean chef's jacket."

"What are you going to do?" Rudy asked.

Daniel replied, changing into the clean jacket, "I am going to welcome them and make them feel at home. Give them a warm feeling." He called over to a waiter, "Do we still have that pink champagne?"

The waiter replied, "You mean that funny tasting wine? I think so; who would order it?"

"Good," Daniel countered. "I want you to open five bottles and pour each person a glass, then add a couple of fresh berries to each glass to hide the flavor."

He winked at Rudy as he walked gallantly through the two swinging doors, accidentally slamming one door into a busboy's face as he was bringing extra plates back to the kitchen. Daniel stopped, adjusted the collar of his jacket, turned his head slightly, and said, "Sorry."

Daniel sauntered over and stood to the side of the head table. In a deep, almost romantic voice, said, "Hello everyone." He paused, making sure he had everyone's attention. "I am Chef Daniel, and I will cook for you today. I will cook various dishes that I hope will appeal to your taste and senses while still highlighting our regional cuisine and fresh ingredients. As a token of our hospitality, as a gift from me to you, I ask that you accept this champagne and join me in a toast."

The waiters brought out glasses and placed one in front of each person. While one poured, another followed along with berries, dropping a few in each glass. A few open bottles were left on the table in silver buckets. A few of the women, not understanding the protocol, drank their champagne as soon as it was poured, prompting jeers from their fellow players, and causing the waiters to back-track to refill their glasses.

Daniel began the toast, "To fine food, and fine friends, I wish you good luck, and good fortune, whether it's on the court or in the jungle. To you."

Rudy and Michelle were in the kitchen and watched through the swinging doors as Daniel made his speech. Both were impressed with his choice of words and professional demeanor. Then he made his toast. Michelle and Rudy looked at each other and repeated, "Jungle?"

Daniel drank his glass, bowed and smiled, then marched back to the kitchen. As he went through the doors, he handed his glass to Michelle, made a face, stuck out his tongue, and said, "Ugh, terrible, there should be an outlaw."

Michelle held her laughter and just agreed, "Yes, there should be an outlaw."

The toast concluded, and the South Koreans applauded as the waiters brought out piping hot kettles of green tea, bowls of rice, and plates of crispy breaded fried chicken. The Korean Coach could be heard saying to the waiters, "Very good, rice, green tea, very good, very happy, thank you."

The South Koreans immediately wolfed down the rice, even though the portions were generous in size, prompting the waiters to ask the kitchen to prepare more. A few of the women seemed to enjoy the champagne, as Daniel called it. The champagne hit these women particularly hard since their stomachs were empty. One woman fell off her chair while reaching to dip her chicken in the garlic-chili-mayonnaise, eliciting hearty laughter from her teammates and a frown from the head coach.

Daniel proved adept at providing flavors pleasing to the South Korean palates. Plate after plate left the kitchen and was quickly devoured by the women. More rice was prepared and served, and even Rudy successfully tried his hand at devising a dish, creating a mushroom, beef, and green onion soup with thick Japanese udon-style noodles.

As the dinner was winding down, the coach asked some team members to entertain everyone with a song. Two girls were selected to sing a duet, which they did without hesitation. They sang in Korean, so all non-Koreans could enjoy the women's pleasant voices, but they had no clue what the two were singing. The South Koreans immediately recognized the song and joined in clapping along, keeping time.

Daniel watched from the sidelines, captivated by the natural grace and beauty of the women. He remarked to Rudy as he joined in watching, "These people have soul, real soul; you can feel it, can't you sense it?"

Rudy, not wanting to get into a heavy philosophical discussion, simply remarked, "They sure do."

The South Koreans noticed the two men watching and insisted they sing a song. Rudy, still wearing his jacket from lunch service, was a mess, apologized, and quickly retreated to the kitchen. Daniel, almost finished with his second cognac, shyly walked into the center of the seating arrangement. He put down his cognac and started the girls clapping. Then in a deep Barry White style voice, mixed in with a good deal of Elvis, he started singing:

Well, bless my heart, what's wrong with me
I feel like an itch from a fuzzy tree
I'm proud to say she's my buttercup
I'm in love, huh
I'm all shook up

The women recognized the song immediately and giggled and swooned as if Elvis himself were standing in front of them singing. They all clapped and swayed to the rhythm.

As Daniel sang, he gyrated like an Elvis impersonator. He grabbed a broom from a passing busboy and sang into it as if it were a microphone while maintaining his Elvis-like gyrations. The women cried out, "Elvis, Elvis, Elvis!"

Daniel enjoyed the attention and attempted a second verse. He didn't know the words but figured he could fake it.

Well, bless my socks they're up in a tree
The winds kind of blowing, and they smell to me
My feet are too big, and that's plain to see
I'm in love, huh
I need to wash up
Ooooh Ooooh Baby
I'm in love, huh
I'm all washed up.

Daniel finally stopped and bowed as the room exploded with applause. Daniel kept his Elvis persona going, saying, "Thank you, thank you very much."

The women cheered and clapped ecstatically, calling out for their favorite Elvis songs. Even the Head Coach could be heard saying as she clapped, "Elvis, very good, very good, we like. "

Daniel bowed once more, graciously declined an encore, made another bow, and exited to the kitchen.

As Daniel entered the kitchen, he was met by a busboy. The busboy handed him a small woolen bundle.

"What's this?" Daniel asked.

"A pair of socks. I heard you were missing a pair of socks." The busboy then hurried out to pick up another tray of dirty plates.

Rudy and Michelle were in stitches.

* * *

Pierre and Maria strolled back to the Tree Trunk. They observed that all of the cars had departed, and the crowd milling around the entrance was now gone, leaving behind a few half-empty cocktail glasses and a mess of extinguished cigarette butts, strown about. Pierre looked at the garbage left behind and commented, "Is this what popularity offers?"

As the two entered, they were greeted by Daniel's Elvis impersonation, gyrating and singing his rendition of "All Shook Up." Maria surprised, asked no one in particular, "Is that my brother Daniel?"

Chapter 15

Maria closed the Tree Trunk after the South Koreans left. and asked the family to stay for an important meeting. She asked that everyone be available at 8:00, and she asked that all be sober. This was directed at Daniel, who must have had four or five cognacs by then and was still doing his Elvis impersonation, singing, and dancing as he cleaned the kitchen.

The meeting started with Maria bringing everybody up to speed. "There is no longer a threat from the Gold Group; the violation has been removed."

Everybody voiced approval.

Maria continued, "To prevent future occurrences of people interfering with our business, I withdrew the inn and Tree Trunk from the program. We will no longer receive payments from the government; subsequently, we no longer need to seek permission for changes, repairs, or additions to the property.

Michelle raised her hand to speak. Maria smiled, recognizing her, "Mother, I take it then, you found a White Knight?"

Maria replied, "I secured funding of 10 million euros to fund the business for five years. At the end of five years, we will evaluate where we are and decide what to do. I also had the lawyers put everyone's name on the deed. By law, we are all partners and equal owners, including Rudy. Rudy, you are now a Villeneuve, whether you like it or not," Maria said with a smile.

Sitting next to Rudy, Daniel patted him on the back and announced to everyone, "Rudy's my brother, you mess with him, and you get the horns. Ehh? My horns." Daniel stuttered for a moment, looking confused, "You know what I mean."

"Congratulations, nephew," Pierre smiled, reached over, and offered his hand. "Congratulations and welcome to the family. You've been with us for close to 20 years, and you've always been family to me, about time we made it official. "

Michelle smiled from across the way and winked.

Rudy spoke, "I guess I can stop calling everyone cousin and use partner instead. Thank you, Maria, everyone, for all you've done for me."

Maria moved on, "I would like everyone's input on two ideas I have for modernizing the dining room. While in Paris, I visited an architect known for his work on historic properties. It will be expensive, but here's what I suggest: first we build a waiter's station to the side of the fireplace. Cooking bread in front of the fire has been very popular but traveling to and from the kitchen with those iron cages, especially when hot, is dangerous, and heaven forbid one is dropped on a guest. The station would have refrigeration, a cutting surface, lighting, and shelves. Bread dough could be stored there, taken out, placed in the cage, baked, sliced, and served. No more back and forth to the kitchen."

"Excellent idea." Pierre was first to respond, "Perhaps we can hire a junior waiter or junior kitchen prep man to be stationed there, to make bread baskets, even simple plates of pate, olives, cheese as well."

Rudy was quick to add his thoughts, "That is an excellent idea. I spend, perhaps waste, a lot of time creating simple pate plates, a slice of pate, a block of cheese, a little garnish. A trained monkey could do it. Maybe we could even refine the process, so the bread is brought to the table along with the pate and sliced right there at the customer's table?"

It was Daniel's turn to speak, "I like the idea, mostly because making the bread as we do is dangerous. There are reasons professionals no longer flambé at the table -- too many accidents, too much liability. But I see two problems; the first problem is coordination. How do I know the table has their bread or pate, and when I should start the entre? Second, we do not have much space; how many tables will we lose to this bread station?"

Everybody nodded in agreement. Maria countered, "Daniel, those are the types of issues I was hoping we would uncover and, together, resolve. Thank you, well said."

Daniel had more, "If safety is the issue, but we want to keep the fireplace and the bread, perhaps it would be wise not to separate the kitchen but to open it up and have some type of oven, maybe even a wood-burning oven, out where everyone could see it."

Rudy perked up. "That would be fantastic. A wood-burning oven; fantastic! Think about how we could expand the menu. We could also offer onion tarts, pizza, and healthy seared vegetables with oil and garlic. I know these ovens. They typically operate at very high temperatures, like 400, 500 degrees C. We could do a small chicken in minutes, bread would be in and out, and we wouldn't have to turn it. Think of what it would do to the atmosphere in the dining room. I mean, if we want to be a cozy, romantic, rustic bistro, what could be more authentic than a wood-fired oven?"

Pierre liked the idea too, adding, "Could we get the wood? Don't you need a special type of wood to burn? You can't just throw in an old table leg or a piece of pine?"

"You're right," Rudy replied, "We must be careful to use only seasoned oak in the fireplace, but occasionally we can use some fruitwood if it's offered to us. I think the farmers have plenty of oak. The important issue is to ensure its dry and all the sap out of it; otherwise, it won't burn, it'll just sizzle."

Maria was happy to watch the discussion. *This is what this family needs,* she thought to herself. Inside, her heart was full of joy as everyone pitched in, adding their thoughts and opinions to the discussion.

"Ok, let's all agree that we need to decide what to do with the bread situation. I want a firm decision by next Saturday. I have borrowed an additional two million euros for building improvements. The money is available; it's waiting to be spent; let's decide and move forward. It would be nice if we could get something done by the winter holiday season."

All nodded in agreement. Rudy had already taken pen to paper and sketched out his vision of a wood-burning fireplace and prep station.

"The next item I want to discuss is an idea introduced by Daniel, and that is the number of tables." Everyone was quiet, giving their full attention, as Maria continued, "You saw today that the kitchen, two waiters, and two busboys could easily handle this room." Then rhetorically, she asked, "Could we handle another three, five, seven or eight tables?"

"We could easily do another seven or ten tables," Daniel said as if it were an obvious conclusion.

"Good, Daniel, that is what I was hoping to hear," she continued. "We currently set fifteen tables, seven more is only twenty-two and not much more work, but Michelle will tell you, it helps the numbers. And if we need to add a waiter or busboy, the additional revenue will easily cover the cost."

Rudy added, "I think we will need two people, a kitchen prep person, and a junior server, perhaps not a waiter, just a server."

Maria took in Rudy's suggestion, "That sounds reasonable, but first, let's decide whether we want to enlarge the dining room."

Again, everyone nodded and voiced their approval, but it was Pierre who finally asked the obvious, "How? I hope you are not thinking of a second floor?"

Maria smiled at Pierre's suggestion, thinking *he really is the clever one.* "No, that would be difficult to manage on a day-to-day basis, but the architect did suggest creating a space for special events on the second floor."

Daniel cut in, "But we don't have that many special events; why travel all this way to rent a space? Suppose they wanted to bring in their own caterers. I am not sharing my kitchen with anybody, well, anybody outside the family."

Maria took out a large, heavy piece of rolled paper, placing it on the table, unrolling it in the process. "After much discussion with the architects, here's what they came up with."

Three views of the Tree Trunk were drawn on paper, with a veranda attached to the outside wall just beside the fireplace. The wall now had antique glass doors, opening from the dining room on one side of the fireplace, leading to the veranda. The base of the veranda was rough stone, and the walking surface was slate. Large rustic beams served as railings, and a central staircase led down to a courtyard containing a fountain. In the artist's rendition, a bar was set up in the courtyard with a picture of a bartender using a shaker while guests mingled about, cocktails in hand. A center aisle was left for guests to come and go, splitting the veranda into two areas, and leaving room for four tables on each side.

Daniel let out a whistle, "It's beautiful."

Maria added, "We did it this way because I envisioned the bread station on the other side of the fireplace. But if we go with the wood-burning oven, we can have two doors, one on each side of the fireplace, instead of one door. Then two aisles leading to the courtyard, and a table configuration of three-two-three or we might try four-two-four."

Daniel replied, "I like that idea. Two doors will bring balance. But I don't think there is amble space for ten tables. I don't think we should crowd our patrons."

Pierre added, "That's a lot of work, structural work. Do you think we'll get the permits, the okay?" Maria turned and smiled, "You should know, you're the mayor."

The room was silent. Pierre glanced at everybody, only to see they were all staring at him. "She's not serious, everybody relax, please. She wants me to put my name in for mayor. I haven't decided yet. Besides, it's up to the people, and we need to get rid of the old one first."

Michelle said it first. "Pierre, you would be perfect. I can't think of a better person for the job. You know the town, and you know the people, the politics, and I understand you have experience with the law…"

Pierre quickly cut in, "Let's not talk about that."

He regained his composure and informed everyone, "The mayor's job in this town is about consensus-building, willingness to be disliked if common ground can't be reached, and juggling many balls in the air at one time. The real challenge is representing the town in front of the regional council in Bordeaux. From what I've heard, they think of us as loafers, always wanting something and unable to pay."

Daniel, who had drifted off, now half asleep from the long day, and a good number of cognacs, spoke with his eyes closed, head resting on his hand, "I have never seen you juggle; can you teach me? I want to juggle; I'll be the juggling chef."

Pierre looked at Daniel, who exhibited all the signs of sleep, "I think we lost him.

* * *

The mayor was having a bad day, again. He had been trying unsuccessfully to get through to the Gold Group all weekend. Michael Goldman didn't answer his cell, and the office number just rang; he couldn't even leave a message. He didn't have DeHaven's personal number, so he would have to wait until Monday to try him. *Well*, he thought, *I'll just have to decide this myself.*

He had passed on the letter from the Ministry, declaring Tree Trunk and the inn in violation of the implicit contract with the Ministry, halting all future payments. He had thought that would get the Villeneuve's attention and bring Maria back to the negotiating table, where he was looking forward to *squashing her like a little bug.* But he had heard nothing and was now wondering how to proceed.

Hopefully, someone has thought of something. He thought as he sat in his empty office and stewed. *I'm in a bit of a precarious position. If word gets around about the deal and what I said about Maria, there'll be fireworks.* He chuckled a bit. *I could face a firing squad.*

The phone rang. He listened and waited as it rang, then remembered Claire, his secretary, had resigned. He quickly picked up the phone. In his best business casual tone, he answered, "Mayor's Office."

"Hello, Arnaud, this is Henri Tremont," came the voice on the other end.

"Hello Henri, what can I do for you?" The mayor said.

Henri spoke with authority, "Myself and a few others would like to see you."

The mayor quickly responded, "Well, it's the weekend. Can it wait for Monday or Tuesday?"

Henri answered, "Yes, Monday morning, 9 a.m. would be fine. Good-bye." The phone went dead.

The mayor placed the phone down and thought, *Oh, boy, here it comes.*

* * *

Six altogether went to meet with the mayor: Henri Tremont, Thomas Raucher, and Paul Stephenson, accompanied by a prosecutor from the local magistrate's office, and two gendarmes from Bordeaux.

As the mayor came out of his office to greet the farmers, he was taken by surprise. "Excuse me, gentlemen, I agreed to a meeting with my constituents. I did not agree to have the police; please wait here." He then led the three into his office.

When the prosecutor tried to enter, the mayor stopped. "Who is this man? You are not a citizen of Saint Charles, and you have no business here. Please leave, or I will call the gendarmes to remove you."

The man smiled and took out a card, presenting it to the mayor. "On the contrary, I have every right to be here. I was asked to be here by your constituents to help clarify what is and what isn't lawful."

Henri Tremont started speaking first, "It has come to our attention that you have attempted to deceive us. "

The mayor cut in, "Henri, gentlemen, please have a seat. May I get you a refreshment, coffee?"

Paul Stephenson spoke, "We don't want to sit. Henri, would you please continue."

"Please tell us of your involvement with the Gold Development Group," Henri asked.

The mayor replied, "My involvement with the Gold Group has nothing to do with you or my job as mayor."

The prosecutor stepped in, "Did you not have a town meeting where you announced the pending sale of the Inn at Saint Charles and The Tree Trunk Bistro to the Gold Development Group?"

"That was a private meeting," The mayor quickly replied.

"Did you not specifically say Madam Villeneuve retained your services to find a buyer, and did you not say you have spoken to representatives of the Gold Development Group?"

The mayor was trying to think of a way out. "Well, I might have said something to that nature, but it's not what I meant. She did not retain me. Talking with her, I just got the impression she did not want to be involved anymore, so I tried to help her by finding some people who would be able to complete a deal."

"Did you have an agreement for compensation?" The prosecutor demanded.

The mayor replied, "What do you mean?"

"Were you to receive a finder's fee or any other type of commission to be paid on the successful completion of the sale of the Inn and Bistro to the Gold Development Group?"

"No", the mayor said.

The prosecutor quickly added, "You're lying. Records found in the Gold Development Group's offices show that you were to receive a set fee of one million euros if the deal was consummated by December first." The mayor was given copies of papers taken from the Gold Group's files.

"That was only to cover my expenses. I had many expenses finding the right buyer. I had to travel to Paris many times. I also met with a representative of the Ministry of Antiquities, John DeHaven. "

"How many times did you travel to Paris?" the prosecutor asked. The mayor replied, "Many times, just ask Mr. DeHaven. Here I have his card; ask him, he'll tell you."

The prosecutor replied, "We can't. He's dead. He committed suicide Friday, leapt from his office window."

The mayor sat back in his chair, stunned.

Henri Tremont offered a document to the mayor. "Mayor, this is a signed and sworn document from the legal citizens of Saint Charles, voicing concern over purported wrongdoings by your office and asking for your immediate removal from office. I present this to you. As of now, you are officially removed from office." Henri then called for the two Gendarmes.

The mayor looked at the document and quietly said, "Is this legal?"

The prosecutor said, "Yes, it is. You have the right to appeal, but you must do so as an ordinary citizen, not from the office of the mayor." As the prosecutor finished, the two Gendarmes came through the door and took up position on either side of the mayor.

Paul Stephenson then spoke, "Mayor, we order you to leave the premises. If you do not do so immediately, these gentlemen will place you under arrest for trespassing and creating a public nuisance."

The mayor, suddenly looking tired, defeated, stood up. "You can have your office and your little village, too. I am through with it. I'm done. Give me a moment to grab my coat, my hat, and my boots." He grabbed some items off his desk, his coat, and his boots. As he was walking out, he turned to the six men now crowding his office, "Good day, gentlemen, good day."

It was still early, barely 10 a.m. Arnaud Martin, the ex-mayor of Saint Charles, now disgraced, walked slowly down the street. He had nowhere to go, nothing to do, no plans, nothing. Wandering the streets, he ended up in front of the Tree Trunk.

Martin went to the front doors of the Bistro, trying unsuccessfully to open the doors and swearing under his breath. He glanced at a small sign on the side of the building listing the hours and cursed again, reading 'Monday – closed.'

As he turned away, he collided with Daniel, who came walking up from the side alley, back from foraging through the woods. "Good morning, mayor," Daniel said happily.

The mayor replied sourly, "I'm not the mayor anymore. The good citizens of Saint Charles just removed me from office. Just call me Arnaud."

"That is too bad, but I will have to admit, good will always win over evil, and the things you did as mayor, were evil."

"You're kidding me. Are you that simple?" Arnaud said sarcastically, "I don't need your silly, naïve observations."

Daniel frowned, "I may be simple and naive, but I have family, a life, I am happy, while you have nothing, and you look it."

Arnaud just looked at Daniel before shouting, "I lost. Yes, I have nothing. Yes, I'm depressed, wouldn't you be?"

Daniel smiled, "But you are lucky. Lucky you still have some friends, such as me, and lucky you are in Saint Charles; people care about people here. Please come with me. Let's have a drink. Maybe I can offer you a job. Have you ever washed dishes, scrubbed a pot? It's easy. I'll show you."

Chapter 16

D aniel brought the ex-mayor into the family kitchen. "Have a seat. Wait while I see what is at the bar," he instructed the mayor, who happily took a seat. As Daniel started for the bar, the mayor replied, "Coffee would be fine," then said as an afterthought, "though I do need a drink, a strong one."

Daniel could be heard as he headed for the bar, "We should have both."

Michelle came bounding down the back stairs, happy the Bistro was closed. She had the whole day to work with Daniel on inventory and developing an order system. The expressway reopened, and Sunday meal service returned to the usual level of traffic. This gave her time to think about the order system. She knew what she wanted to do. She thought of a spreadsheet to start and then a database once she knew the additional requirements. She remembered from her IT class *proto-typing was a viable, cost-effective method to determine functionality when developing new systems.*

As she made the last turn and entered the kitchen, she saw a strange man sitting at the family table. His back was to her, and she had no idea who he was. She spoke loudly, "Good morning," to announce her presence, not necessarily to greet the man. The man turned and replied, "Good Morning, Michelle.

Michelle froze at the sight of the ex-mayor sitting at the family table. Though her body froze, her mind was racing, unable to control her thoughts and form a sentence. The silence was awkward. Finally, Michelle started fumbling for words, "Who, what are…, who let…, is there, how did…".

Daniel returned from the bar with a half-empty bottle of cognac. As he entered the kitchen, he placed the bottle in front of the ex-mayor.

"Good morning, Michelle." Daniel greeted Michelle with a smile and an uplifting tone while removing two glasses from the shelves, "We are having a quick drink, a drink to toast Arnaud's good fortune. Care to join us?"

The ex-mayor looked oddly at Daniel, "My good fortune? A minute ago you were saying I have nothing, now you are saying I have good luck?"

He looked at Michelle, "Is this man all there?"

Michelle, put off by the ex-mayor's insinuation, quickly defended her uncle. "Daniel is brilliant, one of the smartest and most talented people I know. Hear him out."

Daniel smiled, poured a healthy serving of cognac into the two glasses, and became very solemn. "I say you're lucky because yesterday, probably even this morning, a short time ago, you wanted to destroy my family, my most precious possession. Hours, minutes later, you are my guest, and we are sharing a drink at my table. That, my friend, is luck. A less fortunate man would be out on the streets alone and probably looking for a way out."

The two sipped, the ex-mayor, not saying anything, thinking about what he had heard. Michelle stood at the stove, not wanting to be involved.

Daniel interrupted the silence, "Another way to look at it, you are lucky...."

The ex-mayor cut in, "No, I am not lucky. You are kind, generous, forgiving, but I am not lucky. You can put any spin on it you'd like, but the end result is -- I am not lucky. Never have been."

Daniel stopped, waiting for the ex-mayor's negativity to pass. Again, Daniel started, "You are lucky, truthfully lucky because you have fallen, you have hit bottom, there is no direction to go but up. Tomorrow will be a better day."

The ex-mayor looked at Daniel with an incredulous look on his face. He finished his drink in one gulp, stood up, and said, "I appreciate the drink, but you'll have to forgive me if I don't stay and listen to this childish pop psychology. I'm lucky because I've hit bottom and have nowhere to go but up. What bathroom stall did you read that from, or was it from a box of breakfast cereal? I must go. Thank you for the drink."

As the ex-mayor went out the back door, he could be heard saying under his breath, "My word, and I lost to these people. "

Daniel looked at Michelle, a sad look on his face. Michelle had never seen Daniel looking so pitiful. "Michelle, that man has poison in his heart, terrible, terrible poison. He will never get anywhere until he removes it, if it is not already too late. His bad luck is because of this. It is of his own doing. I was going to help him. I sincerely thought I could help him. Sad, very sad."

Michelle sat down next to Daniel and took his hand. "Daniel, everybody deserves a chance. What separates people is what a person does with their chance, once presented to them. Some people are good. They take their opportunities and do good, providing more opportunities for others. Other people are greedy. They take shortcuts, looking for the big score. Those people ultimately lose. It's a law of nature. You can offer them another chance, but most will just try again for the big score, taking shortcuts, and by the laws of nature, will ultimately lose again."

Daniel looked at Michelle, "You are absolutely correct. I did not know you were so wise. Absolutely correct. I agree 100% with everything you just said. Well, good luck, mayor."

Michelle agreed, "Yes, good luck."

* * *

The following Saturday, the town gathered in the basement of the Municipal Building to elect a new mayor. Sign-in sheets were at the front door, and people's names were verified against the official town registration. Henri Tremont once again led the group and called the meeting to order.

"Hello, everyone. Our business today is to elect a new mayor. As you all know, the mayor will be selected for a six-year term, and there are no limitations on the number of consecutive terms a mayor may serve. We have two candidates. The two candidates have drawn straws and will speak in turn. Each will have 30 minutes to speak and answer questions. We will vote by show of hands. If any individual wants to vote privately, they may do so by marking a piece of paper and dropping it in the poll box by the exit door. The first candidate to speak is Paul Stephenson's nephew, Mr. Adam Ryker."

Adam stood up and made his way to the podium, as did his uncle, who agreed to be his interpreter. Adam made a nice speech, not taking any chances, admitting his inexperience but emphasizing his honesty, work ethic, and willingness to learn. He finished his speech by relating his near-death experience with the military. He said it had taught him, "Life is precious, friends and community are precious, they need to be guarded, protected, and treasured.

Daniel, sitting in the third row with Maria and Michelle, said, "I like this guy; he is strong, and you can see it in his eyes; he is honest."

No one really knew what to ask Adam. His lack of language skills seemed to be the key concern on people's minds. When the questioning concluded, he received a standing ovation.

Henri returned to the podium, "The next candidate for mayor is Pierre Villeneuve. Pierre." Polite applause greeted Pierre as he came to the podium. He pulled a few cards out of his coat pocket. He looked at the cards, shuffled them, then placed them back in his pocket. He stared off into the distance for a moment, then started.

"I was up late last night trying to determine what to say, trying to put myself in the shoes of a politician. I wrote some things down, but as I came to the podium just now, I realized we don't want a politician as mayor. We want someone who embodies the soul, the spirit of the town, someone we all can have faith in, who we know will act in the town and residents' best interests. "

Pierre paused for a moment, then continued, "Many of you will vote for me, thinking it will ensure, when you visit me at work, you will get a table by the fireplace. Many will not vote for me, afraid if I win, I will no longer be Maitre'd, and you will lose your favorite table by the fireplace. "

The crowd politely chuckled.

"Either reason should not enter your thinking. You should only vote for me if you sincerely think I am the right man for the job. You should only vote for me if you think we can work together and solve whatever future problems we may encounter. You should only vote for me if you think I can be instrumental in shaping our village, to be the village we want Saint Charles to be, for our families now and the many future generations to come. Thank you, God bless and viva la France."

The crowd was silent, but from the back row came, "Viva la Liberte." One man stood up and started clapping, then another, and another; soon everyone was on their feet clapping. Slowly the clapping was replaced by a chant, "P-ierre, P-ierre, P-ierre." Even Daniel was on his feet, throwing his fist in the air, and yelling his brother's name each time he threw his fist.

Henri finally got the crowd to sit.

As Daniel sat, he looked at Maria, a shocked look on his face, "Oh my God, he just got himself elected mayor. My brother is the mayor."

Maria quickly cut him off, "Stop saying that. We haven't voted yet."

Daniel replied, "You are right. The chickens haven't crossed the road yet."

Maria, paying attention to the proceedings, glanced at Daniel and simply answered, "That too."

Henri Tremont took the vote, and the township overwhelmingly voted for Pierre as mayor. After the vote, Adam stood up first and congratulated Pierre. Adam made his way to the podium and gave a very warm concession speech, agreeing Pierre was the right man for the job.

Then Henri went to the podium, with a broad smile on his face, was obviously satisfied with what had just transpired. He announced loudly, "Ladies and Gentlemen, I present to you the 207th Mayor of Saint Charles en Liberte, the Honorable Pierre T. Villeneuve."

Everyone shouted, clapped, and stomped their feet. Maria stood, a smile on her face, tears of joy streaming from her eyes. Pierre got the crowd to sit and settle down. Once everyone was quiet, a voice from the back interrupted, "I want that table by the fireplace." The crowd roared with laughter.

Pierre, very humbled by his election, looked out at the crowd and said, "Everyone here deserves a table by the fire…but not on the same night."

The crowd once more politely laughed.

He continued, "In all seriousness, thank you. Thank you for entrusting me with such an important responsibility. But there is one person that deserves accolades; there is one person I not only want to, but need to, thank. She says I have stood by her, but it is she who has stood by me. She has given me purpose. Maria Villeneuve. Please, Maria, will you stand."

There was a solid round of applause as Maria stood. She blew Pierre a kiss then quickly took her seat. Pierre spoke for a few minutes, regretting the series of events that caused the removal of the previous mayor. He vowed to "diligently guard the gates to this wonderful place we all call home." Afterward, the town was invited to the Tree Trunk for refreshments and to view the artist's renditions of the veranda.

Everyone loved the idea. Pierre played it up, suggesting the plans will be approved by the Mayor's Office only if there is enough *cash in the envelope.*

Maria stood off by herself, smiling, shaking hands with people as they passed by, and wiping tears of joy from her eyes. Pierre spotted her by herself and went to keep her company. Maria smiled as he approached; Pierre smiled back.

Maria started talking first, "I told you, you could do it, I told you. I am so very happy for you. You have found your calling. Now just be yourself, be the man you were born and raised to be, and you'll be remembered as the best mayor this town has ever had."

Pierre bowed and kissed her hand, "Madam Villeneuve, once again, I am in awe at your ability to see with clarity the world around you. I am forever in your debt." He looked at her, smiled, and then continued, "I have to confess, you don't know how scared I was walking up to the podium. But I must tell you, on the way up, I had a vision."

"A vision?" Maria asked.

"Yes, I saw my brother. I had a vision of Roger, and do you know what he said to me?"

She sniffed and touched her nose with her tissue, her eyes lighting up, "You saw Roger? What did he say? Please, tell me."

He said, 'You're a Villeneuve, act like one, stand tall and make us all proud.'

Maria, tears running down her cheeks, eyes swollen and red, nodded and said softly, "Yes, that's what he would say."

Pierre hugged Maria; they both needed it.

The party wound down with everybody happy and looking forward to having Pierre in the mayor's seat. Pierre left to meet Henri Tremont and Paul Stephenson to get the keys to the Municipal Building and sign the official record book. Claire was persuaded to put in a few hours helping Pierre get organized and to help clean the office. It had been over a week since anyone had been in the office, and it showed.

After the party, Maria asked Michelle to come to her room. There, she confided to her, "We need to prepare for the day when Pierre is no longer with us."

"What do you mean, Mother?" Michelle asked, horrified by what her mother just implied.

"If I know Pierre like I think I do, he is a man with ambition. Correctly harnessed, there are no limits to where his ambition could take him."

Michelle felt relieved at the clarification. "Oh, well, I can back him up and take over if necessary. I enjoyed doing it last Saturday, and after Claire and Rudy get married, we can always count on...."

Maria stopped her, "What did you just say?"

"Claire and Rudy, a little something I'm working on. They both got the hots for each other. I'm working to make it happen. I hope the veranda's finished by the time it happens. It will be a nice place to have the wedding reception, maybe even say their vows," Michelle spoke as if she had it all planned out.

Maria laughed. "Where do you get such notions? Who, what, where do you get these ideas? Do they know you are 'working on it'?"

"Of course not, but you know it's a best friend's responsibility to make things happen when they stall. And, Mother," Michelle said, implying the obvious, "Look at them, have you ever seen two people more perfect for each other?"

Maria sat up on her bed, a curious smile on her face. "They would make a cute couple."

Chapter 17

"Good morning, Sis; what's new in the fabulous world of Hospitality Management?" Rudy asked, feeling spry and energetic after his morning workout.

Sitting at the family table, nursing a cup of coffee and not feeling very positive, Michelle replied, "Morning…"

Rudy immediately got the hint. "Still fretting over the lack of a response from your magazine, or are we depressed no one's invited you to the Governor's Ball?"

"Very funny. I think at a certain level, a person or company needs to respond, even if the answer is no," she said adamantly.

Rudy, sarcastically, answered her back, "Are we talking about the magazine or the Governor's Ball?"

Michelle wasn't 100% sure she would get a response from the magazine, but deep down, she was hoping for something, anything. Any bit of recognition would at least give her some sense of validation. She felt like she had been invited to a party but then told to stand by herself in a corner.

Rudy apologized and tried to console her, "They probably get hundreds of invites and just either lose track of a few or can't respond to everyone. Don't take it personally. Maybe we're not presenting ourselves correctly. Perhaps they'll respond to a glossy color brochure with clever slogans, 'Rest and relax, at the Inn at Saint Charles'."

Michelle looked like she was thinking very intently, her brow wrinkled, and she remained quiet.

"Ok, I give up. Why are you looking so puzzled?" Rudy prompted her, trying to get her out of her mood.

She looked up at Rudy. "What rhymes with Saint Charles? I can't think of anything that rhymes with Saint Charles."

Rudy laughed but quickly stopped once he saw Michelle was serious. He answered her, "I can't help you there. Maybe you should emphasize 'Tree Trunk.' Should be easy to find something that rhymes with Tree Trunk."

"Of all the possible names to choose, our ancestors chose two of the most incredibly awkward, two of the most impossible names." Michelle bemoaned, "Why couldn't they have chosen something like 'The Outlook Inn,' or 'The Liberty Inn' or even 'The Saint Charles Inn.'"

Rudy looked oddly at Michelle, "The Saint Charles Inn'; what is that? Oh, I know, it's the place with the bistro next door, named 'Charlie's Place'. Yeah, that would work if we were renting rooms by the hour. Let's try to maintain some dignity, some class. Look, it will come. Trust me, it won't happen overnight, but it will happen. Let the laws of nature work things out. Mark my words, things will change, and you will look fondly back at the days when the dining room was filled with people you knew by their first names."

Michelle looked at Rudy, thinking he was probably right, but still, "Rudy, how do you control the laws of nature? I mean, how can we influence our fate?"

Rudy, surprised by the depth of his sister's question, had never been asked, nor had he ever contemplated how to influence fate. "Well, I'm not sure you can," He started speaking, more thinking out loud than providing an answer. "I think as soon as you try, you violate the laws."

Rudy sat down at the table, "I think, in all honesty, you can influence your fate by the things you do. Being humble, patient, and understanding of the world around you creates the positive energy that then influences your destiny. I think nature will recognize that you are doing the right thing and will reward you. I think you control your fate by being cognizant of who you are, what you are, and understanding where you fit in."

To lighten up the conversation a bit, he added, "You can't go out and behead a chicken or make some other sacrifice; that won't work. I think nature will penalize you for that."

Michelle thought about what Rudy said. "Then it sounds like you are in control of your life."

Rudy answered tentatively, not sure if Michelle's statement contradicted everything he just said, "Well, some are, and some are not. I think it depends on how conscious you are."

"Good morning, everybody." Michelle and Rudy's discussion was interrupted by Daniel's enthusiastic greeting as he entered the family kitchen from the back stairs. "A nice sunny day we have. I will work this morning on the root cellar. The more I think about it, the more I think it's important to cure some meat and perhaps offer a charcuterie board. What is a country bistro without a charcuterie board? What do you think?"

Daniel moved to the stove. "Coffee anybody?" He asked, not waiting for an answer to his original question.

"There are some croissants left over from yesterday in the pantry. I'll go get them." Rudy responded.

Daniel was quick, "Sit, I'll get them." He flew out the door and was back before his water had boiled. "These look good. Don't we have butter and jam?" He went looking on the shelves and came back with two small cisterns. Meanwhile, his water came to a boil, and the warm, fragrant smell of dark roast wafted through the kitchen as he poured the boiling water over the coffee grounds. "Ah, coffee, a croissant, butter, jam; life is good."

Daniel looked at Rudy as he devoured his croissant. Small crumbs littered the table in front of him. "Will you assist me in the cellar? Your point of view will be invaluable as I get it ready for curing meat. Besides, I have something I want to show you. Michelle, you should join us. I have something to share with both of you." He paused, waiting for an answer.

Rudy was first to reply, "Sure, I'm a little slow getting downstairs, but I'd like to be involved."

Michelle added, "What time?"

Rudy and Michelle met Daniel at the entrance to the root cellar exactly as asked. Michelle wanted to bring Claire, but Daniel asked that Michelle wait before bringing guests to the cellar, telling her, "I have secrets there, very important secrets. Let's decide what we want to do with these secrets before we bring others."

Daniel stepped down the half dozen stairs to the locked cellar door. He took a large ring of keys from his pocket and sorted through them, mumbling, "No, no, not that one, ah, this one." Then, unlocking the large, old padlock, he said to Michelle and Rudy, "Wait here while I turn on the light." Daniel walked into the cellar. A minute later, there was a loud "click."

Daniel shouted, "Come in, come in, please, you can come in."

Michelle carefully helped Rudy step down the stairs, deciding the root cellar wasn't the most wheelchair-friendly place, before leaving it at the top of the cellar stairs.

"Just take it slow, Sis. I can manage if we take it slow, and I have something to lean on."

Michelle replied, "Just lean on me."

Rudy smiled, "That should be a song."

Michelle again replied, "It is."

Rudy groaned, "I know; I thought you had a sense of humor?"

"I do, and you'll see it once you say something funny," Michelle said with more than a bit of sarcasm.

"Ouch slapped around again! Why do I have so many mean women in my life?" Rudy said as if helpless and seeking pity.

Daniel came over, "You two need to work out your issues. I would say kiss and make up, but I am afraid of what that might lead to."

Michelle looked at Daniel, embarrassed, "Daniel, we're joking around, don't take this seriously."

Daniel added, "More like flirting around."

The dim light shone on four long, somewhat narrow, planting tables as the two limped into the old root cellar. Each table looked like it held approximately 15 to 20 centimeters of dirt.

In the dim light, Michelle could barely distinguish what was growing, but it appeared that *something* was growing on three of the tables. The fourth table looked like it was just full of dirt.

"I think I could hang the meat against the back wall," Daniel mentioned while pointing to the dark back wall of the cellar.

Rudy looked at the planting tables. "What are you doing here?"

Daniel replied, still focusing on the back wall, "I am a farmer. I am learning how to coax the earth to provide for us."

Curious, Rudy moved closer, "Are these cepes? These look like morels." Rudy marveled at what Daniel had accomplished, "This is incredible."

Michelle looked closer at the last table. The earth was moist; there was a large amount of wood chips mixed in with the soil. "What are you trying to grow here?" she inquired.

"Daniel walked over to the table, "Growing, yes, but I call it sustaining. This is my sustaining table."

"What do you mean?" she asked, looking closer at the dirt and now noticing that there were many humps, humps of various sizes, randomly placed about, reflecting purpose to the otherwise flatly rolled dirt.

"Why is the dirt lumpy?" Michelle asked.

Rudy answered for Daniel, having already put two and two together, "That's what he is farming, or rather, sustaining."

"Ok, well, let's play riddles," Michelle countered, a bit frustrated her questions weren't being answered.

Having a bit of fun, Rudy tried her again, "In the morning, the very early morning, where does Daniel go?"

"I guess he goes to the forest," she said tentatively.

"And what does he go for, what is he hunting?" Rudy continued.

"He goes hunting. I've never seen him with a gun."

Rudy couldn't believe she wasn't getting it, "Not that type of hunting. Look, what does he bring back?"

Michelle, tired of being made fun of, shuffled her feet to show she was losing patience. "I don't know; I've never seen him return. Look, forget I asked. I don't want to know. It's very nice, Daniel, whatever it is."

She turned to leave, but Rudy stopped her, "Michelle, please, it's truffles. Daniel has figured out a way to farm truffles. He goes out in the forest and somehow finds truffles. Truffles are best when fresh out of the ground, so he picks the truffles, brings them back here, and replants them in his garden, where they remain alive and fresh. Then, when he's cooking and needs a truffle, he comes back here and harvests what he needs."

Surprised by Rudy's knowledge, Daniel replied, "How did you know that? You figured that out by just standing there?" He turned to Michelle, "He is very smart, very intuitive. That's why I like him. That's why we get along."

Daniel then looked back at Rudy, "I sustain them until ready to harvest. I know when I planted them, so I can see if they are taking to the dirt. I have taken soil from the forest and, along with other elements, I try to duplicate their environment. So far, it seems to be working. "

Michelle was in awe. "So, where are the truffles?"

Daniel answered her. "There in the dirt."

"Can I see one?" Michelle asked. Daniel was quick with his answer, anticipating Michelle's question, "I don't want to disturb them. They are very sensitive. They are relaxing and continuing to grow. Let's not interrupt. The next time I harvest, I will let you know, and I will show you."

"Do they actually grow once transplanted; do they actually increase in size?" Rudy was curious.

"Yes, sometimes, the truffles I find are very small. I bring them here and give them nutrition. In a couple of months, I have a nice size truffle, the size of a golf ball," Daniel boasted.

Rudy, leaning on the table and putting his eye down to the dirt, simply said, "Remarkable." Then he stood up, leaning slightly on Michelle but standing as much as he could on his own, looked straight at Daniel. "Brilliant, Daniel, absolutely brilliant. Simple in its design, brilliant in its conception, and best of all, successful in its application."

Daniel smiled and looked again at Michelle, "Sounds like real science."

Rudy reached over, offering his hand. Daniel took it, and as they shook, Rudy said as sincerely as he could, "Well done, Daniel, well done."

Daniel, with a bit of swagger, smiled and thanked Rudy, "Nothing to it. It's all very logical. I just transferred from the forest." Then Daniel's face lit up, "You want to see my special project?"

Rudy looked at Michelle, then back at Daniel. "You have something that will top this? This I got to see."

Daniel went over to a large pot sitting in the corner and motioned them to come closer. The pot, filled with dirt, had a large lump protruding from the center.

"Meet Josephine," Daniel said proudly.

Rudy looked down at the pot, not understanding. "So, you have a pot, and you are growing a truffle. Ok, why is this special?"

Daniel gave one of those 'I got you' smiles and said, "I'll show you."

He reached down into the pot, saying, "Come on, girl, this will only take a minute," and pulled out the largest black truffle Rudy had ever seen. It was nicely round, and the size of a small grapefruit.

"Good lord!" Rudy exclaimed as Daniel held it up to the light. Daniel began telling the story of Josephine: "I found Josephine three years ago in a very dangerous spot, prone to flooding. I carefully removed her from the soil, brought her back and nurtured her over the years. She has at least tripled in size. She is my baby. I am very proud of her."

Michelle, not understanding, asked, "Oh, so that's what a truffle looks like." Daniel let Michelle hold Josephine, handing the giant truffle to Michelle as if it were his child. Michelle held the truffle, looking it over. It wasn't too heavy, but it felt dense, solid. She wondered and finally asked, "When will you harvest it?"

Daniel quickly took Josephine back from Michelle, now with a smug look on his face. He gently placed the truffle back in its pot, quietly talking to the truffle as he covered it with dirt and then sprayed the dirt with a light mist of water.

"I don't know if I can. She's my friend, how can I eat her? How can I take my friend and slice her into pieces and serve her to my patrons? How? I ask you?" Daniel said with a level of agitation, surprising to both Michelle and Rudy.

Michelle gave Rudy one of those 'did you hear what I just heard' looks; Rudy remained silent, knowing this was not the time, this was definitely not the time.

Rudy was quiet as he and Michelle climbed out of the cellar. He spoke once they reached the top of the stairs, "Daniel, I think what you have created is brilliant. But I think the climate required to successfully farm mushrooms is different from what you need to cure meat. The humidity is wrong, the light is wrong, there's no airflow, and as the mushrooms grow and release their spores, they'll latch onto the meat, creating bacteria."

Daniel locked the door and followed Michelle and Rudy back into the house. "I think you're right. I think I must find another solution if I want to cure meat."

Rudy tried to cheer him up, "Maybe we could buy a special cooler, one that you can set the temperature, humidity, and even has fans to circulate the air. I mean, specially fabricated for curing meats. I am sure many commercial kitchens have them."

He wasn't interested. "We cannot take shortcuts. We must do things correctly. Think about all that is lost by putting meat in a metal box for six months. What you have is something that tastes like, like, like it was, it was in a metal box for six months. Terrible, I could not serve it. I could not face myself in the morning. I could not sleep at night. I'd rather put a gun to my head than serve such nonsense. I'll find a solution. The answer is right in front of me," Daniel lamented as he ambled from the family kitchen to the Tree Trunk.

Chapter 18

T ime passed. Michelle's mood toward her magazine changed from bewilderment to frustration to loathing. Though she began to hate what once was her favorite woman's magazine, she still wrote, again and again, letters inviting the publication to visit Saint Charles. She hoped this time, it would be different; she'd get an answer.

Perhaps Rudy was right, *A person always wants what they can't have.* But she was sure the inn was perfect for young professionals wanting to get away together for a distraction-free weekend; it was obvious the inn would be a popular destination. *Why couldn't the magazine see it?* she thought. *There must be something wrong. Being ignored like this just doesn't make sense.* So, Michelle wrote again and again.

One morning, she wasn't feeling her best. She felt bothered by everything and everyone. It was a Tuesday, and the Bistro was closed except for a simple brunch of fruit, pastries, and coffee set out for guests staying at the inn.

Michelle left her room and went downstairs to check on the brunch service, intending to return to her room. It was a typical late October day. The sun was out, but the wind blew cold from the northwest, making the day seem much bleaker than it really was. *A good day to stay in bed,* she thought.

She was checking the front desk when Claire arrived. "Good morning, Michelle. I am glad I ran into you. Here, I have this for you." Claire handed Michelle a small piece of paper.

Michelle looked at it. It had the name "Louisa Duggart" and a phone number. Michelle had spent enough time in Paris to recognize it was a Paris phone number.

"What's this?" she asked.

Claire replied, "Louisa is the writer of the 'Away for The Weekend' travel column, and that's her corporate number. I know how it's been bothering you, so I did a little digging."

"Really? You went to all that trouble. Do you want me to call? I mean, should I call?" Michelle said, quite pleased by Claire's initiative, but not sure what to do next.

"If you don't, I will. You could spend the rest of your life sending letters and postcards and never know the true story. Call to find out yes or no, and accept it, get it over with. I think it is bothering you too much. It is affecting your senses." Claire replied with a stern voice.

"Claire, you are a true friend. Thank you so much. You know, I am in just the right mood. I think I will call." Michelle's mood quickly changed as the two went into the small office behind the inn's reception desk.

Claire asked Michelle to wait while she fetched coffee for the two of them; returning, she brought the magazine's latest issue. The newest travel article was titled "Basking in Basque Country." As they read, both were entertained and amused by the many innuendos and double meanings in the article.

"Louisa certainly is clever and inventive with her writing," Michelle commented, breaking the silence but just calming her nerves as she prepared to make the call.

Claire said casually, "I wonder if she visits the places she writes about, or if it's all her fantasy. Like 'I wish this would happen to me.'"

Michelle lifted her eyebrows, "That's an interesting point. All these perfect weekends, who has such luck? Maybe we'll find out."

Michelle pulled the phone closer, finished her coffee, smiled at Claire, and whispered, "Here goes. Time, we dive into the deep end," and dialed the number.

The phone rang once, rang twice, and on the third ring, "Good Morning, this is Louisa. How may I help you?"

Michelle stumbled a bit, surprised she got through; took a second to regain her composure. "Hello, is this Louisa Duggart?"

"Yes, it is. How may I help you?" the pleasant voice asked again.

"Ms. Duggart, my name is…." Michelle started but was interrupted.

"Please, darling, call me Louisa; everybody calls me Louisa, you may too."

"Thank you," Michelle added, trying to continue, but the woman interrupted again.

"Now, to whom may I be speaking?"

Michelle tried again, "My name is Michelle Villeneuve. I am calling…" but the woman interrupted once more.

"Michelle Villeneuve? I know that name. Let's see. Where do I know that name from?" In the background, Michelle could hear the keys of a computer keyboard clicking and then, "Oh, yes, Michelle Villeneuve from the Inn at San Carlos. We were wondering when or if we would ever hear from you."

Michelle was puzzled. "What do you mean?"

"Well, we liked your proposal and intended to visit, but we had no way of contacting you. You didn't include an email; you didn't include a phone, and all our replies to your letters were returned as 'address unknown.' I even had my intern spend the day scoring a map, looking for San Carlos; we couldn't even find you on the map."

Michelle laughed, "San Carlos? Where in heaven's name did you get San Carlos?"

"That's what was in the database. Is that not correct?" Louisa inquired, fearing another clerical error and wondering what else had been entered incorrectly.

"No, it's the 'Inn at Saint Charles en Liberte,'" Michelle corrected and apologized for not including the main phone number, reciting it as Louisa wrote it down. Louisa cursed, using very unladylike terms as she apologized, blaming the error on her interns, who always seemed to be engrossed by their blossoming hormones and incapable of focusing for more than 30 seconds.

Once the record-keeping was out of the way, Louisa began discussing the possibility of a visit with Michelle. "The way we work is this way. We visit two destinations a month. Since we are an integral part of the magazine with a readership that has increased every issue, I might add, we schedule at least six months ahead. This gives us time to deal with cancellations but also gives us two options. We write about the most interesting of the two destinations; we rarely need to take a third trip, but I will say it has happened. Darling, we would rather work overtime, working with a third destination, than promote what we would consider a dud, if you know what I mean."

Michelle, taking it all in, felt like she had just gotten off a roller coaster. Her head was swimming with questions and suggestions. Most importantly, she was elated, walking on air. Michelle finally asked, "What can we provide you? What would it take to get you to spend the weekend?"

"Thank you. Darling, for the asking, not everyone is so generous and helpful. You seem like a very nice person. My assistant is out today, but I believe we are filling in slots for April and May of next year. Would those be good months to visit?"

Michelle suddenly became depressed again, "Next year?" she blurted out. "Next year is a year away. Couldn't you come any sooner? I mean, the winter holidays would be a wonderful time to visit."

Louisa replied, maintaining her business demeanor, "As I mentioned, we try to stay organized and schedule well in advance. I can keep you in mind in case there are cancellations or if we need a third destination. But otherwise, April is probably the earliest we can get to you."

Michelle, trying her hardest to be positive, replied, "Well, okay. Let's go with April. Which weekend?"

Louisa answered, "I'll have my assistant contact you for details. She's out with an awful cold and probably won't be in till next week, but we'll get back to you with the details. I have you down for April. Perfect, I look forward to our visit and a wonderful weekend in San Carlos."

Michelle quickly corrected her, "Saint Charles, please, Saint Charles en Liberte."

"Of course, Darling, Saint Charles it is. Good day and thank you for your inquiry. Ciao." Louisa terminated the call.

Michelle sat for a minute, letting the experience sink in before finally concluding, "Well, at least we have a date."

Claire was ecstatic. "I think it's wonderful. They are coming; April is a nice time, the flowers are blooming, and the weather is nice. It would be a great time to hike. I will contact my cousins and ask them to set trails. It would be good if we had specific trails people could follow. Maybe some easy trails, and then also some difficult trails."

Michelle stood; she felt spent. "Yes, we have lots of time to prepare. I'll inform everyone the next time we have a family meeting. Claire, I want to thank you again. Thank you for giving it your thoughts and making the effort." She gave Claire a warm hug.

Claire was her usual humble self and answered, "No problem, I am glad you have your answer."

Michelle informed every one of the scheduled visit by the 'Away for The Weekend' staff at the next family meeting. Being months away, everyone acknowledged the scheduled visit but otherwise paid little attention to it or asked any questions.

* * *

It was slightly more than a week later, early in November, when Michelle began to smell something. Guests staying on the second floor, occupying rooms towards the rear of the Inn, smelled it first. They complained of an odor, more pronounced during the day and made worse by opening windows. Guests on the third floor complained of a strong, offensive odor in the hallway but less so in their rooms.

Michelle called local plumbers to clean out the old sewage lines and asked the maids to use extra bleach when cleaning bathrooms, but nothing seemed to rid the air of the moldy, decaying, ammonia-like smell. It became stronger on the third floor, making people slightly nauseous as it easily permeated through walls, floors, and under doors. Michelle, at one point, thought stuffing towels underneath her door helped. But by the end of the day, the smell in her room was as bad as it was anywhere.

Maria began to smell it on the fourth floor, the odor slowly spiraling up through the heat ducts and the elevator shaft. No one had any idea where it came from. Maria's best guess was that an animal had somehow climbed into the walls and died. The smell became so bad on the third floor, guests cut their visits short and checked out.

Rudy and Pierre agreed that the smell was from something dead and decaying, but both were at a loss to explain how an animal could have climbed into the walls.

Maria, frustrated, called specialists. Building engineers from Bordeaux were brought in to assess the situation and ascertain where the odor was emanating from and, more importantly, how to remove it. The engineers, fearing a problem much more significant than a decaying animal carcass in the walls, drilled small holes in the outside walls horizontally every two meters and vertically every three meters to vent any potential buildup of hazardous gases. For the holes, scaffolding was erected, completely covering the Inn. Large pneumatic drills were brought in along with industrial compressors to power them.

The inn and the bistro were closed while the workman drilled holes and tested for the presence of various gases. The tests were negative for the more dangerous gases, but there seemed to be a larger-than-normal methane presence; not enough to be combustible or toxic, just enough to make one dread eating eggs.

Maria feared that having the inn closed would affect what little reputation and goodwill the inn possessed. She urged the men to try anything, anything to get to the answer. The consultants, befuddled, called in as a last resort some specially trained dogs to sniff out the origin of the odor.

Three dogs were brought in: a large, strong Black Labrador, a healthy-looking German Shepard, and a large black Standard Poodle. It took two men to handle the three dogs. The dogs were trained on the smell, then led around the infected areas. Handlers led the dogs to the Tree Trunk's kitchen, where only Daniel's scent seemed to be of interest.

Maria followed, answering questions when she could and granting access where she could. The dogs visited the second floor and became more excited as they neared ventilation grates along the walls. Taking that as a positive indication, the handlers took the dogs upstairs to the third floor. There, they became increasingly agitated as they slowly walked down the hall, stopping briefly at doors. They pulled past Michelle's room, past the storage room, and then stopped, wanting very badly to enter Daniel's room.

"What room is this?" one of the dog handlers asked.

Maria replied, "That room is Daniel's room. He is the head chef at the bistro."

"The dogs are very interested. Can we have access?" The man asked, having a difficult time conversing while controlling the dogs.

Maria fumbled with her keys, "Yes, of course; if I may have a minute." Maria searched her sizable key ring, looking for the Master Key to open any lock in the inn. Finally, she fit the key in the lock and gave it one turn to the left; with a loud and deep click, the lock opened, and the door slowly swung open.

As the door opened, the dogs started barking, straining on their leashes. A warm and then decidedly cool breeze swept past Maria and the handler as they stood in Daniel's doorway.

On the tip of the warm breeze was the most putrid, stinging, offensive smell one could imagine. Maria's first whiff as the breeze swirled past caused her to recoil backward. She stepped on one of the dog's feet, causing it to howl in pain, which in turn caused Maria to lose her balance further and fall back onto the floor. The first dog handler, reacting to Maria's recoil backward, dropped the dog's leashes in a vain attempt to catch her, freeing up the two dogs to run as they will through Daniel's room.

Maria lay there in Daniel's doorway. The smell was so strong and offensive that she had difficulty catching her breath, even with a cloth covering her mouth. The first dog handler was in the room, trying to get the two dogs under control. He was having a difficult time breathing, let alone catching the dog's leashes. He half-swore and half-prayed as he struggled to get the dogs under control. Meanwhile, in an aggressive attempt to get to the source of the odor, the dogs were ripping and tearing through frail cloth partitions and corrugated board Daniel had set up in and around his closet as temporary shelves and enclosures.

The second dog handler held a cloth up to his mouth and held tightly to the third dog leash. With much effort, he pulled Maria back to her feet. As she stood, trying to regain her wits, the man said to her with a smile, "I think we found it. I think we know."

Maria stood with her back to Daniel's room, shielding her face from the stench that lingered, heavy in the air, and stung her eyes and nose. Catching her breath, she thought, *What in heaven's name? No, don't tell me. I don't want to know.*

But knowing her brother-in-law and knowing with him, it could be anything, she finally relented, crying out, "Yes, I think you are right, this is it." Then, in a voice much quieter, almost mumbling, she said, "Lord help us if it isn't."

Chapter 19

D aniel was tipped off by one of the waiters that the dogs were being led through the inn and were moving up to the third floor. He quickly got out of his apron and took to the back stairs, taking three stairs at a time. He had just turned the corner of the back stairs leading to the third floor when he saw Maria falling backward as if hit by a cannon blast, the first handler dropping the dogs' leashes, and the dogs charging into his room

In a panic, he shouted, "My cheese. Save the cheese! Save the cheese!" But he feared the worst. When he got closer, he could hear the damage the dogs were doing to his room.

As he stood in his doorway and examined what was left of his room, the second handler walked past carrying two buckets of semi-liquid organic material. Grimacing, he walked with it out into the hallway and carefully down the back stairs. The kitchen door could be heard opening and then closing.

Almost immediately, the odor lightened. Maria went to the maid's closet, found some air freshener, and began spraying the hall, Daniel's room, and even down the stairs. It helped make the air breathable.

Daniel sat dejected, alone on his bed, looking at the destruction in his room.

Maria came over, "Daniel? What were you thinking? Why didn't you tell us? I mean, look at all the men we hired, the time, and the money we spent. Yet all this time, it was you? Why didn't you say something, Daniel, why?"

"How was I to know? People say there is a smell. I don't smell anything, not anything bad. I don't mind this odor. To me, it's good. It is the smell of nature, of nature being creative. "

Maria pushed on, trying to get an understanding of where Daniel was coming from, "The scaffolding, what did you think the scaffolding was for? All the noise and dust."

"I thought you were starting on the Veranda. Didn't you want it finished by the winter holidays? I thought to ask Rudy, but I forgot, we talked about something else," he replied, shrugging his shoulders.

"But Daniel!" Maria hugged Daniel like a mother would hug her son when he was caught misbehaving and couldn't help himself.

Daniel spoke solemnly, "I wanted to make a special cheese, a special Tree Trunk Cheese, only available here and maybe only at certain times of the year. Maybe. I don't know. I wasn't finished, and now I have to start all over again."

Maria smiled at Daniel with tears in her eyes, "Oh, Daniel, I know you have the biggest and sweetest heart. I can't be mad at you; I am not happy, but I can't be mad. But did I hear you correctly? Was that odor acceptable to you? Did you find it pleasant? Please tell me no."

Daniel shrugged. "Well, I didn't think it was that bad. I would leave my window open and then turn on the heater. The air would circulate. I had no trouble sleeping, resting in my room."

Maria couldn't go on. She gave a last hug to Daniel and said she'd be back to help him clean up, then went downstairs to get things settled with the consultants who now had to remove the scaffolding, after first filling in all the holes they drilled.

Just then, Michelle came bouncing into Daniel's room. "I just heard it's over. I heard it was an attempt to cure cheese gone bad?"

Daniel looked up, still dejected and now having to deal with an effervescent Michelle, "An attempt at cheese, yes, gone bad, no I don't think so. Just needed more time."

Michelle looked down at Daniel and could see he needed a friend, so she took a seat next to him. "Daniel, it's brilliant what you did in the cellar, it's brilliant that you try these things. You, we, don't know if they will be successful until you try. The important thing is you try, and I will tell you one thing -- I for one, want you to keep trying. You are very clever and smart; if you get a notion or idea, try it. They don't call it 'trial and error' for nothing. Ok Daniel, is that a deal?" Michelle said as she got up to leave.

Daniel smiled, "Ok, that's a deal. Hey, and the next thing I try, I won't do it on the third floor."

Michelle added, "Or the second, or in the kitchen. Off-premises, Daniel, do it off the premises!"

Everybody opened windows and vents, and soon, the inn was full of fresh, clean air. Maria had Michelle go up and down the halls every hour with air freshener to ensure that the only smell was the smell of roses.

Daniel's room was cleared of the incriminating debris, and the buckets of organic material Daniel was trying to cultivate into cheese were hauled away by consultants who wore HazMat suits and breathed from portable air supplies.

Everything seemed back to normal.

* * *

The last two days, Pierre had been in Bordeaux trying to mend fences and rekindle old alliances lost to neglect by the previous mayor. The previous mayor let many opportunities slip past without even the recognition that an offer had been made. Perhaps he was afraid of quid pro quo, what ultimately would be the price the village would have to pay, or, as Pierre figured, he was just lazy and interested only in the benefits of the job he could personally reap and not in what would benefit the town itself.

Pierre was surprised to hear that Mayor Martin had declined an offer from the region's transportation authorities to widen the road leading into town and apply a new layer of asphalt. This would have been a significant improvement, widening the road to two lanes, allowing for traffic in either direction at the same time.

Another opportunity he declined was an offer to add signs for Saint Charles en Liberte' on the new expressway, indicating the correct exit and route to take into town.

Both would have increased the flow of traffic into town. *Why would the mayor want to keep Saint Charles isolated? Why would he not want to improve traffic?* He wondered. Then, embarrassed by his own naiveté, it came to him, *the mayor wanted to choke the town, make it a failure. Then he could come in with his banking associates, The Gold Group or whoever, and buy the whole town for next to nothing. Then, once he owned the town, he could have the authorities fix the roads and add the exit signs on the expressway.*

Pierre became amazed, and more than a bit troubled, as the mayor's plan became obvious: *Ruin the town, bring it to the brink of failure, then come in like a conquering hero and buy everyone out at distressed prices, making it seem like he was doing everyone a favor.* Pierre was dumbfounded. *Why didn't I see it? It was right in front of my eyes. All along, the mayor was working against us. He did nothing for five years but conspire against us.* Pierre shivered at the audacity, feeling nothing but revulsion for the man.

Before he left Bordeaux, he arranged for the signs to be added to the expressway. The cost was minimal, given the road was funded by the National Transportation Ministry. It was estimated to take approximately two weeks for the signs to be fabricated and installed. The widening of the road would have to wait for spring, but Pierre managed to get it scheduled for early April, weather permitting.

Pierre took the train to the Saint Germaine station, where he left his Citroen. As he drove the curvy single-lane road back to Saint Charles, he thought how nice it would be to have two lanes and fresh asphalt. *With fresh asphalt, a person could roller skate to the train station.* He laughed as he pictured himself in his new maroon tuxedo roller-skating down the middle of the road, waving at friends as they drove by.

He was happy to be back in town but feeling unsettled by his recent discoveries and conclusions; he was glad the odor had been successfully removed and volunteered to be Maître'd for the weekend, starting with dinner on Friday. While in Bordeaux, he had picked up two new tuxedo jackets, a rich dark maroon and a white, both cut very trim. He purchased two pairs of pants for each jacket, six shirts, and two pairs of very comfortable Italian leather loafers in black. He didn't know how much time he had available for Maître'd duties, but he felt prepared. No matter what the obligation, he would look the part.

Friday night came around, and Pierre was feeling quite pretentious in his new maroon tuxedo. He combed his hair back, adding a bit of hair cream, giving him a slick, shiny retro look. He could have easily fit in as Maître'd of a fashionable 1930s Parisian nightclub.

As was his custom, he placed reserved signs on all the tables, allowing him to ham it up, offering guests a table reserved for another party, making them feel special. It also allowed him to refuse service to whomever, citing completely reserved seating.

The only thing left to do before opening the doors was the menu. Pierre dreaded this part of the job. Though Daniel was getting accustomed to the limitations placed on him by a menu, the process always seemed laborious. It changed his mood in many ways, usually not for the better! *I think I really and truly, would rather see my proctologist than pry and cajole a menu out of Daniel.*

Hearing of Michelle's success with Daniel, he requested she be there. She agreed, but only on the condition Pierre lead the effort.

"It's just a matter of adapting; you adapt to Daniel's style, and he, well, he, sincerely tries. I think he tries his best. But understand, his idea of organization is different from ours," she offered as consolation to Pierre.

"Far different, so different as to be virtually unrecognizable," was Pierre's response, giving Michelle a wink in the process and causing both to smile as they waited for the inevitable.

Michelle's writing was the neatest of the three, so as they got down to formulating the evening's menu, she held the board and the chalk.

Pierre started, "Well, let's start with an onion soup. We have no issues, right, served with croutons and Gruyere?"

Daniel replied, "No issues, except let's call it 'Classic French Onion Soup, Moroccan Style.'"

"French Onion Soup Moroccan Style?" Pierre was quick to counter, "If it's French, it can't be Moroccan."

"Well, I think with a simple beef broth, onion soup becomes tedious. Why not just eat onion, bread, and cheese?" Daniel looked at the two with 'who's with me on this?' all over his face.

Not getting any feedback, Daniel continued, "I add spices, spices typically found in Moroccan cuisine. I add a touch of turmeric and cumin, some cinnamon, and black pepper. It livens it up. Now every sip is a dance, a belly dance. See what I mean?" Daniel laughed at his vision of his soup inspiring "belly dancing."

Michelle tried to be diplomatic, "I don't know what to write. Is it still onion soup? Daniel, do you still add croutons and gruyere?"

Daniel replied, "Of course, I add some spice to the croutons as well. I think it matches the cheese well, but I am seeking a more fragrant cheese. Some might say the spices overpower delicate Gruyere."

Pierre added, "Well, I think it's an interesting concept, and who am I to tell the kitchen how to prepare food. But it is winter, it's cold, and many like to start their meals with a hot bowl of soup. So, I ask that we offer two versions of the soup. For the less daring, let's offer a classic onion soup, and for the more intrepid palates, Onion Soup, Moroccan Style."

Daniel was fine with the arrangement, "Ok, I will prepare both. You should try my Moroccan style. I think you will dance." He smiled and shifted his eyebrows in a very flirtatious manner.

Michelle laughed, "Daniel, you are such a flirt, but we must continue with business; the doors will open soon." Using a curvy, ornate script, she wrote the names of the two soups and then started writing 'Plate of pate', leaving room for a number.

Pierre saw what she wrote and asked Daniel, "We have pates?"

Daniel replied, "I have four pates, but we should only offer two on a plate, let the customer order which two."

Pierre liked the idea, and Michelle wrote the four pates with instructions to select two.

Daniel said to add "Fantasy Bread. "

Pierre looked at Daniel and repeated, "Fantasy Bread?"

"Yes, I have made the mousse; now I'm just waiting for the bread to finish proofing before I stuff it. Rudy has been fine-tuning his bread. I think we are ready."

Michelle cut in, "You should taste it, Uncle. It is the most unbelievable taste sensation. I tried it with a glass of chardonnay…."

Daniel corrected her, "You mean that wine I gave you? It was a Rose from Provence. If we want to stay local, I suggest we offer Paul Stephenson's White Blend. It's drinking like a fine Montrachet. It will have the same effect, but better; trust me."

Pierre insisted, "But must we refer to it as Fantasy Bread? This isn't a snack bar for twelve-year-olds. Let's call it stuffed bread or toasted bread with filling. Something adults can relate to."

But Daniel insisted, "We have already served it, once, no, twice. We called it Fantasy Bread. People know it as Fantasy Bread. They ask for it."

"Fine, call it what you will. Let's not get stuck on it," Pierre said, giving in easily.

It wasn't long before the menu was complete. Tables were set; waiters were shown the menu and instructed regarding how best to *describe* the preparations. They stood ready, waiting for the first guests. Busboys were busy helping Rudy with last-minute prep work in the kitchen.

To help create some ambiance, Rudy brought four loaves of bread to the fireplace. Just minutes later, the wholesome, inviting aroma of baking bread filled the dining room.

The first to arrive were four friends and associates of Pierre's, along with their wives. Pierre had met them on his last trip to Bordeaux. They quickly became friends as they conducted the town's business while learning that they shared similar interests in wine, food, and debating.

The men worked at the local branch of the National Transportation Ministry, and though they held lofty titles, such as Deputy Director, Counselor, and Chief of Engineering and Construction, Pierre did not think they had much influence; he genuinely liked the men and invited them to visit The Tree Trunk, solely as an act of friendship.

The couples were eager to try a new dining experience and once invited, were quick to make the drive from Bordeaux. More than one joke was made that evening over the conditions of the roads leading into Saint Charles.

Pierre, embarrassed by the previous mayor's lack of attention, simply joked, "The mayor was primarily interested in eating, eating, and more eating. Though he was here every day, I don't ever recall having a decent discussion with the man. About the only thing I recall is that he knew nothing about a lot, or is that a lot about nothing?"

Pierre's friends laughed at his humor and the irony of the situation, advising the new mayor to look into some much-needed road maintenance, all agreeing that widening the road into town should be his first priority.

Another suggested, if the land was available, "Construct a municipal parking lot. Let people come, park, and stroll around this lovely little village, or hike through the forest. After an active day, what better ending than a wholesome, hearty meal, a glass of cognac, and a good night's rest at the inn?"

Pierre led the large party to a warm table off to the side of the fireplace. Two tables were brought together, creating one long table. Pierre assisted the women with their chairs, helped by one of the waiters. Looking the part in his maroon tuxedo, hair slicked back, and sporting an impeccably trimmed Corsican moustache, Pierre introduced their waiter. It was a charming, somewhat sophisticated introduction. As he was introduced, the handsome young man in a white dinner jacket smiled and bowed while holding a clean, white towel over his arm.

Encouraged by the warmth and openness of his new friends, Pierre insisted they accept champagne on his behalf. Two bottles were brought up from the cellar, opened, and poured. Warm loaves of bread, including a loaf of fantasy bread, were placed on the table.

Pierre lifted his glass in a toast. "Friends, I thank you for making the trip to visit us here in Saint Charles. I hope you...."

From the far end of the table, a woman let out a moan followed by, "Oh my God."

Pierre finished his last word, "enjoy?"

"Dear, are you alright?" Her startled husband asked, while everyone stared.

"My God, yes, try this bread." She looked at Pierre and asked, "What is this?"

Pierre answered, "Try it while sipping your champagne."

The woman did as Pierre instructed and let out an even louder and deeper moan. "It's fantastic. Better than…"

Sitting across from her, her husband quickly and loudly cleared his throat and gave her a look. She corrected herself and repeated, "It's fantastic."

By now, everyone was reaching for the bread, examining it, and taking bigger and bigger bites.

"Marvelous" was one reaction.

"Incredible, may we order more?" was another.

Pierre watched as the table became silent. The patrons, with their eyes closed, savored the bread, opening their eyes only to reach for another slice.

Pierre finally broke the silence, "That's why we call it Fantasy Bread."

"It's appropriate," was the unanimous response.

The night progressed, other guests came and went while Pierre's friends sat and ate, relaxed, and enjoyed the Tree Trunk's hospitality. They directed many compliments to the kitchen. The fantasy bread was an obvious hit, but so was the Classic French Onion Soup, Moroccan Style.

"Onion soup can be so monotonous at times. It's warm and comforting, yes, but ultimately boring. The addition of North African spices was a whole new twist. I enjoyed it thoroughly," one of the women said while asking for the recipe.

After dessert and what must have been the third or fourth round of cognac, Pierre took the initiative, finding Maria and asking if any rooms in the inn were still available. It so happened she had just rented out the last available room on the second floor, but all four rooms were available on the third floor. Pierre quickly reserved the rooms under his name and went back to check on his friends in the dining room.

As Pierre approached the party of eight, he could see they were engaged in an energetic discussion. Apparently, there was disagreement over the new Design Manual for Low-Trafficked New Pavements released just the year before. Pierre couldn't follow the technical nature of the argument, but after listening, wasn't sure even if there was an argument. Everyone seemed to be expressing the same viewpoint.

Pierre stood quietly by, and as the discussion waned, he interrupted, "I hope everyone enjoyed this evening." Everyone smiled and nodded as he continued, "I know it's a long drive back to Bordeaux and not on the best of roads. Because of this, I have reserved four rooms for you at the inn. I hope you will accept my hospitality and stay the night. When you are rested and refreshed in the morning, you may drive at your leisure back to Bordeaux. We serve brunch on weekends starting at 11 a.m. You are, of course, welcome to stay for lunch."

"That's an excellent idea," one man stated, and all the others agreed. "Since we no longer will be making the drive, let's have one more drink before we conclude the evening."

The wives declined, all deciding to go to their rooms. Pierre, wanting the busboys to clean the table and dining room, invited the men to have a cigar and a nightcap in the bar.

The sizable bill for the evening was presented on a small silver platter to one of the men, who took out a credit card issued under the name of the National Transportation Ministry. He was a little wobbly, looking at the card, then at Pierre.

Finally, he spoke, "Excellent food; thank you and your staff for their warm and gracious hospitality."

Then he looked at the others. "We are on a fact-finding mission, are we not?" All the others nodded in agreement, with one saying, "Remarkable trip. I learned quite a bit. These roads, without question, need attention." Again, everyone agreed, and the man placed the card on the silver platter without even so much as a glance at the bill.

Pierre paid for the rooms himself, insisting he couldn't let friends drive after such a meal. Not only were the roads bad, but most were also unlit, making for rather treacherous driving conditions. The party left in the morning after coffee and croissants, but mostly coffee, still feeling very satisfied. Some were still a bit wobbly from the previous evening's celebration.

Pierre agreed to Matre'd all weekend and had just arrived for duty when he saw his friends preparing to leave. He was wearing his new white tuxedo, what he called his weekend tux. He was quite dashing, a 1930's Hollywood film star, with his deep black hair, slicked back and glistening, trimmed moustache, bright white jacket, and Italian loafers, a cigarette constantly between two fingers or nonchalantly dangling from the corner of his mouth. He presented a romantic, nostalgic image, like he was meeting Humphrey Bogart for a night out in Casablanca.

After seeing his friends depart, Pierre returned to the kitchen and found Daniel preparing for Saturday service. Pierre stood by the entrance to the kitchen and motioned his brother over.

Daniel had no idea what he wanted. Pierre looked Daniel straight in the eye and said, "We have our differences, but I am proud to call you my brother." Pierre reached around and gave Daniel a warm brotherly hug while continuing, "I know we will be successful. I know we will be successful because of your talent, skill, and ingenuity. Fantasy Bread, how did you ever?"

Pierre let his voice trail off as he turned and exited to the dining room.

Chapter 20

After working through the weekend, Pierre decided to sleep late Monday and have a nice leisurely morning, maybe joined by a family member or two. He began thinking, *The bistro's closed today; someone should be around to join me for coffee. It would be good to have some company, to catch up with the family gossip.*

Pierre stood alone by the stove in the family kitchen, watching the water as it began to boil, lost in his thoughts, but enjoying the rays of sun on his face as they cascaded through the large multi-paned windows.

"Maybe I should think about getting married." He thought, *I have a good occupation.* He corrected himself, smiling. *I have a great occupation. I'm mayor.* He amused himself further. *What woman wouldn't want to be the first lady of Saint Charles en Liberte?*

His mood brightened. *I should put myself up for auction. But how would I judge the winner? What criteria would I use, the highest bidder? No, I don't require money.* He paused. *The most attractive bidder, well maybe, the most attractive in terms of the complete package. Yes, that's the way to look at it, the complete package.*

Satisfied with how he would judge the winner, he poured steaming water over the ground coffee, filling his nose with its rich fragrance. *I am looking forward to a good, strong cup and...,* he chuckled, feeling quite full of himself, *reviewing the bids.*

Just then, Claire came running into the kitchen, out of breath, a look of panic on her face. "Mayor Pierre, I went to the office this morning to finish the filing," she said, completely out of breath and struggling with her words, "before reporting for duty at the front desk, you must come. It's terrible. You must come quickly; I think they are going to destroy the town."

Pierre set his empty cup down and the coffee he was about to pour and asked, "Who is going to destroy what town? What are you talking about?"

Claire caught her breath long enough to blurt out, "The machines, there are machines, many of them, and men, they are tearing up the street. Come quickly."

Pierre walked out the side door of the family kitchen, down the short alley to the side street, and then out to the main avenue. Because of a slight rise in elevation, Pierre could only hear what sounded like machinery and construction equipment but couldn't make out anything. Occasionally, he saw a man who looked like he was sitting, operating a machine, and wearing a bright yellow construction helmet. He would appear, push or pull a lever or two, reverse course, and disappear.

What in heaven's name? Pierre thought as he hustled down the street towards the sound. As he came over the rise, he could see out in front of him at least a half dozen, giant, bright yellow bulldozers, pushing dirt along, making the street more than twice as wide as it was before. Pierre could see earthmoving equipment; he counted four of them, scraping along and flattening the newly bull-dozed surface. Further down the road, steamrollers, huge machines with giant cylinders at the front and back, could be seen moving slowly along the dirt roadway, packing the earth, getting it ready for paving.

"What is this?" Pierre wondered out loud as a man wearing a construction helmet came walking up to him.

"Mayor Villeneuve?"

Pierre looked at the man, replying, "Yes, that's me."

The man smiled and offered his hand. As they shook hands, the man spoke while handing his card to Pierre, "I'm pleased to meet you. I am the Construction Supervisor."

Pierre examined the man's card, still not sure if this wasn't some type of joke, while the man continued to speak, "You have some very influential friends."

Pierre looked at the man, "Why do you say that?"

"Yesterday afternoon, on a Sunday, mind you, I received a call from my boss, who received a call from his boss, who received a...."

Pierre stopped him, "Yes, I understand; what was the message?"

"The message was, fix the road, do whatever it takes."

Pierre stood there, stunned but hiding it well while the man continued, "Oh, also I'm to ask you...."

"Yes, ask me what?"

The man looked at Pierre, "I've been instructed to ask, where do you want the parking lot?"

Pierre mumbled under his breath, "I must be dreaming." Then he quickly spoke up, "Let me get back to you. I have your card. Let me check with the town council and get back to you. "

The man laughed. "You have a town council?" he then looked around at the handful of buildings making up Saint Charles, "Who's left to be a citizen?"

Pierre shrugged off the remark, "You're a funny man. Be careful, remember, I have friends. "

The two men laughed, recognizing each other's sense of humor. The supervisor then spoke again, "I'm looking to pour concrete and apply asphalt by the end of the week. There's a 50/50 chance of weather coming next week, so we're cutting it close. The sooner you can get back to me with your lot location, the better. I ordered enough asphalt for 500 square meters. That's a lot big enough for about two hundred vehicles. Let me know if I need more. Like I said, you have some very powerful friends..."

"I may have an answer for you by the end of today. Let me make some calls," Pierre said, concluding the conversation and hustling off to his office followed closely by Claire.

Across the street from the Municipal building was a vacant lot. Pierre knew it to be owned by the Villagrosa family. The family was primarily fruit and vegetable farmers and had hundreds of acres devoted to cabbages, various lettuces, carrots, potatoes, melons, strawberries, blueberries, and much more. The family also grew grapes for producing wine and by all accounts, with increasing success. They had recently bottled an excellent Merlot, a very nice Pinot Noir, and a popular, very delicious Bordeaux-style red blend.

The vacant land across from the mayor's office had been purchased to start a Farmer's Market. The family bought the land at the insistence of the previous mayor, who promised to do everything in his power to bring visitors to Saint Charles. But the family never saw any effort or heard of any actions by the mayor to bring traffic into Saint Charles. So, the land sat vacant, unused, while the family fumed, agreeing never to trust another politician.

Pierre knew the family well, having attended school with Giorgio

Villagrosa, currently the head of the family, and his wife, the former Catherine Toussaint.

Pierre called Giorgio, not expecting to get through to him. A man's voice answered. "Hello?"

Pierre immediately replied, "Hello, Giorgio?"

The voice answered back, "No, this is Antonio, his son. He's out in the Winery. We've finished picking and are filtering out the crush. He asked not to be disturbed."

Pierre knew how important winemaking was to the family and hated to interrupt, but he felt the situation warranted. "If you could please tell him it's Pierre Villeneuve. I have something important to discuss. Tell him it won't take but a few minutes."

"Ok, I'll tell him, please hold." The young man put the phone down and could be heard walking away.

A few minutes later, a man's voice came on the line, "Hello Pierre, how are you? Congratulations on becoming mayor; I hope you do a better job than that bum Martin."

Pierre replied, "How could I not? My doing nothing would be an improvement."

Both men chuckled in agreement, then Pierre got down to business, "Giorgio, as we speak, I have construction crews from the Ministry of Transportation widening the main road into town."

"You're kidding me?" Giorgio replied, "That's wonderful."

Pierre continued, "If I just had some land, the crews have agreed to make a parking lot, a municipal parking lot. Tourists could come and have a place to park. We could even have a sign denoting trails, even a walking tour through various farms." Pierre was making it up as he went along, but it sounded good, and he was truly sincere.

Giorgio added, "Well, what about the lot out front of your place?"

"That's reserved for guests. If I allow tourists and hikers, where will my patrons park?"

Giorgio, quiet at first, giving it some thought, "I guess you're right; it sure wouldn't take much to fill your lot. Well, I guess then you're calling about the lot I own across from your office."

Pierre replied, "Yes, will you sell it back to the town?"

"Sell it, that vacant lot? I didn't pay much for it; I couldn't ask much for it. I tell you what. I'd rather have my family known for their generosity, for doing something for the town, rather than like some who just take and take. I will donate the land for use by the town. In return, all I ask is for the town erect a sign, a sign saying this property was a gift to the citizens of Saint Charles, from Giorgio and Catherine Villagrosa and their family."

Pierre was overwhelmed, "That's wonderful Giorgio, and very generous of you. Thank you. I accept your offer, and I will see to it personally, a sign is erected, and your family gets the recognition it deserves. I swear to you, on my mother's grave. "

Giorgio answered back, "Good, thank you. Now, if you would excuse me, I must be getting back to the winery. I don't want the skins left in the juice for too long. I find it adds bitterness. But I must say, I think this year's vintage has all the characteristics of a superior vintage, and it hasn't even gone into oak yet." Giorgio was talking about his wine and the oak barrels he uses to store his wine for months at a time, adding complexity and flavor.

"I look forward to trying it. If it is anything like last year's, The Tree Trunk will buy the whole lot. Thank you, Giorgio, thank you, and God bless," Pierre said calmly and sincerely.

Giorgio replied, "Same to you my friend," and hung up.

Pierre called to Claire, "Claire, is there a recent survey map of Saint Charles, one that shows property lines?" Claire answered, "Yes, that's one thing Mayor Martin was interested in. He had a survey done of the entire downtown district. It was done just last summer."

She removed the large map from storage and rolled it out on her desk. Properties were clearly delineated, with boundaries drawn. The lot across the street was apparent, with the labeling of "Vacant." An easement was drawn on the east side of the property and along the side facing the road. Pierre guessed correctly that it was intended for sidewalks.

Pierre found the construction supervisor, and together the two examined the survey and discussed options and timetables. The supervisor whistled, and a couple of men crowded around him, reading the survey, pointing, and gesturing with their hands. A bulldozer immediately crawled over and started leveling the lot while a team of men planted stakes to mark the perimeter. The supervisor convinced Pierre to add separate entrance and exits to the lot for ease in controlling access, if the town so desired.

The supervisor also agreed to install a sign and gave Pierre the phone number of the Ministry's Sign and Landscaping Department. By the end of the week, the lot was paved, concrete curbs installed, lines, lanes, and arrows painted on the black asphalt, and a sign erected between the entrance and exit, proclaiming in large, bright, white letters 'The Villagrosa Municipal Parking Lot.' Below, in equally bright but not as large letters, was a tribute to Giorgio and Catherine Villagrosa and their family, thanking them for their generous gift to Saint Charles en Liberte. It was all professionally done and looked very classy.

Pierre wanted to have a ceremony, a grand unveiling of The Villagrosa Municipal Parking Lot. "The people of Saint Charles deserve it. They don't get much. They work hard. It is time they receive something. I want to give them a ceremony." he proclaimed.

The bistro is closed on Monday and Tuesday, so Pierre decided the following Tuesday afternoon would be an ideal time to get everyone together and unveil the new parking lot. Afterward, refreshments would be served in the large common room in the basement of the Municipal building. Daniel and Rudy spent Monday baking cookies and small cakes to serve everybody.

Daniel was also tasked with making punch but in two versions, an alcoholic and non-alcoholic version. He made the alcoholic using wine and a couple of bottles of gin he had hidden away in the basement. He added slices of lemons and oranges to both versions for a festive look. Daniel poured the punch into two large cisterns, labeling the alcoholic punch with a piece of tape, marking it with an X. The cisterns, full of punch, were then stored in the meat cooler.

Unfortunately, the cool, dry air of the meat cooler caused the tape to buckle and lose its grip. On the day of the ceremony, the two busboys were sent to fetch the punch and found two identical cisterns. Knowing one was an alcoholic, but neither having any experience with alcohol, nor knowing how to tell, they decided to pour a bit of each one into the punch bowls, combining the alcoholic with the non-alcoholic versions.

At 3 p.m., everyone gathered outside the Municipal Building. It was a good-sized crowd for a Tuesday afternoon. People seemed friendly and sociable, strolling about, occasionally disappearing into the basement to get glasses of punch, a few cookies, and then more punch.

The punch was particularly popular with the crowd. After a short while, a small group of people gathered around the punch bowls, within easy reach of another glass. The busboys stayed busy, refilling the bowls as the punch was consumed. By the time the ceremony began, the whole town was feeling the effects of Daniel's delicious and intoxicating punch, even those intending not to drink, who confined their selection to the supposedly non-alcoholic punch.

There was no stage, so Pierre stood on a table, an old wooden table that buckled noticeably under his weight. A plain white tablecloth covered the table to give it some semblance of a stage, and Pierre's voice was amplified, courtesy of a small portable P.A. system. Another large white tablecloth covered the parking lot sign.

Pierre knew he had to be quick by the creaks and groans the table made every time he shifted his weight. He reached for the sheet covering the sign. As he did, the table let out a groan. "Ladies and Gentlemen, without further due, I give you…."

Almost on cue, the table snapped in half with a loud crack. Pierre fell straight down, landing on his feet, but his knees buckled, and he fell backward, still holding on to the sheet that had covered the sign, but which now floated down slowly, covering him.

Having visited the punch bowls more than a few times and feeling no pain, the crowd was drawn to attention by the loud crack. Pierre then disappeared underneath the sheet, and left standing in full view was this magnificent sign proclaiming 'The Villagrosa Municipal Parking Lot.'

The crowd hesitated, stunned. Then, thinking it was all rehearsed, let out a tremendous roar and went crazy cheering and applauding, slapping Giorgio on the back, eventually lifting him high up on their shoulders and parading him around the new parking lot, while singing the national anthem.

When the anthem concluded, a shout rang out, "to the punch bowl." The crowd roared, "to the punch bowl" in agreement and then headed back to the basement for more punch.

Meanwhile, Pierre sat between two broken pieces of the table, holding a microphone that no longer worked and still covered by the sheet. He managed to pull the sheet off, only to see Maria, Michelle, and Rudy standing over him, trying to hold in their laughter without much success.

Rudy spoke, "Nice work, Mayor, you sure know how to work a crowd."

Chapter 21

Winter had set in. The days were short, the weather inclement; not the best time to travel about the rural southwestern French countryside.

Weeks had passed since road improvements had been completed and expressway signs installed, resulting in increased traffic around and about Saint Charles. Some visitors came to Saint Charles intentionally and were delighted to find a parking lot with plenty of space to park. They spent their visits roaming about; some even hiked through the hills and forests surrounding Saint Charles. Others were unintentional: travelers lost while attempting to navigate the labyrinth of local roads and highways on their way to another destination, pleasantly surprised by what they stumbled upon.

It was late Friday afternoon, slowly dissolving into early evening. The bistro was open, but only a handful of local patrons had arrived for their usual Friday night reprieve. Given the weather, Pierre, working as Maître'd, didn't expect many for the evening and thus had worn his old black tuxedo. He did not have the desire, nor did he foresee the need, to impress anybody.

Maria was in the office behind the inn's front desk, finishing up with paying bills, and was thinking of joining Pierre for a drink, then going upstairs to bed. A long, good night's sleep appealed to her, the foul weather making her feel moody and unenergetic.

Michelle stood at the front desk, having just replaced Claire, who was in no hurry to leave for home given the poor weather outside. She was taking her time, just hanging around, chatting with Michelle, hoping for a break in the weather, but thinking she would stay for a while, perhaps have dinner.

She hadn't seen Rudy in some time and thought if business stayed slow, she'd have a chance to visit with him.

Michelle checked the hotel register and saw two parties had arrived. Reservations had been made for three additional rooms. *Well, five rooms should be enough to pay the bills*, she thought, though she was still trying to come up with a break-even number. Her calculations showed it to be approximately 1,250 euros a day, easily covered by the price of five rooms, but her instincts told her it was more. Like her boss had always told her, *when in doubt, go with your instincts.*

The mood was sedate. Then Claire, standing nearest the front door, thought she heard a noise, metal hitting something, an immovable object, a car colliding noise. She went to look and saw that a somewhat older, large black Mercedes sedan had run straight into one of the large, waist-high, stone pillars, marking the edge of the parking lot. The stone pillars were spaced every few meters apart and doubled as guards, preventing cars from driving out onto the grass and rolling down the embankment.

Two women, garishly dressed, one in a short leopard-skin skirt and bright pink blouse, the other in leather pants with some type of flimsy lingerie for a top, were standing in front of the car, examining the damage as rain poured down upon them. The two wore footwear with large, spiked heels, causing them difficulty in maintaining their balance on the rough pavement and soft, muddy grass.

Claire called Maria and Michelle to come have a look. Maria gasped as she saw how the women were dressed, but she felt pity for the two and instructed the bellboy to go and provide some assistance.

The bellboy ran out to the women, where he could be seen gesturing and shaking his head, finally walking the women to the front entrance of the inn, under the protection of his large umbrella. After he walked the women inside, he returned to the car and managed to drive the vehicle, parking it safely by the inn's front door. He removed two large suitcases from the trunk and, with a bit of strength and balance, was able to bring the luggage into the lobby in one trip. He placed the two large bags neatly and conveniently by the front desk.

The two women shook off the remnants of the weather and walked up to the front desk. Their garish dress, amplified by their messy, rain-drenched hair and the streaks of makeup dripping down their faces. One placed her oversized purse on the counter. It made a noise similar to a grocery bag filled with empty bottles.

"Oh, my word," she said to no one in particular, reaching into her purse and pulling out an empty rum bottle.

She handed it to Michelle, "Be a dear, dispose of this, would you please?" she said with a brief plastic smile, continuing to rummage through her purse, producing yet another empty bottle, "This too, please." Finally, she located the pack of cigarettes she was searching for all along.

As she lit her cigarette and inhaled deeply, she spoke, "Well, you can see I am in somewhat of a pickle. I don't know what shape my vehicle is in after our little mishap. Don't you people believe in lights?" she asked with an attitude Michelle didn't care for.

Michelle, not known for her willingness to take a smart attitude, replied, "Most people around here know how to drive."

"Oh, lovely, now I have to deal with a smartass hotel clerk," the woman said, looking away and exhaling her cigarette loudly. Looking back at Michelle, she inquired, rudely, "I don't suppose this little hamlet has a 24/7 auto repair?"

Michelle replied, "We have excellent mechanics in town, and I will see if they can be reached, but I believe they wouldn't come till morning, especially in this weather."

The woman extinguished the remainder of her cigarette. She immediately lit another, "Oh, wonderful. Just wonderful. There go our plans."

She turned to her companion," Don't make any plans for next weekend. We're going to be on the road."

The second woman, dark-haired and demure, stood quietly, a few steps back, and shrugged her shoulders in response.

"I can offer you a ride to the train station if you need to get somewhere, though you'd have to hurry, the last train to Bordeaux is at 8 p.m.," Michelle offered, finding it difficult to carry on a conversation, really hoping to just get rid of the obnoxious woman.

"What would I do in Bordeaux?" the woman said snidely as if Michelle should know. "Besides, I would just have to come back," the woman replied, then added, "Well, give us a room, two rooms please." The woman began rummaging through her handbag, finally producing her wallet.

"You do have running water? Am I correct in my assumption?"

Michelle answered the woman as kindly as she could, though she had grown tired of her attitude, "Yes, madam, hot and cold running water." Her patience was wearing thin; she couldn't help herself, adding, "Indoor plumbing too, you don't need to go outside to use the toilet."

Claire could be heard in the background, trying to muffle her laughter.

The woman looked at Michelle, "You need to apologize for that remark."

Maria quickly came out of the office, replacing Michelle, "My apologies, Madam, it's been a long day. Let me help you."

The garish, arrogant woman immediately changed her attitude, perhaps recognizing it was her attitude that had caused Michelle's discourteous remark.

"Thank you. All we want is a dry place to stay until we can get back on the road. Is the bistro still serving?" the woman inquired.

Standing to the side, Michelle tried to be nice, but trying too hard, answered, "Yes, it will be serving till 9 p.m. Our Chef Daniel is an excellent chef, and I am sure you will enjoy his cooking."

The woman looked at Michelle with a straight face. After a lengthy period of silence, she took a drag off her cigarette and said, "Honey, you need to find a new occupation. You are *not* good at this one."

Maria cut in, wanting to separate the two as quickly as possible, "Rooms 8 and 9 on the third floor. The rooms have been renovated. I am sure you'll find them comfortable."

The woman handed Maria a charge card, asking, "May we add our food to the room, or must we pay separately?" while taking another drag of her third cigarette in as many minutes.

Maria made an imprint of the card before handing it back to the woman, blinking from the cloud of cigarette smoke that surrounded the front desk. Learning her name from the imprint, she answered, "Thank you, Ms. Duggart, yes, you may add your meal to your room. Just show your waiter your key."

Michelle froze immediately, recognizing the woman's name. She slowly turned her head to look at Claire, who also had recognized the name and now, whose jaw dropped, and face had lost its color.

Ms. Louisa Duggart, popular columnist and author of the 'Away For the Weekend' magazine feature, placed her card and wallet back into her large pocketbook, turned around without recognizing the service Maria had just performed on her behalf, and marched over to the elevator, followed by her companion, and now also by Andre, the Bellboy.

Michelle stood by the counter and watched as the two women waited while Andre summoned the old elevator to come to the Lobby. She wondered, no hoped, the women would have an accident in the elevator, killing one of the occupants instantly but leaving the other unscathed.

Maria was relieved; no further clashes had occurred.

Andre sent the women to the third floor, stating he would follow with their luggage. The last words Maria heard from Ms. Duggart while ascending was, "Is this thing safe?"

Once all were on the third floor, Andre unlocked the first room and asked which bag should be taken inside. Ms. Louisa Duggart claimed the room and asked for the large bag to be brought inside. She neglected to tip Andre or even say thank you as he bowed and closed the door behind him.

Andre opened the second room. The woman was friendly as he brought in the remaining suitcase, turned on the lights, and checked for towels and toiletries inside the bathroom. The second woman, the demure one, was very appreciative, thanking him for helping with the car and bringing up the luggage. She smiled and handed Andre a ten-euro note. He bowed as he exited the room, thanking her for her generosity, and informed her that he would be on duty and to please call the desk if she needed further assistance.

After removing what remained of the intricate but ruined makeup each woman was wearing, both changed into simple jeans and blouses. Louisa, always looking to stand out, unbuttoned half the buttons on her blouse and tied the dangling shirttails in a large knot, reminiscent of what Annette Funicello might have worn while flirting with Elvis Presley on a sunny California beach.

Both women tied their hair back, not wanting to bother with it. Louisa wore simple loafers; her companion wore old sneakers. They looked every bit like the girl next door, the type of young woman you would find hanging around a soda fountain, looking through pop-culture magazines, closely examining pictures of their favorite Beatle or Beach Boy.

Together, the women entered the bistro from the inn's lobby. Pierre greeted them and immediately smiled as he took in the sight. Both were attractive, Louisa was provocative. Pierre had to remind himself not to stare, and especially not to stare where Louisa seemed to be inviting everyone to stare.

Since it was a slow night, there were plenty of choices for tables. Pierre put them at a table close to the fireplace. This allowed them to enjoy the warmth of the fire but also a good view of the crackling logs thrown on the fire, and the wrought-iron cages of toasting bread, brought out by the busboys.

The waiters flipped a coin to see who would serve the table, with Paul winning the toss. Further bets were made on whether the attractive blonde, Louisa, was wearing any undergarments and, if she were, what color?

Rudy and Daniel wondered what all the excitement was about and peeked through the large swinging doors. Both agreed it was a sight not often seen in the dining room of the Tree Trunk or on the streets of Saint Charles and worthy of the thrill it caused.

But Daniel was troubled. He looked at the woman and made a pitying sound under his breath. Saying softly, "That woman, the blonde, she is missing something. She is missing an important part of her life; you can see, she does not care. She is saying, I am nothing, nothing but a schoolboy's fantasy. It is a shame and shows she has no respect for herself or those around her. She did not have a happy childhood."

Rudy looked at Daniel, "Looking at this woman sitting in our dining room, you can tell she didn't have a happy childhood." Rudy continued, "I am getting a completely different feeling. What I get is, here is a woman in command; she knows what her assets are and how to put them to good use. I bet she could stop a train with just a smile."

Daniel smiled, picturing himself a player, "Ha, easy money, I'll take that bet."

About this time, Michelle walked through the dining room, heading for the kitchen, wanting to discuss a menu change with Daniel. Just as Michelle was about to go through the double doors, she was distracted by the women, particularly by Louisa, whose attire, or lack thereof, was fully on display. Distracted, she pushed through the doors where Daniel and Rudy, also distracted, were hunched over, peering out.

The effect was identical to two billiard balls hitting each other. The forces of nature caused Michelle to walk into the door and bounce backward, laying her out flat on the dining room floor, while Daniel and Rudy were also propelled back and laid out flat on the kitchen floor.

Daniel's nose was bleeding, and a large red knot began swelling on Michelle's forehead. Maria came running from the inn, saying she heard a loud bang.

Surprised by the noise, Louisa stood up with a cigarette in her hand and walked over to where Michelle was lying on the floor. Looking at Maria, she asked, "Has she been drinking?"

Louisa bent over and asked Michelle if she was okay, and after a slight pause, asked, in all seriousness, "Would you like another drink?"

The two busboys standing on the opposite side of Michelle looked at each other as Louisa bent over, one saying to the other, "You owe me twenty-five euros."

The waiter helped Daniel to his feet and gave him ice wrapped in a napkin for his nose. It quickly stopped the bleeding, but Daniel's nose was swollen and now had a small but pronounced hump halfway up his nose. The hump in his swollen nose gave him a manly look. Not that he didn't look manly before, but now, he had a masculine, gladiator look to him as if he was ready to take on the lions.

Unfortunately, Daniel's sinus passages were partially blocked by the swelling, resulting in his voice being changed: raised in pitch and quite nasally and squeaky. The result was that Daniel, a tall, lanky, dark-featured, handsome Frenchman, looked rugged, a man's man, but sounded a little like Donald Duck on helium.

Daniel staggered through the doors and ran into Louisa and Maria, who were trying to bring Michelle to her feet. Daniel stepped forward, and in a serious high pitched, duck voice, said, "Please, allow me." He picked her up easily, tossed her over his shoulder, and brought her to the Inn's Lobby, placing her gently in a large plush, cushioned chair.

Concerned over her daughter's accident, Maria said loudly from the dining room, "Thank you, Daniel."

A few steps back, Louisa wasn't sure what she heard and asked, "Did I just hear you call him Duck man?"

Maria laughed, "No, Daniel, his name is Daniel."

Still a bit unsteady, Daniel returned to the dining room and marched over to Louisa's table.

Louisa, having returned to her seat, was lighting another cigarette. She remarked to her associate, "I don't know how good the food's going to be; they haven't yet seemed to have figured out how to navigate a door." Then she said sarcastically, "And the guy in the chef's jacket is named Duck Man."

Daniel walked up to her table and blew out her flame. He grabbed her cigarette and very dramatically, crumbled it, letting the pieces fall to the floor.

Daniel spoke in his nasally duck voice, "Welcome, ladies and friends. "

The women looked at Daniel in disbelief, Louisa remarking, "That can't be your normal voice."

Daniel continued as if it were his normal voice, "My name is Daniel. I am the Head Chef. I want to cook for you. I want to give you what you are missing in life."

Louisa was amused, "Oh Darling, or is it Ducky, whatever; you don't need to be so dramatic."

He continued being very serious, "Some people say I am an artist, a plate is my canvas, a knife my brush, and I create gastronomic beauty. Some say I am a philosopher because I seek true flavor, the true flavor of my ingredients; others call me a shaman because I am in harmony with my ingredients and provide, through my cooking, a mystical experience. But tonight, I will be someone else, I will be your Captain, and I will take you aboard my ship, on a culinary voyage, an experience like you never, ever have experienced before. And who knows," Daniel changed his body's position, adding a bit of swagger, "and who knows, you may never experience again."

Louisa started to light another cigarette, but Daniel quickly interrupted her, "Please, do not smoke, you will not have a good voyage, you will not benefit from what I have planned. If you must smoke, I will take some ground beef, fry it in lard, cover it in tasteless, old cheese, and serve it between slices of stale bread, like an American beef sandwich. You will not taste the difference."

Louisa looked at her companion, "I believe our friend here is serious? Maybe we should accept his offer?" Again, her friend said nothing, just shrugged her shoulders, not saying no.

Louisa turned to Daniel, "Ok, Darling, you caught our attention. The spotlight is on you. Give us a culinary experience like we've never had before."

Daniel, the swelling in his nose diminishing and his normal voice returning, replied, "It will be your pleasure."

He bowed to the women and gave instructions to the waiter, "In the cellar, in the far corner by the back door, is a red crate. Inside are seven bottles. Please take one bottle and place it in the wine cooler. "

Daniel turned to the women, "Please excuse me while I prepare the first destination."

Louisa chuckled, "Is this guy too much? I wish I could have a cigarette."

Daniel departed for the kitchen. He grabbed his keys and went to his root cellar. Looking briefly at the four tables, he picked half a dozen large cepes, and a small basket of morels. Examining his truffles, he reached down and pulled a nice golf ball size truffle from the dirt. Holding the truffle up to the single hanging light, he admired the fungi with intensity in his eyes and whispered loudly, "Yes, you'll do, you'll do just fine."

Daniel locked up his cellar and took his selections to the kitchen. He asked Rudy to fetch the Fantasy bread and a single baguette. Rudy replied, "I just turned them, give them another six minutes."

While he was waiting, Daniel took a large beef tenderloin from the cooler and sliced out a 25-centimeter section from the center. He set his oven to 400 degrees Celsius.

Rudy, observing Daniel's actions, commented, "Wow, that's hot."

Daniel looked at Rudy, "We are going to shock the beef. We will apply generous amounts of garlic butter, shallot, rosemary, and thyme, then place the beef in the oven for approximately 10 minutes, basting it every 2 minutes. It will be sweet and crusty on the outside, beefy, and moist on the inside. I will serve it with a classic wild mushroom sauce with cream and cognac, and add truffle butter at the last moment to give it a great fragrance. But you must tell me, what about an accompaniment? I just don't want to offer potato; that is too ordinary." Daniel invited Rudy to offer suggestions.

Rudy replied, "Give me a minute to think about it." He spun around in his wheelchair and headed out to the dining room to fetch the bread.

Rudy came back with two large cages, each with a couple of loaves of bread. "He handed the cages to Daniel, who expertly extracted the loaves and placed them on a cutting board sitting on a stainless-steel cart. Daniel quickly grabbed a clean white tablecloth, wrapping it around the cart. He took a small pot containing clarified butter, shallot, and herbs off the stove.

Daniel called to the waiter, "Is the wine chilled?" Then corrected, "It doesn't matter, bring it to the table with three glasses."

Daniel walked the cart to the table. Paul, the waiter, placed small plates in front of the ladies and stood off to the side. Daniel first cut two slices of Fantasy bread, with the dark center, while Paul poured the wine.

Placing a piece of bread onto each plate, he lightly brushed the butter onto the bread. He then announced, "For a starter, I offer you Fantasy Bread, partnered with a local late harvest wine, similar to a Sauterne. It intensifies yet complements the flavor while creating texture and complexity, completing the fantasy."

Louisa looked at her plain, white plate with a single piece of lightly buttered bread, "This is it, my unique culinary experience? A piece of buttered baguette?"

Daniel interrupted her, "Please, Madam, this is the start of the journey; you must learn to crawl across the road before you get run over."

Louisa's companion, the dark-haired girl, took a bite, then a sip of the wine. She lifted her head straight up and slowly chewed, and, finally, swallowed her food. She looked at Daniel, and with teary eyes, whispered, "It's beautiful. "

Louisa looked at her companion and said sarcastically, "Oh, please." She then took a large bite of her bread, along with a sip, more like a gulp, of her wine.

"Well, it is good; the flavor's unique." She chewed a few more times and giggled, "Oh, my word, that's very good." She chewed again and said to her friend, astonished, "I can taste colors; did you taste it?" Then fully laughing, she continued, "It was like a rainbow. You served me a rainbow!"

Daniel interrupted her, "Please slow down, take your time. I want you to take a bite, close your eyes, and let the flavor envelope you. Let it take you where it will. Try this one now." Daniel cut slices from the bread with the yellowish, tan center and refilled the women's glasses. "Please, allow me," Daniel said as he brushed the herb butter mixture on the slices.

He stood back and sipped his wine, having poured himself a glass as well. Louisa was first taking a smaller bite this time, careful not to drip butter on herself, then slowly took a sip of wine.

She sat back in her chair and let out a moan. Other than an occasional chew, it looked as if her entire body had gone completely limp. She moaned again as she took another bite, combining it with a small sip of wine. "Incredible, this is incredible," was all she could say.

The dark-haired girl took a bite and a sip. She didn't moan, but her face went into contortions, her body also going limp as she reacted to the flavors of the bread and wine, obviously experiencing it as Daniel described.

Daniel spoke, bringing the two women back from their journey. "With this next piece, I bring you back down to earth." He sliced two pieces from a warm baguette and unfurled a cloth revealing the black truffle he had brought from his cellar. He carefully shaved off two slices of truffle, placing them on the two slices of bread, and then brushed them with herb butter.

Using a silver spatula, he placed the bread in front of the women, who almost immediately reached for it. The bread brought about smiles and slight moans of pleasure, but nothing compared to the Fantasy bread. Daniel urged them to save some emotion for the other courses.

Daniel next prepared a house-cured trout filet. Not cured in the traditional sense but almost pickled, having been bathed in apple cider vinegar. He balanced the acidity with a sweet lemon-butter sauce. He served the women Paul Stephenson's lovely Chardonnay. It was an extraordinary combination of tart, sweet, buttery, and smoky flavors.

As the women feasted on Daniel's cooking, Louisa's demeanor started to change. She lost her edginess and propensity to be hostile and became pleasant, funny, even entertaining. She also started to exhibit a distinct fondness for Daniel, asking if he ever traveled to Paris, and if not, would he like to?

After the fish, Daniel presented his Chateaubriand with wild mushrooms, cream and cognac, and a slight dressing of truffle butter. At Rudy's urging, Daniel kept it simple, roasting fresh seasonal vegetables, served sprinkled with lemon and sugar for an accompaniment. Finally, he opened a bottle of Giorgio Villagrossa's Red Bordeaux-style blend. The wine, though young, showed depth with nicely developed tannins, perfectly matching the luxurious flavor of the beef. Daniel was spot on with his preparation. The extra hot oven made the beef crusty on the outside while keeping it silky smooth, tender, and full of flavor on the inside.

The women cleaned their plates and were nothing but smiles as the waiter came to clear the table for coffee, dessert, and, of course, cognac. Louisa, quite happy, jokingly asked the waiter, "When can we do this again?"

For dessert, Daniel served a light sabayon surrounded by seasonal berries and dusted with bittersweet chocolate. It was gone before the waiter left the table, as were the large glasses of Cognac Daniel had the waiter pour for the ladies.

By the end of the meal, Louisa was floating on air, nothing bothered her, and she loved everyone, especially Daniel. She asked the waiter to combine her food bill with her hotel bill. The waiter agreed and asked her for her room key. A short time later, he returned, key in hand. He started to hand the key back when she stopped him. She wrapped her hand around the waiter's hand. Forcing his fingers to hold tightly onto her key, she looked deep into his eyes, and in a very soft, sultry voice, she asked, "Would you please give it to Daniel?"

Chapter 22

The waiter bowed to Louisa as he left her table, bringing her room key to Daniel, but not without first helping the ladies up from their seats. Louisa staggered slightly, briefly losing her balance, more from sitting, eating, and drinking for the last three hours than from anything else.

As the ladies were exiting the bistro, Daniel came hurriedly from the kitchen, "Excuse me, Madam, may I have a word with you?" Louisa turned and smiled at her man, "Of course, Darling, anything you want."

Daniel walked up to her, "I am sorry, but I cannot take this. It is a great compliment you offer me, but the policy must be that I decline. Again, please understand it is policy, house rules. I am the Head Chef, and I must lead by example."

He placed the key back in her hand, lingering, holding onto her hand with his two hands. Her hand was warm. It was small and fit easily into his large hands. Louisa's face took on a pale strawberry hue. She looked up at Daniel and so badly wanted to kiss him, she said, "I have never met such an elegant man." With that, she reached up and gave him a small kiss on the cheek.

The moment was interrupted by Pierre, who was standing close by at the entrance to the dining room and feeling uncomfortable with the scene that was unfolding in front of him. He loudly cleared his throat and announced sternly, choosing his words carefully, "Excuse me, perhaps certain things, certain emotions are better left to private expression, not public, and definitely not in the main entrance to our dining room."

Both Daniel and Louisa smiled, embarrassed by their flirtatious behavior. Daniel looked at Louisa, who just stared back. He leaned over and hugged her; while doing so, he whispered in her ear, "Third floor, first door on the left."

Daniel took a step back and bowed, "Thank you for joining us this evening. I hope it was an experience you won't soon forget. Please join us again. My kitchen is always open for you."

Louisa and her companion smiled, both turned to Pierre, who was a bit jealous over Daniel's sudden popularity, and simply said, "Thank you and good night." The two women walked to the waiting elevator. On the short stroll to the elevator, Louisa could be heard saying to her companion, "I love that man."

"Yes?" Her friend replied, to acknowledge she was still there.

Louisa continued, "Yes, I am in love with the Duck man."

* * *

Daniel returned to the kitchen to finish closing and cleaning up. As Daniel walked through the swinging doors, the entire kitchen staff was waiting for him and greeted him like a conquering hero, giving him a standing ovation and many pats on the back. Paul, the waiter who had won the toss earlier and was an eyewitness to the entire evening, walked up to Daniel and pinned a make-shift medal on his chest.

Then with all the pomp and ceremony he could muster, Paul announced, "On behalf of the men of Saint Charles, and of the civilized world, I award you the coveted Legion of Manhood for your actions on behalf of men everywhere, on this night." He aggressively shook Daniel's hand and kissed him on both cheeks.

Pierre came into the kitchen, appreciating what was happening. He walked up to Daniel and said, "I have admired your talents in the kitchen, and now I must say, I admire your devotion to duty. To turn down an invitation from that woman is an act of self-discipline the likes of which I have never witnessed in my entire life."

Suddenly everything, everybody, stopped. It was strangely quiet, and even the gas jets could be heard as they pushed gas through tiny pinholes to be ignited. Paul, the waiter, looked at Pierre and then at Daniel, a look of puzzlement and confusion on his face. "You refused her invitation? What did you do? Did you give her back her key? No, tell me you didn't! Why?"

Daniel replied defiantly, as if there was no other choice, "Yes, of course.

Otherwise, I would be taking advantage of the woman. It would not be fair, and suppose my actions became known. What would people think, we run a brothel? Buy dinner and get a free upgrade. Get a room free with your choice of partners? No, I do not want that reputation. We must guard our reputation. It is more important than you think."

Paul looked again at Daniel, incredulous, repeated, "You gave her back her key?" You said 'no' to that woman?" Almost on cue, the two busboys and the two waiters dropped to their knees and started waving their arms, bending down touching their foreheads to the ground, as if Daniel were a god.

Daniel smiled, "Ok, ok, ok, stop it. Look, I thought she was a nice woman; I enjoyed cooking for her. But she really needs a man in her life. I think the man that reaches her, that pushes her levers, will be a very happy man. But please now, stop, get off the floor."

The four young men returned to their feet and returned to their duties. Daniel had one last thing to say, "Look, when you tell people, and I am sure you will, tell the truth. Tell people I was polite, and I respectfully declined. Right? Are we in agreement?"

Everybody agreed and went about their end-of-service duties. The busboys could be seen in the distance, discussing the peculiar series of events, still shaking their heads in disbelief. Pierre, still standing there taking it all in, walked up to Daniel, offering his hand. As the two shook hands, Pierre looked coyly at Daniel, "Respectfully declined? My kitchen is always open? First door on the left?"

Daniel looked around, then at his brother, and whispered, "Shh, be quiet! It is what men in our position must do. You of all people should realize that."

Pierre let go of Daniel's hand and turned to leave the kitchen, looking back at his brother, smiling, and saying, "People underestimate you. I have underestimated you."

* * *

The night over, the staff gone, Rudy retired back to his apartment for a hot shower and some sleep. The doors locked, Daniel and Pierre retreated to the bar for a nightcap. Both knew what was on their minds but tried their best to keep off the subject. Daniel poured a couple of cognacs.

"Late rain, I don't know if that is good for the crops," he said, making small talk.

Pierre took a sip, replying casually, "I guess it depends on whether we get a frost. Then I think it's devastating."

"Yes, you are right," Daniel agreed without further comment.

It was quiet, and then Pierre spoke, "She was gorgeous."

Daniel gulped his cognac and poured another. "Yes, she was." Then correcting, "Rather, she is."

Rather than telling Daniel what to do, giving him advice, Pierre said, "Well, I am tired and going to bed. Don't stay up too late; if the weather clears, tomorrow could be busy."

Daniel replied, "I'm going to bed too. Been a long day. Good night."

"Good night." Pierre said.

Daniel turned off the lights and made his way through the family kitchen and up the back stairs. He made his way to the third floor, and as always, the first door on the left was his. He turned on the light to find his room, just as he had left it. He looked around at the empty space and thought, *Wouldn't it be nice to have more than just a room and a bath? I'd like to have a fireplace where I could put my feet up, and my woman could bring me something warm to drink, maybe a coffee with cognac and cream? She could talk softly to me and rub my shoulders.* He chuckled at his thought. Wouldn't *it be nice to have a woman?*

Daniel slipped out of his clothes and placed them in his dirty laundry, turned on the shower, and stepped into the hot, steaming cascade of water. It was soothing, relaxing. After a short while, fully bathed, he dried off and hopped into bed. He turned off the light and lay there in the darkness, enjoying the warm comfort of his bed.

He could see out his window where the full moon hung there in the dark night amidst stars just as bright, while the clouds from the storm slowly drifted away. He lay there, the moon illuminating his room, just thinking, thinking about nothing, when there came a soft knock on his door. It was so soft, he thought he was hearing things, but it came again, just a bit louder.

Moments before, Louisa had navigated through the door separating the family quarters from rooms for rent. Reaching the first door on the left, she knocked softly once and then again, this time hearing movement and the sound of feet coming towards the door. She held her breath. The door opened. Standing in the dim light was Michelle.

Louisa let out a short, "Ooops."

Michelle, amused by Louisa's embarrassment and knowing full well what was going on, simply pointed. Without saying a word, she merely pointed at Daniel's door.

Louisa smiled and whispered, "Thank you, you're a doll." She tiptoed over to Daniel's door and looked back to see Michelle closing her door.

She knocked once softly, then again, a little harder. Daniel finally opened the door.

Michelle quietly closed her door but couldn't help herself. She peeked out a small crack she left ajar. As Daniel answered his door, the moonlight bathed Louisa and Daniel in its glow, making their bodies silhouettes. They embraced, passionately kissing. Michelle watched as Louisa's robe fell to the floor. Michelle could see their kissing becoming even more passionate as Daniel's robe dropped.

As their passion continued, Michelle was mesmerized and couldn't stop watching until finally, Daniel, using his foot, closed his door.

Michelle took a step away from the door and suddenly realized she was out of breath. She immediately ran to her bathroom and turned on the shower, neglecting to turn on the hot water, on purpose.

As Michelle stood underneath the icy cold water, she thought of everything and anything. She wanted to remove the scene she had just witnessed from her memory. It was wrong to have intruded on Daniel's privacy, but it was so romantic. It was by far the most romantic thing she had ever seen. As she was beginning to get numb from the cold, she turned off the water and stepped out of the tub. She dried herself and walked toward her bed, thinking, I *hope next time it'll be my turn.*

* * *

The next morning everything seemed business as usual. Guests were checking out of the inn, maids were busy preparing the rooms for the next guests, and the busboys were busy preparing the dining room for brunch service. At the bistro's entrance, a small station was set-up providing coffee, croissants, and other pastries to guests who were not planning on staying for brunch or who just wanted a quick bite before beginning their day.

Michelle was at the front desk as Louisa and her companion came down the elevator. Louisa was beaming, nothing short of a ray of sunshine. "Good morning, Darling. Is this not a wonderful day?" She sang, beaming, as she approached the front desk.

Michelle smiled and replied, "It is. It's a wonderful day. How may I help you?"

Louisa went on, "Well, unfortunately, I have to leave to get back to Paris. I hope my vehicle makes it. Maybe if I'm lucky, I'll get stuck and never have to go back. Paris sometimes just seems so dreary, so boring. All those people, all with the same hopes, telling each other the same lies. And the worst of it is, everyone knows it's a lie. Ridiculous. "

Michelle inquired, staying away from anything controversial, "Did you enjoy your stay?"

"Ohh, last night was so refreshing. You don't know how refreshing." She said with a wink, as she lit another cigarette.

Michelle still wasn't comfortable with Louisa and felt the need to be careful. "Daniel was up early this morning."

Louisa cut in, "Yes, I know."

Michelle gave her a look and then continued, "He worked on your car; he said the damage is only cosmetic. He said those big Mercedes are built like army tanks."

Louisa added, "Thank Daniel for me. He is truly a magnificent man. I am forever in his debt. Are you two related?"

Michelle replied, "Daniel is my uncle, on my father's side."

"I see. I don't mean to pry, but who or where is your father, your mother?" Louisa asked, genuinely interested.

"I don't mind your questions. I am very proud of my family. Daniel and Pierre are both my uncles."

Louisa clarified, "Pierre, the Maître d?"

"Yes, Maria is my mother; you met her yesterday. My father passed away years ago when I was only ten."

Louisa was saddened, "Really, how'd that happen?"

"He was killed by terrorists in North Africa while protecting French dignitaries. There was a ceremony, and the terrorists tried to blow everybody up. My father stopped them but lost his life doing so. He was a beautiful man through and through, but first and foremost, he was a patriot and believed in France. God rest his soul."

Louisa, seeing how Michelle was affected by her story, tried her best to comfort her. "Yes, I believe he was a beautiful man. He certainly has a beautiful family, especially his daughter."

Michelle was overwhelmed by Louisa's sincerity. Close to tears, she spoke quietly, "Thank you, that's very kind of you to say."

Louisa signed her receipt and asked if the bellboy would carry out the luggage. She turned to leave but first stopped, looked about, taking in the lobby one last time.

Looking straight into Michelle's eyes, she said, "It's a beautiful place, this place. It is filled with truly beautiful people. Treasure it and protect it. I have been everywhere, I have seen it all, and this place, there is nothing like it. I hope I will see you again."

Louisa was about to exit the lobby when she had one last thought. "I never did get your name?"

Michelle walked from behind the counter. She stood proudly, straight and tall, in front of the desk, "My name is Michelle Villeneuve, and this is the Inn at Saint Charles en Liberte."

A spark of recognition could be seen in Louisa's eyes, but it quickly faded as she shrugged it off. She smiled one last smile and humbly answered, "Thank you, Michelle. Thank you for your hospitality."

* * *

Later that day, when the first wave of diners had subsided and the tempo of business had decreased dramatically, Maria asked if she could speak privately with Daniel.

He met her in the inn's office. Daniel walked in, closed the door, and sat down.

She started, "Daniel, we are adults, and being in the hospitality industry, I know it brings certain opportunities." Maria wasn't comfortable with the topic, so she was trying to be as savvy as possible. We must maintain a reputation that is beyond question. People must not think any member of the staff would ever take advantage of an impaired guest."

Daniel sat quietly and just nodded, when he thought it appropriate.

She continued, "I heard Ms. Duggart enjoyed your cooking and tried to show her appreciation by offering you the key to her room. I heard further that you declined, but you declined as a gentleman should decline."

Daniel again nodded but also shrugged his shoulders as if to say, "Yes, but of course."

"I just want to say, I believe you handled it correctly, and I am very proud of you. I am very happy that you did the right thing. Thank you, Daniel. Thank you for handling this the way you did."

Daniel stood up to leave. With a very serious look on his face, he replied, "I must get back. But I want you to know, you can always have faith in me.

I will always endeavor to do the right thing, even if I do it wrongly and if I ever do the wrong thing, rest assured, it will be done right.

Daniel nodded and marched proudly from the office, leaving Maria behind with a somewhat puzzled look on her face.

Chapter 23

D aniel moped around the kitchen, looking very disturbed, as if he was carrying a heavy burden on his conscience. Rumors were that he was lovesick, disappointed in himself for not making an effort to spend time alone with Louisa, to talk, to see if there was something more than just emotions, caught in the moment.

It affected his work. He seemed distracted. He created flavorless entrees, completely missing required herbs and spices. Rudy was having difficulty trying to patch and cover up Daniel's mistakes, finally throwing his hands up in frustration.

"Look, what has gotten into you? I have never seen you so sloppy and devoid of care," he admonished one morning while the two of them were setting up for lunch service.

Daniel looked at Rudy with no emotion at all, just shrugging his shoulders as if to say, "Who cares? Nothing matters."

Rudy would not go away. "Oh no, don't give me that. As long as I can remember, you have been my role model, my hero. Your passion, your intensity, and your connection with your cooking are what I strive for. You can't just shrug your shoulders and walk away. What is eating you? If it's a woman, then call her, take some time off and go see her. If she doesn't want you, then forget about her. It's clear you are suffering. Don't do this to yourself."

Daniel looked at Rudy and sat down on a small stool by Rudy's prep station. "You are right. I am suffering. I am suffering because I have done a terrible thing."

Rudy countered, "You? I don't believe it."

Daniel looked at Rudy with sad eyes. "I have. I have made a terrible mistake. Let me tell you. It will be a burden off my back."

Rudy sat in his wheelchair, moving things around on his table, doing something with his hands so he wouldn't interrupt Daniel as he spoke.

Daniel looked at Rudy, "I lied."

"What?", Rudy asked.

"I lied," Daniel repeated.

Rudy chuckled a bit, "Daniel, I don't know if that is something...."

Daniel cut in, "No, you don't know all the facts. I lied to my family. I intentionally lied. If I can't trust you, Michelle, Maria, Pierre, my family to be truthful with me, what do we have? We have chaos, Armageddon. The world as we know it ends. It's over. You should understand that by now. Family is the most precious thing. We must protect it from outsiders who have bad intentions; we must ensure that our family is strong, intact, and invincible. We must never cheat each other, steal, or lie, especially lie; I don't care what the circumstances."

Rudy exhaled loudly, "Wow, I guess you feel pretty strongly about family."

Daniel looked at him and jumped to his feet, "Don't joke with me. I am breaking in two, do not joke with me."

Rudy, very apologetic, replied, "I'm sorry, Daniel. I didn't mean it. I think you're absolutely correct. It's family that is important. Perhaps if you tell me the circumstances, I can help you fix the situation or at least offer you some advice."

"Thank you. That's what I need. I am very confused, depressed. I was beginning to think slitting my throat was the answer." Daniel sat back down, a look of grave emotional pain on his face.

"So, what happened?" Rudy said with great solace.

Daniel began, "After the visit by Louisa, Maria took me into her office and said she was proud of me, said I did the right thing."

Rudy knew what Daniel was referring to, but let him talk, allowing him to get it off his chest.

"She said, and I agree, that our reputation must be without question. We must never be accused or suspected of taking advantage of a patron, especially a woman, whose judgment might be impaired by over-indulgence. I do not argue with this. I agree, without question. We must have our reputation."

"You refused Louisa's offer like a gentleman, right? You didn't lie," Rudy replied, following along.

"But I did not tell the truth. Maria said I handled it well. She thanked me. She said she was proud of me," Daniel said, almost in tears.

Rudy was confused, "I don't get it. You declined. What is wrong? Where is the lie?"

"I accepted her compliments. What I did not tell her, what I did not admit, is that later that evening, Louisa came to my room."

Rudy smiled, "No. Tell me that didn't happen? Louisa knocked on your door? You and that incredible blond, holy smokes!"

"Yes, she knocked on my door twice. The first time, I did not hear her. She had to knock again," Daniel confessed.

Rudy looked at Daniel, giving him a quizzical look, letting his last remark pass. Rudy was quiet, getting his thoughts together, then spoke. "Well, you have quite a moral dilemma. I understand why you feel like you have a weight on your shoulders. I believe you have two options. The first option is to be quiet. Keep this to yourself, and eventually, it will pass. The second option is to tell Maria."

As Rudy spoke, he thought about what Daniel said earlier about family; he stopped, correcting his last statement. "I'm sorry, Daniel, I take back what I said. We are family, and we must be honest and treat each other with respect. Being so, there is only one thing you can do. You must admit your mistake because otherwise, you're a hypocrite. I don't know the outcome, but at least you will have admitted it, so your conscience will be clear, and your burden will be lifted. That's my advice."

Daniel looked surprised, "A hypocrite, let's not bring religion into this. I have come to the same conclusion, but I am afraid of what I will see in her eyes. She will be disappointed in me. She will no longer have faith in me. I am very sorry for my actions. But in my defense, I was discreet; we both knew what we were doing. I am a man. I live in one room. I am accomplished, yet I live in one room. How am I supposed to live? How am I to be a man? Tell everyone tonight you must close your eyes. Pretend things like this don't happen? That is not the way. We need to discuss this, all of us."

Rudy simply nodded. He knew he was lucky. Maria had an apartment constructed especially for him on the ground floor of the mill when it was purchased. He had a kitchenette, a large bath, a living area with a large, overstuffed couch, a small study alcove currently used for exercise, and a good-sized bedroom. The entrance to his apartment had a small veranda, beyond which was the rear ally of the inn and the back door of the family kitchen. She had made sure it was all wheelchair accessible.

Rudy knew he was lucky. If he ever wanted company, his company could come and go unnoticed, avoiding any controversy.

"Poor Daniel," Rudy thought. "He has a large room, comfortable, but he's right. To desire the company of another is only natural; it's human. How does a grown man live in a single room and across the hall from his niece?"

The following day Daniel greeted Maria with a bright, sunny, enthusiastic greeting, like a little puppy about to be taken to the park. They were alone, sitting at the large table in the family kitchen. Maria was glad to see he was out of his gloomy mood.

"Maria, I have something I must tell you. I have a problem, and I hope we can discuss like two adults," Daniel said between sips of coffee.

"Of course, Daniel," Maria replied. "Should I summon the rest? Is this something we all need to be part of?"

Daniel quickly answered back, "No. This is between you and me. Later, perhaps, we involve everyone else."

"Ok." Maria had no problem with that.

"What I must tell you is, that, I was not honest with you," Daniel admitted solemnly.

Maria looked at Daniel, giving him time to talk, waiting patiently for him to finish, finally giving him a little nudge, "Yes, Daniel, go on."

"Last Friday night, very late, Louisa came to my room; we had a liaison. I am sorry. But I think it is important to tell you this. When we talked in your office, you said you were proud of me. I felt so ashamed." Daniel spoke again, quietly, and sincerely.

"Daniel, I know." She reached out and took his hand. "When I said you handled it correctly, I was referring to what you presented publicly and what you did privately. Yes, I wanted you to tell me, but I respect your privacy, and whom you have a relationship with is not my business. I am proud of you for protecting the family, protecting our business. It shows you are thoughtful and you care. The fact that you came to me, the fact that you were troubled and needed to talk, shows me something. It shows me that you are good; deep down, you are a good man. I am very proud to call you my brother."

Daniel sat looking at Maria, his eyes watery, before softly replying,

"Thank you, God bless you." He took her hand in his two hands, closed his eyes, and held her hand up to his lips, finally letting it go.

"But how did you know? Did someone tell you? But who knew? We were very discreet," Daniel whispered, astonished by Maria's revelation.

Maria replied gently, looking at Daniel; he could see the wisdom in her eyes, "A woman knows, Daniel, a woman knows." She continued looking at Daniel, then said softly, "I never noticed how beautiful a man you are, and so very elegant. You are a Villeneuve, through and through."

Daniel smiled, got up from his seat, and went to the stove. "Thank you. Let me make more coffee, would you like a croissant?"

Maria replied, "Yes, that would be lovely, Daniel."

Daniel went to the bistro for croissants. When he came back, it was Maria's turn to lead their discussion. "You know, with the signs on the expressway and road improvements, business is picking up. The inn is booked solid on weekends for the next two months, and very few nights are available during the week. If we had more rooms, we could easily rent them, and that would certainly help our profits."

Daniel asked, "So what is your solution? What do you suggest?"

"There is plenty of room in the mill. The whole top floor is unused, and most of the small employee apartments are vacant. I suggest we utilize the space much more efficiently."

"Ok, how do we do that?" Daniel wanted to know.

Maria was getting to the hard part, the part where she needed to pick her words very carefully. "I think the logical thing to do is to move you and Michelle to the mill, making all of the rooms on the third floor available for rent. If fully booked, each of those rooms could easily generate 5,000 euros a month."

"Maria," Daniel replied patiently, "I live in one room, it is difficult, but I manage. Now you want to move me to a smaller room? What have I done to deserve this?"

Maria had already thought through much of her plan. "Daniel, I know you need space; you need your freedom to come and go as you please. When we purchased the mill, it was very sudden, if you recall. We didn't have a plan; we really didn't know what to do with it. Remember, we were going to use some of that space for catering? Well, now I think it is apparent what we must do."

"I don't see it; what must we do?" Daniel inquired.

"What we must do is make family apartments. Leave the inn for guests and use the mill for family accommodations. There is plenty of space; the whole top floor is unused; it could be turned into wonderful rooms with large windows opening up to plenty of sunlight. We don't use the employee apartments. They can be combined for family use, and the ground floor we keep for storage."

Daniel was thinking hard, "And you? You're not going to leave your room, are you?"

Maria smiled, "Yes, there is enough space for me as well."

"Wow, this is a big deal. This is a change. But I suppose it makes sense. You need to talk it over with everybody. Everybody is affected, you know."

During the following week, Michelle was again working the front desk when she received a call from none other than, you know who. "Hello, Michelle? Louisa here. How are you, Darling?"

"Hello, Louisa," Michelle said reluctantly, remembering how quickly Louisa can sting.

Louisa, sensing Michelle's hesitation, quickly added, "Relax, Darling, I'm on your side. You can put down your guard."

Michelle appreciated Louisa's candor and allowed herself to relax, taking off her gloves.

"I'm sorry, Louisa, it takes me a little time to relax and get to know people. I hope I didn't offend you."

"That's so much better. No, not at all, darling. I'm calling to let you know, I just received permission from my Editor to bump my little soiree in Nice, allowing me to feature the inn in next month's issue," Louisa said cheerfully.

Michelle perked up, "That's wonderful, Louisa. Thank you."

"I've already selected a headline; would you like to hear it?" Louisa asked, brimming with enthusiasm.

"Yes, of course."

"'I'm in Love, Love, Love with the Tree Trunk.' Catchy, don't you think?" Louisa asked, looking for compliments and adding, "My editor loved it."

Michelle repeated what she just heard, "'I'm in Love, Love, Love with the Tree Trunk'?" A little perplexed, Michelle asked, "Wouldn't something like 'A Pleasant Evening in Saint Charles' be more appropriate? "

"Only if you want to attract people over 70 who will bring along their own oxygen tanks. You know, those people who are clinically dead but just won't lie down. I think there might be two or three of them left around that still read my column."

Michelle was stunned, "Clinically dead? Oxygen? Who, what are…?"

Louisa cut her off, "Look, I know my readers, and nothing gets their attention like love. We are all searching for it. Aren't we?"

Michelle decided not to fight Louisa's idea because it would be useless, knowing her as she did. "I suppose so."

"That's it for now. Let's talk again. Ciao." Louisa hung up.

* * *

Maria called a family meeting for late Tuesday afternoon, giving plenty of advance notice to allow time for everyone to arrange their schedules.

As everyone sat around the table in the family kitchen, Maria began, "Business has started to pick up, and I want to talk to everyone about two issues. The first is a simple issue. I have been persuaded to get the Internet and have a…" Maria looked at Michelle, "What is it called?"

Michelle quickly answered, "A website, you can refer to it generically as a 'web presence.'" Michelle continued, "We'll all have email too."

Maria added, "Yes, email too. I know everyone has been asking about email. I think it will also make reservations that much more efficient."

She continued, "The second item is accommodations. We are starting to attract attention; traffic, reservations, and visitors are increasing. Thank you, Pierre, for that. Because reservations are increasing, we need to utilize our facilities more efficiently. We have never fully utilized the mill since purchasing it. Frankly, I didn't know what to do with it. What I would like to suggest to everyone now, is that we go back to the beginning; we start again, this time with a goal in mind."

Rudy asked, "And what's that? The goal, I mean?"

"We keep the three retail spaces, and we create five family apartments. Well, we need perhaps two employee rooms, maybe three, but our real goal is five separate spaces similar to what Rudy has now. They would have kitchenettes, living spaces, large baths, studies, bedrooms, separate entrances, maybe even a private rooftop deck for parties or socializing. Maybe that's where we try our luck at catering? But I think we have outgrown our current living arrangement. Let's be adults. Let's allow ourselves the comfort and privacy we, as adults, all need."

"If we have more than two floors, we'll need an elevator, and what about this place?" Rudy gestured over his shoulder, referring to the family kitchen.

"We'll keep it, of course, but it will become less important as time goes on. Maybe we'll continue using it to meet for coffee or an occasional family meal. Perhaps we can turn it into a lounge by removing the stove, the table, and adding some comfortable chairs," Maria spoke, thinking out loud, looking for ideas.

"If we remove the stove and table, then it goes with me. That's a wonderful stove. It belonged to my grandmother and her mother before that. It's wonderful, and we need to keep it," Daniel said loudly.

Pierre spoke up, "It would make a nice library or study. Have coffee, tea, cold drinks available, hiking maps of the area, some books, magazines; just a nice quiet place to unwind before dinner or going out."

Rudy asked one last question, "Five apartments, so that means you will also move to the mill?"

Maria answered humbly, "Of course. I want to be with my family."

Chapter 24

A week later, Maria took a couple of days to travel to Bordeaux to meet with Architects and Construction Managers. She was able to employ the services of the same firm that worked with her on the original renovations. The firm that designed and created the retail spaces, Rudy's apartment, and the small employee lodgings.

The construction manager was the reputable engineering, design, and construction firm of Mornay & Sons. The firm was founded in the 1800s and had successfully built buildings, roads, and bridges throughout southern France, with many still standing and still in use.

Mornay & Sons kept complete records and histories of every job they undertook, so they were familiar with the inn and the mill. Maria was amazed that even at the very first meeting, though it had been years, the architects knew more about her building and past renovations than she remembered.

They cited load-bearing issues, weight limitations caused by the old bricks used to construct the mill, and how structural reinforcement would safely allow for multiple floors of living space, but at a significant cost. They discussed plumbing and water pressure and the need to replace the old iron pipes with new copper and composite materials to allow acceptable water pressure levels for the upper floors. They even had recommendations on how to transform the large flat roof into an outdoor garden and recreation area, complete with an outdoor kitchen.

Lastly, the firm had just completed the renovation of two old warehouses into modern loft-style living accommodations. The project sponsor wanted modern amenities to attract younger, affluent clients, so the firm replaced the old commercial lifts with modern high-tech ones. The construction firm had the old ones stored, thinking they were in excellent mechanical condition and would be useful for some application. The firm made them available to Maria at the cost of installation.

Maria showed the architects the plans for the veranda. They cautioned her on the design, remarking that anchoring the veranda to the outside wall of the Inn would exert pressure, pulling the wall out, with the possibility of the wall eventually collapsing. The architects warned that building inspectors would never grant occupancy permits to a commercial structure built in this manner.

The firm was also concerned about cutting doorways in the exterior wall for the veranda. Older buildings depend on their exterior walls for much of their load-bearing ability. On an old building like the inn, cutting holes in the wall jeopardizes its stability. Special precautions should first be made to ensure the integrity of the building. The firm agreed to dispatch a team of engineers and architects to examine the Inn and devise a viable plan.

The work Maria requested was extensive. The firm assured her they would do the job correctly and quickly.

As the discussion turned to cost, Maria knew she was in trouble when the president of the firm entered the meeting, asking if she would join him for lunch.

Over lunch, the president listened intently to Maria as she described the motivations behind the project and what she hoped to achieve. An architect at the table took notes as she spoke and made many suggestions that she found helpful.

She discussed moving to the mill herself, leaving the sizeable fourth-floor bedroom for guests. The architect cited security, asking what would stop anybody from taking the lift to the fourth floor and entering the space. She agreed with his concerns and asked for some type of security measure to be devised, as well as extending the rear stairs to the fourth floor.

While finishing the meal, the president discussed timing and cost, "I understand the hospitality business, and the need to be open. An empty room is a cost, overhead, so you must keep your rooms occupied. We can do the work quickly, but construction work is dirty, dusty, and noisy. Your guests, looking for a peaceful weekend in the country, for certain, would not take kindly to your renovations and my work crews," he said.

Keeping the same serious tone, the president continued, "Being so, if you want to move forward with this work, my suggestion is to close down, let us work, and then re-open; have a grand re-opening. That would be the most cost-effective way to proceed. I would double the number of people on the job and work 24/7. In terms of time, if we were able to work 24/7…"

He looked at his architect, who answered without hesitation, "Six weeks."

Maria was pleased. The President then added, "Two crews working day and night come with additional costs. I don't need to remind you that time is money."

Maria inquired, "What are your estimates for costs, including the Mill, the Veranda, and alterations to the fourth floor?"

The President took a sip of coffee and replied, "Please don't hold me to this figure. I need to get details to the accountants for accurate estimates, but I would say we are looking at approximately 5.5 million euros. That includes design, engineering, and construction, and a guarantee of approval and granting of occupancy license. I will put our best manager on the job. He's young, but he is very good; I trained him myself. My son, Thomas."

The architect nodded in agreement, "For work of this nature, Thomas is undoubtedly the best we have. He is meticulous, misses nothing."

The president added, "He just finished a job. He led the renovations of the two industrial buildings. If you recall, we mentioned the two lifts that are sitting in the warehouse? Well, he led that project. Finished a week ahead of schedule and on budget. The client is very happy."

Maria liked what she was hearing, had confidence in the president, and gave tentative approval, agreeing to the 5.5-million-euro price tag if the work was completed in six weeks. "I agree, to have two crews working around the clock comes with a cost, but what assurances do I have that the work will be done in six weeks? Suppose there is a national strike or some other dilemma. Do I pay that extra cost? I should have guarantees. If I pay, then you will perform."

The firm president looked at Maria, "That is very astute of you to suggest performance guarantees. Yes, many construction contracts with important time elements have such clauses. I will need to discuss with my people whether we are willing to commit to a deadline. The problem with working with historical renovations is the unexpected. With these types of jobs, there is a high probability of the unexpected. We know the mill, we have worked on it, so that increases our confidence, but the inn, we know very little about the inn, except it was built a very long time ago."

Maria accepted the president's answer, "When will you be able to start?"

"I'd like to give Thomas a few days to get reacquainted with his family. His wife just gave birth to their first child, a son. He'll want to get back to work soon, though; he doesn't do well sitting idle." The President spoke with a wink and continued, "I can have the plans sent to his home. I'll get his opinion on anything we might want to consider or might have missed."

Maria was very pleased with the discussion. The president asked for the firm to be given a day to write contracts, requesting Maria to come the next day to sign. He also asked if she was able to provide a down payment.

She replied, "Would one million euros be sufficient?"

Maria stayed the night at a small but comfortable corporate apartment supplied by the firm. The next day, contracts were signed, and Maria signed a bank draft for one million euros. Construction work was to start in approximately ten days. A team of engineers and architects were dispatched to inspect the site, take pictures, and conduct tests. Plans would be drawn up and sent to Maria within three days.

Maria was thrilled. She felt like she was breaking out of a rut and facing a bright, new future. But as she rode the train on the way home, a question kept nagging her, "*Yes, we'll close for the six weeks, but what do I do with my people, my family? Where do I put them?*"

She knew the town kept a few small apartments on the top floor of the municipal building for emergencies or visiting officials. She hoped Pierre would allow her to stay in one, himself in the other. She wanted to remain close by to monitor the work and knew of no other option.

"*But what about Daniel, Rudy, and Michelle? What to do? I want them out of the way but where do I put them? I'll ask them to pack their personal belongings and place them in storage. But what do I do then?*" She pondered. She remembered a trip her late husband Roger, and she always talked about taking but were always too busy to find the time, "*Perfect.*" She thought and peacefully enjoyed the rest of the train ride out to the country.

The next day, Maria called a family meeting. She explained to everyone the contract she had signed. "It was a very expensive proposition, but I believe we will get our money's worth. Mornay & Sons is an excellent, responsible firm."

Pierre spoke, "I called my friend at the Transportation Ministry; he said there is no one better in the business. He even said the Ministry uses them on very sensitive, high profile projects, knowing they'll get it done and won't screw it up."

Maria was glad to hear that. "Good, I was very pleased by my recent experience. I am glad others agree. You should start to see their men around. They are sending engineers and architects to inspect the buildings; I guess they are looking to see what they must work with. I don't have the plans yet but should have them in a day or two. As soon as I get them, I'll let everyone know."

Rudy asked, "How long is this going to take, and are we going to try and stay open?"

"They're estimating six weeks."

"Whoa, that's a lot to accomplish in six weeks," Rudy added.

"Yes, they are willing to commit to a six-week schedule only if they can have crews working around the clock, 24 hours a day."

Rudy smiled, "Well, that answers my second question."

Daniel spoke up, "What do you mean? That answers your second question?"

"What he means is that, how can you host guests with construction crews and their equipment going all the time?" Pierre answered.

Daniel looked at Rudy and Pierre, "You can't." He then looked at Maria, "Men will be working all the time, even nighttime, two, three a.m.?"

Maria replied, "Yes, Daniel."

"We can't do that. We have guests. How am I to cook or sleep? I can't agree with this. It's impossible unless we close down," Daniel concluded.

Maria added, "Good idea. We will close for six weeks; actually, I would like to close for seven weeks. Six weeks for the work to be completed, add another week for us to move in and get familiar with our new surroundings."

Michelle asked rather tentatively as if something important was being missed, "Mother, what are we supposed to do in the meantime, I mean, for six weeks?"

Rudy laughed, "Michelle, it's vacation time. Time to visit those places you always wanted to visit but never had the money or the time. I suppose you have the money, and well, you certainly now have the time."

Maria brought up her idea, "I have an opportunity for you. I think it will benefit you personally and professionally. It is good for professionals in this business to get out and see what others are doing. I suggest it is even a must. Even if you are cooking traditionally, it is good to see what people are consuming. With that in mind, I think the three of you should rent a car and tour the States. I think we should get you airplane tickets to Vancouver, Canada. Then you spend the next six weeks driving down the west coast of the United States, I guess, then departing for home in six weeks from Arizona." She turned to Pierre, "What is the name of that large city in Arizona?"

Pierre answered back, "You mean Phoenix?"

"Yes, Phoenix," she confirmed. "Since this is business-related, I will pay your expenses. But this is a serious trip. Do not take this lightly. You are collecting data. Information that we will use to our advantage, ultimately making us better competitors." She lectured, but only half-seriously.

Michelle was stunned, "The three of us? Mother, that's wonderful. I never made it out to the West Coast of the states but always wanted to go."

Rudy was beaming, "Thank you, Maria, it sounds great. Sign me up. If it's not asking too much, can we take a little sojourn out to the islands? Island cuisine is interesting: Asian, Polynesian, French, Spanish influences. Great cuisine."

Michelle was ecstatic, "Please, Mother, just a few days on Maui?"

"What or where is Maui?" Maria inquired.

"Hawaii. Yes, I too would like to go to Hawaii. I have heard great things about Hawaii," Daniel spoke up, adding to the discussion.

Maria looked at Michelle, "Well, you are in charge of planning. Plan the trip and give me a number. I am sure we can work it into the budget." Maria said, happy to see everyone on board and so enthused.

"What about Claire? Shouldn't she come too? I feel sorry for her, left alone." Michelle pouted.

Maria turned to Pierre, looking at him with a question on her face, "Well?"

Pierre smiled, "I think I can make do without her for six weeks. I always wanted to learn how to file."

Maria turned to Michelle, "Ask Claire if she would like to go. We would love to have her as our guest."

Rudy mumbled quietly, "*Yessss!*"

* * *

Michelle was excited packing for her trip, making decisions on what to bring, when she suddenly remembered Louisa. Louisa had bumped an article on her journey to Nice to feature the Tree Trunk. *I've got to call her and let her know we'll be closing for six weeks.*

She then thought about Louisa's title. *I'm in Love, Love, Love with the Tree Trunk. Good lord, how did she ever come up with that title?* She said to herself as she folded another blouse to place in her suitcase.

Michelle sat down to take a break. She thought about Louisa's style of writing and how riddled her articles were with sassy, double-meanings, and risqué metaphors. She repeated Louisa's title *I'm in Love, Love, Love, with the Tree Trunk".* "*She's in love with the bistro, could there be a double meaning I'm just not catching? There's got to be.*

Then it dawned on her, *Daniel. She's not in love with the bistro; she's in love with Daniel. No, she's not in love with Daniel; she's in love with his tree trunk. Daniel's the tree trunk. On no! She is writing about her sexual experience with Daniel! That's why she's in love. Oh no, no, no, no. What have we done?*

Michelle quickly ran downstairs, finding Daniel alone in the cellar with his Mushroom farm. "Daniel, I need to talk to you. I need to talk to you privately and on a very personal basis. I don't want you to share this with anybody."

Daniel, in the middle of pushing some dirt around, stopped for a minute and shrugged, "Ok, we are alone. You have my word. I will not repeat anything we discuss."

Michelle fidgeted, very nervous, not certain how to begin, "Daniel, you know how women have certain physical features that men are always talking about or wanting to see, and it seems the larger, well, the more attention the woman gets?"

"Yes, for instance, a woman's bosom. Men, including myself, are attracted to a woman's breasts. That is not news; it's as old as time," he said casually, waiting for her to get to the point.

"Well, a woman also sometimes wonders about certain physical characteristics of men. Some women are very sexually active, and they talk about a man's, huh, talent." She continued but found it more and more difficult to select the right words.

"Yes, I have heard of such a thing," Daniel added, preoccupied with his mushrooms, not paying attention.

"Well, Louisa is doing an article on the Bistro, and I am just wondering…." Michelle was getting frustrated trying to figure out how to say what she wanted to say and ask what she wanted to know. "Well, what I am trying to say…." Finally losing her patience, she just blurted out her question, "Louisa's article is titled 'I'm in Love, Love, Love with the Tree Trunk,' are you the Tree Trunk? I mean not you, but part of you?"

Daniel chuckled, "That Louisa, she is full of mischief. Yes, when we were together, she made many comments, many comparisons. She jokingly called me the Tree Trunk, and at one point, she wondered if the bistro was named after me. "

He stood up in front of her, "I don't want to say more. Some things are better left unsaid. But I will say this, knowing Louisa as I do, her saying she's in Love, Love, Love with the Tree Trunk; she is not talking about the bistro."

Michelle looked at Daniel. Daniel was now back tending his mushrooms. *He handled that very well*, she thought, and then answered, "Thank you, Daniel, I know it's not the easiest topic to discuss. But be forewarned, the article is scheduled to come out next month. You could become a national hero to women."

Daniel shrugged, "If I were a young man, I would brag to my friends. Now, I do not want that type of notoriety, and I do not want that type of woman."

"I can understand, and I admire you for that. I'm going to finish packing. See you later." Michelle was satisfied with the outcome of her sleuthing but still did not know what to do about Louisa. She bounded up the cellar stairs, and as she came out into the midday sun, she paused, squinting and thinking, *Geez, a tree trunk, I wonder how big...*" She then stopped herself, *Michelle, don't go there, just do not even think about it*. She continued to her room to finish packing.

Chapter 25

The renovations to the inn and the mill progressed quickly. Thomas Mornay, son of the president of the construction and engineering firm, was in charge, and as Maria monitored the worksite, she marveled at the respect he received from his men. *Such a young man and already with such a great presence. This man could make history,* she thought to herself as she watched Mornay and his men work.

The men had covered up all the furnishings the best they could with canvas tarps and plastic sheets. They set up large lights on small stands so men could work through the night. As Maria walked across the canvas, through the dining room, she could see parts of the floor had come uncovered. She cringed at the amount of dust and debris that had accumulated on the carpeted floor.

Halfway through the project, Maria traveled once more to Bordeaux to pay an agreed-upon payment and review progress with the engineers. All indications were that the job was on schedule, with three weeks remaining. While in Bordeaux, she arranged for the carpet in the Inn's main dining room and lobby to be replaced. She picked a warm, dark golden color for the bistro and dark green for the lobby and front staircase, rear staircase, and the new library that was once the family kitchen.

The mill was converted into five units with identical floor plans, laid out in a row. Maria asked that the two end units have a slightly larger area, while the middle unit be smaller. She claimed the smaller middle one for herself and one of the large end units for Daniel. She waffled by the day as to who deserved the other large end unit. One moment, she thought Rudy should get it, the next, Michelle, but then Pierre since he is the oldest. So, she was conflicted and thought, *We'll have to sort it out once everyone is back.*

Each apartment had full kitchens and separate systems for heating, cooling, water, and electricity. If the units were unoccupied by family members, they could be rented or left empty with all utilities turned off.

The large commercial lift taken from a warehouse renovation was installed to the rear in the center of the building, with a hallway separating the lift from the living quarters. On each side of the elevator shaft were small studio apartments intended for employees. There were three altogether, two on the first floor, one on the second floor. Instead of a fourth apartment, the space was designated as a conference room. The old family dining table was placed there, and a small kitchenette was installed. Audio/visual equipment was installed, and one wall was painted stark white to double as a projector screen.

Stairs were installed, allowing access to the hallway that led to the entrances to each unit. Emergency stairs were built outside the building at both ends, bringing the building up to code and allowing the roof to be used for commercial purposes.

The roof was reinforced and insulated for sound. Commercial-grade flooring was installed. Electrical and hot- and cold-water outlets were installed, and the periphery was built up. Lastly, the lift was brought up to the roof. It required a special key for rooftop access, allowing for a high degree of security.

While in Bordeaux, Maria purchased two large steam tables with wheels that could be loaded in the kitchen and then brought up to the roof by lift. She also brought a carving station with wheels, a large stainless-steel table fitted with a butcher-block top. She envisioned a pleasant summer afternoon with Daniel carving a large bird or roast while diners watched and enjoyed the sunset.

Maria left nothing to the imagination, and the architects earned every penny of their fee. She had walls moved, brick walls exposed, large windows installed, and fireplaces built. She even had them design and build a wood-burning oven for the Tree Trunk's kitchen so Rudy could continue baking bread, only safely, no longer having to travel across the dining room with hot iron cages.

She considered the veranda a masterpiece. It had a stone base with rustic, old wood beams taken from demolished barns and farmhouses used for railings. Two sets of antique doors led from the dining room, one on each side of the fireplace. The same wood used in the railings framed the doorways, not for structural integrity but for visual appeal.

A stone staircase came off the veranda and down to a cobblestone courtyard. Thomas had his best artisan build a period-perfect fountain at the far end. The courtyard's perimeter was marked by a low stone wall, allowing patrons to sit and enjoy a glass of wine before or after dinner while enjoying the cool evening air and the comforting sound of bubbling water.

Maria surveyed the new layout. She was delighted at the design and very pleased with the quality of work and materials. She was a walking testimonial for Mornay & Sons and Thomas, the construction manager, who, according to Maria, walked on water.

"One week to go, well really two weeks, one week till construction is done, another week for the cleanup, the new carpet, and getting back to normal. I'll have to remember to call someone to get us wood to burn in the oven. I remember Pierre saying it had to be special wood. I'll have to remember to ask him the next time I see him." She went over her mental checklist, adding still another item to the list.

I haven't heard from the family in a few days. I hope all is well. She said to herself. *The last I heard, they were in San Diego and looking for a place to relax before driving to Phoenix.*

So much was going on, but she remembered Michelle mentioning going out to the desert for a couple of days, just wanting to sit by a pool and take in some sun. *I wonder if that's where they went?"*

* * *

With a week to go on their trip, Michelle was tired of moving from place to place, tired of being in the car, tired of getting up in the morning and having to do something, tired of adhering to a schedule. One morning over breakfast, she had an idea. "Hey, guys, let's just go out to a resort somewhere and sit by the pool. They have many resorts and some pretty eclectic dining spots out in the desert, and this is the perfect time to be there. I asked the concierge. He said Palm Springs is a popular spot. What do you say?"

Daniel seemed interested, "Yes, let's go. That's where Elvis retired. Maybe we will meet him? I'd like to ask him where he learned to dance."

"Elvis is dead," Rudy corrected Daniel

"Really, when did he die?"

"A very long time ago," Michelle responded.

"No, no, no. That was only a publicity stunt to sell more records. See, Elvis record sales were not good, so they pretended he has died. People then bought his records because there would be no more. He sold more records dead than when he was alive." Daniel laughed at the irony of the situation he just described.

"Well, I'll go make reservations for five nights at the Hard Rock. It's new, and it's right downtown. If you see Elvis, be sure to point him out to the rest of us." Michelle finished her breakfast. "I'm pretty much packed and ready to go. Let's leave as soon as possible. I'll be in my room."

By noon, they were on the highway, heading toward the desert and Palm Springs.

* * *

Rudy and Claire were getting more and more cozy with each other, even going off by themselves to explore. Rudy was maintaining his strengthening exercises and spending less and less time in his wheelchair.

Late one afternoon, while lounging by the pool, Rudy approached Michelle, "Sis, Claire and I would like to go for a drive. Can I get the keys?"

Rudy and Daniel did most of the driving down from Vancouver, so Michelle had no doubt Rudy would drive responsibly. She also knew not to ask questions.

"Ok, go ahead and take it. I think you'll need to add petrol, the tank's pretty low," she said, digging the keys out of her bag.

The two went off. Michelle noticed Claire's bag was awfully large, for just out for a drive. "I wonder where they're off to?"

Five hours later, Rudy and Claire drove down the main street of Las Vegas, Nevada, stopping finally at the Chapel of the Bells, a 24-hour wedding chapel.

Approximately an hour later, with an Elvis impersonator and a Marilyn Monroe clone as witnesses, Claire Elizabeth Fawcett became Mrs. Rudolf Leopold Villeneuve. The couple paid for pictures and received a gaudy binder with two dozen pictures taken during and after the ten-minute ceremony.

The couple had their choice of characters for witnesses. Rudy sincerely thought Mickey and Minnie Mouse would be perfect, but unfortunately, they would have had to wait while the mice satisfied other obligations.

Rudy's second choice was Elvis, and Claire chose Marilyn Monroe. The couple laughed as they drove home, imagining Daniel's reaction to seeing Elvis as Rudy's best man. They decided to tell Daniel they met Elvis in downtown Palm Springs, and since he was not busy, he drove to Vegas with them to be their witness.

Rudy and Claire looked around Las Vegas, had fun at an all-you-can-eat buffet, and then drove through the night back to Palm Springs, arriving just before the sun started peeking over the horizon. Rudy had purchased an inexpensive bottle of champagne at an all-night grocer, and the two of them sat together in the hotel's hot tub, drinking champagne over ice from two small plastic water glasses while watching the sunrise.

* * *

Michelle became worried when she awoke and saw Claire's bed had not been slept in. She quickly threw on some clothes, went to the front desk, and was relieved there were no messages. *Where could those two be?* She said to herself.

She went down to the garage and found the car. Remembering a trick she had seen watching a police movie, she checked the hood of the vehicle. *Cold, they've been back for a while. Hmm, the restaurant's closed, downtown's closed, Daniel? Why would they be in with Daniel?"*

Daniel eventually answered Michelle's persistent knocking, coming to the door half asleep. "No, not here," answering Michelle's question, then looking over at Rudy's neatly made bed. "Doesn't look like he's been here all night. Want me to get dressed and help you look?"

"No, the car's here, and there are no messages at the desk. I suppose they are just wandering around. They'll show up." Then with an afterthought, she said, "I hope."

Michelle was still worried and felt tense. She thought a nice soothing swim, a couple of laps in the pool, then maybe 15 minutes in the hot tub would help relieve her tension.

She put on her swimsuit and went to the pool, swimming back and forth, the water gurgling around her head. While she did her laps, she occasionally heard laughter, familiar laughter, but the sounds of water muted it.

She finished her swim and walked over to the hot tub, drying her hair, her face buried in a towel. The chlorine stinging her eyes, she only began to see as she reached the edge of the hot tub. Opening her eyes, she saw in front of her, literally up to their necks in hot water, were Rudy and Claire.

"Hello, Sis," Rudy chimed, "Care for a glass of cheap champagne over ice?"

"Where have you two been? I've been looking all over. I didn't know what to think. Where did you go? "Michelle was flabbergasted, a little perturbed but relieved to find them safe and unharmed. "Good Lord. Gone all night. What did you do? Drive to Vegas, or something?"

"Yes, that's exactly what we did." Rudy answered.

"But why? There are casinos and gambling here, right across the street."

"Well, we wanted to."

"The only reason people go to Vegas is to elope." Michelle stated.

Claire held up her left hand to show the gold band and diamond she now wore while Rudy answered, feeling the effects of the cheap champagne, "Good guess, and the prize goes to the winner. That's exactly what we did. Have some champagne. Let's have a toast to the newlyweds."

Michelle was speechless. "*Nooooo*, you didn't? Did you? I am so happy for you. "She jumped into the hot tub and made her way over to the couple. She embraced both in a tight group hug.

Just then, an older couple came around the corner, wearing robes and flip-flops, heading for the hot tub. They stopped as they saw Rudy, Claire, and Michelle, in their group hug, giggling and giving each other loud, pronounced kisses.

Startled, the woman shouted, "Oh, my lord, Henry, look. They're having an orgy in the hot tub!" They quickly turned around and walked swiftly away. The woman continued loudly, lambasting the man, "I told you we should have stayed at the Hilton. I told you. Don't these young people have any sense?"

All three left the hot tub a short time later. Michelle agreed to switch and share a room with Daniel giving the newlyweds some privacy. Rudy and Claire, both feeling the effects of the champagne and having been up all night, retreated into their room after placing a Do Not Disturb sign on the door.

Daniel was having breakfast when all the switching occurred and was surprised when he returned to find Michelle in the shower. He waited patiently for her to finish. "Why do you take a shower here? Does your shower not work?" he asked nicely.

"I gave my room to the newlyweds," Michelle coyly replied.

"The newlyweds? Why did we have to give your room to the newlyweds? Does this now mean we will be four in this room? That is a little much. Maybe we can find another place to stay?" Daniel replied, very concerned. "What kind of policy is that? You must give up your room for newlyweds? America, sometimes I just don't understand how she works."

"It's not a hotel policy; it was my decision. If you were newly married, wouldn't you want to spend time with your bride?" Michelle kept baiting Daniel.

"Yes, but I would not expect complete strangers to…" Daniel stumbled, looking for the right words.

"What if they're not complete strangers?" Michelle interrupted, asking innocently.

Daniel finally caught on, "Not strangers, who then? Did Rudy, no, don't tell me, did Rudy and Claire? When did this happen?"

"They eloped last night. They drove all night to Las Vegas, got hitched, and drove back. I found them this morning, drinking champagne in the hot tub. She's wearing his ring, Mr. and Mrs. Rudy Villenueve."

Daniel sat down on the bed, a faraway look in his eyes. He was quiet for a long time, finally speaking, "I am happy for them. I am very happy for them. Before too long, I will be a grandfather." He looked up and smiled.

"Well, I don't know what you'll be, but it will be wonderful, three generations of Villeneuve. I can hardly wait." She smiled and rolled onto the bed. "What about you, Daniel? When are you going to do your part? When are you going to add another branch to the family tree?"

Daniel smiled, slightly embarrassed, "I don't know. There are many things to consider. But soon, I hope. I am keeping my options open. I don't want to make a mistake, but I don't want to live alone."

Michelle felt sad for Daniel. "You are never alone. We, family, are always here for you. If you ever feel lonely and need company, come to me. No matter what the circumstances, I will be there for you."

Daniel's eyes were teary, and he was feeling very sentimental. "Thank you, Michelle. I am here for you as well. I do want to meet someone. I do."

On the last night of their trip, all four went out to celebrate. Michelle still hadn't told her mother the news, and Claire hadn't yet told her family. Talk that night included family, children, and who will and when to tell Maria and Pierre.

Michelle owed her mother a phone call. She hadn't spoken to her in a couple of days, and she needed to remind her of their plans for arrival back home. She hesitated to call because she didn't know if she would be able to keep Rudy's and Claire's secret.

"I have to call mother. She must be wondering why I haven't called," she mentioned at the table.

"So call, it is nothing. But you should leave it up to Rudy and Claire to decide when to tell everybody," Daniel advised. "Claire must decide when to call and tell her family, too."

"I am going to wait and tell them in person. They have only met Rudy briefly. I will take Rudy with me and introduce him." She giggled, "I will say, meet Rudy. Oh, and by the way, he is my husband. If they kill me, then at least I have a witness."

"What if they kill me?" Rudy replied, surprised by her suggestion.

"I was only joking. They know your family. They know you have a very bright future ahead of you. They will be happy for us." She smiled, kissing him on the cheek.

Claire continued, "My mother has been after me to decide what to do. Go to University, help with the farm, or work in an office. I have received many lectures, too many lectures, about what her mother told her and how she got married at seventeen years of age. It's incredible, but my mother already had three children by the time she was my age."

Rudy added, "That's life on a farm; more children means more work can get done."

"I remember when I was five. That's when I started helping my mother with laundry, cleaning, and kitchen work. It was constant. If you weren't doing something, you must be lazy," Claire reminisced.

"You had a good upbringing. You respect people, and you respect yourself. I have seen you do things without being asked. You might criticize the system, but everyone would benefit from a couple of years working a farm," Daniel observed.

Michelle, listening, got the conversation back on track. "Back to my original dilemma, I just don't know if I can keep the secret from Mother. She knows me too well. She will ask, what's new, what have you four been doing. I'm afraid my answer will make her suspicious. If she probes, I'm in trouble. I cannot hide anything from Mother."

"Why don't you call and then give me the phone. I'll tell her and ask her not to mention this to anyone. We want it to be a surprise. She's good with secrets," Rudy suggested.

"Thank you. That's what I was hoping you'd say. It's too late to call this evening, but we'll call first thing in the morning," Michelle suggested, relieved the pressure was off. "Oh, by the way, I called the airline and got our tickets changed. Originally, we were set to fly from Phoenix to New York, then to Paris. Phoenix is a five-hour drive. I don't think I can do another five more hours by car. I have had enough of traveling by car. So, I switched us to a Los Angeles to Paris non-stop. It's only about two hours back to Los Angeles airport. "

"Way to go, Sis. I hate having to walk around airports, looking for your flight, your gate, then waiting to board. Non-stop is great; you hop on and hop off," Rudy replied.

"Our travel time is reduced from sixteen hours down to eleven, so that works out nicely. There is just one problem," Michelle said smiling, giving all the cues, hoping someone would ask.

But Rudy just continued, oblivious to Michelle's body language, "Plus, to spend that much time in an airport means you will have to eat airport food, and here in the States, it is so bad, worse than bad. Steamed beef patties wrapped in foil."

Daniel finally spoke, interrupting Rudy's ranting, "And what is the problem? Do we need to stay another day? I don't mind. I have been eating this wonderful Mexican food, very spicy, very different. I can eat more."

Michelle enthusiastically replied, "No, the only seats available were business class, so I splurged. We are going home in style!"

"I don't call that a problem. I call that an appropriate close to our trip, a grand finale, and the only way newlyweds should be allowed to travel," Daniel replied while raising his glass for a toast.

Michelle then looked at Daniel. "I'm responsible for the budget, and I had to spend five thousand euros for the upgrades. If I don't say it's a problem, then Mother will be furious."

Daniel, looking serious, replied, "A toast! I hereby dedicate this toast to splurging. Without splurging, we would be eating airport food." Daniel then looked at Michelle. "Tell her I insisted. Tell her I would have broken out in a rash if I had to eat this lousy food. And remind her, there is nowhere to go if you have a rash over the Atlantic. Who knows? Maybe they would ask me to leave, open the door and tell me to jump, afraid everyone would get the rash."

Michelle looked at Daniel with a look of disbelief, "Right, you want me to tell my mother that I spent five thousand euros so my uncle wouldn't be asked to leave the plane while traveling out, high over the Atlantic?" She laughed. "Daniel, where do you get this stuff? How do you make it up?"

After a bit, Michelle was able to hold in her laughter. "I'll remind Mother we'll arrive in Paris at 11:30 a.m., five hours earlier than expected. We'll take the high-speed express to Bordeaux and the afternoon train to Saint Germaine. If Claire's brother picks us up on time, we'll be back in Saint Charles by 8 p.m. That should make her happy. I will bet she is just dying to show us all the new renovations to the inn and bistro."

Rudy added, "I wonder if she'll be five thousand euros happier. And don't forget the mill. I am dying to see what she has done to the mill. My wife may be a farm girl, but she deserves to live someplace respectable."

"Don't worry about me. As long as I am with my husband," Claire said sincerely, showing her affection and placing another kiss on Rudy's cheek.

Rudy beamed and kissed her on her exposed shoulder, "Is this woman the greatest? I feel like the luckiest man on the planet." He reached over and hugged Claire, whispering, "You are mine, all mine, and I love you."

The signs of affection between Claire and Rudy were occurring more frequently and were starting to be a little out of control, prompting Michelle to speak up. "Hey, you two, I know you're just married, but save it for later. Let's enjoy the meal first; then you two can go on your honeymoon."

"Yes, I agree. It's wonderful to be in love. But you do not need to demonstrate. We all know this," Daniel added. Then he tried to start a new conversation. "I am looking forward to being home," he continued, showing a bit of homesickness. "I am looking forward to getting back to work. I have some ideas on incorporating West Coast cuisine into our menu."

"Me, too. I think we should incorporate more peppers. I think a little heat will enliven dull palates," Rudy observed. He had cooled off and was back in control of his senses.

Daniel nodded in agreement, "Yes, peppers, especially roasting, then stuffing them with cheese or even spinach, and serving them with a spicy tomato sauce or maybe even a curry sauce. Exotic flavors like nutmeg, curry, and cumin are becoming very popular. It's a way to make classic dishes exciting. I would be willing to wager a great sum, most of our patrons have never tasted anything like Mexican food."

"I also like the idea of ceviche. Instead of using oil like in escabeche or raw like tartar, add raw fish to citrus juice to cure it, giving it a nice acidic tartness to match the saltiness. I think if we can get the fish, it would be popular," Rudy stated, excited by the prospects. He thought for a moment and then continued, "Maybe we can try a ceviche, but add capers and olives, appealing to someone more accustomed to Mediterranean flavors. Thinking about it, wouldn't that work with fresh sardines?"

"Yes, you are right. That's perfect for sardines. We will call it citrus cured sardines with olives and capers. Brilliant. You've been thinking. That's good. I enjoy ceviche too. We should put our heads together and come up with some new items to serve." Daniel replied. "Maybe we could start a revolution, a revolution in French Cuisine. The world thinks French cooking is nothing but garlic and heavy sauces of butter and cream. We can show that it is the freshest of ingredients, matched with fresh herbs and spices, which are intended to work in perfect harmony with the food to bring out the natural flavors. We can do this. We will do this. This is how my cooking will be."

Daniel emphasized his last statements with a loud voice and several slaps on the table with his open palm, causing most in the small dining room to pause and look.

Rudy was smiling, nodding his head with Daniel, "I am with you 110 percent. I think we need to start a revolution. I am with you, Daniel. Let's leave our mark. Let's turn French Cooking upside/down. Let's make history."

Daniel, very excited now over the prospects of leading a revolution, cautioned, "We must be careful. We must respect tradition; we French are very big on tradition. But while we respect tradition, we will be very clever, very discreet, and introduce new ways of preparing, new ways of presenting, and most importantly, introduce new flavors that are actually just uncovering old flavors in ways that were never really understood or exploited. That is what will get people excited. If we just add a handful of chiles to beef stew, people will revolt; but for example, if we roast a chicken, baste it constantly with an herb-infused butter, and serve a pan gravy flavored with a bit of chili and turmeric, then accompanied by fresh roasted and pureed squash with a bit of nutmeg and curry, there will be fireworks. That will get people's attention."

Rudy was listening intently, sitting on the edge of his seat, "Daniel, I got something even better. Part of the kitchen renovation was the installation of a wood-burning oven, at least, I hope it was. I think of a small chicken cooked at 500 degrees Celsius, basted with butter; the breast meat is moist and buttery, and the skin crispy like a cracker. It now has a slightly smoky flavor, served with roasted root vegetables drizzled with oil infused with chili, cumin, and nutmeg. Then add the pan drippings as you suggest with maybe a splash of Spanish sherry?"

"My God. You think like me. I want to go home and cook. My dear friend, my dear nephew, we will make history. Mark my words, we will make history," Daniel said pointedly at Rudy in such a way that they all believed every word he said.

Rudy raised his glass for a toast, "Vive La France."

Daniel replied, "Vive La Tree Trunk."

All four toasted, "Vive La Tree Trunk."

The group laughed and drank as Daniel and Rudy continued plotting their French Cuisine Revolution, occasionally joined by Claire and Michelle. They were just happy to hear how motivated, excited, and happy the two men were.

Claire leaned over to Michelle and said quietly, not wanting to interrupt the discussion, "I will call my family from Paris. They are expecting us, so there shouldn't be any issues. One of my brothers, or maybe my father, will be at the station, waiting."

When the meal was over, Michelle went with Daniel, and the newlyweds went off to spend their first evening alone.

Before saying good night, Michelle reminded everyone, "We'll leave about 9 a.m. for the airport; our flight's at 4:25 P.M. We must return the car, go through security and customs. I'd rather be a little early than a little late. Oh, and remember, we must call Mother before we go.

Chapter 26

❧

"Hello Mother, this is Michelle," Michelle said a bit nervously while Rudy, Claire, and Daniel stood by.

"Hello, Michelle, how is everyone? I was hoping I would hear from you today. You are coming home today, are you not? I mean, your flight leaves today, but you'll be back tomorrow?" Maria said warmly, welcoming the call from her family.

"Everyone's fine. I think we are all a bit sick of traveling, especially traveling by car, and are *so* looking forward to coming home. I made some changes to our travel plans." Michelle informed her mother. "I changed our flight to a non-stop out of Los Angeles, arriving tomorrow at 11:30 A.M. We'll call Claire's family from Paris to let them know."

"I can call them. Will you take the high-speed to Bordeaux?" Maria asked.

Michelle floundered when Maria suggested she would call Claire's family. "No, Mother, let Claire tell them."

Rudy let out a moan as soon as he heard Michelle's answer. Michelle herself cringed, knowing she had just let the cat out of the bag.

"Tell them what? It's only to let them know she's on her way home. Is there more? Michelle, what are you saying?" Maria became curious.

"Mother, I think you need to talk to Rudy." Michelle surrendered and handed the phone over to Rudy.

"Hi, Mom." Rudy was cheerful as he greeted Maria. "Well, the good news is we had a great trip. We experienced some great cooking and are full of ideas. I'll let Daniel tell you more."

Maria wasn't so easily swayed, "That's wonderful, Rudy. Is Claire okay? Is she in one piece? Is she happy?"

"Let me ask her." Rudy could be heard asking Claire, "Mom wants to know if you are okay?"

Maria could hear laughter and giggling in the background. She was relieved when she recognized Claire's voice but couldn't hear enough to understand what she was saying.

Rudy spoke again, "Claire said she is wonderful. She said she is wonderful because she just married the most wonderful man."

Rudy could hear rumbling and noise over the phone as Maria let it slip out of her hands, then the sound of fumbling as she attempted to pick it up.

"Rudy, who did she marry?" Maria asked in a very staid, patient voice.

"Me," was his reply.

Maria burst into tears and could barely speak. She had spent the last six weeks overseeing the renovation. Six weeks of little sleep, dirt, and noise everywhere, alone making decision after decision. Now, given a chance, she let all of her pent-up emotions go, and the tears streamed down her cheeks. "Don't kid like this. Did you really? Claire is such a wonderful girl. Tell her she is most welcome to our family, and I am so proud and happy to call her daughter. "

Rudy confirmed their marriage and said they would like to have a formal ceremony to confirm their vows once back and settled. Rudy then asked for Maria to remain quiet until Claire informed her family.

Maria could be heard crying over the phone. "I hope those are tears of joy, "Rudy said comically, trying to elevate the mood.

"Of course, they are. I am so happy. I must go tell Pierre. Being mayor, perhaps he could preside over your ceremony?" She said between sniffs and the sound of tissues drying her eyes.

"That's a great idea. Well, look, we have to get going to the airport, so we will see you tomorrow evening. Take care, Mother." Rudy waited to hear Maria's acknowledgment, which came with a few more sniffs, then hung up.

The trip home for the weary four started uneventfully. The business class seats were large and comfortable, acceptable by even Daniel's standards, and the wine flowed freely.

Daniel complained a bit. Bored by the taste and lack of complexity of the fruit-forward, immature Californian, Washington, and Chilean wines he had been drinking for the last six weeks and was being offered again, he craved something more palatable. He wanted French wine. "Please, I have been drinking this grape juice for the last six weeks. Please, serve me a French Wine, a second or third growth will do."

He pleaded at every opportunity. Finally, three hours into the flight somewhere over the Canadian wilderness, a cabin attendant, feeling sorry for him, sneaked a bottle of 22-year-old Chateau Lafite-Rothschild Margaux from the first-class galley. Daniel was overjoyed, relishing in the sublime dark chocolate and tobacco-rich flavor of the wine, tasting its relaxation as it reacted to oxygen hitting it for the first time in two decades. Daniel promised the woman that he would cook a special meal for her and her husband if she ever came to Saint Charles.

"But I am not married. I don't even have a boyfriend. It is difficult to maintain a relationship when you travel like I do." She joked with Daniel, smiling a warm, inviting smile that Daniel interpreted as an invitation.

"I can imagine. I do not travel. As a chef, I work constantly, but I shouldn't complain since it is my passion," he replied, smitten by the woman, who was very polite and well-spoken.

She asked him, "Do you have a family? Where is Saint Charles? I cannot say I ever heard of it."

Daniel laughed politely. He relaxed more as the conversation continued, "Many cannot even find it on a map. We are about 200 kilometers northwest of Bordeaux. Farm country, agriculture, not just wine, but wonderful produce and meat. I am not married. I have a wonderful family, nieces and nephews, brothers, sisters, but no, I am not married either. In Saint Charles, I am not presented with many opportunities. I tell people, I am married to my work."

The attendant smiled, "Let me refresh your glass." She left and returned with the Lafite, but she also carried another bottle. "Let me pour you this. It seems to be the most popular with our First-Class passengers. I'd like to get your opinion."

She poured a glass for Daniel. He first tried to get a sense of it from its bouquet, but not detecting much, he took a mouthful. His eyes shot open, his cheeks bulged out, and he quickly unbuckled his seat belt and ran to the lavatory. Not even closing the door, he spit his mouthful into the toilet, flushed, and then gave a brief washing to his mouth.

Daniel slowly made his way back to his seat, apologizing to people as they gave him the strangest of looks. The attendant, still standing by his seat, but now laughing. Michelle, Rudy, and Claire were wondering what was happening with Daniel.

"I'm sorry, I should have warned you. I agree. I think this is terrible, but for some reason, the First-Class passengers are drinking it as if it were honey from heaven," she mentioned to Daniel as he sat back in his seat.

"They are definitely not French. Yes, please warn me next time," he requested, but he enjoyed the joke all the same.

She got close and whispered, "Brits and Americans."

Rudy leaned in, "A little flight sickness?"

Daniel corrected him, "Wine sickness. "Then, speaking to the attendant that lingered nearby, he said, "This is my family. My nephew. Sitting next to him is his wife. They have just been married, and this is my niece."

"Very pleased to meet you. Congratulations on your wedding. I will see if I can get another bottle of Lafite. I will tell the Senior Attendant that it is a special occasion. Besides, no one in first class is drinking it." she said with a smile and a wink.

When the attendant disappeared behind the curtain separating business class from first-class, Daniel turned to Michelle, "Do you like her? I think she is lovely, so nicely mannered, well-spoken, and she has an intelligent palate. I like that in a woman. I think she is capable of making a man feel like a man."

"Didn't you also think that of Louisa?" Michelle looked at Daniel with a sly grin on her face.

"No, Louisa, ah, well, Louisa..." Daniel stumbled with his thoughts, attempting to put his thoughts into words. The right words to describe a very desirable woman, but not one a man could have a successful relationship with. "Louisa is a complicated woman. She is a rose with many thorns. She is greedy; she wants it all and thinks it should all be put on a plate for her choosing."

"That's a very complicated assessment of a woman you only spent one night with," Michelle stated, taking the position a therapist would take while trying to understand a client.

Daniel's eyebrows went up, "You mean the evening she visited? I was in the kitchen most of the time, but I could sense. I had an idea what she was about."

"No, I mean from the evening you two spent together," she said, the sly grin returning to her face.

Daniel's naturally loud voice suddenly became very low, almost inaudible, "That's right. You know. I meant to ask you this before, but how do you know, and who else have you told? Was it you that told Maria?"

"Daniel, relax. "Michelle's voice also became very soft and quiet, "I have told no one. That evening late, Louisa first knocked on my door. I answered and pointed to your door. Forgive me, but I watched as she knocked and went in."

"She is not the smartest. She may be clever and political, but not the smartest. I am sorry, but I told her first door on the left...." Daniel stopped in mid-sentence, and then with a smile, said, "First door on the left if you are coming from the back stairs." He started laughing louder, and then in his natural, loud voice, "I sent her to your room! Oh, my word. The first door on the left, through the partition, is your room. I sent her to your room." Daniel laughed until he had tears in his eyes.

Michelle appreciated the irony, though she didn't find it as funny as Daniel did. "Is that what happened? I was wondering if she did it on her own or had an invitation. Now I know, right instructions from the wrong direction."

The attendant returned, carrying two bottles. Seeing Daniel in stitches, she stopped. "Well, I guess you are enjoying the flight? I brought two bottles, the last Lafite and a Latour. It's a bit younger, but I was told from a reputable source, "she added with a smile and a bounce in her eyebrows, "that it is drinking very nicely."

She turned to face Rudy, giving Daniel time to compose himself, and said, "What can I offer the newlyweds?"

Rudy smiled, "Thank you. Daniel has already started with the Lafite, so if I may get two glasses of the Latour?"

"You may have the whole bottle." She expertly opened the bottle and poured a taste for Rudy. He smiled as he took in its budding aroma, then allowed the attendant to pour a glass for each. She then whispered, "Here, place this down by your feet, in between your seats. I don't want to tempt other passengers by walking back and forth with the bottle."

Rudy and Claire both thanked her and enjoyed the wine. They giggled at each other as they began to feel the effects of high altitude and wine.

Meanwhile, the attendant had returned her attention to Daniel while opening the bottle of Lafite. Michelle asked for a glass. She usually slept on long flights, but she didn't want to miss tasting a 22-year-old Lafite. "I can always sleep, but how often do you get served a Lafite? Too bad we don't have a little pungent cheese and bread." Then thinking of what she would eat at home, she added, "It's going to be so good to get home."

"We'll be serving dinner in about 90 minutes. But if you like, I can get you something now. Would you care for a cheese platter? It would not be a problem." She smiled sincerely, wanting to make her passengers happy.

Michelle looked at Daniel. Daniel nodded and replied, "That would be nice. I always think of a fine Bordeaux as a wine that should be served with food."

The attendant smiled at Daniel, "I agree; you and I think alike. Excuse me for a moment." She disappeared behind the curtain into the first-class cabin and returned shortly, pushing a beverage cart. She filled several glasses of other business class passengers, stopped to take an order or two, and then disappeared again before coming back with her hands full of bottles. She poured one here, the other there, and then fit them onto her cart. She locked the cart's wheels while unfolding white linen napkins and placing them in front of passengers, utilizing them as tablecloths. Another attendant helped her place small glasses of nuts and pretzels in front of the passengers. Moving down the aisle, checking on each row of passengers, she finally reached Daniel's row.

"Here you are," she said, placing a platter of bread, cheese, and grapes in front of Daniel and Michelle and another in front of Rudy and Claire. She smiled and asked, "Could you lift the plate? I need to place a cloth down. It will help if there is turbulence."

Daniel lifted the plate while Michelle held their glasses. With the efficiency of years on the job, the attendant unfolded two white napkins with a pop and covered the folding trays. The same procedure was repeated for Rudy and Claire.

"How's everybody doing?" she asked before moving to the next row.

Daniel was quick to speak up. "Everything is wonderful. This brie is not bad, and the gouda is nice and nutty, but I don't recognize this other one?"

"It's an American cheddar. It's not bad, don't you think?" the attendant said to Daniel.

"American cheddar? I am glad you didn't tell me before I tried it. I probably wouldn't have, but now that I have, I like it. It goes well with the wine. It's a bit salty and dissolves nicely on the tongue. It's good but not great. I think it's a little bland, needs more flavor. I think cheddar originated in the UK," Daniel said, thinking more out loud than really conversing.

The attendant added, "A stronger cheddar is called a sharp cheddar."

Daniel laughed and took another bite of the cheddar. Michelle asked, "Why do you laugh?"

"I laugh because I find the taste of cheddar dull, boring. The blander the flavor and Americans think of it as sharp." He laughed again

"So?" Michelle asked, thinking there's got to be more.

"Don't you see, it's dull, so it's sharp. Only Americans would use such contradictions. It is as if great is mediocre and mediocre is great, only in America."

"I'm not 100% with you. Maybe a better example would be if it's cool, it's hot, and if it's hot, it's cool, "Michelle said, finishing her wine and using her elbow to prompt Daniel to pour her another glass. "I like good wine. I agree with you, though. California wines are good but lack a degree of subtlety, elegance. What's that saying? Oh, yea, 'in your face; that's what California wines are, 'in your face.'"

"Yea, I think they are sharp." Daniel poured her a glass of the Margaux, giving her a wink.

The flight continued with more wine, dinner, and dessert. Finally, Daniel settled in after finishing his second cognac, placing his seat in the prone position and turning off his light. It was just minutes later when Michelle heard a mild rumble as Daniel fell into a deep sleep. His breathing produced a deep, even nasal tone, often referred to as snoring.

Michelle covered Daniel with another extra blanket. Looking around, she found most passengers were already asleep, so she ignored his snoring, put on her headphones, and started watching her third movie.

The attendant was extremely nice, offering Michelle cognac and other after-dinner liquors. Michelle declined but was elated when the attendant brought her a large mug of hot chocolate and a few warm cookies. "Oh, that's so nice of you. Thank you. Perfect. Just what I wanted, but I was too embarrassed to ask. "

"You looked like you needed a nice hot mug of something other than coffee." The attendant offered. "You and your family are very nice. Is it true Daniel is the Head Chef?" she asked.

"Yes, and he is fabulous. His creativity is remarkable. I don't know how he does it, but he communicates with his ingredients and knows just the right amount of seasoning," Michelle remarked.

"Did I hear you right? Communicate?" she asked Michelle to clarify.

"That's right. His ability to understand ingredients, to create combinations, to make the right preparation is nothing less than astounding." Michelle, sensing an opportunity, decided to do, as they say in America, 'grease the wheels.' She spoke quietly and personally to the attendant, almost whispering, "Please don't tell Daniel I mentioned this, but he is lonely. He wants very badly to meet someone who shares his passion, old-fashioned in a way, but non-traditional. It's hard to explain, but he wants someone who shares his vision, shares his vision of life."

"Oh," The attendant replied, surprised at Michelle's candor.

"Yes, we live a wonderful life. Daniel is so involved and so happy at what he does, but you know how men are? Daniel needs someone to live for, someone to share his life. He has all this success, but at the end of the day, he goes home alone." Michelle was stoking the fires for Daniel. She could see that the attendant was interested, but she realized that she was also describing herself.

The attendant talked a little about herself. "I am looking to settle down. I have traveled enough. I still enjoy traveling and meeting people, but the sense of adventure is no longer there, and slowly it is becoming routine. I am senior, so I have choices of where I go, but no new routes interest me. There are opportunities flying new routes to the Middle East and Africa, but the restrictions on women I cannot accept, so I won't go there."

She continued, "It was announced recently that the airline would begin offering buyouts to senior personnel. I have enough years to receive a handsome sum. I am wondering if I should. If I had somewhere to go, someone to be with, if I had the right opportunity, I would file my papers tomorrow." The woman stopped and looked at Michelle, surprised she had volunteered so much, but the attendant found Michelle warm and easy to talk to.

Michelle saw that the attendant was suddenly a little uncomfortable. "You can confide in me. Daniel is my Uncle, and I love him dearly. If I thought I had to protect him, I would. But you seem very genuine." Michelle looked over at Daniel, checking to see if he was still asleep, and seeing he was, she continued, "And Daniel noticed too. He is quite smitten. He is a great man, and he's got a good heart and a good eye. "

"I like him very much. I like his outlook on life. He seems a little edgy, a little unusual, but passionate; that makes life interesting. Unusual people, for some reason, attract me. I will write him a note. I will also give you my information; maybe you can keep me informed. Let me know if he's not interested. I don't want to waste my time or look foolish."

Michelle smiled, "I'm pretty good at match-making. I think you should start thinking about filing those papers."

The attendant smiled, patted Michelle on the arm, and left to see to other passengers. Michelle was happy with the conversation she just had. She turned off her light, turned off her video, and just sat back in the comfortable seats, staring into the darkness, listening to the drone of the aircraft, and sipping her hot chocolate. She started to cry, not a big heavy cry but a soft, melancholy one, with just a few tears coming from her eyes. As she cried, she thought, *If I'm such a good matchmaker, why am I so all alone?*

Later, when the flight was starting to awaken and was just hours away from landing, the attendant came by and gave two slips of paper to Michelle. One was folded and had Daniel's name on it; the other said "Hi, I'm Gabrielle," along with a Paris phone number.

Michelle quickly retrieved a pen and wrote her name and phone on a napkin along with "Tree Trunk Bistro." "If she loses this paper, she should be able to remember Tree Trunk Bistro." She then thought, *We really need to change that name. What kind of name is Tree Trunk Bistro?*

Chapter 21

Claire's brothers, Marco and Phillip, were waiting with the van at the Saint Germaine rail station when the 7 p.m. train pulled in at 8:30. They had arrived a short time earlier and just had enough time to stretch their legs and have a cigarette when they saw the train approaching the station.

Home at last, the four travelers climbed off the train, gathered their luggage, and moved slowly down the platform, Claire by Rudy's side as he managed to move along in his chair. Marco and Phillip approached, smiling, happy to see everyone back from their long trip.

Claire stepped forward and gave her brothers a warm hug. "Hello Marco, Phillip, so good to see you and so good to be home. Thank you for meeting us." She said exuberantly, "Do you know Daniel, Michelle, and Rudy?"

They made introductions all around, and then the conversation returned to Claire. "Now that we are all acquainted, brothers, I would like you to meet my husband." She once more lifted her finger, showing her ring to her brothers as if to dispel any doubt. Rudy came forward in his wheelchair, slowly stood up, and shook Claire's brothers' hands once more. The brothers let their hands be shaken but stood motionless on the platform, a look of disbelief on their faces.

After an awkward moment of silence, the brothers looked at each other and then back at their baby sister. Marco, the eldest brother, spoke, "You got married? How'd you do that? It's not legal, is it? Father said he had a funny feeling about this trip. He said a lot could happen in six weeks. Boy, was he right."

"Let's get you all home. Then we should call Mother and Father. If anything, we should do a little celebrating tonight," Phillip added, seemingly much happier with the news than Marco.

Marco stopped, looked at his brother, "You are right. What am I talking about?" He walked over to his sister, reached down, and gave her a suffocating hug, "Congratulations, Sis. I am happy for you." He then went to Rudy, who had remained with his chair, took his hand, and said in all sincerity, "I have lost my sister but gained a brother. Best wishes and welcome to the family."

Claire had to get a tissue from her purse to dry her eyes. She loved Rudy, and she loved her family. Though she never doubted it, she was relieved to see her brothers accept Rudy as their own.

The drive back was smooth, even though they were riding in a large van meant for farmhands and equipment. Many questions were asked, and many stories were told. Phillip said the winter holiday was uneventful; with the inn and bistro being closed, there wasn't much opportunity for socializing. Pierre hosted a New Year's Eve celebration, but there wasn't much food, and the punch wasn't so good; the party barely made it to midnight.

Dozing off in the far back seat, Michelle now remembered Gabrielle's note. She took it out of her pocket and handed it over to Daniel. He looked down at her hand. "What's this?"

"I don't know. Something the cabin attendant wanted me to give you," Michelle said, half asleep, shrugging her shoulders, and trying to hold back a yawn.

"The flight attendant, that nice woman? When did you receive this? Why did you not give it to me sooner, so I could say something?" he said, irritated, but more so from traveling, jet lag, and the effort needed to focus than from the delay in receiving the note

"She asked me to give it to you later. She didn't want to create a scene or make you feel uncomfortable," she replied, not really wanting to get into it with Daniel. She felt drained of energy to the point even casual conversations were a chore.

Daniel unfolded the note. It was short. It simply said, "*Like you, I have been looking. I think I have found it. Have you? Gabrielle.*" Her phone number was there and underneath her number was the imprint of her lips, in dark red lipstick.

Daniel took the letter, carefully folded it, and placed it in his wallet. His mood changed completely. He had a strange look on his face, in his eyes. Michelle couldn't see clearly as the only light was the occasional streetlight, but his eyes were shiny, a sure sign of tears.

"What's the matter, Daniel? What's wrong?" She said softly, placing her hand on his shoulder and rubbing gently, feeling a bit motherly towards him.

"I am sorry. I am tired and too emotional," he replied, looking down and rubbing his eyes, embarrassed by his uncharacteristic emotional display. "Remember on the plane. I asked you what you thought. Well, I had a feeling. I knew when I saw her, and then first spoke with her. I knew it," he said softly, pulling out a handkerchief and drying his eyes.

"Knew what? What? I don't understand. Please, talk to me, Daniel," Michelle said, thinking he needed to talk. He needed to get something, whatever, off his chest. To this day, she doesn't know why she said it, she's never said it to anybody before or since that day, but she just blurted out, jokingly, "What, does she want to have your baby?"

"Ha, Very funny. I am laughing," Daniel said in the darkness, an edge to his voice.

"I'm sorry, Daniel. But you know me; I have a very weird sense of humor. Please, I apologize. Please talk to me. I will never again make light of your feelings." Michelle was sincerely sorry and kicking herself for being so callous toward her uncle.

Daniel really didn't care. He needed to get it out. "She's the one. Her name is Gabrielle. I think I will marry this woman," he said as if a great weight had been lifted from his shoulders and a decision that was plaguing him had been decided. He could now move on with the rest of his life. "She is beautiful, classy, so well-mannered, and has excellent taste, an exquisite palate. I have known her only a short time, but I know what she is about, and she's it, the one. This woman was made for me. I have found her." He chuckled, feeling better now that this great pent-up emotion had been released. He looked down at Michele and smiled, "Or maybe it is better said, she found me!"

Michelle knew not to take Daniel's words lightly. She knew he was serious, very serious. "That's great, Daniel; I'm happy for you. You really think she is the one?" she asked, letting him talk but giving him clues that he didn't have to answer if he didn't want to.

Daniel looked again at Michelle. "You should have given this to me earlier." He looked out into the distance, lost for the moment in thought and memories. "No, you are right. It would have been uncomfortable. I would have bothered her. She would not have been able to get her work done. It was a good decision," he looked at her in the darkness and put his arm around her, "Thank you."

Daniel was quiet for the remainder of the ride home, as was everyone else. Michelle felt relaxed from Daniel's warmth and safe in his arms. She was soon asleep.

* * *

The inn looked about the same as it always did: a large, imposing stone structure, with a few outdoor lights, almost obliterated by the ivy growing down the façade. The light shining through the windows of the front doors gave the only indication of the possibility of inhabitants. Marco pulled the van up to the front entrance. Andre, the busboy, immediately came out to help with the luggage. Daniel removed his long lanky frame from the confines of the van, stretched, yawned, then knelt and kissed the ground.

Everyone seemed to just pile through the front doors. Almost on cue, all stopped and gasped as they surveyed the inn's renovated lobby. The floor was covered in a dark, luxurious green carpet contrasting nicely with the light strawberry-colored walls. The dark brown wood chair rail, accents, and beams across the ceiling did an excellent job of softening the contrast, as did the gold sconces that added small amounts of light around the perimeter of the room. Hanging from the ceiling in the center of the room was a very impressive silver and gold chandelier. The chandelier's style and the many sconces were perfectly matched.

Along the far wall, separating the small office from the lobby, was the inn's desk. Michelle thought it looked slightly larger than she remembered, but what amazed her, and made her smile, was that she could see the back of a computer monitor sitting down below the counter, just peeking up over the edge. She could tell the computer was on from the slight glow provided by its screen.

Maria, hearing the van pull up, the sound of voices, and the lobby door open, quickly finished what she was doing and came out from behind the Inn's front desk. "Welcome home, everybody. Welcome home, Michelle, Daniel; good to have you back. Rudy and Claire, the newlyweds, welcome home and welcome to our family." She hugged everyone and gave Claire an extra special hug and kiss.

Claire introduced her brothers, who jokingly called Maria *Aunty*. Everyone was joyful, happy to be home, happy with Rudy and Claire's marriage, and truly impressed with the lobby's transformation. All agreed. It was rustic, sophisticated, and elegant. Michelle's description was especially noteworthy, describing the lobby as 'under-stated elegance'; she didn't mention that she borrowed the phrase from an American Auto Company. She had seen the slogan used in a poster while traveling through Los Angeles's airport and thought it clever. But overall, everyone was impressed by the transformation.

Daniel was standing by the door, taking in the lobby but also thinking about Gabrielle. Maria interrupted his thoughts, "Daniel, I am sure you want to see your bistro? Everybody, should we look?"

Maria led everyone into The Tree Trunk's dining room. The outdoor lights cast interesting patterns of light and dark through the newly installed, old-fashioned, leaded glass-paned doors leading to the Veranda. The room was cozy, warmed by the fire. The crackle and pop from the wood-burning in the fireplace sounded comforting and reminded everyone that they were safe, and finally home.

Rudy was the first to speak, spotting the large beehive-shaped dome in the far corner of the dining room, next to the doors leading to the kitchen. He wheeled over to the chest-high counter that separated the dome from the dining space, slowly stood, and placed his elbows on the counter. He examined the prep space on the other side of the counter, the brand-new refrigerator, and the service table with small compartments for various ingredients. He turned to Maria, "It's beautiful. It's exactly what I pictured. Thank you so much, Maria. I really can't thank you enough." He turned back to take it all in again. He spoke out loud but seemed to choke on his words. "We have ourselves a wood-burning oven. Game on, baby, game on."

For the first time anyone could remember, even in the past, through the toughest of times, it hadn't happened, but at that moment, that night, as everybody witnessed, Rudy became emotional.

Maria walked over to him. "You thought I forgot, didn't you? I wanted it to be a surprise. It was built just last week. We hunted high and low in Bordeaux, Toulouse, and finally Nice for the right expertise. We couldn't find an artisan with the right experience, so we brought one in from Italy. He came all the way from Naples. It took him a little over a week to build it. He cut the stone right where you're standing. It was quite a mess. It's the main reason why you are standing on a new carpet. You simply cannot remove brick dust from the carpet," Maria lectured to remind all, in case they ever wanted to try it themselves.

"I can't wait to light the fire." Rudy added, "Are there instructions on how to season it?"

"Yes, Antonio left many notes on seasoning the oven, operating, cleaning, and repairing, if there are problems. But it's all written in Italian. I was never good with Italian. My German is passable, but my Italian is terrible," Maria added.

Claire spoke up, "I speak Italian. I learned it from my grandmother."

"Great, I knew there was a good reason to keep you around," Rudy said with a smile and a wink as Maria handed a large folder of handwritten notes to Claire.

"Don't mind him; he gets upset when he doesn't know everything.", Maria smiled, having a little fun at Rudy's expense.

Claire opened the folder, looked at the first page, then gasped loudly, drawing everyone's attention, curious as to what she discovered, "My word, it says if your name is Rudy, do not use this oven. It will not work for you." She looked up at Rudy and smiled, then continued, "It says here to let your intelligent, beautiful wife take care of it since we all know lighting a match is a challenge for you."

Everybody, including Rudy, had a good laugh. Rudy looked at his wife, "You're not going to let me get away with anything, are you?"

Michelle made her contribution, "That will teach you. Well done, Claire." The two girls gave each other a high-five salute.

"I know all the tricks; I was raised with four brothers. Believe me; I can stand on my own two feet."

Maria got everyone back on track. "I had a lengthy conversation with Antonio before he left. He said he'd built many of these, and the design is very efficient. It will easily produce a steady 500 degrees Celsius and run all day on five to ten kilos of oak. That's another thing; he suggested we use only seasoned hardwood, like oak. Softer woods don't burn well and will leave residue in the cooking chamber, giving the food a horrible flavor."

Rudy looked at Maria, "How do you know all this? I mean, that's a lot to comprehend. I'm impressed."

"There's more...he also said that in a week or so, after we have lit our first two or three fires, and the oven is fully seasoned, we should hire a good tile man to tile the outside, making the oven attractive for people to look at. But he said, make sure the man knows what he's doing. Make sure he knows it's an oven."

"Yes, good idea. It could use a little sprucing up," Rudy replied, examining the rough, pale brown clay exterior of the oven.

Suddenly, a gust of cold night air swept through the dining room as Daniel opened one of the glass doors leading to the veranda. Examining the door, swinging it back and forth, he spoke to no one in particular, "Very nice work. I am impressed. The door operates very smoothly and is very solid, heavy for a glass door. It can even be locked from the inside. That is good. These people knew what they were doing."

Maria cried out, "Daniel, it's cold. Let's do that in the morning. Please shut the door."

"Hello, hello?" came from the inn's lobby. Claire immediately recognized the voice.

"Hello, father. Come to the dining room," she cried out and started walking towards the voice, stopping halfway as Claire's mother, father, and brothers, Claude and Edmund, entered the dining area.

Claire greeted her family with traditional hugs and kisses. Mr. Fawcett, Peter to his friends, was a fifth-generation landowner and farmer. His great-great-great-grandfather Andre Fawcett, purchased title to the land when it was taken away from German aristocrats during the French Revolution. Andre was a wealthy lawyer living in Paris with his wife and children, but he thought the mobs in the streets were too bloodthirsty. Afraid he might lose his head for stating his opinion, he purchased the land and moved his family out of Paris as quickly as he could.

The hard life of a farmer showed on Peter's face and hands. His face was weathered, and his fingers were bent, gnarled, and calloused. But his eyes were deep and focused, intense. He had the look of a man who did his job and expected you to do yours. He trusted a man's word and did not suffer fools wisely. The two sons by his side, Claude and Edmund, had the same intense look.

"I was told to come, to bring everybody, that there was a celebration," Peter said to his daughter Claire.

Phillip, one of the brothers that met Claire at the station, spoke up, "Yes, Father. I think it's about to start. At least it should."

"I do not understand. What am I missing?" Peter asked, looking a little confused by all the innuendo.

"What he means, Father...." Claire stepped up in front of her parents, took hold of her mother's hand and her father's. "What he means is that we have reason to celebrate. While on the trip, Rudy proposed to me, and I accepted. We were bored and had some time, so we drove to Las Vegas and got married."

Claire's father looked at his wife, looked back at Claire, and smiled, saying patiently and respectfully, "Your mother and I would like to meet this young man."

Rudy stepped forward, a little wobbly at first but managed to stand straight; he stood next to Claire, "Mother, father, may I present Rudolph Leopold Villeneuve, my husband, and your new son-in-law."

Peter Fawcett looked at Rudy and offered him a chair, "Here, sit down, son. Don't strain yourself for us. We know your family; we know you were raised right, and you'll take good care of our daughter. We couldn't be happier. Welcome to the family."

Claire's father shook Rudy's hand vigorously, and her mother hugged him. "She's my only daughter. I raised her to think for herself, to understand duty and loyalty. Respect her, and she will respect you. I know you two will have a wonderful life together. I am so happy for you two. Welcome to our family."

Peter Fawcett took out his handkerchief, wiped a few tears from his eyes, and blew his nose. "Well, why aren't we celebrating? It's bad luck not to toast newlyweds. Daniel, can we get some champagne?"

Daniel turned to Maria, "I don't know. I just got back. Maria, is there any champagne in the storeroom?"

"Yes, as soon as I heard the news, I ordered six cases, express delivery. They are in the meat cooler," Maria said and started to walk in that direction.

"Please, Maria, allow me." Daniel stopped her.

"I'll be happy to help." Peter Fawcett followed Daniel, each returning with two bottles. "This will get us started," Peter announced loudly.

Pierre came walking in and apologized for working so late. He saw Rudy and Claire and the champagne being poured and shouted, "I am so happy my assistant has returned from her honeymoon. Now tell us, when can we expect Pierre the 2nd to arrive?"

Claire kissed him on the cheek as he hugged her and voiced his best wishes for the newlyweds, also saying how jealous he was that Rudy found such an attractive and wonderful young lady. "Right in front of our noses," and asking Claire, in between sips of champagne, "Are there any more like you around?"

Peter Fawcett, feeling no pain and finding no reason not to be jovial, took his wife in his arms, protecting her from Pierre's imaginary clutches, saying, "You can't have this one..." leaving the thought hanging in the air. "I just got her trained, and I would hate to have to start all over again."

Everybody laughed as Claire's mother gave her husband a good swat on the shoulder, saying sarcastically, "I think you had better look again to see who has who trained."

Claire leaned over to Rudy, "They are always playing like this. I don't think there is a couple better suited for each other than my mother and father."

Rudy looked at her, "Well, there's you and me."

Claire smiled, leaning against Rudy as he placed his arm around her. Feeling comfortable and at ease, she replied, "That may be true."

After many handshakes, and hugs and kisses, a few more introductions and slaps on the back, laughs and chuckles, and a few more bottles of champagne, Maria announced, "Doesn't anyone want to see your new apartments?"

Maria first took out a black pen. She had five key rings. Each keyring had six or seven keys and a single tag on each, labeled A, B, C, D, and E. She described the layout, five apartments in a row with the two end units, the larger units. She explained how she assigned A, a large end unit, to Daniel. She wrote Daniel on the tag and handed it to Daniel. She also said the keys on the ring were for the inn's lobby door and the Tree Trunk's front door. There was also a lift security key, giving everyone access to the roof via the lift.

She then described how she was uncertain who should get the other large end unit. Her first thought was giving it to the eldest. "But Pierre is finding that the Mayor's job done correctly requires frequent trips to Bordeaux and Toulouse. Why assign a large unit if he will be gone a great deal of the time? "

Maria continued, "That leaves Rudy and Michelle. I think the answer is obvious. I think, or I hope, the next generation of Villeneuve will soon be on the way, hence the need for more space. Forgive me, Michelle, but I am giving the other large unit to the newlyweds."

There was a round of applause as she wrote R & C on the label and handed the keys to Rudy.

"I am in apartment C. I am in the middle. Pierre, Michelle, one is on the right, next to Daniel, the other on the left next to Rudy and Claire." She queried. "Any preference?"

Michelle and Pierre started talking at the same time, stopped and looked at each other, and then started talking again at the same time.

Pierre said to Michelle, "Go ahead. You start."

Michelle said to Pierre, "No, you can start."

"Ok, I'm traveling quite a bit these days. Unit D between Maria and the newlyweds will probably be on the noisy side, especially when my grandson arrives, so why don't I take that one?" Pierre volunteered.

Maria countered, "Noise shouldn't be a problem. Thomas had the men line the interior walls with brick. The walls are very solid. Noise shouldn't be a concern."

"Ok, then, I'll take the unit on Daniel's end. We'll have the two old guys on one end, the young people on the other end." Pierre adjusted his decision accordingly, just trying to get a decision made.

Maria added with a smile, "That seems reasonable." Then looking at Michelle, she asked, "Are you ok with apartment D?"

"Yes, fine. This is great, Mother. I've never had my own apartment. Can we decorate? I mean, can we do things we want to do? Like, add colors, motifs, carpets?"

"Well, yes, of course, you are free to do as you wish. But first, you must look. I had everyone's bed moved along with what furniture you had, but you might want to think about buying some additional furnishings. But have a look first. "

Everyone filed back to the mill. An entrance leading to the mill was cut through the wall in the old family kitchen. The short passageway led to a hallway that had five doors in a row. Two other doors stood opposite the five. The freight elevator was between the two doors, made civilized by a large metal gate that easily slid from side to side.

They all hopped in the lift and rode it up one floor. Everyone was amazed the elevator worked so smoothly while carrying so many passengers.

Upon exiting, they were in a lovely wide carpeted hallway with five attractive wooden apartment doors. On each entry was a letter, A through E. To one side of the elevator was another closed door, unmarked, and on the other side was the meeting room with the old family table. Michelle remarked, "Oh, that's excellent! A place to meet, and you kept the family table. That's lovely, mother. That's so right."

Maria smiled, "Yes, everybody. This is the conference room. It has a kitchenette; we can make coffee or snacks. There's a small fridge and audio-visual equipment. Michelle can now show us what it's like to be in the corporate world."

"It will be helpful. Trust me," Michelle said quickly, not wanting to keep everyone from seeing the new apartments.

"Well, everyone, let's go in," Maria announced. Maria joined Michelle as she entered her new apartment for the first time.

As the doors opened, Maria could hear the emotional gasps as everyone took in their new accommodations. Michelle's gasp was especially prominent because she was standing right in front of Maria.

Michelle looked at her unit and immediately turned and wrapped her arms around her mother. "It's beautiful, Mother. It's gorgeous. It's so wonderful. Is it really mine?"

Chapter 28

T ime flew by as the family settled into their new surroundings and got down to work. Claire read to Rudy the instructions on how best to season the oven. It called for three fires over as many days. He was instructed to make a small fire and let the oven cool, then a larger fire and let the oven cool, then an even larger fire, and again, to let the oven cool.

Once the oven had cooled after the third fire, the oven needed to be thoroughly cleaned of any ash or suet. After the cleaning procedure, the oven was ready to use.

A load of newly cut oak was stacked in the rear of the bistro, but it needed to be split into much smaller pieces. Smaller pieces would season quicker and would be better suited for use in the oven.

Having moved back in, the waiters were looking for something to do while the bistro remained closed. They had spent their days cleaning and stacking dishes and cleaning some more. Being young and energetic, they jumped at the chance to wield an axe and split the large oak logs.

Success at log splitting wasn't easy, nor was it quick. The two young men struggled and finally determined that by using a large chisel, the heavy, dense wood could easily be split by a few hits with the back of the axe. Before long, the two men had the entire stack split down into smaller logs, easily placed into the oven as needed.

As the wood dried, armfuls of split wood were placed in the small cubbyhole underneath the oven, created for just that purpose.

To try out the oven, Rudy first placed as much wood as could fit into the two large kitchen ovens and set the oven thermostats on 65 degrees

Celsius, letting the wood bake overnight. After 24 hours, the wood was perfectly seasoned and ready to be used in his oven.

While the wood dried and a series of fires seasoned the oven, Rudy made bread dough, adding a little more yeast for a crispy crust and a chewier center. He also brought out a bottle of old sourdough yeast he received from Claire's mother and was dying to try. He let the dough proof overnight while the wood dried; the dough was ready to go in the morning, as was the wood.

When the oven was cleaned and ready, Rudy stacked a few of the split logs in the oven, being careful to note how many pieces of wood and how they were positioned. This way, he could understand how quickly the wood caught and how long the oven took to reach temperature. He could then work out how much wood the oven needed to stay at temperature.

Rudy monitored the oven's temperature through what the builder's notes referred to as the control box. The control box did not so much control as monitor. Inside the oven were three temperature probes. The probes had electric leads leading to and plugging into the back of the control box. Three small led displays on the front of the box displayed the temperature of the oven.

The instructions the artisan left behind noted that most chefs, after working with the oven, began to understand it and, after a short time, established a rapport with the oven, no longer requiring the use of the controller.

Rudy brought the fire up. When the logs were ash, he placed two additional pieces of oak in position. Then, monitoring the temperature and using a large metal peel, he managed to place four baguettes, side by side, in the center of the oven. *Boy, this takes some getting used to*, he said to himself as he watched the bread bake. He let the loaves go for an extra minute, then slid the peel underneath them, twisted them, rotating them 180 degrees, and placed them back in the oven.

Exactly two and one-half minutes later, he placed four piping hot loaves of bread on the counter. "Pickup," he yelled to no one in particular, but hoping someone would hear and come to investigate.

Daniel came from the kitchen, not into the dining room, but into the prep area. "Ah, so we have our first bread, fresh from the oven." He picked up a loaf with a napkin-covered hand and tore off an end piece. "Very nice, good crust." He placed the loaf back down and tore a portion off the piece. "Excellent flavor. Yes, good, I like it chewy like this, and it's very nice tasting, not too salty, not too yeasty. Excellent. I hope you can produce this consistently. Excellent, now which one, huh, which one is the sourdough?"

By this time, Andre the bellboy smelled the bread and came over for a taste. Rudy cut slices off the loaf for all to try. Andre took a piece, then another, "Fresh bread, there is no other sensation like it."

Rudy smiled, "Thank you. Enjoy, eat as much as you like."

Paul, the waiter, had noticed the small crowd gathering, as well as the warm, delectable smell of baking bread. He came from the kitchen but first stopped to fetch a large cistern of butter, not the butter usually placed on tables, but the rich, high-fat content, sweet butter Daniel required in his cooking.

Large gobs of the butter were loaded on the warm bread and savored by all in attendance. Maria passed by and stopped. "Fresh bread and butter, you can always include me," she enthusiastically added, selecting a modest-sized piece but loading it down with a good dollop of the soft butter.

Finally answering Daniel's question, Rudy announced, "Let's try the sourdough."

Rudy took one of the loaves, slicing it slightly on the diagonal, and stacked the pieces on his cutting board within easy reach. Everyone reached for a piece but then had to wait as, one by one, they applied butter.

"Hmm...", Daniel murmured, "I like this even better. It's saltier, but comes with tartness, almost like English Fish and Chips. It tastes of sublime salt and vinegar. What do you think?" he asked anybody who cared to respond.

"I agree," Maria answered. "It is saltier, but you really have to look for the saltiness. But I taste the tartness. I think tartness is very noticeable."

Rudy added, "That's the sourdough yeast. It's typical bread yeast, but with additional bacteria, Lactobacillus, to be exact, which ferments into Lactic Acid, giving us the tartness."

Daniel replied, "Interesting."

Maria smiled and added, "Thank you, Rudy. Lactobacillus?" then let her voice trail off, not knowing what to say next. She took another piece of sourdough, added butter, and retorted smartly, "Hmmm, but it's certainly delicious, bacilli or no bacilli." Finishing her bread, she knew she had to get away from all that butter; otherwise, she'd never fit in any of her clothes, "Well, excuse me, everyone, I must head off. Well done, Rudy. I'm looking forward to your next oven test."

Rudy made a few more loaves, quickly becoming adept at handling the long-handled peel, raw dough, and loaves of the finished bread. He was getting accustomed to working with the oven and was turning out perfect baguettes consistently.

The family arrived home on a Wednesday. Over breakfast two days later, everyone agreed the following Thursday should be the grand re-opening, allowing everyone to get back into sync. They could work the kinks out for Friday night, historically the busiest day of the week. Maria also asked that Sunday be reserved as family day. Only families would be seated, and the hours of operation were limited to 1 p.m. to 8 p.m.

Given the increase in business from the new expressway, normal hours of operation were expanded on weekdays till 10 p.m. with Friday and Saturday till midnight. Daniel didn't seem to mind the extra-long hours, finding that he could prep for Friday and Saturday the night before. "Just a matter of staying organized, keeping one's ducks all crossing in a row," seemed to be his favorite saying.

As Daniel and Rudy prepared for the grand re-opening, it became apparent that Rudy could not be in two places at one time. He could not be in the kitchen preparing sauces, prepping appetizers, or setting up plates with the appropriate accompaniments to Daniel's entrées, while also minding the bread and other various food items intended for the wood-burning oven.

Rudy was perplexed as to how to move forward. He loved formal cooking and was amazed at Daniel's technique, learning much from just observing. Daniel was also very good at explaining how to make corrections, like fixing over-seasoning or ensuring cream does not scald when heating it quickly.

But the wood-burning oven was just so much darn fun. To Rudy, it was like playing in a sandbox, better yet, noting how quickly items cooked in the intense 500-degree Celsius temperature; he likened it to instant gratification. He could watch the bread turn golden brown right before his eyes, turn it around with the long-handled, large paddle-like peel, and watch again as the other end turned color.

He loved inventing. Even though Daniel did not want pizza on the menu, Rudy loved making them, using bread dough, rolling it thin, even figuring out how to toss it, like in the movies, adding garlic, olive oil, and whatever else he had around. People raved about the pizzas he made, especially those with garlic, mozzarella, roasted fennel, and cured black Nicoise olives, all locally grown.

Rudy finally struck a deal with Daniel. Paul would train to bake the various loaves of bread they served, and Rudy would work as he traditionally did in the kitchen. Taking Paul's place as a waitress, on the nights they needed two waiters, would be Claire or Michelle. But on slow nights, such as Wednesday and Thursdays, Daniel would allow Rudy to work out front, and the Bistro would feature offerings from the wood-burning oven, such as roast squab or rack of lamb -- but no pizza of any type.

For some reason, serving pizza was not an option for Daniel. "If we place a pizza on the menu, then what next, chicken wings from Antelopes, or maybe corn chips and tomato relish? We no longer must cook. We no longer need waiters; just call out a number. "Table 23, your chili-beef taco sandwich is ready for pickup.' Then we will need to line the walls with tubes, so we can all watch sports, nothing but sports 24 hours a day. I think I will look for another job. Please, no pizza. If you want pizza, hire another chef. I am not the right man for the job."

Maria took note, "Please, Daniel, you are the right man. I back you 100%. It is your kitchen, and if you say no pizza, there will be no pizza."

For the grand re-opening, they sent invitations to all the local populace and some good friends that lived far away. The inn quickly filled up with all rooms taken, including the two additional rooms on the third floor and the new penthouse suite. Pierre had reserved the penthouse for the newly appointed Regional Minister of Transportation, whom he hoped to convince to schedule a twice-daily, intercity bus route through Saint Charles.

They offered two seatings with a fixed-price three-course and five-course menu. The Tree Trunk was sold out, with people starting to be turned away.

The weather was cold for even this time of year, upsetting Maria and her plans to utilize the veranda. She couldn't picture even the hardiest of souls enjoying dinner out in the frigid weather.

While on their trip, Michelle had noticed that when the temperature dipped, restaurants in California would utilize several gas heaters, mounted high up on poles, and placed around outdoor seating areas. These devices emitted an immense amount of heat, making chilly nights rather pleasant.

Maria liked the idea and had Michelle and Claire search for a retailer. The two women searched high and low and finally found something suitable at a construction equipment wholesaler in Toulouse. Still, with Michelle nor Claire having a construction license or even a permit, the firm could not offer them to the women.

Finally, exasperated with what seemed like endless requests and continuous denials, Maria contacted Thomas Mornay, her contractor from the recent renovation.

Thomas was sympathetic and volunteered to step in, asking how many she needed. Less than 30 minutes later, Thomas called Maria back, informing her six units, with fuel, were on their way to her, but coming from Toulouse by truck would take about four hours. Thomas said the driver would have an invoice and treat him well; it was his brother-in-law.

Maria couldn't thank him enough and asked if he was attending the re-opening. Thomas apologized, saying, "With a new baby, our first, we do not get out much. But as soon as we are able, my wife and I would love to join you for dinner. I gave the invitation to my father, but he is traveling to Spain these days to expand the business. I don't know if he will be back in town. In fact, the last I saw, the invitation was sitting on his desk. I don't even know if he has been back long enough to check his mail."

Maria was gracious, "I'm sorry to hear you won't be attending. Everybody has been overwhelmed by the quality of your work. I was hoping I could introduce you. But there will always be another time. I would like to thank you again for everything, and please, come to Saint Charles when you can and enjoy our hospitality as my guest."

Thomas was thankful, wishing all his clients appreciated his efforts like Maria did. "Thank you, Madam Villeneuve, that is very gracious and generous. I will tell my wife that we must schedule a visit sooner rather than later. Meanwhile, knowing my father, I better brush up on my Spanish."

Maria laughed at Thomas's suggestion and concluded the call, "Thank you, Thomas. Stay in touch. Goodbye." Maria hung up. "Such a really nice, pleasant young man. I couldn't begin to repay him for all he's done for my family and me."

Maria called for Michelle and Claire, "We can start taking reservations for the veranda. Thomas Mornay has arranged for six large outdoor heaters to be delivered. They're coming by truck from Toulouse, so at least four hours."

"That's fine, mother. We don't need them until Thursday night. If they come today, we can start them and see how well they work. Maybe we'll only need four," Michelle said while trying to figure out a spreadsheet problem.

The truck pulled up in front of the Tree Trunk approximately five hours and 20 minutes later. The driver jumped down from the cab with a clipboard and went inside while another man started to undo ropes and straps holding the six large, square boxes to the truck's bed.

"Hello, hello, delivery for the Tree Trunk. Is there a Madam Villeneuve around?" the driver called out.

One of the busboys quickly found Maria, who was happy to hear the truck had arrived and quickly made her way to the bistro's entrance. "Hello, I'm Maria," she said cordially, extending her hand.

The driver shook her hand, introduced himself, and informed her that her delivery of six large industrial heaters was sitting out in the truck. He asked, "where would you like me to unload them?"

Maria explained the purpose of the heaters, how they would allow diners to enjoy dining on the veranda in the chilly weather. She wanted them to be placed around the veranda so they would warm but not be intrusive.

The man laughed, "Warm, they certainly will but not be intrusive? Not a chance. Madam, these units are capable of ten, maybe twenty thousand BTU. You have six of them. That's enough BTU to warm a small football stadium. In terms of noise, I wouldn't stand next to one unless I was wearing protection."

"Oh, my word. I don't think this is what we wanted. This is a restaurant, not a football stadium. You spoke with Thomas Mornay, did you not?" Maria asked, concerned, somewhere, somehow, the message was lost.

"Yes, he called in the order. Said it was a rush job." The man volunteered, "If he weren't related, I would have shipped it commercial, but you know, you try to take care of family."

"Yes, of course," Maria replied, uncertain how to deal with the young man.

The driver stepped to the edge of the dining room, "So this a restaurant?" The man looked about. "Very nice. Tommy did this?" the man asked, familiar with Thomas Mornay to the point he referred to him as Tommy. "We haven't eaten in hours, what with loading and driving through the traffic. Is there any possibility of getting some food? We'll pay; we don't mind."

"Yes, of course, we always try to take care of our own," Maria replied, cringing a bit at her smart answer, hoping he wouldn't pick up on it.

"Thank you. I'll get my associate and call Tommy as we sit and eat. Is there a washroom we could use to get rid of this road dirt?" the man asked, happy knowing food was on its way but still a little concerned over the six large heaters in the back of his truck.

The Inn was still closed, and Maria felt sorry for the hungry, road-weary men. She offered them each one of the studio apartments out back. "Here are the keys to units 1 and 2. Just follow the corridor through the library, and you'll find the units to the left and right of the lift. There are fresh towels and linens on the bed if you want to rest. Unfortunately, I can't offer you a fresh change of clothes."

The young man smiled, "Thank you, that's very generous—a hot shower, some food, maybe even a little rest before we must drive back. Madam, I wish all my deliveries were this way. Thank you."

Maria smiled, "That's quite all right. One favor deserves another. Let me know when you get through to Thomas."

"Thank you. I will," the man replied as he and his associate went off to clean up.

Maria made a note to ask the maids to clean the two studios and went to the kitchen to arrange food for the two men.

She found Daniel and Rudy in the kitchen, trying to perfect a simple pot-au-feu with the southwest American flavors they had enjoyed while on their trip. "What can we offer them that's fast and easy? They haven't eaten in a while, so fast, easy and substantial would work," she suggested, hoping for a simple answer.

"The wood-burning oven is still hot. I'll need about twenty minutes to get it back to the correct temperature, but that's no problem. I can roast some chickens, some root vegetables, bread, and a fruit tart for dessert. It won't take long. I wouldn't mind the practice. I'll start them with a couple of small, simple pizzas, just garlic, cheese, maybe some anchovy," Rudy volunteered.

"That sounds perfect. Is that ok, Daniel?" Maria asked, relieved the solution was simple.

"Yes, of course. My ovens haven't been on all day. It would take them an hour to get to temperature, and what for, two small chickens? No, give this to Rudy. It's fine," Daniel replied, adding, "Here, let me get the chickens from the cooler. Start the fire, and I'll bring them to you."

The men showered and came back to the dining room. Paul, the waiter, set the table, and the two were treated as guests, served as any other patron would be served, and even given a glass of cognac with dessert. The young men joked that they felt like royalty, the service was good, but the food, "fit for a king" was their assessment.

After the meal, the driver called Thomas Mornay to figure out what to do. The exchange seemed heated at times, and the driver had to interrupt the call with a call to his warehouse, which concluded quickly. He then called Thomas back.

Maria stood off to the side, not wanting to pry or influence events either way. The only thing she knew was that the heaters were utterly useless to her.

The call concluded, and the driver began speaking with his associate, who seemed surprised at what he was hearing. Midway through the discussion, both men asked for another cognac. Before pouring, Paul the waiter looked at Maria, who nodded, letting the men have another. She thought, *These guys drove all this way here for nothing; they deserve a drink or two.*

Once they finished, both men stood up and asked for the bill. Maria took the statement from Paul and told the men they were her guests, and it was her pleasure.

The driver, shyly, obviously embarrassed, spoke to Maria, "Madam, I don't know where the problem occurred, but there was a problem with your order. We have the type of commercial outdoor heaters you desire. You thought you needed six, but I can tell you based on my experience and seeing the size of your space, four would do, possibly even just three, but I would start with four."

Maria took note, "Ok, can I get the four delivered? I have a grand opening on Thursday, and we have already started taking reservations for tables out on the veranda. If we don't have the heaters, we won't be able to seat people, and that will not be good."

"I understand," the man replied, "We will drive to Bordeaux and drop off these units at Mornay's warehouse, drive back to my warehouse in Toulouse, pick up the correct heaters, then drive back to Saint Charles."

Maria was startled, "What? That is a tremendous amount of driving."

The man smiled, "Driving is what we do. You have been very kind, very hospitable; the least I can do is make sure your order is correct, and you get it on time."

"Thank you" was the only thing Maria could think of saying.

The man continued with one more request, "It's 3 p.m. We would not make Bordeaux and Mornay's warehouse in time, not with evening business traffic. Let us stay and rest. We will leave approximately 2 a.m., arrive in Bordeaux, unload, and get back to Toulouse by 9 a.m. My warehouse will be waiting. We'll load quickly and be back by this time tomorrow, one full day to spare."

"Fine, if you think you can do it," was Maria's reply.

"I must keep my customers happy. I can do it. I must do it." He smiled, bowed, and asked to be excused as he and his partner went off to lock the truck and grab some much-needed sleep.

Chapter 21

T he two men arrived late Wednesday afternoon with the four heaters for the veranda. After so many hours of driving, they were exhausted. Maria fed them again and let them rest up in the two empty studio apartments.

Waking early Thursday, the men assembled the heaters, tested them, and placed them on the veranda where they would be most useful. Maria was impressed with the amount of heat they gave off. She was sitting out in the cool, winter midday sun, in her short-sleeved shirt and sunglasses, feeling like a Hollywood star lounging on the Riviera. "Well, now I know how the stars live. What are they called? Oh, yes, the other half." She said with a heavy drollness as if it were such a chore to exist. Her comment elicited laughs from the two young men who were still moving about, making sure everything worked perfectly and that Maria was satisfied with their work.

Michelle and Claire joined Maria and learned how to refuel the heaters and get them started again. The heaters were fueled by propane gas, and a large tank was good for about four hours of moderate heat. At the setting generating the greatest amount of heat, a gas tank only lasted approximately two hours.

The large tanks were obstructions to the flow of foot traffic around the veranda, which worried Maria. First, her vision of a sophisticated alfresco dining location was marred by the sight of several large bulbous metal tanks connected by hoses to each upright heater. The hoses connecting each tank to its heater were not very long, so the heater's tank sat on the floor next to the heater. This was not Maria's idea of sophistication.

Secondly, she had just removed, at great expense, a safety hazard created by baking bread in the fireplace; the wood-burning oven remedied this situation.

Now she felt she was creating another hazard with the heaters, gas tanks, and hoses. If a person wasn't looking, they could easily bump into a tank, trip, and fall. Heaven forbid, if the off-balance patron brought down a lit heater on unsuspecting diners nearby. The result would be catastrophic.

She became distressed as she envisioned her waiters trying to maneuver around the heater tanks with trays of plates. *This is not good*, she thought. *This is an accident in the making.*

Maria called Pierre, Michelle, and Claire over to help her figure how to use the heaters without hurting anyone.

"Well, is the issue not enough room to navigate, or is the issue placement? I mean, do you want the heaters out in the middle of the floor? If the answer is a simple matter of moving them, then we should move them. But if moving them makes them useless as heaters, then the question is how to create more room, so people don't trip?" Pierre spoke as he tried to figure out what Maria wanted. It was an easy solution to move the large aluminum poles, but he wasn't sure that was what she really wanted. He suspected she wanted the heaters to stay exactly where they were and just wanted to get rid of the tanks.

"I notice all the tables here are tables of four. What would happen if we substituted smaller tables?" he said, throwing out an idea to see if it sparked an interest.

Michelle caught on immediately, "Yes, that would work. Mother look, if we take these two tables and replace them with smaller tables of two, we create an aisle."

"Then all we need to do is figure out how to hide the tanks or cover them. Claire, would you mind going to the linen closet and fetching a white and a red tablecloth?"

Claire answered, "Certainly." She was gone before Pierre could say thank you.

Returning, she handed the two tablecloths to Pierre, who first placed the red one on one of the tanks, disguising it well. "I like the red cloth. It's discreet, but it's red for a reason. It is a warning."

"Let's now try the white one," Maria asked. They watched Pierre as he removed the red, replacing it with the white, carefully wrapping it around the tank and the pole for the greatest effect.

"I like the white one. It's more sophisticated. It reminds a patron we are conscious of the visual appeal of our dining space," Maria stated, not sure if she conveyed her feelings coherently. She tried again by adding, "If I see the red cloth, I see a poor attempt at hiding the tank. It's like putting up a flag, like a janitor would do when warning of a wet floor. But the white blends in; it recognizes an eyesore and shows we are attempting to alleviate it. Does that make sense?"

Michelle answered her mother's question slowly, "I see your point. Yes, I understand, and I agree. Let's use white tablecloths to wrap the tanks. We need to change out two tables here and those two tables for smaller tables, then wrap the tanks in white tablecloths," She said while pointing to the other side of the veranda where a heater stood center, like a flagpole, in a cluster of tables.

"Should we look at the reservations?" Claire asked, "I mean, should we make sure that reservations for the veranda are for parties of two? Suppose we only have parties of four? What will we do, separate them?"

"Yes, that's a very good point." Pierre added, "If we are taking reservations specifically for the veranda, we have to make sure we match the seating with the number in the party."

"Maybe if it's just parties of two, we can replace all the tables. That would leave plenty of room," Michelle said.

"Filling the main dining room with parties of four would be wonderful and lucrative. The more, the merrier, for obvious reasons," Pierre said with a nod and a sly smile.

"I'll go check the reservations," Michelle added and ran off to the Inn's reception desk, where the reservations were taken and kept on the computer.

The reservation system was easy to navigate and understand; the dining room was represented graphically with the exact number of tables. When a reservation was taken, it was assigned to a table, and the little graphic on the screen then changed color. Each table was defined in the set-up process. The program would not allow a large party to be assigned a small table; the number of seats had to equal or exceed the size of the party. Once all the tables were reserved, any further reservations went on the waitlist.

She checked the veranda and saw that only three tables were unreserved for the first seating; the second had two unreserved tables. "That's good. We're almost sold out," she thought and continued checking the seating. Of the five reserved tables, only one was a party of four. The second seating had two parties of four.

"This is good," she said to herself as she closed the computer window and hustled back to the veranda. "Good news," she announced as she walked through the antique doors leading to the veranda. "There's only one table of four in the first seating, two tables of four in the second seating."

"Are we sold out?" Pierre asked.

"Almost. Three tables left in the first, two in the second," Michelle answered.

"Good, once again, our luck has held up," Pierre announced. "Let's get these tables arranged. Claire, could you ask someone from the kitchen to help move tables?"

Daniel soon came, along with Paul. They quickly maneuvered the larger tables around the heaters and replaced them with smaller tables from the dining room. Paul grabbed fresh table clothes and set the tables for two.

The veranda was split into two sections, with each having two tables of four and three tables of two. This provided enough space to walk to and from a table without being obstructed by a heater and its tank or another table.

Meanwhile, Maria took several white table clothes and tried as best she could to cover the tanks. She was pleased with her handiwork. She surveyed the tables around her, feeling happy with the outcome overall. "Now if the weather would just cooperate.," she lamented.

As the day went on, guests began arriving for their stay at the Inn. Many were like old friends showing up for a reunion. The Zieglers came all the way from Munich, wanting to see the renovations to their very most favorite retreat while escaping the harsh weather back home. As they walked into the lobby, they were immediately astonished by the warmth and casual country sophistication. "Every time we come here, it seems more and more like home. The renovations are very nice, very warm, "Mr. Ziegler said while registering at the desk. "May I inquire? Would it be possible to rent an apartment? My wife and I enjoy it so much here; we would like to move here or at least stay for an extended period. Perhaps we spend the winter? The winters here are much milder than what we experience in Germany."

Maria politely laughed at Mr. Ziegler's inquiry and then, seeing he wasn't joking, replied, "We have never been faced with such a suggestion. I really don't know how to respond except to say we are very flattered. I see you are staying for four days. May we discuss this later, before you depart? Today we are very busy, and I would find it impossible to find the time to think this through."

"Of course, Madam Villeneuve, my apologies. I did not consider that in my behavior. Please, when you have time, my wife and I would enjoy the opportunity to sit and discuss. Perhaps over tea, one day?"

"That would be very nice," Maria responded. "It would be a much more meaningful and useful discussion." She checked him off in the reservation, called over to Andre, and asked him to show the Zieglers to their room, the Master Suite on the second floor.

Maria checked their dinner reservation and saw they had a table for four, off to the side in the main dining room. She thought they would enjoy dining on the veranda. She waited until Andre returned to the lobby and then called the Ziegler's room.

Mr. Ziegler thought it was a wonderful idea to have a table on the new veranda. Mrs. Ziegler wasn't so sure until Maria mentioned the heaters. Mr. Ziegler mentioned his wife's niece and husband would join them tonight. They lived nearby and were driving in for the gala. He said the niece takes a bit getting used to but ultimately has a good heart and is fun to be around."

* * *

That settled and no other parties to be checked in, Maria went to the kitchen to check on the menu and food preparation.

She found Daniel in tears as he sat on a small stool in the corner of the kitchen. A large flowerpot, draped with a white tablecloth, sat on the floor between his legs. He cried the tears of distress and great loss.

"Daniel, why are you crying? It's almost 2:00 p.m. We have our first seating at 6:00 p.m. Why are you not preparing? What's the matter?" she questioned him, sincerely concerned over his troubles.

Daniel slowly raised his head, showing his red, swollen eyes. "She's gone. Josephine. This morning, she said it was time, and now she's gone."

Maria tried as best she could to comfort him, never having heard the name before today. "I have never heard of Josephine. Have I met her? Have you brought her around and introduced her to people? Who is she?"

"No, you have never met. I found her years ago, alone, in the forest. I took her in, nourished her, treated her like my own, and now she is gone." Daniel broke down, covering his face with a napkin to muffle his sorrow.

"You found her alone in the woods?" Maria repeated, starting to really wonder what was going on. But she did what she thought she should do and comforted her grieving brother-in-law. "Daniel, our lives come to an end at some point. All we can hope for is that our passing is peaceful, and we are with loved ones." she stopped for a moment. She had to stop. She was beginning to feel depressed as if a good cry was coming. *Wait a moment. This is ridiculous*, she told herself. She had no idea who this person was and, knowing Daniel, if she even existed. She told herself to straighten up, act responsibly.

"Well, Daniel, perhaps we can grieve at a more suitable place and time. For now, we have over 150 guests coming this evening, and we must be prepared. Can you help me, Daniel? Perhaps what we can do is place a small plaque near the fireplace in honor of her memory," She said softly, trying anything to comfort him, put a smile on his face, and bring him back to reality.

"She would like that. I know she would," he replied, slowly coming out of his funk. He started to get up and then spoke softly, "I am sorry, Josephine. I must leave you, but I will be back, and I will make sure your contribution is noted. I will make sure your flavor is remembered by all."

"Flavor? Josephine has flavor? Daniel what is in the flowerpot?" Maria became concerned. *Josephine had passed, and she was in the pot. Why would she have flavor? Good heavens.*

Daniel looked at Maria solemnly and said one word, "Josephine." Then continued, "I'd introduce her, but…."

Maria didn't know what to do next. "Has she been cremated? Are those her ashes? Don't you dare tell me you found someone in the woods and then had them cremated, and they are now sitting in the kitchen."

Not knowing what else they could be, she was furious. "Daniel, what are someone's ashes doing in the kitchen? If anyone found out, we would be closed before we even opened."

Rudy came by at that moment. "Oh, I see you've decided to bring Josephine to the big opening event. I was wondering when you would bring her out of the cellar and introduce her to everybody."

Maria turned to Rudy with smoldering eyes, "You knew about Josephine?" Then turning back to Daniel, "You kept her in the cellar? Daniel, how could you?"

"Oops, I have to finish prepping. Daniel, let me know when you want me to start braising the beef." Rudy turned quickly and sped off to the other side of the kitchen, where he became lost amid the clatter of pots and stainless steel.

"Yes, I kept her in the cellar. If I put her in my room, you may get the dogs after her, like you did with my cheese." Daniel's voice and stance were becoming arrogant and aggressive.

Maria quickly snapped, "Daniel, don't use that tone of voice with me. It's opening day, we must perform, and the only way we are successful is if we perform together. I don't need your shenanigans. I do not have time to indulge you in some childish prank. Now you tell me in as few words as possible: Who is Josephine and what is in that pot?"

Daniel sat back down, looking weary. "I am sorry. I get emotional. I realize I lack, as a person, what many others naturally have. I can't explain it, but I get attached to people and things around me. I seem to understand and build a rapport with the things around me."

Maria felt sorry for her outburst. She should never have yelled and lost her temper, not at poor Daniel. *Lord knows, he tries, and the success we've enjoyed so far has been mostly due to his skill and talent*, she thought. She then replied, "I must apologize, too, Daniel. It was rude of me to say the things I said. They were hurtful, and I am deeply humiliated by my behavior. Please forgive me." She leaned over and kissed him on the cheek.

Daniel smiled, accepting her apologies. Then he held the pot, pulled the napkin back, and pushed the pot forward in the direction of Maria. "Josephine."

Maria looked in the pot and saw only dirt. She looked at Daniel. "Dirt? Josephine is dirt?"

Daniel reached into the dirt with his two hands. With a grimace on his face, he pulled out the large black truffle he had named Josephine and had nurtured for the last three years. Brushing off the dirt and holding it up for Maria to see, he repeated, "Josephine."

Maria gave a quick examination to the large fungi in his hands, looked back at him for clarification, repeating, "Josephine?"

Daniel nodded, "Josephine."

Maria collapsed to the floor in a large heap, her head down and hidden between long strands of her hair and the folds of her skirt, which went every which way. Her feet were drawn up into a ball. A muffled sound came from somewhere inside this human ball of hair and cloth. An onlooker could make out shoulders, moving up and down in unison with the sound.

Daniel looked, "Maria, are you alright? The floor is not that clean. You should not be on the floor. Let me help you up."

A head slowly rose from the heap on the floor. "Leave me, Daniel. I'll be all right." She laughed, and then she laughed again. Looking at Daniel sitting there with a giant truffle in his hand, she couldn't control herself and

244

burst out laughing. Not a funny joke, polite laugh, but a gut-wrenching, 'laugh so hard it hurts' laugh.

Finally, she caught her breath, "Josephine, Josephine, the truffle. I should have known." Maria then started crying.

Chapter 30

As Daniel flipped the contents of his sauté pan, he couldn't help thinking, *There is no other place for me. There is nothing like being in front of a stove. This is where I belong.*

He began imagining himself a famous ballet impresario, the principal dancer of the renowned Tree Trunk dance ensemble. He moved the pans around with a flourish. He made great efforts to mimic a swan, standing on his toes, imagining his arm the bird's long neck, as he added seasoning. He did pirouettes and little jumps as he plated his preparations, imagining rounds of applause. He bowed again and again as the audience called for encore, encore.

He stopped for a moment, interrupted by arriving orders. In the background, he could still hear clapping and calls for an encore. Looking up, he saw an audience of Rudy, Claire, Michelle, and Paul nearby, applauding. Rudy and Claire were holding sheets of paper with large number 10's, both also insisting on an encore.

Embarrassed, Daniel smiled, bowed once more, stating, "Perhaps you can say I am immersed in my work?"

"That was beautiful. I believe you have missed your calling," Michelle added and went back out to the dining room.

Claire smiled and kissed her husband on the cheek, adding as she left, "Daniel, you are fantastic. You are truly a great artisan. You have tremendous balance."

"Thank you, everyone. Unfortunately, the show is over. Rudy, we need four onion soups and four loaves of fantasy bread." Daniel continued preparing the dishes he needed to complete the order.

Rudy ladled onion soup into four large ornate bowls. Rudy added a pinch of cumin, cinnamon, and freshly grated fire roasted ancho chili to add a bit of complexity. He then added a large flat, toasted, buttered crouton, covering it generously with a mixture of grated Gruyere and mozzarella cheese. Daniel insisted on having mozzarella in the mix so the long strings of melted cheese attached to their spoons would entertain diners.

Rudy placed the bowls under an open flame and waited while the cheese turned a golden brown and tiny bubbles formed. Before calling for pickup, he liberally doused each serving with Spanish dry sherry. He dusted with the grated ancho chili, accenting the Gruyere and giving the soups a nutty flavor and a savory aroma.

Rudy then hustled out to the front station, retrieved four loaves of the Fantasy bread from the refrigerator, and slid them into the oven. He waited for three, four minutes, turned the bread around, and waited. A minute or so from finishing, he slathered on his garlic-mayo-gruyere cheese mixture and watched how the bread slowly turned mahogany brown. He turned one more time, gave it 30 seconds, and the bread was done.

The grand re-opening's three and five-course menu didn't seem to work with most patrons. Most of the diners were old friends, and they wanted their usual. So, it was decided early on to abandon the fixed price menu.

Daniel didn't mind, "How would you like to cook the same thing, 150 times in one night? Fixed-price menus tend to lead one to drink," Daniel lamented as he took another sip of his cognac.

Claire and Michelle shared the responsibility of extracting a suitable menu out of Daniel. Seeing the dining room was full of people, it had to be done quickly. A menu was a difficult task even when Daniel sat and focused. It became next to impossible while he was in front of the stove and engrossed in his cooking.

While Michelle cleaned off the board, she spoke loudly to Daniel to catch and keep his attention. "I saw onion soup, so we have onion soup, right?" Michelle was already writing it when Daniel gave her his answer.

"I think so. Rudy, did you make a fresh pot of onion soup today?" he asked.

Rudy came through the doors with warm baguettes and Fantasy Bread. "No, I didn't have time, and besides, it's not on the menu."

"It is now," Michelle quickly replied.

"Better start preparing immediately. How many servings do we have left?" Daniel asked.

Rudy placed the bread on a cutting board. Paul came by, started cutting, filled small baskets, and took them out to the tables needing bread.

Rudy peered into a large pot on the back of the stove, "I'd say six, maybe eight."

"That's not good. It'll take me 20 minutes to get the soup ready," Daniel said and then cried out to the busboys, "Peel me a dozen large white and red onions quickly; I want them yesterday, now, please."

Michelle turned to Claire, "We need to stay out of the way. Then she said to Daniel, "We'll be back." He didn't answer as the girls left the kitchen.

Daniel took a large pot from the rack, filled it half full of water, and tossed in some carrots, celery, beef bones and trimmings, and a few chicken carcasses. He looked at Rudy and spoke, "You didn't see this," while taking two large spoons of beef extract and stirring the paste into the water. Finally, he dumped the contents of a bottle of red wine into the soup, bay leaves and two whole heads of garlic after first crushing them with the side of his knife. Moments later, the first hints of heat appeared as tiny bubbles started to rise to the surface of the soup.

"We need to let it boil for at least 15 minutes, so the flavors come out of the bone. Once we get the flavor, we can add the onion, but first, I must sweat them," Daniel said intently, as if he were on a mission, calling out to the busboys in his next breath, "Can I get those onions, please?"

It took Daniel mere seconds to chop an onion. Rudy assisted, taking slightly longer. Together, in a matter of minutes, they had a huge sauté pan filled with slices of red and white onion. Daniel added a large block of butter and half a bottle of white wine. Once the butter started to melt, Daniel lowered the flame. "We do not want to burn the onions or the butter. We want nice succulent onions. This is why it takes so long to make onion soup."

Meanwhile, Thomas entered the kitchen with an order for two onion soups. Then Paul entered with an order for four.

"That's it on the onion soup. We are preparing more, but it will be at least fifteen, maybe twenty minutes," Rudy reported as he pulled out six bowls and started constructing the dishes.

Daniel called out to the busboys, just finishing peeling the last onions, "Please, one of you, grate cheese. I want 1/3 mozzarella, 2/3 gruyere blend. Please. The other can check the dining room."

As the onions slowly sweated down, Daniel prepared other dishes while closely watching the onions.

Rudy informed the waiters that their soup was ready and then surveyed the scene. Onions were sweating on the stove, the broth was boiling, and Daniel had a half dozen entrees in various stages of preparation. *This guy is a master. No doubt. We went from a possible disaster to almost back to normal. Daniel can really get things done.*

Daniel saw Rudy looking about, "You can make more croutons and skim the broth. You know how beef produces film; remove the film. It must be removed."

Rudy replied, "Will do. Daniel, I have to say thank you. I thought I was in trouble, but you got everything back on track. Thank you."

"We have to help each other. Being mad or belittling you is a worthless exercise. It is a better education showing you how to solve a problem than punishing you for creating it." Daniel smiled and started plating an entrée.

Rudy smiled, "Yes, and to be honest, I do not respond positively to the caveman approach to management."

Daniel looked at Rudy with a curious look on his face, "Caveman? Cavemen had management. How do they know this? Did they find pay stubs, organization records?"

Rudy looked the other way, trying to stifle a laugh, not sure if Daniel was serious or not, finally answering when it got too quiet. "Just a figure of speech, you know, cavemen, they pounded their chests like apes, trying to intimidate. I don't do well in that environment."

"Oh, Tarzan. I used to like to hear Tarzan scream. That was a great scream," Daniel concluded. "Let's go ahead and strain the soup; the onions are almost ready."

Rudy readily agreed, relieved the conversation was over.

The two incorporated the onions into the strained broth. Daniel tasted before adding a few dozen bay leaves, salt, and pepper. He tasted again, "Not bad. Let's add the beef bones back in, then give the soup ten minutes."

Michelle and Claire came back into the kitchen. "Can we continue with the menu? Please? It's starting to be a little crazy out there. Everyone's waiting for the menu, drinking wine, and eating bread. The good news is wine sales are up; the bad news is people will start passing out any minute now."

"Ok, Rudy, do you want to try out your oven?" Daniel asked, thinking he would jump at the opportunity.

"Sure, of course. What can I do?" he replied smiling, eager to try his ideas and to show he was capable.

"Let's do as you suggested: a small roast chicken, basted in butter and herbs, and served with a simple medley of roasted root vegetables. Very tasty, very healthy," Daniel offered, his eyebrows lifting as if making an obvious suggestion.

"Excellent," Michelle replied, writing the menu item in her ornate script.

"I think you should make a separate menu section, a section perhaps "From the Wood-Fired Oven," Claire suggested, smiling that little girl smile everyone loved.

Daniel spoke, "We will need another entrée or two. But I don't want pizza, please no pizza."

Rudy then spoke, almost shouting, like he had just won the lottery, "How about a tart? Can we do a tart, a wild mushroom tart, with garlic, oil, and, I don't know, roasted peppers?"

"That's intriguing. Yes, tarts are fine. I think tarts are appropriate." Daniel added, "Let's do this; we'll do two tarts, a wild mushroom with gruyere, and an asparagus with roasted peppers and goat cheese. Perhaps add some thin slices of garlic. Please be careful. Do not get too complex. We want robust, simple flavors.

"Perfect, I understand", Rudy was ecstatic.

"Take your station out front. I'll have the busboys bring you what you need. Oh, lastly, let's put a filet with Gorgonzola and roasted vegetables with a port wine reduction on the side." Daniel was in his element. He was in charge, and no one doubted for a minute his purpose or his orders.

Daniel gave some quick instructions to Rudy before continuing with the menu. "What I want you to do is roast about 300 grams of filet, and when it is just past rare, almost medium-rare, place the meat on a serving plate. Put a large slice of gorgonzola on the meat and leave it in the oven until it has fully melted and enveloped the meat. At 500 degrees Celsius, that should only take 30 seconds. Careful; the plate will be hot. Place the vegetables on the plate with a small flask of reduction. Some will use it; others won't. Later, we will get feedback and decide what to do. Now go stoke your fire, get ready."

"Ok, let me get some aromatics first. Placing sprigs of rosemary and thyme in the bird's cavity would certainly be enticing," he said, moving off to the vegetable and fruit cooler.

Daniel turned to Michelle with a wink. "It is best to nurture a man, let him grow, and experience, than to shut him down through intimidation or neglect. I would like Rudy to remember me being a good teacher rather than someone who stood in his way."

"Oh, one other thing," Daniel mentioned to Michelle, "Tell the waiters, if anyone orders the filet, to make sure they serve Villagrosa's red blend or his Merlot. Either one would be perfect with the dish." He paused for a moment, then continued, "I think we need a sommelier, and I have an idea who we can hire."

"Ok, but a good sommelier would be expensive. I mean, in Paris, they are considered superstars," Michelle said while continuing to write, adding a few chicken dishes, the usual crowd-pleasers, two additional beef dishes, a pork chop, and, finally, Daniel's and Rudy's take on ceviche made with fresh sardines, along with a simple salad of fresh greens.

"Not if she's my wife," Daniel said with a wink and smile.

Michelle didn't put two and two together until much later; for now, she focused on finishing the menu and inquiring about pates.

"I have a country pate; it's coarse and hardy. Some will like it. I also have a very fine duck liver mouse, it's like silk - a nice contrast. Yes, add a plate of two pates with cornichon and olives. Oh, and the onion soup is now ready." Daniel exhaled, glad that was over with. He instructed the busboy to fetch him another cognac and began cutting root vegetables for Rudy's plates.

As Michelle and Claire exited the kitchen carrying the menu, the crowd roared with appreciation, with half the crowd on their feet trying to peek at the menu. Paul and Thomas were busy taking orders for meals, while Michelle and Claire helped by filling glasses and offering bread.

Daniel called Claire to the kitchen. "With Rudy out front, I need help. Please grab an apron and do exactly what I tell you."

Claire obeyed instantly and stood by as Daniel first demonstrated how to fix a bowl of onion soup. Then he showed her how to plate pates, and finally how to plate the sardine appetizer.

Claire proved herself to be quite adept at food preparation. She only needed instructions once. She assembled the many plates without error and never stumbled or became confused. When Rudy came back to the kitchen to replenish his ingredients, he saw his wife quickly manipulating soup bowls oozing with melted cheese, assembling plates of cured sardines, and organizing blocks of pate, counting the number of little pickles and olives, making sure she did not cheat anyone.

He smiled and joked, "Now you know what being married to a Villeneuve is all about."

She looked up and smiled at her husband. "I never thought being married would mean I'd become a chef."

Rudy smiled back at her and thought to himself as he made his way to the meat and dairy cooler. *You must learn to wear many different hats in this family.*

The first sitting went by without a hitch. The new menu was appreciated, and Rudy kept busy pushing small chickens, chunks of filet, and loaves of bread into his oven.

The tarts turned out to be extremely popular, with many parties opting to sit and relax and catch up with the latest gossip while sipping wine and munching on a tart or two.

Maria was beginning to get worried. The second seating was at 9 p.m., and at 8:30, many patrons still hadn't ordered their meals. They sat and ordered bottles of wine, loaves of bread, pate, and an occasional tart.

She tried everything, even offering free dessert, hoping that would end the meal, but most parties thanked her and continued as they were, oblivious to time and the message Maria was trying to convey.

Finally, Maria pulled Michelle, Pierre, and Paul aside and asked for suggestions. Paul was flabbergasted, "I have never seen people so involved. I have one gentleman who's on his third bottle of wine and second pack of cigarettes. I am afraid if he doesn't stop soon, we will have to call paramedics to take him away."

Maria was incredulous, "Three hours is enough time for a meal. Don't you think?"

Pierre volunteered to do the talking, "I'm the Maitre'd, I'm in charge of the dining room. I will see to it that the parties finish and move out."

Michelle added, "I'll help you, Pierre. I'll go with you."

With that, the two went to the first table. Pierre started, "Hello, please excuse me. We have the second seating at 9 p.m. We will need this table. Can we ask you to please finish your meal, settle the bill and leave the table? Thank you."

The patrons were embarrassed, having sat for three hours and having not even ordered dinner. Yet, they admitted to being full and feeling quite satisfied. They immediately asked for coffee, the bill and inquired if the bar was open.

Pierre looked at Michelle as they moved to the second table, "That was easy, let's see how this one goes."

"Let me do the talking," Michelle volunteered.

"Certainly, it will be good practice for you," Pierre allowed.

The two walked to the next table, a party of four young men. "Excuse me, gentlemen. Our second seating is at 9 p.m. We must clear the table and prepare for our next seating. May we ask you to finish your meal, settle the bill, and leave the table?" Michelle said in a sugary voice, a voice that many might find a bit patronizing.

"We're still thinking about dinner. We need more time to decide," one of the men replied, obviously feeling little pain.

Pierre stepped in, "Gentlemen, unless you have reservations for the second seating, the first seating is over, and we ask that you move from the table."

"Who do we see about reservations for the second seating? We like it here and would like to try the food," another said, just as inebriated as the other.

"I'm sorry, but the second seating is full. We have no available tables." Pierre said, glad to get rid of these drunks.

"Wait, I know you. I know. I saw your picture; you're the mayor. That's not fair; why did you call the mayor to ask us to leave?" the first man spoke again, while the others chuckled, that senseless chuckle indicative of drunk men.

"We voted for you, so I hope we can stay. Didn't we vote?" a third man added.

"No, but if we would have, we could have," the first man said, laughing and slurring and getting the words backward.

"Look, boys…" Pierre tried one more time to ask them to cooperate, "Let's be reasonable. We run a restaurant. We like it to be a nice place. This isn't a place to drink your dinner. This isn't a place for you to sit for hours on end, drinking. We ask nicely that you settle your bill and leave, allowing us to prepare for the next seating."

"Your girl is awfully cute. Is that your girl? I think we should become acquainted." One of the men reached for Michelle's hand.

Michelle saw it coming and moved out of the man's way, causing him to miss. Suspended in air and grasping for support, he fell out of his chair onto the dining room floor. He emitted a loud moan. The man nearest

Pierre, shouted "Aldo, why did you hit my brother?" He rose from his chair, with a clenched fist and with all the force he could muster, struck Pierre on the side of the head, snapping his head to the side, taking him off his feet and causing him to fall to the floor, where he lay unconscious.

Another one of the men, surprised and not understanding what was happening, quickly stood up, tipping the table over onto his friend, who didn't appreciate losing his glass of cognac, especially all over his lap. He stood up and threw a punch as hard as he could at his dinner companion, missing the man by a good half a meter and hitting the brick wall. He screamed loudly at the pain from what must have been a dozen broken bones in his hand. He recoiled and literally jumped on his friend. The two fell backward onto the next table and rolled to the floor, tipping over a third table, smashing glasses, chairs, and plates.

The man called Aldo stood up, wavering a bit, not recalling fully what had happened. He looked at Michelle and smiled, leaning over, trying to make contact, "You're awfully cute. Let me have a kiss, just one little kiss?"

Michelle slapped the man across the face. "Don't ever touch me," she said with a vengeance and stood back.

Aldo, surprised and not anticipating her rejection, suddenly turned from adoration to meanness and hate. He slapped Michelle hard, with the back of his hand, turning her face bright red as it started to swell. "Don't ever tell me what I can and can't touch. You started this. You and this clown in the suit."

Peter Fawcett, Claire's father, had just entered the front door with his four sons, four large strapping farm boys. He wasn't sure what was going on, but he jumped in without hesitating when he saw the man strike Michelle. He walked up to the man called Aldo, grabbed him by the collar, and said, "You are a brave man hitting a woman, now hit me. I dare you to hit me. I will tear your head off like a chicken's, you coward."

Aldo gave Peter a smirk and tried to twist out of his grip. Peter Fawcett became so enraged he couldn't control himself. He struck Aldo twice with his fist, wanting to wipe the silly drunken grin off his face. Without much effort, Peter dragged the young man up the stairs by the scruff of the neck and out into the parking lot, throwing him to the ground. His sons followed along, dragging the other three men. All four rolled and writhed on the ground, one of them grabbing his swollen and broken hand. Aldo was clutching his jaw where Peter Fawcett had landed his blows. In the distance, sirens could be heard as gendarmes from the next town over signaled they're on their way.

"You don't know what you just did," one man said, talking to the crowd that had gathered. "We were sitting there innocently enough, trying to order dinner, when this idiot in a red suit attacked us. I saw it all. He hit my brother hard enough he fell out of his seat onto the floor. Then the girl kicked him. I saw it with my own two eyes. You people are in trouble. Do you know who I am? Somebody, call my agent."

Michelle came out of the Bistro and stood over the men, her face nicely swollen from Aldo's hand. "How dare you create a disturbance in our place of business? I hope the law puts you behind bars where you belong. Here's your bill. Pay it, or are you nothing but drunken deadbeats?"

The man laughed, "I'm not paying anything. You'll be behind bars before I am, cupcake. Maybe if you apologize, I won't press charges." The man paused for a minute, then laughed and continued, "Yeah. I tell you what, here's the deal. You apologize, fix me dinner, and then we'll get cozy, know what I mean? And then, maybe, I'll drop charges. "

Michelle was about to spit on the man when a boot came out of nowhere, hitting the man squarely in the chest, knocking him flat over. "You really need to be taught manners." A man's voice spoke.

Michelle turned to find Marco Fawcett, Claire's eldest brother, standing next to her, shaking his head in disgust at the four animals.

"Thank you," she said quietly.

"Entirely, my pleasure," he said, looking at the man in disgust.

The man sat up, trying to shake the cobwebs from his head, "You people have no clue. Don't you have any idea? You people really don't recognize who I am? This is going to be painful, but not for me. Somebody, call my agent."

Inside, Maria and Daniel knelt over Pierre. Maria held Pierre's head in her hands. She was in shock, "No, please no, please no, oh God." She repeated, over and over again.

Daniel was busy cutting steak when the violence erupted. Hearing screams and furniture breaking, he came from the kitchen, only to see Peter hit a man twice and drag him out the door. He saw Pierre's maroon jacket on the floor and ran to his side, meat clever still in his hand, beef blood all over his apron. "Who did this? I want to know. Who did this?" he screamed.

Daniel started to go outside, but Maria, afraid of what Daniel might do with the large meat cleaver, stopped him. "Please, Daniel, stay with me. Stay with me, please."

Daniel stopped and turned around, coming back to stand by Pierre's unconscious body. He set the meat clever down, and with tears in his eyes, said, "Why would someone want to do this to Pierre? My loving brother. Why?"

Daniel fell to his knees next to Maria, wrapping his arm around her. She leaned over and cried into his shoulder.

Chapter 31

The Gendarmes arrived, as did an ambulance filled with paramedics. Pierre remained unconscious on the dining room floor. The paramedics, fearing possible spinal injuries or brain trauma and swelling, called for a medical helicopter. The helicopter was there in 35 minutes and airlifted Pierre to the large, modern regional hospital in Bordeaux. A team of doctors and nurses worked all night, stabilizing his vital signs and reducing the swelling in his brain. By morning, he was moved to intensive care, where he remained unconscious, in critical but stable condition.

The officer-in-charge asked everybody to wait until told to leave. This was a serious incident, and the officer wanted everybody's account of events. After listening to a few eyewitness accounts and taking statements from a few patrons who were seated nearby, it became apparent the four men were lying. The officer-in-charge was experienced and separated all involved before taking their statements. While the eyewitnesses and Michelle gave nearly identical accounts, each of the four young men gave a different account of the events leading up to, during, and after the incident.

The man with the swollen, broken hand claimed Michelle pushed him to the floor, after which she deliberately stepped on his hand, crushing it into pieces. The gendarmes laughed at the man's insistence that a 52-kilogram woman was able to crush his hand while the man lay there on the floor, unwilling or unable to do anything about it.

"Well, she's a woman; what am I supposed to do? I was taught to respect women," the man insisted.

"Too bad your friend didn't have the same upbringing," The gendarme replied, a look of disbelief and disdain on his face.

Aldo, the man who slapped Michelle, claimed she had tripped over Pierre, who had fallen because he was drunk. He claimed she hit her face when she fell, and he was trying to help her up when suddenly this ape of a man started hitting him. He told the interviewing officer, "We were getting along nicely; she even asked if I was doing anything later. I think that guy is too old to have such a young girlfriend. I bet she needs a good…"

The gendarme stood up, smacked Aldo across his face with his glove, and ordered, "Shut your mouth, or the ride to jail will not be so pleasant."

Aldo smiled at the man, "I'll make sure you pay for that." Aldo spit something from his mouth onto the pavement. "You are brave when I am handcuffed but take the shackles off and let's see how brave you are. I will kill you without hesitation."

"Threatening an officer? I will add that to your charges. Would you care to dig a deeper hole for yourself?" the officer smirked at Aldo, hoping to have a chance to teach this man a lesson.

The man that hit Pierre, Sameed Monsour, claimed they were just getting up to leave when this man in the red jacket bumped into him and fell. "He must have hit his head on the table. I heard a bang, and the man was there on the floor, unconscious."

Sameed further claimed, he never laid a hand on him. He also stated that Peter was jealous, jealous that Aldo was flirting with his girl. He said Peter hit Aldo repeatedly out of jealousy. "I saw it with my own two eyes. Right in front of me, boom, boom, boom. The man kept punching Aldo. I tried to step in, but these four farmer-looking goons held me back. A good thing too, or I would have killed that man. No one attacks my brother and gets away with it, no one."

The last man had no idea what had happened. "One minute I'm sitting there, enjoying a conversation with friends, the next minute I'm on the ground, with my friend laying on top of me. It happened so fast. I don't really recall anything. But we were peaceful, minding our own business, getting ready to leave. We weren't looking for trouble."

The gendarme asked how the tables were knocked over and broken. "I don't know what happened to the tables. Someone must have pushed them over on top of us," the man said innocently.

The four men were handcuffed, formally charged with numerous serious crimes, and driven away in a police van. Later, the prisoners were handed over to the Federal Police, the Carabinieri, and placed in a regional prison till Monday, when formal charges would be filed.

Meanwhile, Maria closed the Tree Trunk until further notice. Photographers came and took more pictures of the crime scene and more pictures of Michelle's bruised face.

The inn stayed open, but Maria asked everyone to respect her wishes and let the bistro remain closed. She found it difficult to enter the dining room. Everything reminded her of Pierre and the events that had transpired that evening. She found it difficult to stand where Pierre stood and received the blow that may have ended his life. She sat for hours staring at the large fireplace, a small fire still burning. She cried and prayed. *Why, why our family? Oh, Lord, haven't we sacrificed enough? Please, Lord, take me, take anything from me, but don't harm my family. They are innocent and mean well. Please.* She prayed and cried, cried some more, and prayed.

The next day, Maria and Michelle took Pierre's Citroen and drove to the hospital in Bordeaux. There the two sat by Pierre's bedside, waiting, hoping, praying for him to wake up.

Michelle sat and read to Pierre. Sometimes, she talked to him, "Uncle Pierre, if you can hear me, this is Michelle. Did I ever tell you that you are my favorite uncle? I love Daniel and the entire family, but when I need help and guidance, I think about what my Uncle Pierre would do. You don't know this, but you have helped me so many times, and I want to thank you. I wish you would wake up so I can tell you in person."

The two women sat for days by Pierre's side, taking turns to freshen up in the hospital lavatory, going out and finding something to bring back to the hospital to eat, neither one of them having much of an appetite, nor feeling the urge or need to sleep. Frequently, they called home to update everyone on Pierre's condition.

Pierre's vital signs were stable, and tests showed somewhat normal brain activity, showing he could breathe on his own. He just wasn't waking up. The hospital moved him out of intensive care to a small room by himself. The hospital also brought in a small cot so that Michelle and Maria could nap if they desired.

Five days after the incident, a doctor appeared, accompanied by a priest.

"Hello, I am Doctor Miranda. I am the Head Trauma Physician for the hospital. May I speak with you for a moment?" he said while standing in the doorway, wanting to establish respect and give Maria and Michelle all the personal space they needed.

"Yes, please come in, Doctor," Maria replied.

"Hello, I am Father Constantine. The Archbishop assigned me to attend to the patient's spiritual needs. May I join you as well?"

"Certainly, thank you, Father," Maria said. "This is my daughter, Michelle, and my name is Maria. The gentleman, eh, the patient, is my brother-in-law, Pierre."

The Father, getting a closer look at the emotionally drained faces of the two women, spoke as he pulled up a chair. "There is a small chapel on the top floor, which is always available if you need a moment for prayer or solace."

Maria managed to eke out a smile, "Thank you, Father."

The doctor pulled up a chair near the two women, "What I want to discuss, and determine, if possible, well, … The human body is remarkable for its resilience and its ability to replenish and heal itself. "

The Doctor never liked this part of his job, finding it difficult to judge people's emotional state. It seemed he was always too cold, too business-oriented, when he should have been warm and compassionate, and then too compassionate when he needed to be non-emotional and business-like.

The doctor continued, trying to find the middle ground, "But sometimes the task is too difficult, and the body cannot cope. Like a shop at the end of the day, it shuts itself off, closes down. The medical profession can do many things to keep the body going, but at the end of the day, if a body decides to shut down, it will. I speak metaphorically, but I hope you understand."

Maria asked politely, "Has Pierre's body decided to shut down?"

The doctor answered, "No, remarkably not. His body appears to be fighting back, trying to stay alive, but we are concerned about his brain. Tests have shown normal activity, there is blood flowing to his brain, and we have thinned his blood to prevent clots, but swelling is never good. We don't know if the swelling caused any permanent damage, and we don't know if he will ever come out of the coma."

"I see," Maria said to the doctor, her eyes wet. She tried to maintain her composure, but she found it difficult. As she listened, tears came slowly down her cheeks.

Michelle, sensing that the point of the visit was about to be revealed and it wasn't going to be pleasant, started crying softly at first. She found that her tears flowed easily. She lowered her head, hiding her face in her handkerchief, as wave after wave of grief racked her body. She wished this would all go away. How she wished!

The doctor paused for a moment while Maria reached for the box of tissues, pulling once, twice, three times to get the tissues she thought she needed for what she sensed was coming next.

"The longer the body is in this state, the more susceptible it becomes to various medical dilemmas. While certain parts are healing, other parts are having difficulty maintaining."

The doctor paused, trying to put this as humanely as possible. "I am here to ask you."

Here it comes, Maria thought to herself, *Be strong. Be strong for Pierre, for Michelle, for the family.*

"To what extent do you want us to help Pierre? If his body decides it's had enough and starts to shut down, do you want us to intervene?" The doctor looked straight at Maria, not showing any emotion, waiting for the tidal wave that just hit the woman to subside.

Father Constantine then spoke, "Or do you wish for God to show his mercy and compassion and take his child home?"

Maria looked away, focusing on nothing, and said, "Oh, God."

She took a minute to compose herself. Thinking about Pierre. *Now I really need you.* She finally spoke, "He is the second son of Roger and Patrice Villeneuve. I married the eldest, and I lost him to a terrorist attack. Pierre is the only real link I have to the past. He was the best man at our wedding. Now with my husband gone, I rely on him for so much; he keeps me grounded. I can't let him go." The tears were streaming down Maria's cheeks as she spoke, causing the doctor to hold out the box of tissues. She took another three, four tissues.

Michelle took a few tissues, quietly saying, "Thank you."

Maria continued after drying her eyes, "But he is a man of faith. I know he believes, and I know if he is called, he will answer. I know he would want me to give him to God's grace and love. I know he will recognize when it is time, and he would want me to let him go."

With that, the emotions erupted in her heart; she dropped her head and cried loudly, her body convulsing.

Father Constantine drew his chair closer and wrapped his arms around Maria. "Why, Father? Why Pierre? He is such a good man. He was trying so hard; all he wanted was to give. He wanted nothing in return. A smile perhaps; is it too much to ask for a smile?"

The doctor stood up and quietly said, "I will have a nurse draw up the papers. We will need your signature. Thank you, and I am very sorry. But he is a strong man. It is good that you sit with him, talk to him. People who have recovered from similar situations have reported that they were aware of what was happening around them but could not respond. So perhaps he is listening right now. "

Maria felt weak and totally drained. She felt so insecure; she needed to have her decision reaffirmed. She pulled her chair over closer to Pierre and brushed his hair. Fluffing his pillow and pulling his blanket up to his chest, she held his hand and looked at him, her heart full of love. She whispered, "I want you to stay. I so badly need you; the family needs you, but if you must go, I understand. If you feel it is time, then I won't stop you. It would be wrong for me to stop you. I want you to remember I will always love you like a brother, and I will always be there for you."

The nurse then entered the room with a clipboard, "Madam Villeneuve, would you please sign these papers?"

"Yes, what am I signing?" Maria asked.

"These are 'Do Not Resuscitate' orders. Didn't you just speak with Doctor Miranda?" she replied.

"Yes, I did. I am sorry." Maria took the papers and signed as required.

The nurse looked at the two women, "Madam, if I may make a suggestion?"

"Yes, of course," Maria said while handing the clipboard back to the nurse.

"Go home and sleep. Eat something, get some sleep, have a hot bath. Then in a day or two, come back. You are slowly torturing yourself and doing so won't change anything. You need to be strong. Don't you have a family? You should remember that other family members also have needs." The nurse attempted to remind Maria that life goes on, and she must continue for the sake of others.

"Yes, you are right." Maria looked at Michelle. Michelle looked back at her mother, her face completely void of color except for her large red, droopy eyes.

Maria spoke softly, pleading, "Sweetheart, let's go home."

The nurse interrupted Maria, "We have your phone. We will contact you immediately if there are any changes to the patient's condition."

"Yes, thank you." Maria turned and kissed Pierre on the cheek, whispering, "We will be back shortly." Then, amazingly, she joked, saying adamantly, "Don't go anywhere."

Michelle had to laugh. It felt so good after days of crying. She repeated the sentiment, "Yes, Uncle, don't go anywhere; we'll be back." Then Michelle got an eerie feeling, a strange feeling, stopping her in mid-step. She would swear she heard Pierre reply, "I'll be right here."

* * *

As the four men were transferred to the Federal Police and booked, several officers recognized two of the men. Sameer was Riki Rivage, and Aldo Monsour, Sameer's brother, was his singing partner, Aldo Aldo.

The two were pop music sensations across the French-speaking world and had recently made successful film debuts in the French remake of the Elvis Presley hit, "Beach Blanket Bingo."

Sameer contacted their agent, who immediately went into crisis mode, releasing press releases calling Michelle a liar and labeling her an old spinster who was just seeking money and attention. News stories were released stating the evidence clearly shows 'she assaulted Aldo and that Aldo never lifted a finger against her.' The press releases also said Michelle had a history of mental illness, starting while in University, where she had sought counseling.

The releases classified Pierre as a drunkard and womanizer who wanted to be mayor just to impress women. The releases claimed that Pierre had stumbled into Riki Rivage in a vain attempt to get his autograph and a picture taken with him.

The news releases were vicious, citing rumors and obvious falsehoods, but they succeeded in their goals with public opinion swinging back and forth but trending more and more in defense of the brothers.

Contrary to expectations, sales of Riki Rivage's and Aldo Aldo's music soared, and theaters showing their movie were sold out for weeks on end.

In a phone conversation from prison, Sameer's agent said this might have been the best thing to happen to his career. There were even inquiries from Hollywood, and studios were sending scripts, anticipating a quick trial, acquittal, and a boom in popularity.

Feeling confident with the positive direction of public opinion, Sameer and Aldo, with special permission from the Head Magistrate, held a press conference from the prison.

The two were held in special confinement for their safety and were not informed of recent events or the many press releases issued by their agent. In captivity, they were not allowed visitors except for barristers. The men had no time to be prepped by their agent; hence, they told what they knew when asked.

It was a fatal mistake.

Starting off, a member of the press asked, "Do you feel the legal system is singling you out?"

Both men replied, "Yes, very much so. We did none of these horrendous things, or at least we were provoked."

"Provoked? How so?" asked another reporter.

"I saw my brother attacked," said Sameer.

"By whom?" The reporter asked.

"By the woman and the big guy. You know the farmer," Sameer replied, trying to remember the story he gave to the police.

"The woman attacked your brother? He states that the woman tripped, and he helped her up." The reporter asked for clarification.

Sameer looked at his agent, "Yes, but once she was on her feet, she hit my brother."

Another reporter asked, "Aldo, what did you do when the woman attacked?"

"I hit her back," Aldo said with a smirk as if it was his right to do so.

"So, you did hit the woman," the reporter clarified.

"Yes. I slapped her across the face," Aldo said

The agent could be seen on the side vigorously shaking his head and mouthing the words, "No, no, no."

A murmur went through the press corps. Aldo, full of bravado on most days, thought, "I can handle this."

"Look, she slapped me first," he volunteered. "So, I slapped her back. In my culture, where I come from, it's appropriate to discipline a woman. My father slapped my mother on many occasions. It's how women learn to respect and do what they're told," he said proudly.

The reporter was amazed at Aldo's candid but totally insensitive statement. "What, if anything, did you do to provoke the woman into slapping you?"

"Nothing. Oh, I think, maybe, I wanted a kiss, or something like that. I had a few drinks, and she was friendly and attractive, so I thought, hey she might want to kiss a movie star. I thought I was doing her a favor, and so I went to kiss her, and she slapped me. So, like I was taught, I slapped her back. It was just a reaction. Nothing personal."

Still another reporter asked, "Sameer, were you provoked when you hit Mr. Villeneuve?"

"I don't recall hitting anybody," Sameer replied.

"Evidence points to you hitting Mr. Villeneuve unprovoked and actually hitting him quite hard. The man is still in the hospital," the reporter informed Sameer and watched for a reaction.

"The guy was drunk and fell," Sameer insisted.

"But there are several eye-witnesses who saw you strike the man with your fist," a reporter asked.

"They're lying," again, Sameer insisted.

The same reporter cut in, "Are you aware the man is in a coma and lucky the blow did not detach his head from his spine?"

"Serves him right," Sameer replied.

"Serves him right, how so?" a reporter asked.

"He attacked my brother. Nobody, nobody hurts my family without answering to me," Sameer said, agitated by the incessant questions. In his mind, he did the right thing in defending his family's honor.

"Aldo is your brother. Who attacked him?" a reporter, writing furiously, asked.

"The drunk man, the one in the red jacket. I saw him go after my brother, so I protected him," Sameer said proudly as if to say who wouldn't.

"How did you protect Aldo?" still another reporter asked.

"I hit the man as hard as I could on the side of the head. As he lay there, I looked at him and said, 'Don't you ever come after my family or me again,'" Sameer admitted proudly.

A reporter was confused, "So it is your contention that the man, Mr. Villeneuve, attacked your brother, so you hit him to protect your brother?"

"Yes, I was provoked," Sameer said as if that made all the difference.

The reporter spoke to Aldo, "Aldo, were you attacked by Mr. Villeneuve?"

"Yes, I guess so. If my brother says so, then it must be true," Aldo replied.

"But you have no recollection of being attacked by Mr. Villeneuve?" the reporter pressed on.

"Well, no, but that doesn't mean it's not true." Aldo tried to work his way around the increasingly uncomfortable situation.

The reporters laughed. One asked, "Aldo, if you don't recall it happening, but your brother said it did, you want us to believe your brother and not you?"

Aldo replied, "Look, I was drunk. It happened so fast. I don't know what happened every second. Give us a little leeway."

On the sidelines, Aldo's agent closed his eyes, put his head down, and shook it gently back and forth.

"You admit you were drunk?" a reporter asked.

"Yea, it was a Thursday night, and we'd been sitting there for almost three hours. We had some excellent wine, like five bottles: we were feeling no pain. Then this jerk comes along and says we must leave," Aldo stated while lighting a cigarette.

"So, you were drunk, not Mr. Villeneuve?

"Well, he was probably drunk too. Why else would he ask us to leave?" Aldo said as if it was obvious.

"In earlier statements, it was reported Mr. Villeneuve was drunk and stumbled into your party," a reporter reiterated.

"Yea, that too," Aldo said as he inhaled and blew smoke rings, apparently bored with the whole ordeal, bored with the details.

The reporter was amazed by the lack of consistency in their stories and pushed on, "Aldo, a gentleman sitting at your table stated to the police that he was pushed to the ground by Michelle Villeneuve and then his hand was deliberately crushed by means of her stepping on it. Did this happen before or after you slapped her?"

"I don't know. It must have been before, or maybe it was after," Aldo admitted, trying to look interested but not really caring.

"Do you recall it happening?" the reporter asked.

"Oh, yea, I remember, she ground her heel into his hand, like she was putting out a cigarette," Aldo answered, thinking that should make for good press.

"Yet, you did nothing?" the reporter asked Aldo point-blank.

"Well, I respect women. Sure, we give them a good slap every once in a while, to keep them in line. But if a woman is really putting it to my friend, I stand clear. I don't want any part of it," he admitted.

"Did you see this happen?" another reporter chimed in.

"Well, not really; I saw my friend holding his hand, saying it was broken. I assume it was the woman. How else could he come by a broken hand? I mean, Sameer had already laid out the old man, so it had to be the woman," Aldo stated, thinking it was obvious.

The reporter, not believing the absurdity of what was being said, clarified once more, "So again, just because you didn't see it doesn't mean it's not true."

Aldo, mistakenly thinking the reporters were on his side, replied ecstatically, "Exactly, now you're getting it." He was proud, proud in the clever way he had manipulated the press.

But their agent, fearing even worse, sprang into action and stepped onto the stage, "Ok, enough. That's all the time we have for questions. The conference is over, keep in mind that these recollections are not indicative of what really happened. They are only for entertainment purposes. "

The reporters all laughed as they filed out of the room, repeating what they just heard, "What does that mean, only for entertainment purposes?"

Feeling like a fool, the agent watched the reporters leave, and the guards enter and handcuff Sameer and Aldo. "Well, boys, that's it, you just admitted to assault and possibly murder. There is nothing else I can do for you except issue an apology to your fans. I'm sorry, good luck."

The Agent watched as guards led the two away, Sameer cursing under his breath and saying to Aldo, "What did you have to say that for?"

An hour later, charges of giving false evidence to police were added to the men's long list of charges.

Chapter 32

Maria and Michelle drove solemnly back to Saint Charles early Friday morning, two weeks and one day since the incident. As they entered the lobby, they could barely get to the front desk because of all the baskets of fruit and flower arrangements that lined the lobby walls. On the inn's counter were stacks of letters and cards. It was amazing to Maria and Michelle; many were sent not only from friends and acquaintances but also from complete strangers. Maria didn't realize how big this whole thing had become until they started sorting through the cards and letters, noticing postmarks from faraway places such as Australia, Japan, and the United States.

Maria and Michelle vowed to get back to the hospital and Pierre's side as soon as they were rested and felt confident leaving the inn and bistro. Maria wanted to re-open the bistro, knowing for many people it was the only diversion they had from their tough lives, eking out a living from the earth. She also knew she couldn't leave Daniel and Rudy just to sit and wait. She chided herself, "That would be asking for trouble."

She called a family meeting to get everyone's thoughts on opening the bistro. Daniel, as usual, was passionate about the choices the family must make. Not surprisingly, Rudy and Claire also shared his sentiment.

"We must open if only to have a limited menu. This town, these people, we care for each other, and we rely on each other. We need to be there for them, as they were for us. We are, for many folks, their only connection to the world. How can we remain closed? That is not what a Villeneuve would do. It is not what Roger would do. It is not what Pierre would do. I am Daniel Villeneuve, and I owe it to my brothers. I will not remain closed."

Tears formed in Maria's eyes as she listened to Daniel rant about justice and duty. She wasn't sure what sent her over the edge; the mention of Roger, of Pierre, perhaps just the thought, the possibility, Daniel, was the last of a family of truly magnificent men. Whatever it was, it overwhelmed her. For a minute, she felt hatred for the world. She wanted to scream. She wanted someone to tell her the world's a beautiful place, so she could scream and call them liars. She felt incapable, useless, and confused.

Maria shivered. It was more shaking off the lingering feelings of self-pity than a reaction to the temperature. As everyone looked at her, waiting for her decision, her advice, she thought to herself, *The family needs me now, stand up, be yourself, be someone.*

She remembered something Roger told her, years and years ago, "Being a leader must come from the heart. It is loving, caring for the people around you, and making decisions for the benefit of those you love while guiding them down a common path."

Daniel broke the silence, once again loud and defiant, "Are we cowards? Have we ever quit because of a setback? No, and we will not quit now. These animals ruined their lives. I will not let them ruin *mine* or *yours* or *yours* or *yours*," Daniel said as he pointed his finger at family members, one at a time, emphasizing the word *yours*.

Maria tried her best to be coherent. "What do you mean by a limited menu?" she asked.

"I could fire up the wood-burning oven." Rudy chimed in, "We could do simple preparations like chicken and beef filet. It was working well opening night."

Daniel added his thoughts, "We would do a limited menu because it will just be Rudy, Claire, and myself, and Claire is needed at the front desk.

Maria countered, "You will have Paul and Thomas. I am sure both of them would like to get back to work."

"Yes, but it is not the same." Daniel replied without hesitation, "Who will be Maître d'?"

"Paul is the most experienced. He can seat people. He knows what to do," Maria answered Daniel's question.

"Ok, but I will still want to have a limited menu. Pate, soup, a chicken dish or two, beef bourguignon, perhaps short rib, or a simple pot-au-feu. Then we have tarts, chicken, and filet from the wood-fired oven." Daniel thought for a second, then, looking up at everyone, announced, "If I add dessert, we have a complete menu; what am I talking about?"

Daniel laughed along with everyone, providing a moment of levity to the past days of sorrow and sadness. As everyone smiled and laughed, Maria could feel the stress level dropping, the tension easing. Then and there, it became obvious to her. She had to open the Tree Trunk.

"Ok, it's 9:30 a.m. Can we open for lunch? Let's aim for opening the doors at noon. Where are Paul and Thomas and the busboys?" Maria started to get into her stride again.

"I think they're out back playing cards. Thomas will be glad to get back to work; the busboys are killing him playing five-card," Rudy replied happily.

"Good. Claire, could you fetch the boys? Rudy, could you light a fire in your oven, and if you have a moment, throw a couple of logs in the fireplace," Maria spoke, and people moved.

"Daniel?" Maria asked.

"Yes, that's me. What can I do for you?" Daniel stopped as he was walking to the kitchen, in his mind sorting through what he needed to do first.

Maria walked up to tall, lanky masculine Daniel, looked up to him, and smiled warmly. "Thank you," she said.

Daniel looked down at her, knowing what she meant, knowing she was sincere, genuinely thankful. He put his arms around her, giving her a bit of a hug, and whispered, "I am here for you and the family."

Just then, Claire came bounding around the corner. "The boys said they would just need to get cleaned up and dressed. They'll be here in 30 minutes."

"Good." Maria surveyed the dining room, "Let's get the busboys to do a quick sweep and straighten out the tables. Also, can we open the doors to the veranda? A little fresh air and sunshine will do us all good."

Claire went over to the veranda doors, opening them and locking them in place. A light, warm breeze swept into the dining room, refreshing the air and giving it a slightly sweet taste.

"*Wonderful,*" was Claire's sentiment.

"Perfect," was Maria's response as she smiled back at Claire.

"I am glad the doors will open." Claire confided to Maria, "People sitting idle helps no one. It gives people more time to cry, to pity themselves. Pierre is a fine man, and I pray he recovers, but meanwhile, we must continue. I think you are correct. and I want you to know I admire your decision."

"Thank you, Claire, that's very nice of you to say." Maria smiled, and together they walked from the dining room to the inn's lobby, where Michelle had already started to sort the mail and remove some of the older, less healthy-looking flower arrangements.

"Well, we sure have a lot to do here." Maria stopped, looking over what was once her elegant, clutter-free lobby. "Why don't we start by moving the flower arrangements to the entrance of the bistro? That's where Pierre worked; that was his world. When I go back to the hospital, I will bring some of the flowers with me. His room needs a bit of color. But for now, let's put them in the entranceway of the Tree Trunk, next to his podium. "

Maria laughed, "*Needing a bit of color,*" she repeated. It was a phrase she heard Pierre say many times.

Rested, bathed, and replenished, Maria and Michelle loaded Pierre's Citroen with flower arrangements and get-well cards. Obviously, Pierre couldn't read the cards, but Maria wanted them there for when he woke up.

Michelle went to Pierre's apartment and took a few books from his collection to read to him. She remembered he always liked adventure stories; looking at his titles, she found Robison Crusoe, Tarzan of the Apes, and The Count of Monte Cristo. "Three ought to do it," she thought as she grabbed the books and headed back out to the car.

On the way to the hospital, Michelle got to thinking, "Mother, how do you suppose Riki Rivage came to attend opening night? I mean, doesn't it seem odd that Riki and Aldo and their entourage just happened to be driving around remote farmlands, far from any civilized town, far from what guys like that look for; they come upon our place, on opening night, and get a table for four? They must have had an invitation. But who sent it, or how did they get it? I made the guest list, and for sure, I did not invite Riki Rivage."

"Well, they got there and got in, somehow." Michelle's mother was driving and daydreaming, not paying much attention to what Michelle was getting at.

Hearing her mother's reply, Michelle wanted her to pay attention. Michelle was serious and thought her questions important and deserving of answers. "Really, Mother, think about it. We stage an event and invite all our friends. These thugs show up, ruin the party, and even put one of us in the hospital. Something just doesn't add up. I'm beginning to think we were sabotaged."

Maria politely laughed at her daughter's ideas and choice of words. "Sabotaged. You think someone deliberately came to our opening to what? Harm us?"

"I don't know; putting it that way does sound a little odd, far-fetched. "Michelle sat quietly for a moment, wondering if she was just paranoid. She remembered from her college days, *Just because you are paranoid doesn't mean they are not out to get you*. She smiled, thinking about all those old weird sayings from college days.

She let her mind wander, going off on a tangent. *What were some of those funny sayings; some of them were too true. Oh, I remember; the only certainty in life* is *death and taxes*. She liked that one. Michelle then remembered Murphy's law, *Anything that can go wrong, will,* and then as a follow-up, she and her friends would always reply that *Murphy was an optimist*. She smiled, thinking of her circle of friends at the university, how they swore they would always be friends, and how quickly everyone went their separate ways. "*Well, that's life*," she thought.

"I guess we'll have to wait to find out," Maria added, keeping the conversation going.

"What? What do you mean, Mother?" Michelle was suddenly brought back to the present from her dreaming of her past.

"Well, Pierre was Maitre'd. He would have accepted their invitation and seated them. Wouldn't he have?" Maria asked rhetorically.

"Sure, or at least crossed them off the guest list. You are right. They couldn't have been walk-ins. We were fully booked. We'll have to wait to get Pierre's story. I wonder what happened to his clipboard. Have you seen it?" Michelle asked her mother.

After thinking for a minute, Maria answered, "No, but to be honest, I haven't really looked for it. It could be sitting there at the podium."

"It probably is. I don't remember him carrying it. I wonder if he made any notations. Well, at least we can see the names that were crossed off," Michelle added.

Just as a lark, not even half-serious, but perhaps as a direction worth exploring, Michelle wondered out loud, "I wonder if Louisa had anything to do with this?"

Maria smiled, "I had thought that, but was hoping it wasn't so."

"Yes, it's ugly to think, but she is in Paris, and you know, she considers herself *quite the celebrity*, "Michelle said with a bit of a flourish, causing Maria to laugh. Then more seriously, she added, "She's a big enough jerk herself; she could easily have other jerks, like Aldo Aldo and Riki Rivage as friends." She looked out the window, disgusted, but more so in herself for being petty and calling people names.

"I can't picture Louisa sending people to us with instructions to disrupt the evening. It doesn't make sense. She left the inn wanting to come back, telling us we were special," Maria replied seriously.

"Maybe we insulted her?" Michelle guessed. "She bumped an article to give us publicity, and without telling her, we closed down for seven weeks and took off for the States." Michelle then laughed, "Maybe she was insulted we didn't ask her to come too. Can you imagine six weeks with Louisa? What a disaster."

"You didn't call and tell her?" Maria asked.

"No, I was about to, but reading Louisa's articles, everything has a double meaning. She read me the title of her article. It sounded funny. Something about it sounded odd. When I finally figured out what her title meant, I couldn't; I just couldn't speak with her," Michelle admitted, again feeling petty but justified. She knew, though, her notion, her actions were meaningless unless Louisa was informed. She just didn't dare to confront her because Louisa was much more valuable as a friend.

The two drove along, picturing Louisa joining them on their trip.

Maria and Michelle giggled at the thought of a half-dressed Louisa riding in the back seat with her gaudy sunglasses, taking large gulps from a bottle of rum, and smoking one cigarette after another, referring to everyone as 'Darling' or 'Doll.'

"She probably would have insisted on stopping every five minutes to use a restroom," Maria said.

Michelle added, "Or stopping to buy more cigarettes. Can you imagine if she ever ran out? She'd go crazy." Michelle paused, then continued, "I can just picture Daniel, fed up, and wanting to sneak away in the middle of the night, leaving her behind in some flea-infested motor court." Michelle laughed, adding, "I bet she wouldn't have made it out of Canada. I can picture Daniel slipping the border guard 100 euros to detain her."

Maria laughed, "Can you imagine Daniel insisting to the authorities, 'keep her, don't send her back to France, please, we don't want her, you keep her.'"

The two women had a good laugh at Louisa's expense as they barreled down the road, the city of Bordeaux off in the distance.

* * *

Daniel looked again at the note Gabriella had given Michelle to give to him. Before folding it up for what seemed like the 100th time, he repeated her words over and over again. He kept asking himself, *Why am I hesitating? She is the perfect woman, and she is willing. Why can't I simply call her?* Late into the night, he sat by himself in the main dining room, warm fire at his feet, nursing a glass of cognac, the bottle not far away.

He felt hands on his shoulders, comforting hands. He turned to see Claire, "Oh, hello Claire, I didn't hear you come in. You startled me. Pull up a chair; let me pour you a Cognac." He pulled a chair closer, relieved to have some company. It allowed him to forget for the moment, Gabrielle, freeing his mind from the agony he was putting himself through.

"No, please, I am fine. Thank you. I couldn't sleep, so I thought I would check the front desk and make sure the doors were locked. I hope I didn't interrupt you," she said softly, immediately putting Daniel at ease. He wondered what made her voice so soothing. It was soft, clear, emotional, loving. *Gabrielle's voice is very similar,* he thought, grimacing, as once again, she was on his mind.

"Why the funny face? Is something troubling you? Would you like to talk about it?" Claire acknowledged, seeing the look Daniel just made.

"It's just Gabrielle. I don't know what to do. I want to connect with her, but I am acting like a coward. I don't know what to do?" Daniel admitted, staring into the fire.

"Well, I tell you. Men always have trouble with women, and women always have trouble with men; it's inevitable. Women see the world in entirely different ways from men, so of course, there will be misunderstandings." She tried to comfort Daniel, letting him know it's just part of life.

"Yes, I realize that, but why am I afraid to contact her? I am spineless. I am like a young boy who has a crush on his teacher. I think about her all the time, but I cannot find the courage to talk with her. What is wrong with me?" Daniel replied.

"Daniel, I know you are not bashful. Why you hesitate, I believe, is because, in your mind, this woman is perfect, and the more you think about her, the greater she becomes to the point she is beyond perfection. I think you are afraid she will not be perfect," Claire counseled Daniel.

"Is that what you think? I wonder if it is true?" Daniel looked surprised, not really thinking about the rationale Claire just exposed.

"My advice: call her. Be honest. Tell her you cannot stop thinking of her. She will appreciate your honesty and tell you things that she wants you to know. There is no reason to lie; trust me, she doesn't want to be impressed.

There is no reason to tell her things to impress her. Your being honest will impress her. Tell her how you feel, how you felt when you first saw her. That is what she wants to hear. Then if there is an attraction between you two, it will come out. But don't be concerned about perfection. It is for fairy tales." Claire spoke to Daniel, giving him all the warmth and kindness she had.

"But remember, she is a woman, and you are a man. It is simple. She needs you, and you need her." She smiled as Daniel got up and finished his cognac.

"Thank you, Claire; it's late, but are the phones working?" Daniel asked.

"Of course, the phones work all the time," she replied.

"I want to call her now. I cannot wait any longer. I must call her," Daniel insisted. "Show me how to work the phones, please; here is her number." Daniel handed the note to Claire.

Claire looked at the note, "Daniel, this woman, Gabrielle, she wrote this, and you hesitate? Can't you see her desire? This woman is very passionate," she scolded Daniel. "Men. Sometimes I think you are all children, deaf, dumb, and blind children."

Claire led Daniel to the office, where she told him to "sit, get comfortable, it may be a long conversation." She took his empty glass and went to the kitchen to make cappuccinos, returning shortly.

"Ok, are you ready?" she asked Daniel while sipping her cappuccino, wishing she had added a bit more cinnamon.

"Yes, please. Call her," Daniel replied.

Claire dialed the number and handed the phone to Daniel, slowly moving outside the office but staying within hearing distance.

The phone rang several times before finally, "Hello?"

"Hello, Gabrielle? Daniel here. How are you?" Daniel replied.

"Daniel, what a pleasant surprise. I didn't expect to hear from you. Well, I thought, or rather hoped, you would call sooner," Gabrielle said softly, unsure of where she stood.

"Yes, I wanted to call sooner. I have been thinking about you. Every day I have been thinking of you. Every minute of every day, I have been thinking of you. But I had some issues I had to work out with myself. I am sorry, I was a coward, and I was afraid to call," Daniel said, thinking he's never admitted this to a woman, but it was true, and he felt stronger after admitting it.

"I have been thinking about you. I put in my papers. I am retiring from flying, and my last flight is in two weeks," she replied.

"That's great. You must come to Saint Charles. I will reserve you a room at the inn. I want to show you my kitchen, and we just had the dining room renovated and a veranda built. It is beautiful and romantic. I sit out on the veranda, and I picture you sitting next to me, holding my hand. I want you to come. Please say you will."

"That's wonderful, Daniel. Of course, I will come, but I fly to Los Angeles tomorrow, and I layover a day before I fly back. I won't be back till Thursday. May I come for the weekend? I can drive to you Friday and return Monday. My last flight leaves that Tuesday."

"I will make a reservation for you, three nights, Friday, Saturday, Sunday. I don't know how busy I will be, but I will make time for you. We are on reduced hours. We had an incident, and we are still recovering." Daniel informed her, then thinking out loud, "Perhaps I can drive with you back to Paris and wait for you to return. I have many friends working in the hospitality industry; it has been a while since I last saw them. I want to visit them."

"But your kitchen? Won't you be missed?" Gabrielle asked.

"I will need to make arrangements, but it can be done. Again, we are on limited hours. We had an incident, a fight. Some thugs came to our opening and caused trouble. My brother is in a coma. It is terrible," Daniel replied.

"Oh, my Lord, I heard about this. That was your place? The two drunken rock stars who attacked the Maitre'd. That was your brother?"

"Yes, and remember Michelle, sitting next to me on the flight?" Daniel asked.

"Yes, of course, she was very nice. I liked her immediately," Gabrielle replied.

"She was the one they slapped. Her face is still bruised," Daniel told her.

"Terrible. I'm so sorry" was all Gabrielle could say, feeling very apologetic. She had believed the papers and the original story, thinking the boys were being provoked and taken advantage of.

"Pray for my brother's recovery. He is a good man. But now, it is late. I must go, but I am very happy we talked. Very happy we have made plans," Daniel said, tired from the stress he put himself through and relieved she seemed exactly as he remembered.

"I am very happy, too, Daniel. Thank you for calling. I look forward to my visit. I look forward to spending time with you."

"Thank you. Goodbye for now," Daniel said as he hung up.

Daniel looked at Claire, "I need a cognac."

Claire laughed, "I am sorry, Daniel, for eavesdropping, but listening to your conversation…."

"Yes?" Daniel opened his eyes wide, looking at Claire.

"It sounded like two people in love," she said, smiling at Daniel, whose cheeks blushed brightly with cherry-pink color.

Chapter 33

The women returned to Saint Charles late Thursday afternoon after spending the week at Pierre's side. He had shown little change during the week, and that worried Maria.

She was beginning to think of *what*-ifs, the unspeakable scenarios. What if he never recovers? What if his condition deteriorates? She didn't want to think about it, but she supposed someone had to. She was the head of the family, and it was her responsibility to make sure everyone was cared for, was safe, was fed, and sheltered. *Besides...* she thought, *if not her, then who?*

After spending the last three nights at the hospital, Maria relaxed in bed, feeling warm and safe the first night at home. She pondered, "*Why was this burden put upon me? Why was I singled out? Of all the people that existed, of all the family members, if I had to choose someone for the role as head of the family, I would be the last person I would choose. What was it about me that I was singled out? Why did I have to prove myself, or is that why? Is this my test?*

She contemplated lying quietly in bed and viewing the stars from her loft out the large front window of her unit. All the units had tall ceilings in the living areas that were cut off by lofts, intended to be sleeping areas. Large front windows allowed buckets of light to enter, illuminating the space practically all day. At night, those same windows gave spectacular views of the dark sky and the celestial dance that played out every night amongst the planets and stars.

She thought of her late husband. She had spent so much time thinking of Pierre; she had overlooked Roger. She smiled at his memory. *He's somewhere out there. I know he is. And I know he is in touch with Pierre, telling him, 'it's not time. I will let you know, but for now, it is not time.'* Maria tucked her head under the blankets, feeling snug and secure. She closed her eyes, knowing that soon, soon, she would have Pierre back. She fell off to sleep, a peaceful smile on her face.

Maria woke early, feeling refreshed and ambitious. *Today is a fine day, a day to get things done*, she thought to herself, sitting at her small dining table, sipping her coffee, watching the shadows dissipate, and the sky brighten as the sun rose higher and higher in the morning sky. *I have no idea what needs to get done, but I'm sure there's something.*

Michelle also woke early, but unlike her mother, Michelle felt lazy, not wanting to get out of bed. She cried out to the world as she stretched underneath her covers. *Go away. Not interested. Come back another time.*

Michelle felt tortured, singled out as she finally got out of bed and made her way to the bath for a hot shower she hoped would take away the cobwebs that spun through her head and influenced her thoughts. "Oh, why me? *Why me?*" she said out loud, knowing there was no one to provide an answer but not caring.

It wasn't till 9 a.m. that Michelle finally made it to the inn's front desk. A few guests were in the process of checking out. Claire was busy stapling copies of receipts together and having people sign for the various charges incurred during their stay.

It all seemed routine, even a bit mundane to Michelle, as she tried to be perky and energetic but failed, "Good morning Claire, anything interesting to report?"

"No, just the usual, oh, I forgot to mention. While you were gone, Louisa called for you. I tried to take a message, but she wanted to talk to you. She was especially eager to talk just to you."

"Ok, I'll call her. It's still early; I'll call in an hour or so," Michelle replied, starting to feel depressed, gloomy.

"Are you alright, tired? I don't mind working if you want to go back to bed," Claire advised Michelle, noticing Michelle's sagging shoulders and less-than-usual upbeat disposition.

"No, if I lay in bed all day, then I'd really get depressed. I just need to do something. I need to do something challenging, mentally challenging. My brain just needs a good workout," Michelle admitted as she did the best she could and smiled an insincere smile.

"Well, thank you for trying to be cheerful," Claire said sincerely. "I wish I could help you."

"I'm so sorry Claire, you are a sweetheart, and I appreciate your asking and caring. I don't mean to be ugly with you or anybody. I guess I just think about my potential, and then I look at my job as a hotel clerk. I wonder what all my education was for. Why didn't I just do like Rudy and spend the time and money backpacking through the Himalayas? I tell you, Rudy seems so balanced, so at peace with himself. He's brilliant and so even-tempered. Nothing fazes him. Nothing. Why couldn't I be like Rudy?" Michelle blurted out almost in frustration.

"You couldn't be like Rudy because you were busy being Michelle." Claire seemed to be so good at simple answers that made a lot of sense. She continued, but was more serious, probing, "I don't mean to get too personal; I love you as my sister, and I want the very best for you. So please don't hate me for saying this, but have you ever thought you might have come back too soon? That maybe you should have stayed in the States a few more years? I mean, it seems like you go through this self-hatred occasionally, and lately, this mood of yours has appeared many times, much more frequently. I wonder if that is what is causing this. You prepared for Wall Street...." Claire was talking, slowly following Michelle when Michelle cut her off.

Michelle was in tears, tears that Claire hadn't noticed, "Stop, please stop. Don't say anymore. You are right. I am so ashamed. I am so ashamed and frustrated. This is a lovely place; the family is so supportive, kind, loving. It is what I needed at the time. But I can't help thinking, I spent so much money and time, sweat and sacrifice, building a resume, creating a skill set, and now that I have it, I'm letting it go, and in favor of what? Choosing whether a party of four should be given to Thomas or Paul? Is that now my primary skill?" Michelle astonished Claire with the sharpness of her ridicule and self-loathing.

"Maitre'd is nothing to be ashamed of," Claire said softly but firmly. "But if it bothers you, then just remember, it's your family business. Everything you do is for your family. I wouldn't care if I had to clean toilets. If it were for the family, I'd clean that toilet like it's never been cleaned before, and when I finished, I'd stand tall and say, I did my best. Believe me."

Michelle laughed. She laughed because she was so tired of crying. And amazingly, Claire made sense; she made so much sense. Michelle remembered thinking she would get the best education money could buy, get the best job, and work for the most exclusive of investment banks. What motivated her? She didn't know, but it seemed everyone had opportunities, and she didn't want to be left behind. *No, it could not be?"* she said to herself, sitting in the office. *Did I do all that out of sheer peer pressure? Because I didn't know what else to do? Everyone else was going in that direction, so I just followed along. But I didn't know what else to do.*

She had admitted it to herself before but thought it nonsense, just a poor mood. She was capable; she was smart, more intelligent than many others. But banking was an alien world. She wanted prestige, entrance to the magical world of high finance, and she got it, but she felt so out of place, awkward and alone once there. No one was like her, no one to talk to, to lean on; she couldn't wait to get out.

Michelle sat in the quiet office, one minute self-doubting, the next self-loathing, the next self-pitying. *I am so confused. I wish I were stupid. I really do, stupid with no ability to look inward. I swear I am going to investigate getting a lobotomy.*

The phone rang. Michelle picked up, "Hello, the Inn at Saint Charles en Libertee'. How may I help you?" she said pleasantly, glad to be distracted from her phobias.

"Hello, this is Louisa Duggart calling for Michelle Villeneuve. Is she available, please?" Louisa's unmistakable voice pierced into Michelle's so-so mood.

"Hi, Louisa. This is Michelle. Please accept my apologies for not being available to accept your calls. I have been spending a lot of time at the hospital with my uncle."

"No issues, my dear woman. Please, that is what I am calling about. I have been utterly sleepless myself. My conscience would not let me rest until I expressed my sincere apologies and best wishes for your dear uncle's speedy recovery," Louisa said in her perfectly practiced voice, choosing the right words as if she were reading from a script.

"Thank you for your thoughts and prayers, but no apologies needed. There was nothing that was your fault," Michelle replied, thinking it odd Louisa would admit to anything.

"Well, that's where you are wrong. You will hate me for what I am about to say, but I swear on the apostle's graves that I will make it up to you. I will make it right, as my name is Louisa Heloise Malvasia Duggart."

Michelle believed Louisa had something important to say; she just wasn't sure she wanted to hear it. She just wasn't sure, but then finally decided. "Well, if you have something you need to get off your conscience, I'm listening, all ears."

"I received your invitation to the re-opening and RSVP'd intending to go. But then, at the last minute, I got a chance to go aboard this Prince's royal yacht for a weekend cruise to La-La land, if you know what I mean. An opportunity like that comes only once in a lifetime," she said to Michelle.

"No problem, I understand. I'm not offended," Michelle replied, actually happy she didn't show up.

"Well, I thought it would be crass to cancel my reservation at the last moment, and I didn't want you to have an empty table on your big night," she added, not yet finished with what she had to say.

"Thank you. That's considerate of you," Michelle replied, waiting for the punch line.

"So I sent Riki Ravage and Aldo Aldo in my place instead," Louisa said quickly, hoping Michelle wouldn't react. But there was silence. A silence so thick, so immense, it would smother a herd of elephants.

Michelle's face went completely white; her hands trembled. She wanted to say so many things, but it was all flashing through her mind at once. She tried to say everything, and there was just too much to say. Stunned, she just stared into the wall as if she were looking far into the distance. Finally, she spoke slowly and softly, "Thank you, Louisa, thank you for the call. Have a good day," ending the call.

As she hung up the phone, Louisa could be heard saying, "Michelle, I'm so sorry. I'll make it up to you, I promise. Michelle?"

Michelle, feeling dead to the world, confused, and sick to her stomach, slowly got up from the desk. She found Claire in the kitchen flirting with Rudy, "Claire, could you fill in for me at the front desk? I need time alone," Michelle said to Claire.

"Certainly. What's the matter? You don't look so good," Claire responded, concerned with what had come over Michelle. She followed her out of the kitchen.

"I just need time alone. I just want to be alone." She walked to the front desk, leaving Claire in charge, and then went through the back to her apartment. Inside, Michelle went to her bath, fell on her knees, and became painfully ill.

Afterward, she washed her face and hands, brushed her teeth, and lay down to take a nap, all the while wondering if her family will ever forgive her.

* * *

Michelle didn't really nap; she just lay on her bed, with a blank face and a blank mind. She stared out the window, only occasionally noticing a bird flying by or a plane way off in the distance. But she didn't want to think. Thinking meant remembering, and she didn't want to remember. She finally sat up, stretched, yawned, and thought about poor Claire. Checking the time, she saw that two and half hours had passed by.

"Poor Claire. She's going to hate me for abandoning her. Well, everyone else will soon hate me, so why not her too? "

Michelle took a quick shower and dressed. Feeling much better, she went to the hotel lobby where Claire sat patiently in the office, reading the previous month's issue of her favorite women's magazine.

"Hi, thanks for sitting in for me," Michelle said, with a relaxed demeanor but still not feeling as chipper as she'd like to.

"Hi, feeling better?" Claire asked.

"Better, but not my best," Michelle answered, "Give me some time. I have issues I've got to come to terms with."

Claire grinned, "Honor the Gods but make friends with your demons. You'll live a longer, happier life." Claire looked up at Michelle, "My grandmother used to say that. She lived to 103. "

"I like that. I agree. I have long ago stopped running from them, though I have not yet learned to live with them. I guess you can say I still need to make friends," Michelle said seriously, going along with Claire's grandmother. Michelle knew her demons were there but just couldn't deal with them.

Claire sat around the office helping Michelle when and where she could, occasionally going back to see her husband. Michelle asked Claire why she went back to see him so often. She replied, "Because I love him, and I just like to see him. I like to see his smile and seeing him makes me smile," she admitted cheerfully.

Claire's effervescent happiness briefly repulsed Michelle. But she fought it, telling herself, "Don't be a witch. Just because I can't be happy doesn't mean I have to ruin it for others. Be happy that they are happy." Finally thinking, *I hate myself sometimes, I really do.*

"Well, since you like to visit the kitchen, can I send you back to ask what the guys are planning to feed us for lunch? If Rudy's oven is hot, ask if we could split a small chicken or a mushroom tart would be good. I'd love a small salad. How about a salad and a tart?" Michelle asked.

Michelle had just checked in the last reservation for the evening when Claire returned with a tray full of dishes. "That looks wonderful, thank you, Claire," Michelle said as she peeked under a few of the metal lids covering the plates.

The two women dug into the plates that crowded the large waiter's tray. They had fresh asparagus, slightly grilled, with a wonderful lemon balsamic dressing. They split an appetizer of citrus cured sardines, with a hint of coriander, zest of lime, and just enough heat from local chilies to appeal to sensitive palates. Finally, they gorged on slices of tart, piled high with wild mushrooms, goat cheese, roasted peppers, and small, salty black Nicoise olives.

The two women couldn't believe how satisfying these dishes were and how the flavors blended so well, making them want to take another and another bite. That is until they tasted the next dish, which was even more delicious than the previous, then the next dish, and so on.

When every plate was empty, the two women sat back in their office chairs, sipped a glass of wine, and swore they would never eat again. "Well, I could eat another slice of tart," Michelle admitted as she sipped.

"I agree. I couldn't eat another bite; except I thought the asparagus was very refreshing. I think another slice of tart and just a small portion of asparagus," Claire thought would be perfect.

Michelle, silent for a moment, spoke, "But wasn't that sardine good? How do those guys do it? I could eat another sardine. I couldn't eat another bite of anything else, except I could eat another slice of tart, a small portion of asparagus, and another sardine. But that's it," Michelle admitted, looking over at Claire with a frown.

The two girls burst into laughter, "That's the whole meal. We couldn't eat another bite except for the whole meal! We have become pigs." Claire laughed at their hypocrisy.

Michelle was also laughing, "My word, we are turning into big fat sows. But can we help it? The food is so good. "

The girls were just cleaning up the office area from their feast when the phone rang. Michelle answered it, hoping she wouldn't burp in the middle of her conversation. "Good afternoon, the Inn at Saint Charles en Liberte. How may I help you?"

"Hello, may I speak with Ms. Michelle Villeneuve?" The man's voice was clear and distinctly American.

Michelle recognized the voice immediately, "Hello John; this is Michelle. How are you? How is life treating you in New York?"

John Reynolds, Michelle's boss from New York, was surprised he didn't recognize Michelle's voice. "Hello, Michelle. I didn't recognize your voice. Life is good, getting better. I ran into a little family money, and with some seed money from friends and associates, I'm hanging out my shingle, going it alone."

Michelle was genuinely happy for her old boss, "That's great, congratulations."

"Thank you. I also got some deal flow going, doing some secondary offerings from the mid-stream operators we took public." John Reynolds spoke enthusiastically about the promising start of his business. "We'll be lead underwriter, and I've got commitments from some old friends for distribution," Reynolds stated as if it was all going to plan.

"Makes sense, but to get the marquee names, the real lucrative deals, you'll need to have your own distribution. Clients don't want a lot of paperwork; they want to talk to one person, one firm, that's it." Michelle was in the business long enough to know how things worked and how deals were made.

Reynolds continued, "But you know as well as I do, you have to keep the deal flow going. If you fall behind or get lost in the shuffle, that's it. So, I'm constantly on the road. I need someone to take charge of the back office. Someone I can trust and who knows what they are doing. Someone that I know will ensure all the T's are crossed and the I's dotted." Reynolds didn't half-step or beat around the bush. "You want to come work for me? You can name your price, within reason, give yourself whatever title you want. I offer profit sharing and a piece of the action; every year you're with the firm, I'll give you one half of one percent, up to a max of five percent."

"Why stop at five percent?' Michelle asked.

"Michelle, if you are still with me after ten years, you'll have so much money you'll be buying your own energy companies. Fifty basis points of equity in my bank will be chump change," Reynolds stated flatly.

Michelle laughed; she was giddy; out of nowhere, a once-in-a-lifetime opportunity had presented itself. John Reynolds, her old boss, knew everybody in the energy business. He received Christmas cards from CEOs, birthday wishes from CFOs, and played tennis with all the movers and shakers in the Investment Banking Industry. This guy was a star, and he wanted her. She was dizzy over the sudden attention.

"Hello, Michelle, are you still there?" Reynolds asked as Michelle pinched herself, making sure it wasn't a dream.

"Yes, I am here. John, I need time to think this through. I am here helping my family, and my uncle is in the hospital. I am inclined to accept your offer, but you understand family. I just can't hop on the next plane to New York," Michelle cautioned but wishing she could do precisely that.

"I understand. Take a few days, a week. I'm speaking at the Partner's Energy Conference in Houston next month. I could use your help putting my presentation together," Reynolds replied.

"What's your topic?" Michelle asked.

"Mid-Stream Investment Opportunities," Reynolds answered her.

"That's interesting. They want you to show all your cards." She laughed politely but was genuinely curious how he would make a presentation to an auditorium full of bankers on opportunities in the market segment he hoped to capitalize on.

"I agreed to do the presentation before I was assigned the topic. I won't make that mistake again," Reynolds admitted, impressed Michelle caught on so quickly, recognizing what he was being asked to do.

"Let me get my head around this; can we talk next week?" Michelle requested.

"Sure, you still have my number?" Reynolds asked.

"Yes," Michelle replied.

"Ok, I'll call you Thursday. I'll be on the road, but if you have any questions, call. If I don't answer, leave a message, and I'll get back to you," Reynolds advised.

"Thank you, John, I will. Talk to you," Michelle finished.

"Thank you, Michelle." Reynolds hung up.

* * *

Gabrielle parked her late-model Peugeot out front in what looked like bistro parking. Not seeing any signs or other impediments, she took her bag from the trunk, locked the car, and walked to the inn, figuring she would check in first and then look for Daniel.

She was strikingly good-looking; some would say a handsome woman. She had high, prominent cheekbones, lovely bright green eyes, and a very straight, slender nose, making her face perfectly symmetrical. Her striking facial features were accented by rich, thick, shoulder-length black hair. If asked, though, she would say her lips were too small, and she would go through great lengths to accentuate and make them look fuller and plumper. This did nothing but enhance her appearance.

She had perfect posture, courtesy of years and years of ballet lessons. She had been educated in private schools by nuns who insisted on proper diction and grammar. She spoke properly and rather elegantly.

She dressed conservatively, feeling she would rather have the attention of the few that listened to what she said, instead of the many attracted to what she bared. She was as tall as Michelle, if not a few centimeters taller.

She entered the inn, and Andre, the bellboy, rushed to her side. "Please excuse me, Madam. I did not hear the door open. How may I assist you?" Andre hoped this woman was pleasant. She was so beautiful; it would be wonderful if she were friendly as well.

"Thank you. I believe there is a room reserved for me. My name is Gabrielle. I am an acquaintance of Daniel's." She spoke warmly, kindly to Andre.

Andre was immediately in love. "Let me help you to the desk, and someone will, of course, help you with any questions. I will look for Daniel and return shortly."

Andre brought her bag to the front desk. He rang the bell. Claire and Michelle came from inside the office. Michelle spoke, "Gabrielle, so nice to see you. I didn't know you were coming. Does Daniel know?" she asked.

"I hope so. I spoke with him earlier in the week. He said to come to visit for the weekend. So here I am," she answered, smiling and hoping her visit wasn't a mistake.

"You are here for the weekend? Excellent. I am going to give you the best room in the house, the Penthouse. It has lovely views, bright light, and fantastic woodwork. My great-great-grandfather actually had the room built for his son and his wife when they were first married," she explained, so happy to see Gabrielle.

Andre came back to the Lobby, "Chef Daniel will be with you shortly. He is tending to a culinary issue."

Michelle laughed, "A what?"

"Well, not really; he is putting on long pants and a fresh jacket," Andre admitted, himself grinning, half laughing.

Gabrielle thought it was cute and waited patiently.

Daniel came bounding around the corner, looking down to watch his step. When he got to the inn's desk, he stopped and looked up into Gabrielle's beautiful green eyes.

"Hello, Gabrielle," Daniel said softly and tentatively.

"Hello, Daniel," Gabrielle said softly, tentatively.

Gabrielle was tall, but Daniel was still a good 30 centimeters taller, even though she had on heels.

Michelle took Claire's hand and motioned for her to come back into the office.

Claire, in turn, looked at Andre and cleared her throat. Andre took the cue and retreated to the dining room.

Daniel and Gabrielle were left standing alone. Daniel took a step toward her, staring into her eyes. She didn't move; she just stared back.

Daniel took another step toward her. She could feel his breath. She could hear her own heart race; her own breathing seemed loud. Her knees felt weak like she could easily fall over.

Daniel took her two hands and held them together in his hands. He brought them up to his mouth and softly kissed them. "I am not the handsomest man, I am not the richest man, nor the most intelligent, or the bravest; I am a simple, honest, hardworking man. You will never have to question my feelings for you; I will always be here for you, and I swear on the graves of my ancestors, you will want for nothing." He gently kissed her hands again.

Daniel looked up again into Gabrielle's eyes and smiled, stating nonchalantly, "I also look pretty good in a tux."

Gabrielle smiled and laughed. As she laughed, a tear that had formed in the corner of her eye rolled down her cheek, happy and thankful Daniel had lightened the mood.

Daniel caught her tear with the sleeve of his jacket. "I will never wash this jacket."

She took Daniel's face in her hands and gently kissed him. She pulled back and whispered, "I have waited a long time. I think the wait has been worth it but I do not want to wait any longer. Please, Daniel, take me to my room."

Daniel took Gabrielle's bag, and the two headed for the elevator. Daniel had his arm over her shoulder; she was leaning into him, her arm around his waist. Daniel summoned the elevator, and as they waited, they embraced and kissed again.

Michelle and Claire came out of the office and saw the two enter the elevator, ascending to the fourth floor, the Penthouse floor.

Hearing the elevator, Andre the bellboy came from the dining room. Seeing Michelle and Claire, he had to ask, "Who was that woman? I have never seen such a woman. I mean, she moved like a cat, so graceful, tall and straight, like a marble statue, and her voice, her voice was that of an angel's, so full of compassion and love. What was her name? I have to know."

Michelle smiled, "Careful, Andre. Her name is Gabrielle, but you must admire her from a distance. That is the future Mrs. Daniel Villeneuve."

Chapter 34

J ust having the opportunity offered by her old boss elevated Michelle's mood. *At least someone knows I'm still alive,* she thought to herself, adding *And believes I'm still capable.*

But her elevated mood didn't last long as she started contemplating the decision she needed to make. She wanted the recognition, the title, the conferences, the headlines, all that came with a career in banking; she wanted it so bad, but *was it the right choice?*

She felt like the character Faust, her old boss, the devil. She questioned herself. *Am I willing to sell my soul for success? What is the price of recognition? What is lacking in my life that motivates me to make a pact with the devil?*

Michelle sat for hours, late at night, and stared out the window. *Maybe I can be happy in New York? But can I be happy without my family? Can't I have both? Why can't I have both? Why can't I have my family and have my career, title, and recognition? Can't they co-exist?*

The more Michelle thought, the more conflicted and confused she became, and she was frustrated that she couldn't come to a rational decision that satisfied all her inner conflicts. *Ah, one more sleepless night,* she thought to herself, lying in bed, as she watched the first hints of light peek over the horizon.

She rolled over and somehow fell asleep. She slept soundly and dreamed. She was standing in the lobby, dressed in a suit, bags packed. Everyone was there saying goodbye and good luck. Everyone was happy for her, supporting her decision, telling her it was the right decision, patting her on the back, and wishing her all the luck in the world. A jet plane waited out in the parking lot to take her to New York, her boss, John Reynolds was standing in the plane's door beckoning her to hop on board.

Everyone was happy for her, except Pierre. Pierre sat in the conference room, wearing his marooned tuxedo, smoking. There was a large ashtray full of smoking embers in front of him; though there were burning cigarettes in the ashtray, he lit another.

Pierre summoned her to the conference room. "Do you think this time it will be different? Think again. You'll be stuck in an office, day in and day out, nothing but numbers, numbers, numbers," Pierre said sternly.

"No, it'll be different. I know it'll be different. I know what to do," she said, correcting Pierre.

"It'll be different? Ha, famous last words. No, it won't be. A title doesn't make things different. Your own office just means a bigger cubicle. Your boss will take all the successes and blame you for all his failures, just like before." Pierre smiled.

Michelle tried to talk, "But, but, I won't let that happen."

"There will be nothing you can do about it. You will be powerless. You'll feel trapped, and there will be no one to turn to. Your boss doesn't love you. He won't marry you. He won't, you understand? Face it; he doesn't want to marry you. To him, you're nothing but a…."

"*STOP!!!!!!*" Michelle woke, screaming, and bolted into a sitting position. Her bed was a mess like she had been wrestling, her mouth was dry, and she was soaked in sweat. The feeling of panic remained but slowly disappeared as Michelle realized, *It was only a dream. But my God, what a dream.*

She lay back down and stared at the ceiling, thinking, *Pierre was right, I am in love with my boss, and the only reason I want to go back is to get another chance. I want title and recognition, yes, but only so he recognizes it so that we're equals. Once we're equal, that will make him want me.*

But isn't that a basic tenet of human nature, the need to be recognized by peers? But I have that. Everyone says I'm good. I have that. I am really doing this just for him. She repeated it. *I am really doing this just for him. Just for him. Oh my God. What a silly goose. I am pathetic.* She grinned and felt light and alive, recognizing that she had finally stumbled upon the truth.

Thank you, Uncle Pierre. Thank you so much.

* * *

Michelle bathed and dressed. She went to the front desk. Realizing she was early, she went to the kitchen and made herself a Cappuccino, this time remembering to add a touch more cinnamon.

Andre came in, and together they set up the coffee station so guests with early departures didn't have to leave on an empty stomach. Michelle brought out a large basket full of croissants and sweet rolls Rudy had baked earlier that morning. She didn't expect Rudy to still be around. Now that he was married, he woke early, did his baking, and then liked to return to the warm, comfortable confines of his wife and bed.

Andre filled two large cisterns with fruit preserves and brought along a large block of sweet butter, some small plates, and appropriate cutlery.

A short time later, Michelle was back at the desk as the first guests were coming down the elevators, looking for coffee and wanting to check out.

Michelle, to this day, remembers the time. It was 9:10 a.m., Saturday morning, when she got the call.

"Good Morning, The Inn at Saint Charles en Liberte'. How may I help you?" Michelle greeted the caller.

"Yes, this is Doctor Michaud at the Medical Center in Bordeaux. Is this Maria Villeneuve?" the voice inquired in a very official tone.

"Oh, God. No, this is Michelle Villeneuve. Pierre, the patient, is my uncle. Oh God, is he alright?" Michelle cried, praying this was not bad news.

"Yes, I see your name here on the approved list. I am calling to inform you that your uncle woke from his coma this morning and appears to be doing fine. We are conducting tests, but other than a few minor issues associated with not moving for three weeks, he is in excellent shape and is responding to stimuli. He has been asking for Maria and Michelle, which I imagine is you?" The doctor said, still using his official voice.

"Thank God," Michelle said, relieved the message was not what she initially feared. "That's wonderful. Can we come today? Will we be allowed to see him?" Michelle begged.

"Yes, of course. We will sedate him so that he doesn't overexert himself, but we will make sure he remains conscious," The doctor explained, then concluded the call.

"Thank you, doctor." Michelle hung up and told Andre to watch the desk. Michelle ran as fast as she could to the family's apartments and rang her mother's bell.

Maria answered the door, looking comfortable in her robe with big fluffy pink slippers on her feet, a large cup of coffee in her hand, and the TV droning on in the background. The news channel, sedately reporting the latest global tragedy.

"Mother, Pierre's alive. I mean, he's conscious. The hospital just called, and he's awake. They're doing tests, but so far, he's ok." Michelle spoke quickly and excitedly.

Maria fell against the door, almost dropping her coffee; she smiled, "Thank God. Our prayers have been answered."

"I have to get back to the front desk. I just had to let you know," Michelle added.

"Yes, thank you. I'll get dressed. We need to go see him. Can Claire watch the desk for you?" Maria asked.

"I'm sure she will. I'll find out, but if not, Andre will watch it. I don't need to change. I'm ready when you are," Michelle replied.

"Andre? Yes, fine. Just give me 30 minutes. I'll see you at the front desk," Maria added, then closed her door.

Claire readily agreed to watch the desk, and less than 30 minutes later, the two women were on their way to Bordeaux.

Michelle drove. She wanted to because she thought her Mother drove like an old lady. "But I am an old lady. I think it's important that I act accordingly."

"Yes, Mother, but it will take us twice as long to get there if you drive," Michelle asserted.

Defending herself, Maria spoke up, "Don't be silly. The way you drive. We might not get there alive."

"Very funny. I'm careful," Michelle said as she slammed on the brakes, barely avoiding a tractor pulling out of a dirt path, a large cart full of bales of hay in tow. "Lots of surprises on this road," Michelle added.

"Yes. Lots of surprises, so stay alert," her mother replied.

The women managed to arrive at the hospital in a timely fashion and without any further incidents involving man or beast. They rushed to the ward where Pierre was being kept only to find an empty bed.

"Excuse me, nurse," Maria inquired to a passing orderly. "Where is the patient? His name is Pierre Villeneuve. He just woke from a coma."

"I am not sure; this is not usually where I work. But I know recently there was a patient who suffered a massive heart attack. You can check with cardiology or try the morgue," he said casually as if he were giving directions to the nearest ice cream shop.

"Oh, dear God," Maria cried as she contemplated what she had just heard.

"No, absolutely incorrect. Mother, do not pay any attention to what he said. He doesn't know anything. What an idiot for saying something like that, 'check the morgue,' Idiot." Michelle tried to ease her mother's concern and hide her own, but she was feeling her own panic building up inside as she looked for someone in authority, someone who might know where her uncle could be.

"Come, Mother, let's check the nurse's station," Michelle said to her mother, taking her by the arm and walking down the stark, white corridor towards a group of nurses clustered around computer screens, each carrying a clipboard, their eyeglasses on hefty nylon tethers.

"Excuse me," Michelle said as the two women got closer. "We're looking for a patient. Can someone help us?"

"Sure, what's the patient's name?" came a reply from one of the nurses sitting in front of a computer.

"Villeneuve, Pierre Villeneuve," Maria replied.

The nurse typed in a few commands and quickly replied, "He's just down the corridor in room 332B. I'll take you there; I need to take his vitals," she said as she stood up and grabbed her clipboard, walking briskly down the corridor. She spoke to Maria and Michelle, "This way, please," in case there was any confusion.

The women turned the corner, entering room 332B, only to find it empty. Flowers and cards were lying about, proving that the room had been occupied. But as for the patient, he was missing.

The nurse was a hearty-looking woman who appeared to be someone not interested in nonsense and other forms of tomfoolery. She placed her hands on her hips, bit her lip, and said, "That man. I told him to stay in bed. We even gave him a little extra sedative. The doctor is not going to be happy when he hears about this," she said as she placed her glasses on her nose and made some notations on her clipboard. Then she turned around and said, "I know where he is. Follow me, please."

Michelle and Maria followed the nurse. She led them down an adjacent dimly lit corridor, then through large double doors leading to a series of stairs. The nurse led them down the stairs to the basement. There were large pipes, some painted yellow with warning signs, others painted black, and some painted grey. They walked down the corridor, up a small flight of concrete stairs, and finally through a fire door that led to a courtyard.

In the middle of the courtyard was a cement bench surrounded by basic landscaping typical of government buildings and institutions. Standing in the middle of the courtyard were three barefoot men, all wearing hospital gowns that were open in the back, exposing more than any sane person would want to see. Oblivious to their exposure, each man smoked a cigarette, taking great puffs and blowing the smoke whimsically in the air.

The men seemed to be in an argument. "No, fish in the Mediterranean have it too easy. Life is good; they do not stress or want for anything. But North Atlantic fish must work to stay alive. The flesh is heartier, fattier; there is more flavor." Pierre's voice rose above the rest.

Two of the men noticed the women approaching and quickly put out their cigarettes. Pierre, his back turned, was unaware and kept smoking and talking. "I don't care whether the water is hot or cold. I tell you, it is what they eat that makes the difference. North Atlantic…"

The nurse stopped, interrupting Pierre's latest observation, "Mr. Villeneuve, you know the rules about smoking?"

Pierre quickly turned, blowing smoke out of the side of his mouth. Then, seeing Maria and Michelle, he said, "Maria, Michelle, I am so glad to see you."

He took another puff of his cigarette, put it out in a small puddle of water nearby, and then added the butt to the growing collection of spent cigarettes the three men had formed.

Before Pierre could say more, the nurse spoke again. "You men should not be out here in your bare feet. You will catch cold, and no telling what germs you will drag back with you into the ward. Let's go inside, but you will need to wash your feet before going upstairs. "

Pierre stepped over to Maria and gave her a big hug. "I am so happy to see you," Pierre said quietly. "Michelle, I am so glad to see you. Actually, I am quite surprised to see you," Pierre said while giving her a big hug.

"Why are you surprised?" Michelle asked, then added, "I have been here frequently. I read to you, brought you flowers, and even spoke with you. The conversations were somewhat lopsided, but I was by your side, as much as I could be."

Pierre put his arms out for the ladies. Michelle on one side, Maria on the other, Pierre spoke as they sauntered back into the building. "I woke this morning, not knowing where I was. I have no recollection of what has happened, why I am here, nothing! The last thing I remember it was our grand re-opening, and we were getting ready for the second seating. But when I woke this morning, I had a strange premonition; I had this feeling that you were on your way back to New York or packing to leave for New York. I don't remember saying it, but I was told, the first words I spoke were, "Why do you go? He doesn't care."

"I am not sure what it means, so perhaps you can tell me?" Pierre asked.

Startled, Michelle didn't know where to start. She had time to think as the three returned to the building and found orderlies waiting with towels, soap, hot water, and slippers. His feet finally cleaned, Pierre showed the nurse a shortcut back to his room after bidding his new friends goodbye.

Back in his room, a young doctor was waiting. "Mr. Villeneuve, I told you explicitly to stay in bed. Your body has been through a traumatic experience and needs to rest. Please follow our instructions."

"My apologies, Doctor. I just wanted to get out and smell the fresh air," Pierre said coyly.

"No, you wanted to go have a smoke—no more smoking. Once we release you, you may do as you wish. While in our care, you follow the rules. Rule number one, no smoking; rule number two, stay in bed; rule number...."

"Ok, ok, ok. I understand. You'll have no more problems with me," Pierre said while looking at Maria, rolling his eyes, and hopping back into bed.

"Good, thank you. Nurse, please take his vitals. I'll be in my office," The young doctor instructed.

"Yes, doctor." The nurse complied.

When the nurse had left, Maria asked Pierre, "You have no recollection of what has happened?"

Pierre replied, "No, none whatsoever. But I remember everything that has happened since 5 a.m. this morning when I woke."

"You woke at 5 a.m. They didn't call us till 9 a.m." Michelle said, amazed that the hospital waited so long.

"Well, they needed to do tests and things like that. They did a lot of brainwork. Apparently, according to experts, my brain is healthy, very healthy. They did tests. You know, I have near photographic memory now."

Maria replied, "No, you are joking with us."

Pierre countered, "No, it's true. Here, grab one of those books." Pierre pointed to the three books Michelle had brought from his library.

Michelle took the first book, Tarzan, from the stack and handed it to Pierre.

"Ok, I'm turning to page 37." Pierre then made a motion with his finger, looking like he scanned the contents of the page.

Handing the book back to Michelle, he instructed, "Now countdown to any word, and give me the number, like the 22nd word, or tenth word, whatever you choose."

Michelle counted to eighteen. "Ok, Uncle, what's the 18th word?"

"Ape." Pierre then added, "The passage is 'the great ape looked at the frail human child.'"

Michelle laughed, "Perfect. That's remarkable." She turned to another page. "Let's try this page," handing the book over to Pierre.

Pierre spent a minute scanning the page, then handed it back to Michelle.

Michelle asked, "What's the twelfth word?"

"Rain." Pierre replied, "The passage is 'as the rain fell, Tarzan looked over at'."

Michelle looked at her mother. "Mother, his memory is perfect."

"They gave me an EKG; they had to call in experts to verify the readings. The experts said they had never seen so much activity. But I feel fine, no headaches, a little stiff in the knees, but otherwise, I feel fine."

Maria asked, "When can you come home? When will they release you?"

"I don't know. They just said they want to monitor me. Maybe they'll tell you?" Pierre replied.

"I'll go check with the doctor, see what they want to do," Maria spoke as she went out the door, leaving Pierre and Michelle alone.

"I am so happy you are back with us. I was so afraid, Uncle. I couldn't sleep. I had a hard time focusing." Michelle leaned forward, giving her uncle another hug.

"Thank you, Michelle. It's good to be back, awake, from wherever I was," Pierre answered, wanting to know the answers to the many questions he had. "But tell me about New York? What happened? Why is that on my mind?"

"Pierre, I haven't mentioned this to Mother, so keep it to yourself," she asked Pierre.

"Of course. I won't repeat it. But something tells me I already know," he replied.

"I received a call from my former boss the other day. It couldn't have come at a better time. I was feeling very depressed, rejected, and insecure. My old boss offered me a job in his new bank. He said I could name my price, give myself any title I wanted, and he'd give me equity. Everything I ever wanted," she recalled.

"So, what did you do? Why are you still here?" Pierre asked, curious as to why she didn't jump at the opportunity.

"Because I had a conversation, not really a conversation, a dream. In this dream, a very trusted person told me something, something about myself, I was too afraid to admit," she said quietly to Pierre, carefully, as if her telling it incorrectly would make it somehow untrue.

"That conversation was with me," Pierre said seriously. "I advised you not to go. I remember now."

"Yes. You said 'he doesn't love you. He'll never marry you," Michelle said tearfully, not knowing why she was getting emotional.

"Your boss is named James, Jim, or ..." Pierre asked.

"John," she replied.

"Yes, John. His family name is Metals? Petals?" Pierre, a little confused, asked.

"Reynolds, John Reynolds," Michelle corrected him.

"Yes, I had a conversation with him. He said some very disparaging things about you. I told him I would not allow my niece to work for such a scoundrel. He said women like you were a dime a dozen. He said he doesn't lie; he just lets them believe what they want to believe. He's got a dozen women who will do anything he asks because they think he's going to marry them. He admitted that. I had to warn you," Pierre recalled.

"Oh, my God. That's so true. He strings people along. He doesn't commit either way; he just gets people to go along. Do you know what he does? He makes false promises." Michelle cried out, "Oh my god. But how, Uncle, how do you know all this?"

"I don't know. But I woke this morning thinking it's important that I stop you before you ruin your life," he said calmly, almost sadly. He then spoke like a father would speak to his daughter, "Michelle, please believe me when I say I want the best for you. If you feel your greatest contribution in life, your greatest happiness, will be in banking, New York, Boston, or Timbuktu, then I will wholeheartedly support your decision. But this man meant you no good. He does not have your best interests in mind. If you want to get back into banking, look around; find the right opportunity. Don't jump on the first one that comes along, especially if it involves this man."

Maria entered the room. "My goodness, the mood has certainly turned somber. Why are you two looking so serious?" she asked.

"Just talking about career moves, feelings. Pierre has given me some excellent advice," Michelle said to her mother, then turned back to Pierre.

"You were always the best when it came to understanding me," Michelle said, lightening the mood.

"Well, I had a nice conversation with the doctor. They want to keep you for the weekend. If all goes according to plan, they'll release you Monday morning." Maria announced, "And by the way, they are impressed with your mental agility, their words, not mine, and are closely monitoring your brain activity in case there are side effects."

Just then, a nurse entered with a large syringe, instructing Maria and Michelle, "Visiting hours are over. The doctor wants the patient to rest."

Maria and Michelle gave hugs and said goodbye as the nurse administered a sedative, and Pierre slowly closed his eyes.

The drive back to Saint Charles was uneventful. Michelle had a lot on her mind. She let Maria drive, so she could let her mind wander.

Chapter 35

D aniel and Gabrielle descended the lift to the lobby. Claire was filling in for Michelle, as Michelle and Maria had hurried off to Bordeaux when they received word Pierre had come out of his coma. Daniel introduced Gabrielle to Claire, even though the two women had met and immediately recognized each other.

Claire informed Daniel that Pierre had woken, but she hadn't received any other news. Daniel, of course, was very happy and asked her to let him know immediately of any further developments.

Daniel took Gabrielle on a tour, first showing her his kitchen. He introduced her to Rudy, though like Claire, the two immediately recognized each other.

"Hi, nice to see you again. I want to thank you for the Latour," Rudy said. "It was a great bottle. I didn't expect to be served such a quality wine on a flight," he added with a grin.

"It was my pleasure. It makes me happy to see someone appreciate a good wine," Gabrielle replied with a smile.

Gabrielle was impressed with the kitchen, and she thought the wood-burning oven was a wonderful idea. "The wood-burning oven technique will bring real authenticity to your cooking and menu," she observed.

Daniel beamed, "Isn't she wonderful?"

Gabrielle smiled, happy she could be herself, and that everyone she met seemed so genuine. She liked these people; they made it easy to be friendly. As she and Daniel spent time together, she became more and more relaxed.

She felt like she had finally found a place where she could spend time, perhaps even become a part of.

Daniel took her to his mushroom farm, and she was amazed at what he had accomplished. "Fresh mushrooms? Are you able to just walk a short distance from your kitchen and pull mushrooms right from the dirt? Truffles too? You are a magician. I would call you a god, but I am afraid it will go to your head." She smiled coyly at Daniel, who smiled back.

"I am not a god and not a trickster. I work at it and just keep working at it until I get it. I am showing you my successes; of course, I have had twice as many failures. But I am a lucky individual. My family supports me. They want me to fail. They know if I am failing, I am learning, and sooner or later, I will succeed." Daniel took Gabrielle in his arms and said, intentionally being overly dramatic, "I want to warn you, I am a failure, but I am a man, proud of my failures."

Gabrielle laughed. She was getting to know him and starting to recognize his playfulness, "I have met many important men, very successful men. They all try to impress me with their accomplishments. But the more they try to impress, the more I start to feel it was only luck, not talent, skill, or hard work, just luck. You are the first man I have ever met who spoke proudly of his failures, which impresses me. I am impressed because you tried, and though you failed, you want to keep trying. That tells me something about you." She looked seriously at Daniel. "It really shows your depth, your character. I find you a very, very attractive man." Gabrielle stood there in the dim light, hoping she wasn't revealing too much, but Daniel made her feel comfortable, and she sincerely wanted to tell him. Tell him that she was falling in love with him.

Daniel broke the brief silence, "Come, I have one more thing to show you."

He quickly walked up the cellar stairs, pulling Gabrielle behind him. He placed the lock on the door and once more said, "Come with me."

He took her down into the basement of the bistro, where extra tables, chairs, and boxes of various supplies were stored. He turned on the lights, illuminating the space. It was dusty and only partially organized. There were a few cases of wine against one wall. Gabrielle looked and saw a few cases of champagne against another wall. In the corner, she could see stacks of wine crates, and finally, going the length of the large room, from floor to ceiling, were rows of empty wine racks.

"What's this?" Gabrielle asked.

Daniel took a bottle out of one of the crates against the wall. He took two glasses from one of the boxes, examined them quickly, and, satisfied they were clean, he placed them on a small table. He pulled two chairs from a stack and gestured to Gabrielle, saying, "Please sit down."

He took a corkscrew out of his pocket and quickly removed the foil from around the cork before removing the cork itself. He poured the deep red garnet wine into her glass.

"Oh, my God, I can smell the wine's aroma from here," she said before he finished pouring.

He poured her a sample and stood by, waiting for her reaction.

Gabrielle picked up the glass and held it up to the light while giving it a flick of her wrist. "This wine has very nice legs," she suggested. Then placing her nose into the glass, tilting it just a bit, she looked at Daniel, "Superb, very nice, how are the tannins?"

"See for yourself," he suggested.

She tasted. Daniel watched as she rolled it around her tongue, then swallowed. "My word," She said giddily, almost laughing. "This wine is huge. It's magnificent. It tastes of blackberry, tobacco, lavender and, and a taste of…."

Daniel cut in, "Truffle?"

"Yes, yes, black truffle. It then explodes with mature, lingering tannins. It's absolutely delightful," Gabrielle exclaimed. "Please, pour yourself a glass and tell me if I imagine this. Pour me another glass as well, if you please."

"So you enjoy wine?" Daniel asked casually.

"Yes, of course. I used to dream of having some land, some vines, a small winery, produce a few varietals, maybe 30, 40 cases each. Enough for local bistros. Enough to keep me going, and who knows? Maybe even open my own bistro. A small place, simple dishes, but very fresh local ingredients."

"What happened to that dream?" Daniel asked.

"Time, reality, pressures of living. Land is not cheap. If I work to earn, who works the land?" Gabrielle spoke, her tone very sentimental, as if she wished she could do it all again.

"Gabrielle, I will speak honestly. I will speak from my heart, but as you recognize, I must also be realistic, rational," Daniel said as he sipped and enjoyed the wine, thinking it's better than he remembered.

"Please, Daniel. I want to hear what you have to say," Gabrielle replied, wanting to know his thoughts.

"I want you in my life, very badly in my life. I will not pretend and say I love you. But I will say, in time, I could easily fall in love with you."

"Thank you, Daniel. I feel similar. I think the word love is used too freely. I think it is used as a ploy to get others in bed," Gabrielle admitted.

"Yes, that is probably true," Daniel replied. "I want you to stay here in Saint Charles, but I am worried. Worried that you will see your life pass you by. You are intelligent, energetic, and curious. I think over time, you will become bored, restless. I think you will begin to think you made a mistake. I have my work; what will you have?" Daniel asked, wondering if she had thought about this already.

"Thank you. You are insightful. My experience has been when talk turns to commitment, a man wants nothing but to possess. You have not spoken of possession. Instead, you are concerned about whether I will feel whole, if I will have a purpose. Daniel, that is an essential aspect of life, and you are right. I will not be satisfied cleaning house every day. I, like you, want to leave my mark. When it's time, I want to go to my maker knowing I accomplished something. I appreciate your concern greatly. I did notice, driving up here, that Saint Charles is, is, remote. I do not know what opportunities are here; I assume there are not many?" she said honestly, while continuing, happy to have this conversation. She was relieved that Daniel considered more, was looking for more than just a pretty face.

"But I have a feeling you have already resolved this issue," she added. "What are you proposing?"

"Look at the shelves behind you," Daniel instructed.

"Yes, they are empty, dusty, and empty. It looks like you have space for 1,000 bottles, maybe more if you update the space, easily another 1,000 bottles if you put in another stack of shelves," Gabrielle observed.

"And what else?" Daniel asked.

"Well, I guess you could have quite a cellar if you just found someone to…." Gabrielle stopped; her eyes shot wide open. Almost dropping her glass, she continued slowly, "If you just found someone interested in putting it together."

Daniel looked at her and smiled.

"You don't mean…are you offering…do you want me to…oh my God. You're not kidding me? You are serious?"

Daniel sat, looked at her, and nodded affirmatively. "We need a cellar, and we need a sommelier. I think we need you. I am confident we do.

Gabrielle burst into tears. "Daniel, you just made me the happiest person on earth." She reached over and took his hand. "It has been my dream. Oh, Daniel. I can visit the local farmers and find the best bottles. We could be known for having incredible wines, available no other place, and with your cooking and the wood-burning oven, we could become known throughout France. Oh, Daniel, let's do it. Let's set the culinary world on fire. You, me, the others, let's make history."

"Yes, I want to start a revolution, the second French revolution. Viva la revolution." Daniel held his glass up in a toast.

"Viva la France," Gabrielle answered back.

Then Daniel did one more, "To you, Gabrielle."

She smiled back, responding, "To us."

"Yes, to us," he replied.

They both drank, emptying the glasses; Daniel poured another. She looked at him, her face glowing and her eyes bright. She whispered, "Daniel, take me home."

Daniel looked confused, "What, to Paris? I was hoping...."

"No, Daniel. This is home. Take me to your apartment," she said, laughing lightly, giving him a wink.

"Yes, of course. It will be my pleasure. But let's not forget the wine, and you know..." He handed the opened bottle to her and gave her the cork; then, reaching into the wooden crate, he pulled out another bottle.

"As head chef, before I offer any wine to my patrons, I have to be sure it is consistent, and the only way I can do that is by opening another bottle," he said, rising to his feet and offering Gabrielle his arm. "I know it's work, but we all must chip in, make a contribution."

She laughed, "Yes, and as sommelier, I agree. Wine must be consistent in appearance and taste. We need to ensure it is. Our reputation is at stake."

"How very true," Daniel said, putting his nose in the air, pretending to be a snob.

They walked together up the wide stairs into the light. As they walked towards Daniel's apartment, he looked over at her, still pretending to be a snob, "Have you ever thought about being someone's wife? I guess the phrase commonly used is 'taking a husband'?"

Gabrielle was charmed and entertained by Daniel's clowning around, replying, "Only recently."

"Oh, I see, hmm, lucky man," Daniel added as he unlocked his apartment door.

* * *

The women arrived back in Saint Charles in time for closing. Rudy had worked alone for most of the night, which was fine by him. It gave him time to hone his skills with the wood-burning oven, and most of the patrons were locals, hungry, thirsty, and wanting to know the latest news concerning Pierre.

The locals loved his roasted fennel tart and wild mushroom tart, causing him to experiment even more. Knowing onion soup was a favorite, he devised an onion and Gruyere tart, brushing on garlic butter just before serving and sprinkling it with just a breath of Spanish sherry. It was a huge hit, with many patrons not bothering to drop the soup label when ordering. Paul and Thomas, the two waiters, went along with it, placing their orders as "onion soup tart."

But only a handful of locals showed up, those needing a change of scenery from their own homes. Having spent Friday nights at The Tree Trunk for years, they knew of nothing else.

Both women were famished and immediately went to the Bistro. They asked Rudy what, if anything, he could fix for them. Claire, who had sat for hours at the front desk, took a break and joined Maria and Michelle for some much-needed sustenance.

Rudy was happy to oblige and happy to hear Pierre was doing fine. The women sat nearby so they could carry on a conversation while Rudy worked.

Michelle told him about Pierre's memory. Rudy had read several scientific journals that discussed changes to people's personalities after experiencing trauma to the head. He seemed to remember that it was not uncommon for people to suffer memory losses and gains. Rudy was glad it was the latter and not the former.

Rudy asked Claire to get two small chickens or a single large bird from the cooler. She brought back a somewhat large bird. Rudy butterflied it, placed it on a bed of wild mushrooms with slices of lemon, slathered on butter and herbs, and slid it into his oven.

He basted the bird every other minute or so, finally pulling it out as the skin became crispy and the breast meat firm. He cut the bird into manageable pieces, placed it on a platter with the mushrooms, roasted fennel, asparagus, spring onion, and carrot. He finished it with a drizzle of the pan juices.

The ladies dug in, relishing every bite. Halfway through the feast, Maria stopped for a moment, "Has anyone seen Daniel? Where is my wayward brother-in-law? Is he around? Has anybody seen him?" She then added, "By the way, this is a lovely chardonnay. Where did it come from?"

Claire spoke up. "My father dropped it off. It is his third vintage. Long ago, he said he could never compete with Villagrosa's reds, but he said he could make a respectable showing in white. This is his third attempt. He dropped off a case. I placed it in the cellar, by the stairs."

"I think it's absolutely lovely. Pleasant on the palate, tastes of green apple, fig, and a tinge of sweetness, honey. Thank your father for me and ask him if we may order additional cases. I don't think we have much in the line of whites in the cellar, and with warmer weather coming up, I am sure people will be asking for them. "

Michelle added, "And please tell him to invoice. We will pay by check or have the bank transfer funds, whichever he chooses."

"How many cases shall I ask him for?" Claire asked.

"I think sixteen. The summer season is June, July, and August. That's twelve weeks. Add another four weeks for May, and assuming a case a week, that's sixteen cases." Maria explained her thinking. "But if he has more, we'll take twenty. I'm sure this will cellar well, and you can never have enough of something good."

It was quiet as the three women enjoyed their meal. There was an occasional sound from the kitchen of a pot being moved, cleaned, or stored, but otherwise, it was quiet.

Daniel and Gabrielle entered the dining room from the inn's Lobby. "Hello, everyone. Hello, Maria, I am glad you are here. I would like you to meet Gabrielle Lucerne."

Maria and Gabrielle exchanged greetings. Maria's first impressions were very good. Nobody had told her much, only that Daniel was interested in a woman named Gabrielle. She didn't have much to go on, and she would never have guessed Gabrielle would be so poised, well-mannered, and obviously beautiful.

After all the pleasantries, Daniel stood up and spoke, "I think it is an excellent time to have a family meeting. Well, a family meeting plus one guest. I first want to say that I believe all the pieces are coming together. The kitchen, our cooking, the recent renovations, even our new dialog with local farmers has been paying off. Plus, Rudy and I have lots of ideas obtained from our recent trip. Thank you, Maria.

"I believe we are missing just one piece of the puzzle. If we find this one piece, we will be complete, and there will be nothing we cannot accomplish. In fact, if we have the right piece, the right fit, I believe, deep down in my intestine…"

"Daniel, say 'gut,' not 'intestine,'" Michelle admonished.

"My apologies, ok then, I believe in my gout…" Daniel tried again.

"Whatever, what do you feel?" Michelle wanted him just to move on.

Gabrielle was laughing, laughing with Daniel, not at him.

"I feel one piece is missing. But I believe, confidently believe, I have found that piece." Daniel smiled, waiting for someone to ask him to reveal what he was talking about.

Michelle was relieved. She was afraid Daniel would say something about her like, "we need to find a husband for Michelle." Michelle spoke, "Ok, Daniel. Tell us the piece that is missing and how Gabrielle can be that piece."

"You are right, yet only half right. Yes, Gabrielle is the missing piece. But what role shall she play? Think about it? What are we missing?"

Everyone sat looking at each other, puzzled.

"What about wine? Who is going out there and talking to farmers about their wines? Who do we have to tell our patrons what we have in the cellar that will enhance their dining experience?" Daniel asked, walking about, his arms accentuating his point.

Rudy was first, "We really could use a sommelier. We really could use someone that loves wines and will visit with locals, ensuring we get the best."

"Exactly, exactly." Daniel turned to Gabrielle, "See, that is why I love my nephew. He is smart, and we think on the same frequency."

Daniel then stood in the center of the room, and with all the fake bravado he could muster, "Ladies and gentlemen, I would like to present to you a woman that I have come to admire and, of course, adore. I give you the sommelier of the famous Tree Trunk Bistro, a woman whose bounds has no taste, Gabrielle."

"Daniel," Michelle tried to correct his error, "her 'taste has no bounds.'"

"Yes, we know that. Thank you, Michelle," Daniel replied.

Daniel took Gabrielle by the hand and brought her to her feet, leading her to the center of the room. "Please, Madam Sommelier, if you could say a few words."

"I don't know what to say. This is very unexpected. But I will say, I would love the opportunity to be part of something. Something unique that has the potential to be great. I see that here. I think you are wonderful people, and you have something special here, very special." She said sincerely, everybody listening, enchanted by her charming personality.

"I have been a flight attendant for more years than I like to count, and in those years, I have learned much about food, wine, and most importantly, people. I have been interested in wine. Though I would never brag about my palate, I am confident in my ability to recognize a good wine and pair the wine with the appropriate foods and flavors. I am suitable for the position of sommelier, but I recognize the challenge. I always strive to be better at what I do." Gabrielle looked at everyone while everyone looked at her, enamored by the way she spoke, how she presented herself, and how she moved about.

"I don't know what else I can say. I will do a good job, and I am ready to start right away," she added.

Maria spoke, "Gabrielle, I don't know how you found us or how we found you. I just don't know, but I am glad our paths have crossed. I think you will be an invaluable asset. I think Daniel is right; there are very good wines being made in this area; we need somebody to hunt them down. We need someone to establish a rapport with local vintners, a wine cellar, and a wine list.

Most importantly, we need someone that can present our wines to our patrons. Daniel is right; we need a sommelier. I am a good judge of character. I think you have what it takes. Welcome to the Tree Trunk."

Maria walked over to Gabrielle, and the two women hugged. Michelle stood up, walked over to Gabrielle, and hugged her while whispering, "bulls' eye" in her ear. Claire was next, offering a hug while offering congratulations.

Maria then asked the question that was on everybody's mind, "Do you two have plans for a future together?"

Gabrielle knew the question was coming but was still caught off guard. "I don't know. We are very fond of each other. This has been our first day together, and everything is very new to me. I have one more flight, one more obligation I must attend to. I will leave Monday and come back the following Friday. That time apart will allow us time to think. When I come back, we will have a more meaningful conversation about a life together."

Daniel, listening to Gabrielle, smiled and added, "Notice, she did not say no."

Gabrielle smiled and laughed politely, "Yes, I did not say no."

Chapter 36

Maria drove Pierre's Citroen to Bordeaux Monday morning, leaving Michelle behind, fearing the back seat was not large enough to comfortably hold a 175 cm tall woman or a 185 cm tall man.

The day was bright and sunny, and Maria became so lost in her thoughts that it seemed to her that she was only on the road for a little over an hour. As she pulled into the hospital's parking lot, she could see the large clock across the way. She realized it had taken her almost three hours.

The hospital staff brought Pierre to the discharge area in a wheelchair while Maria signed forms and received instructions and medications for his care. Pierre was smiling, wearing his casual clothes, which Maria had brought on a previous visit. She had already sent his brand-new maroon tuxedo to the cleaners.

"Good morning." Pierre greeted Maria, happy to see her and happy to be leaving the hospital. "You didn't happen to bring cigarettes, did you?"

"Of course not. I don't think the doctor wants you to be smoking," Maria advised her brother-in-law as she took the stack of papers, Pierre's copies of his medical records, and placed them in her valise.

"Well, we can always stop. I am sure there is a café nearby. An espresso sounds inviting too. Don't you think?" Pierre suggested.

"Pierre, let's go home. I would think after all we've been through, you will want to get home and stay home," Maria replied, flabbergasted that Pierre wasn't as homesick as she expected.

"Well, let us depart then. Shall I drive?" he said in all seriousness.

"Heaven's no!" Maria said, correcting Pierre and leaving no room for debate.

Pierre was helped into the passenger seat while Maria climbed into the driver's seat. The backseat was filled with flowers, Pierre's books, and Maria's valise, making Maria think it was a good thing she came alone.

The radio, long ago had stopped working. Well, it worked actually, but it wouldn't bring in any signals. The only noise it emitted was a steady static sound, no matter what station it was tuned to. So the two made small talk as they rode along.

"How are Claire and Rudy?" Pierre asked.

"Like two peas in a pod," Maria answered. "They are obviously in love."

"Still on their honeymoon?" Pierre said a trifle sarcastically.

"They both have big hearts, they'll never fight; you'll never see them argue," Maria concluded, hoping Pierre's cynicism would disappear. "Daniel has met a woman. Her name is Gabrielle. He won't admit it, but he has fallen in love with her. I think she is in love with him too."

"Really, go figure. It just goes to show, there is someone for everyone," Pierre replied, still being a bit sarcastic, too sarcastic for Maria.

"That was a terribly mean thing to say about your brother," Maria admonished.

"Well, let's be real; it's a mean world," Pierre explained. He sighed and was quiet for the remainder of the ride home.

* * *

Michelle was glad John Reynolds didn't answer his phone when her call went to his voicemail. Still, she didn't want to leave a message, especially a message declining his offer. So, she hung up before his recording finished, before she heard the ubiquitous beep. *I'll try again later*, she thought, and then tried to decide how many more times she would attempt to reach him before leaving a message. *I'll try three times. After the third time, if I still get his voicemail, I'll just leave a message. The heck with it, at some point, we all must move on*, she told herself.

Michelle had the early front desk duty. She didn't mind; it was quiet, and her head was usually clear in the early morning. She went through the reservation software, satisfied with its performance and features, until she found something quite peculiar. In April, almost the entire third floor, five rooms in total, were reserved under the Duggart name. It was booked again two weeks later and then once again, three weeks later. The first reservations were for Thursday and Friday, the second for Friday and Saturday, and the third back to Thursday and Friday. *Was this the same Duggart?* Michelle wondered. *It's not that common of a name. Wouldn't she contact us before making the reservations? Knowing Louisa, she'd insist on a reduction in rate, reserving five rooms for six nights,* she thought.

Michelle decided to dig a little deeper and brought up the charge card. The name on the charge card, reserving the rooms, was indeed Louisa Duggart. *After all the trouble she caused, and then my hanging up on her. I thought she would have too much pride ever to show her face here again. And five rooms, why does she want five rooms for two nights, weeks apart, on three occasions? This looks odd. I don't know what she's up to; I'd better get Mother's opinion.*

* * *

It was nearly 1 p.m. by the time Maria and Pierre made it back to Saint Charles. Pierre managed to extricate himself from the passenger seat when Maria had climbed out and walked around to his door. He was standing there when Andre the bellboy, came out of the Inn.

"Welcome home Monsieur Villeneuve. It is so good to see you healthy and standing tall." Andre was all smiles as he gave Pierre a customary hug.

"Thank you, Andre. It is good to be home, and I feel healthy, but I could use a cigarette," Pierre replied after returning Andre's greeting.

"Here, allow me," Andre said, pulling a pack of cigarettes from his pocket, offering one to Pierre, and then fishing around in his pocket for a light.

Pierre inhaled deeply and then exhaled a large cloud of blue-grey smoke, immediately feeling the large dose of nicotine he had just self-administered. "Ah, wonderful," he said to no one in particular.

"I thought it would be a good time for you to quit," Maria said, watching him smoke his cigarette.

"I enjoy it. Why would I stop something I enjoy?" Pierre answered. "I just spent three weeks in the hospital. They did every test imaginable; they had me swallow little metal capsules and watched as they went through my system."

Pierre turned to Andre smiling, "I would hate to be the one that had to retrieve those," causing Andre to laugh loudly. "After everything was finished, the results show I am as healthy as anybody. In fact, the doctor said that I am in remarkable shape for a 56-year-old man. Good lord, that sounds horrific," Pierre said, with a curious look on his face.

He then repeated, "56 years old…" and after a short contemplation, Pierre looked over at Maria, "I better start living."

He finished his cigarette and said to all, "Well, should we go in?" then opened the door to the inn lobby, holding it open for Maria and bowing as she went past.

As Maria walked past Pierre, she examined him out of the corner of her eye. *There is something odd about him. Something very odd. He is more brazen, cavalier. I am not sure if I like this new Pierre.*

Michelle was still at the desk when Maria, followed by Pierre, walked through the door. "Pierre!" she cried and ran around the desk, giving him the hardiest of hugs. "Welcome home. It is so good to have you back."

"Hello, Michelle, it is good to be back. How has life been treating you?" Pierre asked.

"Well, I feel oddly at peace with myself," was Michelle's answer.

"Good, that's important. Now the challenge is to stay that way. You have a lot of living left to do, with a lot of decision-making. It will be a challenge," he advised, smiling and giving her a wink.

Pierre then announced, "Well, I am going to take a long, hot shower, put on fresh clothes, and then see what's going on at City Hall. Should we agree to meet for a late lunch, or shall we wait and have an early dinner?"

Maria spoke up. "I'm a bit tired from the drive and would like to rest. Given the time, why don't we try for an early dinner? Our guests will be checked in, and we won't need to keep anybody at the desk. How does 7 p.m. sound?"

"Sounds very good to me," Pierre replied. "I will see everyone then. Maria, thank you for picking me up and for all the hours you kept vigil. I know it wasn't easy on you. I don't know if I will ever be able to pay you back." Pierre reached over and gave Maria a long, lingering hug.

"You are welcome. Our prayers were answered. It is wonderful to have you back," Maria replied while thinking, *That sounds like the Pierre I once knew.*

As Pierre walked off, Maria and Michelle watched him go, noticing something odd with his walk. He walked stiffly, and from his waist up, nothing moved as he walked. There was a slight lean to one side, Pierre's left side.

Maria and Michelle quickly looked at each other and then looked back at Pierre as he marched out of the lobby.

Maria asked quietly, "Did you notice something odd about Pierre's walk?"

Michelle replied solemnly, "Yes, very odd. He walks very rigidly, almost as if he was glued or hammered together."

"But his legs move," Maria observed.

"Yes," Michelle added, "but nothing else."

After a moment of silence, Michelle then added, "It's too bad."

"Too bad? What do you mean?" Maria quizzed.

"Too bad he's too old to be a soldier. He'd be perfect. Just give him a rifle," she replied.

"Michelle, that's terrible." Maria scolded her daughter while trying to hold in her laughter. Finally, both women broke up laughing, as each pictured in their minds Pierre's stiff walk, visualizing him marching along in a military parade.

Maria finally pulled herself together, observing, "Well, we don't have to worry. Besides his age, that distinctive lean to the left will surely get him disqualified."

Michelle, agreeing with her mother, added, "Yes, perhaps if it were a lean to the right, the military would make concessions."

Both women laughed hysterically as they transformed Pierre's odd walk into a humorous political statement.

* * *

At dinner that night, everyone was happy to have Pierre back and in good spirits, including Pierre. Rudy started the meal off with his onion soup tarts, and Daniel, sensing everyone's mood for a celebration, brought out four bottles of the good stuff, a vintage Villagrosa Bordeaux Blend. It was one of the first vintages produced by Villagrosa and had sat in the far corner of the cellar for years. Daniel had just noticed it when he sat in the cellar with Gabriella.

It stood up well to the large pieces of beef and lamb Rudy roasted in his oven. Daniel sipped and relaxed while examining the wine, holding it up to the light and spinning it around in his glass by moving his wrist.

"Truly remarkable, what mother nature will do if given a chance," he pondered as light spun its way through the dark garnet-colored liquid. "How the fruit of a simple plant, a vine, becomes a complex, flavorful elixir, worthy of a man devoting his whole life to its creation. It is nothing less than a miracle. It is the true essence of religion. This, my dear family, my loved ones, this…" Daniel held up his glass of wine, "this is truly, the manifestation of God. "

"That was very poignant, Daniel," Maria commented at Daniel's narrative and characterization. "I don't know if I agree with everything you said, but what you said, how you said it, was very touching, romantic in an odd way."

"It is only my opinion," Daniel answered.

"So, Pierre, how is the management of the town going? Anything happened worthy of discussion?" Maria asked, changing the subject.

"No, but we are running low on revenues. We have citizens that have not paid fees and taxes in years. The previous mayor left things in a mess. I don't know what he did all day, but he certainly didn't manage the books. I am even more troubled when I think about Mayor Martin's supposed background," Pierre replied to Maria.

"That's right," Michelle cut in, "I remember him saying his background was banking."

"Some banker. I doubt if he could add," Pierre stated sarcastically and continued, "I think we either raise taxes or we petition the government for help. But if we do the latter, bureaucrats will swarm all over this place. After forming committee after committee and installing draconian spending measures, they will insist the town raise taxes. Do you know what I am in favor of doing?" Pierre insisted, knowing full well it would not be a popular solution and an almost impossible task to get the citizenry to go along.

Still fascinated with his glass of wine, Daniel casually replied, "No, what are you in favor of doing?"

Everybody stopped and looked at Daniel. He looked up, noticing everyone staring at him. "What, I want to know, what do you favor?"

Pierre replied, "Daniel, my dear bother, all I ask is that if you decide to participate in the discussion, that you pay attention. "

Daniel sipped his wine and put his glass down, "I will pay attention when something is being said."

"Boys, boys, let's be civil. This is our first dinner together in months. Let's be happy we're together," Maria pleaded.

"Of course. I apologize, Daniel. Raise taxes. It will be a herculean task to get approval to do so but I am afraid it has to be done," Pierre politely answered Daniel's question.

"I apologize as well. Sometimes my mind wanders. I will try to focus," Daniel replied.

Michelle then asked, "Are there any assets to sell? Doesn't the town own some properties?"

"Yes, one thing Mayor Martin did was have the town surveyed to establish property lines for all the town-owned real estate. The town owns quite a bit of real estate, but who wants it? We don't want developers to come in, so we can't just sell it on the open market." Pierre had thought of this option only briefly, thinking he didn't want to deal with strangers purchasing town land and seeking development permits.

"Next door, the meadow, and the grassy hill, it is town property, is it not?" Daniel asked.

"Yes, it is. It's about a six hectares parcel. It includes the meadow and the hill up to the crest. There is an easement out to the main road, next to where the parking lot is. It's a nice piece of property. We should buy it." Pierre described the land correctly but was only half-joking when he mentioned the purchase, seeing if anyone else had an interest.

Michelle, curious, asked, "What would we do with it?"

"Well, first of all," Pierre was now serious, very serious, "buying it would prevent anyone else from buying it. Secondly…"

Daniel interrupted Pierre, "We could plant grapes, eventually bottle and sell our own wine. If the family doesn't want it, I will buy it. I will make it a wedding present for Gabrielle, but of course, it will belong to both of us. We will call it 'Chateau Gabrielle'; our first bottling will be a cabernet and merlot blend." Daniel chuckled and then added, "Saint Charles Cuvee."

Everyone was stunned. Claire looked at Rudy, who looked at Pierre, who looked at Michelle, who looked at Maria.

"Yes, I have decided. When Gabrielle returns, I will ask for her hand. Her dream and one of my fondest wishes is to grow my own grapes and make my own wine. The meadow and the hill are perfect, sun all day. The hill drains to the meadow. Gabrielle and I will plant pinot noir and merlot on the rocky slopes; we will grow cabernet in the meadow, where the soil is richer and moist.

"Who would like to join me?" Daniel asked.

Michelle seemed eager, "Let's get a price and see what we can do. I have a fairly large sum sitting in the bank. I'd rather buy a real asset with potential than let my money languish in a savings account. Besides, I always wanted to jump in a tank of grapes and crush them between my toes." She said, causing everyone to laugh.

"I'm in," Rudy replied before looking at Claire and getting her approval. Then he corrected his terminology. "My apologies, count *us* in."

"The family should buy it if the price is right. Well, I would hope it would be reasonable. We would be doing the town a favor," Maria suggested, having never thought of purchasing the adjacent property, but having known it belonged to the town. She always assumed it eventually would be turned into a park of some kind, but the more she thought about it, the more she liked the idea of a family winery.

"It really is a brilliant idea. Daniel mentioned having a sommelier as the final piece; I think having a vineyard, our own label, maybe even an orchard with a dozen or so apple trees or cherry trees is the final piece. We would be ready then. I mean, really ready," Maria suggested to the family.

"As Mayor, I cannot sell town assets to members of my family, even if the family pays double the normal price. I will have to contact Council Members, and they will have to set the price and make the sale," Pierre stated firmly. "I can contact members and see what they think. Most are our suppliers. They know if we succeed, they will too. The land has been owned for years. Nobody else has expressed an interest in it. But to be ethical, this transaction must be done on what's referred to as an 'arm's length transaction.' I can have no part in it, except of course in an administrative capacity."

"Yes, I understand your concern," Maria admitted. "Well, see what you can do."

"First thing tomorrow morning, I will get on the phone," Pierre agreed.

"Daniel, if the family buys this land, tell Gabrielle we bought it so she may realize her dream," Maria said, smiling at Daniel.

"So, you are quite smitten?" Pierre asked Daniel, continuing, "Congratulations, I look forward to meeting her, and I guess if she is sommelier, I'll be working with her."

Daniel was excited, telling Pierre about Gabrielle, "Yes, she is wonderful; poised, so articulate and intelligent; you will fall in love with her, but you better not." Daniel smiled mischievously, "She is taken."

Pierre laughed in return, "I am dying to meet her, and Daniel, please trust me, I would never, ever, get between my brother and his woman."

"I know, I was only kidding. But thank you for saying so," Daniel replied, sheepishly, a little embarrassed by the misunderstanding of his joke.

Pierre continued, "Good, that's settled. Now, when are we opening for business?"

"I'd like to mention something before we move on. I noticed this morning something a little peculiar." Michelle asked for the floor.

"The floor is yours," Pierre yielded and went back to enjoying his meal.

"Everyone remembers Louisa Duggart?" Michelle asked.

Pierre spoke first, "Where do I know that name from? Oh, I remember, the blonde with the large…"

"Pierre!" Maria stopped him before he could describe more.

"I mean, the nice-looking blonde." Pierre smiled, a devilish smile, winking at Daniel, who smiled back in return.

"Well, she has reserved five rooms for two nights on three different occasions. The first nights are mid-April, then two weeks later, then three weeks later. This is a new one on me. Can anybody shed some light as to what might be going on?" Michelle glanced around, seeing if anybody had any idea.

Daniel asked, "Each time it's two nights?"

"Yes," Michelle replied.

Pierre continued for Daniel, "The visits are two, three weeks apart?"

"Yes." Again, Michelle replied.

Daniel looked alarmingly at Pierre. Pierre looked curiously at Daniel, and both then said in unison, "We're being evaluated."

"Evaluated. What do you mean?" Michelle asked, alarmed by the sudden joint admission.

Pierre explained, "There are numerous culinary societies; people who have taken it upon themselves to judge the quality of food and service at public eating establishments. Some are national, some global. They all go out, not together, of course, and provide ratings. The public can review the ratings and determine if the establishment is worth frequenting."

Daniel had to add his opinion, "Much of it is nonsense, but the more widely followed Societies can make a star out of the chef or destroy him, make him wish he was never born."

"Yes, I have heard of these ratings. Some people follow them as if it were a religion," Michelle said, somewhat unsteadily, wondering what Louisa has gotten us into. "What do we do?" she asked.

Pierre offered his advice, "Let's not panic. Contact Louisa and see if she will provide you with some information. We could be wrong. It could be completely innocent."

"Innocent? No, not Louisa," Michelle replied.

Daniel then spoke, "I remember once there was a star chef in Paris. Everybody loved his food. His restaurant was very popular. I don't know what happened, he was on a holiday or something, while a Society came and visited his restaurant. The review was horrible. I think the Society said they would rather go to Ireland and eat pub food, bangers, and mash than eat at his restaurant."

Michelle, sensing drama, was eager for the conclusion, "So what happened? Did the chef quit, was he ruined, did he jump off a bridge and commit suicide?"

"No, he moved to the UK and opened an Irish pub," Daniel said smiling.

Chapter 37

"Hello, Louisa here. How may I help you?" Louisa's contrived voice came over the phone.

"Hello, Louisa. This is Michelle Villeneuve. How are you?" Michelle replied as calmly and controlled as she could, even though deep inside, she wanted to take Louisa's head off.

"Michelle, good to hear from you. Honestly, I am so happy you called. After that fiasco with Riki Rivage and entourage, I didn't know if you would ever be willing to speak with me again."

"I understand, Louisa. You didn't do anything on purpose. You tried to do the right thing. I cannot fault you for that. I can be critical of your choice of friends, but who am I to do that? You should see some of my mistakes."

Both girls chuckled. Louisa continued, "Well if it makes you feel any better, my Prince, the one I went cruising with, turned out to be a real frog, an absolute toad.

"That's unfortunate. Well, we can't all be princesses," Michelle consoled.

"How true. What can I do for you?" Louisa asked as the women concluded their small talk.

"You reserved several rooms. It just seemed odd. Is there anything you want to tell me?" Michelle asked as delicately as she wanted to be.

"About the reservations? No, just some relatives looking to buy some land; perhaps retire someday and, like your family, establish an inn, bistro, perhaps a winery. They're looking for property closer to Bordeaux, though, so I wouldn't worry about competition. It will be a drive for them, staying at your place, but I convinced them staying at your inn would be worth it. I made the reservations. Otherwise, they'd still be debating where to stay," Louisa calmly informed Michelle.

"Ok, I was worried…." Michelle started to say but was cut-off.

"No need to worry. Must run. Shall we talk again? I must come for the weekend and see the renovations. Let's put that on the schedule. Bye for now. Ciao." Louisa terminated the call.

Michelle thought about her conversation with Louisa. It seemed plausible, her relatives looking to buy land. *I should warn Pierre*, she thought, considering the conversation she had with the family concerning the land next door.

But Michelle had one lingering thought, *Should I believe Louisa? She has never lied to me, but for some reason, I always think she is.*

* * *

The bistro, closed on Monday and Tuesday, opened for business as usual on Wednesday. There was not much fanfare or celebration except for locals who were happy to see the bistro open and glad to see Pierre back and on his feet.

Pierre's odd walk was pronounced and noticed by almost everyone, but no one dared to mention it.

Rudy manned the wood-burning oven offering bread, tarts, and roasted vegetables to accompany Daniel's traditional entrees. The evening wasn't slow, but business was steady, making the workload manageable and causing the time to go by quickly. It was closing time before anyone realized it.

Maria was happy the evening went by smoothly without incident or mistakes. Pierre also felt good and was pleased to get back into the swing of things. He remarked, "If you're afraid of water, the only remedy is to be thrown into the pool."

The wood-burning oven became very popular among the patrons. Daniel and Rudy originally agreed that Paul and Thomas, the waiters, would be taught to use the oven for baking bread. This way, on busy nights, Thursday through Saturday, the oven could be used for bread while Rudy returned to the kitchen to assume his traditional role as sous chef. Thus, Rudy was allowed to use the oven for other than bread baking only on Wednesday evenings and occasionally during lunch service. It was not an ideal solution, but it would have to do until they could devise some other arrangement.

"We have to revisit this arrangement," Maria insisted. "Our patrons are increasingly asking for dishes prepared in the wood-burning oven. I asked them what they found so appealing, and everyone liked the additional smoke flavor and simplicity of the preparation. I think we need to consider how to offer dishes from the wood-burning oven every night. We can limit it to bread for lunch service, but it is important to have it operating every night and for brunch. Rudy, can we devise an egg dish or two, maybe an egg tart to serve for brunch?"

"Yes, it would be simple. I also have an idea for a tart made with goat cheese and honey, simple and satisfying. It would be excellent for those seeking something light early in the day," Rudy stated.

"Sounds delicious. I imagine it would pair well with a pinot noir or even a sweeter white, such as a German Riesling," Pierre observed.

"Whatever goes well with Goat Cheese, that's the dominant flavor. I was thinking of adding seasonal fruits, maybe even figs, but let's keep it simple for now," Rudy further suggested.

"Ok, great, now back to our original dilemma. How do we manage the kitchen? Rudy cannot be in two places at once?" Maria looked about for suggestions.

"It worked well when Claire filled in for Rudy," Daniel offered, then asked, "Claire, do you have any interest in working in the kitchen?"

"Rudy and I have discussed this. I also have an interest in baking. I would like to be trained as a pastry chef. But I understand that we are managing a large, complex enterprise and that we all must do what we can. I would be happy to be trained as a sous chef," Claire responded to Daniel's question in her typical gracious, yet matter-of-fact, way.

"Complex enterprise?" Daniel asked rhetorically, "If I didn't know any better, I'd say you spend a lot of time with Rudy. He is wearing off on you."

"In a good way," Claire replied with her cute little girl grin.

Maria wanted to make sure Claire knew what she was getting into. "Claire, you understand that to assume the role of Sous Chef at the Bistro, you are obligating yourself to a Wednesday through Sunday schedule. You will have Mondays and Tuesdays off, but, of course, you will see a substantial increase in your salary."

"Yes, I understand. I don't mind the hours, and I like having Monday and Tuesday off. Those happen to be the days my husband has off," she said as if Maria didn't know.

Rudy cried out, all in fun, "Nuts, there goes my night out with the guys."

Maria laughed politely, recognizing Rudy's sense of humor. "Ok. You start tomorrow. We open at noon. Daniel, what time do you want her to report to work?" Maria asked, very business-like as if she was really running a complex enterprise and trying to be serious and reinforce the principle of responsibility.

"I think 10 a.m. would be appropriate." Then, looking to Claire, he added, "Please dress accordingly, casual slacks, no dresses, comfortable shoes. Wear your hair up and out of the way. Also, please provide me your sizes so I can order you Chef's uniforms."

Daniel continued, "I will discuss with you the prep that needs to be done, and together the three of us will discuss the menu. We will need to discuss the menu for the whole weekend so we can get our orders out to our suppliers. Now that we will permanently be offering items from the wood-burning oven, we will need to adjust our orders." Daniel spoke directly. Mimicking Maria's style, he spoke seriously and with great responsibility.

"Has anybody offered us capons? We need to talk to someone about getting in some capons," Rudy finally remembered to ask. "Also, duck. If we want to start offering healthier food, duck is a great alternative to beef."

"Yes, it is considered an alternative to beef because the meat is dark red in color. But the flavor, the flavor is minimal. Duck does not come near the flavor of beef. We have supplies of very tasty beef. If we want to be healthy, we should offer leaner cuts of beef," Daniel admonished.

Maria added her thoughts to the discussion, "I agree. I never understood why Duck was so popular. I find it tough and not enjoyable to eat. You either must prepare it almost raw or cook it till it is nothing but tasteless protein. I don't think anyone has ever asked for or criticized us for not having duck on the menu."

Pierre spoke, "I like a roasted piece of duck, but I also agree, Duck takes most of its flavor from the sauce. But, capon, I think capon is delicious. I think it would become a very popular dish. We should seek out a steady supplier of capon."

"My father can do capon," Claire volunteered. "He used to raise them when I was young but stopped because no one would pay the additional price over chicken. I remember my father being distraught because merchants in Bordeaux would sell his capons for much more than chicken, but they were only willing to pay him the price of chicken. Finally, after arguing over and over again, he said enough and stopped raising them. But I know he'd be happy to start again. I think he enjoys eating them himself."

Maria took over, "Ok, Claire, if you could call your father and ask him to raise a flock of capons, perhaps 30 or 40 to start. We will pay his price, of course, within reason."

"Wait," Daniel interrupted. "I think Pierre is right. I think people will want it if they see it on the menu. It is not something people prepare at home, so they will order it. I think more like 100 birds. We will sell them, and besides they freeze well. Freezing them for a short time does not take away the flavor," Daniel added.

"But I remember, they are big birds. A capon, once harvested, weighs in excess of two or three kilos," Claire said, thinking 100 birds is quite a bit of meat.

"Yes, let's start small. Ask him to raise a flock of no more than 50. If they sell well, we will order more. Now, we need to determine how best to prepare it. At 3 kilos, we can't just throw it in Rudy's oven," Maria insisted.

"That is my job, and I will do it. Give me a little time. It would help if I had a bird to test my theories. It is difficult to say I will do it this way or that way, when I don't have a bird to demonstrate. But if the birds are as large as Claire says, then if we want to roast, perhaps we cut pieces like we cut steaks. My memory tells me a Capon has fat, so roasting by the piece may be an option." Daniel paused for a minute, then added, "We can always serve with red wine or chasseur," he advised, suggesting a capon cooked Hunter's style with mushrooms and red wine.

"Yes, I agree. We leave it up to Daniel to decide," Maria corrected, happy to turn the capon issue over to Daniel.

"Will Gabrielle return Friday?" Maria added.

"Yes, as much as I know, that is what we talked about. I have not been informed of any changes," Daniel replied.

"Good, I am eager to get her started on the cellar, and I would like to take her around to meet a few winegrowers. It would be wonderful to have a wine list, appropriate vintages, and varietals. I think our patrons will like it, too. They will be able to try each other's products. Maybe we could even start a rivalry or two," Maria said. "Gabrielle must be careful she doesn't bruise any egos. This will certainly be a test for her political skills. No doubt she's had the training and experience."

"I think she is anxious to get started," Daniel replied.

"I am looking forward to her being sommelier. I am running out of jokes to tell when guests ask for the wine list. Today I was offering red, and a 'don't even think about' white, an excellent vintage, of course," Pierre said, smiling but serious. "It will be nice to have an organized cellar instead of going to the basement and wondering what's in this crate or that box. Having racks of bottles organized will be marvelous, as will knowing what we have ahead of time. Who would have thought? "

Everyone chuckled at Pierre's comments. Everyone knew Pierre was accurate in his description of the past wine service at the Tree Trunk. It was an area neglected for years, with obvious missed opportunities. Maria had lost count at the number of times local vintners had offered her superb wines at bottled prices that were so low she doubted they covered the price of the bottles. Unfortunately, she was stretched too thin and too focused on some other problem needing immediate attention that she was unable to participate.

Pierre continued, "It was an excellent idea on your part Daniel, and from what I hear, Gabrielle is the perfect person for the task. Well done. And to entice her to take the job by offering her marriage; that is duty beyond what anyone could ask for."

Daniel perked up, not sure if he liked Pierre's insinuation, "That is not funny. I offered her the job because she knows wine. She has an excellent palate. I want her to be near me, and here in Saint Charles, there are too few opportunities. She would grow bored and leave. Don't talk like that," Daniel said heatedly, adamant Gabrielle deserves the job and will be successful at it.

"Yes, Pierre. I don't know what your reasons are, but they are not welcome. Please, respect your brother, especially in front of the family." Maria frowned at her brother-in-law.

"My apologies. I only meant it as a joke. Like I said before, I understand Gabrielle is a very presentable and smart woman. I look forward to working with her. Please, Daniel, please accept my apology."

Daniel replied, "No issues. It was only a bad joke."

"Well, if you would excuse me. I need to take my medications and head to bed. I need to be up early tomorrow. I must see about selling some land. Good night everyone." Pierre stood, took his plate to the kitchen, and disappeared.

"You know, he has a point if you read between the lines," Rudy suggested. "Is Gabrielle joining us so she can be Sommelier, or is she being Sommelier so she can marry Daniel? Suppose after some time she no longer is interested in working seven days a week? Suppose after some time, she or Daniel decide marriage is not for them. Forgive me, everyone, but we know nothing of this woman, nothing at all. I admit she is a tremendous combination of intelligence, personality and looks, but I keep wondering.

How could she be living in Paris for so long and not have accomplished something? How could she not have ties to someone or something?"

"She seems genuine, down to earth," Michelle observed but also wondering who Gabrielle is.

"I am a good judge of character," Daniel spoke, trying to think of some way to defend his feelings towards Gabrielle. "I agree, we know little of this woman, but I also think she is genuine, honest. Maybe she is leaving or running away from something, a bad marriage or relationship. Many people have that problem, and they seek an opportunity to start over. Can we blame her if she wants to start over? Can we blame her if she woke up one day and said, 'This is not my dream. This is not my idea of life. I think we should help her become what she wants to be. "

Rudy looked a little askew at Daniel, wondering what it was about this woman that made Daniel turn a blind eye to the many obvious warning signs. "But we are not a rehabilitation center for confused and misguided flight attendants. Yes, she has a dream. We all have desires, ambitions, and dreams, but what lengths should we go to ensure a total stranger realizes hers? We're about to spend a lot of money on a parcel of land. Why? Because your sweetie wants to grow grapes?"

Rudy didn't mean to be so smart with Daniel, but the more he talked about it, the more he convinced himself there was a problem. Many questions needed answering.

"I agree. I think we all have become smitten by Gabrielle's charm; I know I certainly have. But it's her charm that makes her successful at what she does," Maria spoke, more thinking out loud. "I want to move forward and purchase the land before someone else does, but let's keep it a family matter," Maria added, instructing everyone to keep quiet about it. "Let's sleep on the other issues. I am not sure what the answers are. Perhaps we just need to take it one day at a time. "

* * *

Claire did well on her first day, adjusting to her duties as second chef to Daniel. She found Daniel humorous, silly, and incredibly insightful about food, its ingredients, and its preparation. Amazingly, he was also in complete control of his kitchen.

She did as she was told, easily taking instructions from Daniel. She assisted in washing and cutting vegetables for roasting and parboiling; she patiently watched Daniel as he demonstrated how to cut steaks and neatly de-bone chickens. She was tasked with breaking open dozens of eggs, separating the yolks for Daniel's Crème Brulee.

Lunch that day was busier than usual. No doubt many people came to see Pierre and afterward stayed for lunch. Claire spent much of her time preparing plates for Daniel's entrées and soon understood the various codes and signals he used when requesting plates.

Daniel always used numbers. The numbers one through five were for potato accompaniments, the numbers six through ten were for various vegetables. Claire soon understood Daniel needed one plate with mashed potatoes and asparagus, the other pan-roasted potato and asparagus when he ordered "two plates 17 and 37".

Claire marveled at Daniel's ability to maintain control under pressure. The busier it got, the more controlled he became. On the other hand, Rudy would come charging through the door between the wood-burning oven and the kitchen, scream unintelligibly, and return to his oven. This caused Claire or one of the busboys to drop what they were doing and ask what he needed.

The evening meal went by without any significant problems. Rudy underestimated the demand for Fantasy Bread and his tarts, now offering five different combinations. With an hour left to dinner service, he ran out of proofed dough, causing him to use dough that he had made earlier that day, and not fully developed. The flavor of the wood-burning oven and a generous slather of mayo mixed with garlic and fragrant gruyere cheese saved the day.

Daniel admonished him. "You will need to be better prepared. You underestimate your own popularity. The dough takes a long time to prepare properly. From now on, make one and one half as much as what you have in the past. If you still stock out, prepare twice as much. Daniel then added good-heartedly, "Not having enough, selling too much…that's a problem many chefs wish they had."

Chapter 38

Michelle assumed the duties of Maitre'd, giving Pierre time to catch up on his mayoral responsibilities. Those duties included rounding up the council members, reporting on the town's poor fiscal condition, and suggesting ways to generate some cash quickly.

Gabrielle arrived back in Saint Charles late Friday morning and walked into the lobby of the Inn, this time with a large suitcase that she could barely handle. Andre came running over as soon he spotted her. "Hello, and welcome back, Gabrielle."

"Thank you, Andre. It's good to be back. I can guess Daniel is in the kitchen?" she asked.

"Yes, we started service at noon. He is usually in the kitchen by 10 a.m. and stays there until closing. He is a dedicated, hard-working man," Andre mentioned, thinking pretty women always make him say too much.

"Thank you, Andre. Yes, he is a very hard-working man who is dedicated as well," she replied, wondering if she should check in or wait.

Maria, hearing the conversation, came from out of the office. "Hello, Gabrielle. Welcome back." She smiled, offering a warm welcome, complete with a hug.

"Hello, Maria. You don't know how wonderful it is to be back. You look absolutely radiant," Gabrielle offered, admiring Maria's natural beauty.

"Thank you. That's very kind of you. Daniel is in the kitchen. Lunch service just started, so he will be focused, very focused," she said, raising her eyebrows and making Gabrielle laugh. "Why don't we go and say hello to

Michelle. Then maybe you'd like to join me for coffee or perhaps freshen up from your drive. Meanwhile, I'll tell Daniel you are here."

Maria brought her to the bistro's entrance through the inn's lobby, dropping her off with Michelle and informing Daniel she had arrived.

"It is not a good time. Could you entertain her until the service concludes? It's busy today. I don't think I will be able to leave the kitchen until at least 3 p.m. If you would, please give her my apologies, "Daniel said between the numerous tasks he was attempting to accomplish all at once.

Paul came hustling in to drop off an order. Daniel read the order and then barked instructions to Claire, "Two onion soup, a goat cheese tart, and four plates 17, 17, 37, 38."

An hour into service, and the dining room was almost full. The place hummed with activity. The two waiters, Paul and Thomas, sprinted to get food to diners, obviously becoming overwhelmed.

Gabrielle looked out at the pandemonium. "My word!"

"Yes, it's been hectic," Michelle spoke honestly without hesitation, "The real problem is that we haven't worked out the coordination between Rudy's station and the kitchen. If a table orders a dish from the wood-burning oven, the kitchen doesn't have any way to track it and vice-versa. So we have to work on that. Plus, we need a third person. We need a wine steward or a…." Michelle was interrupted.

"Or a Sommelier?" Gabrielle spoke for her.

"Yes, a Sommelier," Michelle agreed.

"Well, here I am. Give me an apron," Gabrielle insisted.

Michelle went to the kitchen and grabbed Gabrielle an apron which she quickly tied around her waist. She went to the side table where the waiters had placed bottles of wine, ordered but not yet delivered to tables. Gabrielle started opening bottles. As the waiters went by, they shouted meaningless table numbers at her.

Seeing the concern on Gabrielle's face, Michelle pointed out the tables and clarified the table numbering arrangement. Soon Gabrielle was pouring wine, chatting with patrons, discussing favorite Chateaus and vintages, and even helping to serve a few plates from the wood-burning oven. Gabrielle was all smiles, and more importantly, patrons seemed to enjoy smiling with her.

The pace of the room calmed measurably, and activity seemed to settle into a nice easy rhythm. With Gabrielle involved, things just seemed to move more efficiently, at a nice, even tempo.

Michelle looked out over the dining room, full of what looked like very happy people, and the room seemed full of joyful sounds, people eating, enjoying each other, and genuinely delighted sounds. *Way to go, Gabrielle. Way to go*, Michelle thought to herself.

At the end of the service, when the room had but a few parties remaining, Paul fetched a bottle of red wine from the basement. He opened it and offered a glass to Michelle, Gabrielle, and Thomas. Paul poured each glass, including one for himself. He then offered a toast, "To Gabrielle, a woman whose mere presence turns chaos into order, disarray into poetry, and catastrophe into triumph. Madam, thank you for your efforts today. To Gabrielle."

"Thank you, Paul. That is wonderful of you to say. You and Thomas looked like you were struggling, so I could not stand and watch. I had to step in," Gabrielle replied.

"Thank you. Any time you wish to join us on the floor, please, you are most welcome," Paul said cheerfully and sincerely. He was certainly grateful for her efforts but couldn't help thinking how much difference it made when someone participated, who really knew what they were doing.

Daniel had heard from the busboys that Gabrielle had passed her first test with excellent evaluations. As soon as he was able, he left the kitchen for the dining room. Passing through the large double doors, he came upon the four having a glass of wine and toasting to Gabrielle.

As he got closer, he said with all the authority he could muster, "Gabrielle, one thing we do not permit is drinking during business hours, and especially drinking with the help."

Gabrielle's face went flush white, while Paul very sheepishly handed a glass to Daniel, "Here's your glass, Daniel," giving him a healthy pour.

"Ah, thank you. "Then putting on airs, Daniel asked, "what are we drinking today, the blend or the merlot?"

"You are joking," Gabrielle laughed, not minding at all bearing the brunt of Daniel's humor. "You had me there for a moment. You are a good actor. "She then reached over and gave Daniel a hug and a brief but passionate kiss. "How are you, sweetheart. I missed you."

"I missed you, too. How was your trip?" he asked.

"Just another trip. They use large planes on these long routes, so there were eleven attendants. Of those eleven, four of us were eligible for buyouts, and all four of us filed our papers. We went out in Los Angeles and had a nice dinner with champagne. We are not allowed to drink twelve hours from our flight, so our celebration was somewhat sedate."

Daniel smiled, "We will have time to celebrate later. On Sunday, we have a single service at 1 p.m., lasting till 8 p.m. Then we close till Wednesday. We will have plenty of time to celebrate."

Gabrielle smiled, "Wonderful."

"I must get back. We will be busy this evening. Maybe you will want to start on the cellar? There is still time to order more wine for this evening. Peter Fawcett was supposed to deliver 20 cases of Chardonnay. I don't know why he is taking so long."

"Who is taking so long?" a man's voice sounded from across the room. Peter Fawcett stood in the entranceway that separated the bistro's lobby from the inn's. "I took a little longer so I could prepare you a sample of my capon. I have eight birds on ice, plus twenty cases of white wine that, I believe, will earn respect no matter where it's poured."

Daniel smiled, "Hello, Peter. Good to see you and thank you for bringing presents."

"Well, they are not really presents. I have costs to cover, but I'll give you a good price. I brought you smaller birds. I thought that is what you'd prefer," Peter said.

"Thank you. Yes, smaller birds would be a good beginning. Whatever price you think is fair, you need to make a profit. Please charge us accordingly," Daniel replied, thankful to have such a good rapport with his suppliers.

Michelle added, "Hello, Peter. Could you please invoice us? I will write you a check or have the bank transfer funds, whatever you prefer."

"Whichever takes the least effort. I understand we will soon be competitors?" Fawcett added while shaking Daniel's hand.

"I am not sure I understand?" Daniel replied, thinking he knew what he meant but not wanting to discuss the matter with Gabrielle or the waiters present. "Did you see Maria as you came in? She mentioned to me that she had something very important to discuss with you. Here let me take you to her office," Daniel said quickly, fumbling along, just trying to separate Peter from everybody.

"Good, I also have a proposition to make to her," Peter added.

Paul, the waiter, looked at Michelle for clarification, "Competitors?"

"Don't look at me. I have no idea," Michelle said with a shrug.

When Daniel had Peter alone, he turned to him. "I am sorry to be so rude, but we do not want anybody to know we are purchasing land to grow grapes and perhaps establish a winery."

"What? This is news to me," Peter replied.

"That is not what you meant? Being competitors?" Daniel said, a look of surprise on his face.

"No, heavens no, but I think it's a good idea. When Claire called asking about Capons, she also mentioned fruit trees. She wanted to surprise Maria with a couple of mature fruit trees. She thought planting them around the veranda would be nice. Patrons could enjoy an apple tart, with apples picked just minutes before. I market my apples and bring you a bushel every now and then. "

"Yes, I know," Daniel admitted.

"I was only joking about competitors. That's my sense of humor. You'll get used to it," Peter said, slightly frustrated, thinking that if humor takes this much effort, I'll keep my jokes to myself.

"But I must be completely honest." Peter continued, rubbing his chin as he spoke, "Claire asked if I still had extra vines. I asked what she would do with them. She told me she could not say, and I let it go at that. But now that you've mentioned it, the more I think about it, the more I like the idea."

"Think about what? What idea is that?" Daniel asked.

"Growing your own grapes. Making your own wine," Peter said without hesitation.

Daniel was again alarmed Peter had mentioned what they were doing, even though he had just told him. "Yes. But please do not speak of it, please tell no one. Not until we make an announcement."

"Of course. I do not gossip," Peter said, slightly confused, "I have been thinking quite a bit about winemaking. I have a proposition to make to Maria."

"I will take you to her office." Daniel led the way to Maria's office, where she sat, opening correspondence and figuring out how to respond to an email.

"Maria?" Daniel stuck his head through the door. "Do you have a minute for Peter Fawcett?"

"Yes, of course, come in, sit," Maria said as she put down what she was doing. "Hello, Peter, what is on your mind?"

Peter entered, sitting in one of the comfortable chairs opposite but facing Maria's desk. "Claire called and asked about capons, so I brought you some fresh birds," Peter started.

"Wonderful. Thank you. Please charge us what you think is reasonable. I think Michelle would like an invoice if that is not too much trouble?" Maria was very polite and personable with her request. Peter was now family, albeit remotely, but she still lacked experience doing business with him. So far, though, she liked the man, and the more she talked with him, the easier it became.

"No, not at all," Peter replied. He then continued, "Claire also asked if I still had extra vines. She did not mention who or what they were for but, of course, I assumed."

Maria laughed politely, "Very good guess, Peter. Yes, we are interested in producing our own wines. We just need the land and the vines. Well, I must say we are also missing what is, probably, the most important piece," Maria responded, leaving something for him to ponder.

`"What may that be, if I might ask?" Peter inquired, already knowing what she was getting at and thinking this was the perfect opportunity for him to strike a deal.

Maria laughed again, "Expertise. We are looking into obtaining some vacant land from the town, and perhaps we can purchase some vines on the market. Bordeaux being Bordeaux, I'm sure a person could buy anything and everything they need related to wine and winemaking. All that we need then is the expertise."

Peter added, "Don't forget, you also have the outlet. You have buyers. It's difficult to be an unknown and sell wine in this market. People like proven names, names they know will sell. If your vintages are good, you can serve them, and if they are very good, you can also offer bottles at retail. Are you still selling bread?"

"We stopped when we underwent renovations. Now that life is getting back to normal, I'd like to re-open our retail store," Maria admitted, liking Peter more and more as the conversation went on.

"You should re-open as a bread, wine, and cheese shop. Many families have been making wonderful cheeses for generations, wines too. They would welcome a friendly outlet. I say friendly because we all have tried to take our products to the markets in Saint Germaine and even Bordeaux. We know our products are of the highest quality, better quality than products sold in those markets, but we are not treated with respect. Merchants offer us crumbs. I have seen my friends give their products to the nuns and orphanages rather than take the ridiculous prices those rogues offer. It is a shame that we do not get the recognition and respect we deserve."

"Peter, my heart goes out to you and all the families. I know you have all worked hard and feel frustrated and cheated. I think you are on to something.

A Bread, Wine, and Cheese Shop is an excellent idea. We are getting more and more traffic through Saint Charles, and we need to give people a reason to stop. We should even organize a wine and cheese fair. The Tree Trunk will provide free bread so visitors can try all the different cheeses, and then we can offer a refreshing glass of Saint Charles Cuvee." Maria laughed at the notion of offering her own label, but she was excited over the possibilities.

Maria's motivation heartened Peter. "Thank you. You have excellent ideas as well. But first, let's get the doors of the store open. I'll contact my friends and get the word around. Would we be able to meet some night or morning at the Tree Trunk? Maybe have a nice, pleasant morning meeting talking about the products and the possibilities?" Peter asked.

"Yes, but a Monday or a Tuesday. The bistro is closed those days so that we won't interrupt the preparation for lunch service," Maria suggested.

"Good. I have something else I'd like to discuss with you."

"Yes?" Maria listened.

"We started this conversation discussing wine," Peter stated, confident his idea was a good one. "I suggest we start a partnership. You commit your resources, I'll commit mine, and, well, let's see what we can do together."

"What can we do together?" Maria asked rhetorically. "I need to know first what we are trying to do?" she offered, feeling like she was missing the main point.

"I've been making wine for a few years now. My whites are showing well; my reds still need work. The fact is, I don't have the right soil for red. But you know the hillside to the west of the mill? I bet that soil would be perfect for pinot noir and the meadow? I think it'll need a little irrigation, but I would bet my last ounce of gold, if you planted cabernet sauvignon, cabernet franc, and even Merlot, the vines would grow like weeds. If you're looking to buy some land, look no further. So, my offer is this: we'll be partners. We'll do whites at my place, we'll do reds at yours, and at the end of the day, we'll share in the prize money." Peter smiled and slapped his hand on her desk, signifying he was all in and ready to deal.

"Why did you mention the hill and the meadow?" Maria asked, slightly perturbed that he should know about the property when she had asked everyone to keep it a family matter.

"It's the best and one of the largest pieces of land the town owns. Besides, it's next door. Why would you want land down the street when there's a nice lot adjacent to your property? I may be from the country, but

I still have some sense," Peter said adamantly, adding, "So what do you think?"

"Sounds very good. I like it. It gets us up and running quickly, but still, I'll have to check with the family." Maria said smiling, "That includes Claire."

"She's got a good head on her shoulders. She'll tell you; I am a man of my word. You keep up your end of the deal, and I'll take care of mine," Peter said, in case Maria had any doubt.

"I believe you are. Let's talk in a day or two. Meanwhile, let's set a meeting regarding the retail store as soon as possible," she reminded Peter.

"I'll try for this coming Tuesday," Peter answered.

"I'll write that down and relay the news to the family. Thank you for everything, Peter," she said as she got up.

Peter stood. "By the way, I have twenty cases of my chardonnay. Where would you like me to place it?"

"Ask Daniel, no, no, ask Gabrielle where to put it," Maria replied.

* * *

It was Louisa's Uncle Claude's birthday. She had to call him and offer love and best wishes, especially after he had agreed to take his committee to someplace named Saint Charles and review a country bistro named The Tree Trunk.

Typically, an eating establishment must submit its credentials, including menus, and the kitchen staff's resumes to be considered for review by The French Culinary Society. Once submitted, there are no guarantees if or when the committee will visit and review the establishment.

It is considered an accomplishment to be reviewed. A review indicates the committee perceived something unique or interesting, in terms of cuisine, that warranted investigation.

Louisa pleaded with her uncle to take the committee to Saint Charles. When he finally relented, she made the arrangements for the committee members to stay at the Inn.

To properly review and grade an establishment, the committee visits over a series of evenings. The review must be held blind; that is, the establishment has no idea of their identities or the purpose of their visit.

Louisa placed the reservations under her name, successfully hiding the identities of the committee.

To say the committee is difficult to impress is an understatement. But their strict allegiance to the highest standards is what makes their opinions all the more popular. The committee uses a five-star scale with one star the lowest and five the highest. It is worth noting that no establishment has ever been awarded more than a three-star rating in the 200-year history of the Society. One restaurant, twice reviewed and awarded three stars, was thought to be a contender for a fourth star. But unfortunately, a salad fork went missing from a place setting, and was subsequently replaced with a dirty utensil, resulting in the restaurant's rating being reduced to only two stars.

According to one past committee member, "Five Stars infers perfection. The Committee commonly considers perfection an ideal so grandiose that it is considered virtually unobtainable through human effort."

Each year the committee is formed with various members of the culinary industry. The membership is kept secret until the review season has concluded. Once the season is concluded, the committee goes into seclusion to determine if a star or stars should be awarded. Afterward, a large ceremony is held and televised, similar to the American Film Industry's Academy Awards. The committee members are introduced, and the ratings are then carefully announced. Typically, the establishment's Head Chef attends and is brought up on stage to accept the award.

Once an establishment is rated, it keeps the rating for three years, after which it must submit another application. An establishment can only be reviewed once every three years. Thus, each review and rating is treated as a new award.

Louisa's Uncle Claude is the committee head, elected by Society members for an unprecedented third five-year term. He had heard about the Riki Rivage incident and agreed to take the Committee to The Tree Trunk as a special favor for Louisa.

"Hello, Uncle Claude?" Louisa asked respectfully.

"Yes, Louisa, how are you, child?" the man's voice answered and perked up as he recognized who was calling.

"Well, all grown up. How are things with you?" Louisa inquired.

"Busy, very busy. Our schedule is filling up. Our reviews have become very popular, and we are inundated with applications. We have created a second committee to help us get through our backlog," Claude commented.

"Well, that's good," Louisa said, not really knowing what else to say on the subject. "I'm just calling to let you know that you are all set with reservations for the sixteenth and seventeenth of April, the first and second of May, and then again for the twentieth and twenty-first of May. You'll love

Saint Charles. It's so quaint and charming, like out of a children's story, and the food is perfect, fresh and well-prepared," she told him once again, even though she knew she could never influence his opinion.

"That's wonderful. I firmly believe simple country-style cooking with the simple usage and presentation of fresh ingredients should be the cornerstone of contemporary French cuisine. I know the committee looks forward to visiting. Now, management is not aware of our plans or who we are? That is very important, you know," he reminded his favorite niece.

"No. Someone asked, but I just told them you were relatives in the area looking to buy property," she replied.

"That's good. Excellent. Well, let me run. As always, it was wonderful to hear your voice," Claude said, needing to get back to business.

"Oh, Uncle, Happy Birthday! I hope you have many more," Louisa just barely remembered why she had called in the first place.

"Thank you, dear. Ciao." Claude was happy, she remembered, as he concluded the call.

Chapter 31

G abrielle enjoyed participating in Friday evening service. With Daniel working, she had little else to do. Before the doors opened, she spent some time in the cellar, placing fifteen cases of Fawcett's white on the racks and another five in the meat cooler. She counted twenty-two cases of Villagrosa's red wine but other than having either blue or red foil sealing the cork, the bottles had no distinguishing features. She had no idea what the vintage was or whether the bottles contained a blend or were a single varietal. She opened half of the cases and arranged them neatly on the shelves, storing the unopened cases nearby. It seemed easy until she found a third color and then a fourth. Thinking about her previous week's experience when Daniel first introduced her to Villagrosa's red wine, she remembered Daniel was taking bottles from a case that displayed still another color foil. She had five different bottles from Villagrosa's winery and no idea what they were.

She brought a blue and a red foil to the dining room. She also brought a green and a purple. The bottle she shared with Daniel was a great wine. She didn't know how much was available, so she wisely left that out of the offerings.

She gathered Michelle and Claire, Paul and Thomas, and asked Daniel and Rudy for a minute of their time. When all had gathered, she announced her intentions: "The cellar contains twenty-two cases of various red wines: bottles with red, blue, green, and purple foil, no other markings. Before we open to try and determine what they are, I thought I'd ask for input. Does anyone know anything about what these bottles are?"

Daniel stepped over to the station where the four bottles were on display. "The red is a Bordeaux blend, seven, maybe eight years old, drinking nicely, very mature for its age. The blue is a merlot from the same year, very smooth, like velvet. The green is a three-year-old Rhone-style red. It's a big red, very big. The purple is a five-year-old Bordeaux blend, tasting of mature fruit but still developing tannins, so it needs a few more years. "

He continued, "Villagrosa also has a decent pinot noir that we should order. He told me he would put a few dozen cases away for us. We need to follow up. Maria has his contact information. Ask her to call him for you."

Daniel then walked back to the kitchen, followed by Rudy. The two disappeared behind the large swinging doors.

Gabrielle looked at Michelle and Claire, "How does he do that? My Lord, that was impressive."

Michelle just smirked, "Daniel certainly has his moments."

Gabrielle did as Daniel asked and went to Maria. "Excuse me, Maria, may I have a word with you?"

"Hello, Gabrielle, certainly, come in, sit. What can I do for you? Oh, and before I forget, thank you for your efforts today. Would you like to work this evening?"

"Yes, very much so. I was hoping so," Gabrielle replied. "But the reason I am here is Daniel asked me to ask you to get in touch with Villagrosa and have him deliver the Pinot Noir he has reserved for us."

"Oh, wonderful. Many people have asked for Pinot Noir. It appears its time has come. When I was young, we would just call it Burgundy," Maria offered.

Gabrielle was relaxed, feeling congenial. "I agree; it is easy on the palate, always seems to go along nicely with whatever is being served even if it's a pungent cheese."

Maria smiled and nodded. "Give me a few moments to finish what I was doing and then I'll call and see if he can deliver a few cases."

"Thank you. I'll get back to the dining room and see if I can help set up. Thank you again." Gabrielle smiled and left Maria's office.

Gabrielle was immensely helpful to Paul and Thomas and the busboys in setting up the dining room. Her assistance allowed Paul and Thomas to fill the gas tanks for the outdoor heaters and arrange them on the veranda. Michelle hadn't received any reservations explicitly asking for the veranda, but it would be nice if they could offer outdoor seating.

As service began, Gabrielle noticed cases of champagne in the cooler while retrieving a bottle of chardonnay. She received the okay from Maria to offer it to guests. "Not bad," Gabrielle thought, "Three very good reds, an excellent white, and champagne. Not a bad start." She purposely left out the young Bordeaux blend, following Daniel's recommendation that it needed more time.

The night moved along, and Gabrielle proved to be quite adept at handling the many conflicting demands on her attention. Paul commented later that evening, "I don't know what it is; things just seem to go smoothly when she is involved."

She was quickly making friends with many guests, commenting on how wonderful she had treated them. Locals dropping by for the usual night out also commented on how Gabrielle seemed to add a great deal of elegance to the dining room, with one long-time patron saying, "I am really beginning to enjoy this place." Another said to Maria in passing, "At last, it seems like a real first-class restaurant."

* * *

Michelle continued as Maitre'd, while Pierre worked fervently on the land acquisition. After all was said and done, the Town Council voted overwhelmingly to sell the parcel of land to the Villeneuve family, agreeing to allow the cultivation of grapes and the establishment of a winery, complete with a public tasting room. The price was steep, but Maria was happy to pay it if it meant quickly consummating the deal. This allowed her to get back to more pressing matters, and besides, the money was going to a good cause: returning Saint Charles to a sound fiscal footing.

Pierre worked late into the evening to get the land appraised and a contract drawn up. He went back and forth with Town Council members concerning mineral rights, water rights, easements, and the adjustment of zoning restrictions.

The lawyers were concerned with the zoning. Because the property was zoned for commercial use, a winery, construed as an agricultural enterprise, would violate town zoning ordinances. This prompted Pierre to make what seemed like endless phone calls to get the Town Council to waive zoning restrictions. At one point, he found himself driving out to Tremont's farm to get his signature after first stopping to pick up Stephenson to witness the signing.

Maria hired Mornay & Sons to draw up plans for a winery building. At Peter's request, she asked the architects to include plans for digging a cavern deep into the hill and lining it with brick and stone to maintain an even temperature for the aging and storage of barrels of wine, as well as already bottled vintages. For the time being, though, every inch of soil was to be planted, and once the fruit was harvested, it would be trucked to Fawcett's facility for crushing, aging, and bottling.

Eventually, when the budget permitted, the winery would be established and opened to the public.

Maria wasn't in a hurry to build the winery. They had no wines to offer the public, and if they did, she'd like first to offer them through the retail Wine, Bread, and Cheese store she was about to start with help from the community. She was satisfied to let the architects take their time and think about suitable designs for the Winery.

After the purchase had been made and all legalities settled, Peter Fawcett sent two of his sons and some hired hands to clear the land, lay down pipes for irrigation, and erect trestles to eventually hold the vines upright.

Fawcett himself tested the soil every other meter till he was confident of his earlier assumption, pinot noir on the hillside, other red varietals in the meadow. He brought the vines, and planting began just days after purchasing the land.

* * *

One week after planting, on a sunny Monday afternoon, Daniel took Gabrielle to the vineyard. "Come, I want to take you for lunch," he said as he took her hand and picked up a backpack. A baguette poked out one side, and the sound of tinkling glasses accompanied each step.

They followed a wide path leading from the parking lot and stopping at the vineyard's edge, halfway up the hill. They continued along the edge of the vineyard to the crest of the hill, where they came upon a small clearing. Two picnic tables with benches had been placed there by Fawcett's ground crew. It was where they usually ate lunch and took their breaks.

It wasn't much of a hill, but there was enough elevation to see the whole vineyard, row after row of plantings. Daniel could easily make out the color markers at the end of each row, signifying the type of grape planted. On the hill itself, getting the full benefit of the afternoon sun, Daniel could see a single color, red.

"Well, what do you think?" he asked Gabrielle as he started to remove items from his pack.

"It's beautiful. The sun feels so good. The skies are blue, and look at the plantings, so neat and organized. What do the colors mean? The little pendants at the end of each row?" she asked.

Daniel started taking items out of his pack. He handed her a small round of cheese, and another small packet of cheese, two apples, and a small block of pate. Then he took out the bread, a knife, and a small cutting board. He looked out over the vineyard, "The colors signify the type of grape, the type of vine planted in that row. Notice on the hill it is all one color."

"Yes, I see," she answered and then asked, "What varietal is red?"

"Pinot Noir," he answered, pulling out two bottles of red wine. She could tell by the color of the foil that it was the same wine Daniel had opened the day he showed her the cellar.

When she saw the wine, she immediately smiled, "Oh, the good stuff."

Daniel smiled back, "Yes, the good stuff." He reached back into his pack, and a look of despair came over his face, "Oh no, I only brought one glass."

"Did you really? Oh well, who needs glasses? We have two bottles. One for each of us," she replied.

Daniel then pulled out a second glass, smiling, "Oh, here's the other. My mistake."

"You were joking? I was about to throw the one in the trash," Gabrielle said excitedly. "I will have to remember to keep my guard up."

Daniel opened one bottle and poured her a taste, "You would have consumed this wine straight from the bottle?"

"Sure," she replied.

"So would I," he admitted and winked.

She laughed that charming laugh of hers. Once again, she felt confident she had found a good man.

They enjoyed the wine, cheese, pate, and each other's company. Daniel was silly, making her laugh; she talked of personal desires and dreams, making him fall in love.

"So, do you like the vineyard?" he asked while opening the second bottle of wine.

"Yes, I can't wait to see it at the end of summer, when it's green and lush," She replied, picturing how it will look.

"This is our vineyard," he said to her.

"What do you mean, 'our vineyard'?" she asked.

"The family's. We bought the land and joined with Peter Fawcett. He supplied the vines and did the planting. They are mature vines and will yield mature fruit; maybe not this year, but certainly in a year or two. Eventually, we will build a winery and allow people to visit and taste our wine."

"That's wonderful, Daniel. If you have fruit next year, who will do the winemaking?" she asked, wondering if she could help in some way or at least observe and learn.

"Fawcett will. He's been producing chardonnay. He very much desires to produce a red. It seems there is a friendly rivalry between Fawcett and Villagrosa." Daniel replied. Getting philosophical, he added, "I wonder what it is about wine-making that drives a man to expel all his energies, to be so emotional?"

"Don't you know?" she said to him, knowing he wouldn't have an answer. "Wine is the most beautiful woman a man has ever dreamed of, but she is trapped; her soul is trapped within all these tiny little pieces of fruit. Man needs to extract the essence of the woman so that she becomes one, whole, and beautiful. He creates a tasteless monster without appeal if he doesn't get all the pieces correct and leaves out an ingredient. But if his assumptions are correct, if he is right in his intuition, then this gorgeous woman, a seductive temptress, emerges every time a bottle is opened. Men desire her, want to possess her, but are greedy, so he lets his woman go each year and seeks to create another. But he thinks, 'this time, I will create an even more seductive, passionate, and beautiful woman.' In a way, winemaking is man's noble pursuit of pure beauty but in another way, creating wine is man's folly. Each year he searches, creates, and desires perfection, perfect beauty that he never obtains. "

Daniel smiled, "That is remarkable. I have never thought of it that way, but indeed, the perfect wine is what we seek, but there is no such thing. It makes sense. You know, at one time, I wanted to make wine."

"You did?" Gabrielle asked.

"Yes, until I met you. Then I said to myself, 'Why do I need all these beautiful women? I just need one. I will let the world fight over the others, and I will keep one. So, I have made my choice." Daniel laughed slightly and grinned. He looked at Gabrielle and thought she is everything he ever wanted. "There is no perfect wine, but I have found a perfect woman."

"You have? And who would that be?" she said coyly, a mischievous grin on her face.

Daniel took her in his arms and kissed her passionately, then replied softly, "I think I have made that obvious."

* * *

Two weeks had gone by, and Maria was still waiting to hear from Fawcett concerning the retail store. The vines had all been planted, and every day she saw a man walking the vineyard, usually later in the afternoon. At times, she recognized one of the sons. Sometimes, Peter himself walked along the property, occasionally picking up a handful of dirt and straightening up a trestle. It didn't look like there was any intent. It made her curious.

Coming up on almost three weeks, Maria began to worry. If everybody was so interested in selling products, why were we not talking, meeting, planning, doing something?

Maria approached Claire, "Claire, has your father mentioned anything to you about organizing a meeting? Organizing a meeting with other farmers?"

"I have not spoken with my parents in weeks. It is a very busy time for them. They harvest spring crops, ready the ground for summer crops, and then plant the summer crops. All this must be done between late March and early April to allow time for a decent summer growing season. This is the busiest time all year for my family," she replied with a look of concern on her face.

Claire was concerned. It was the first time she was away from home and not helping, and it didn't feel right. She hoped her mother wasn't struggling.

"Is there any way we can help? You are welcome to go and help your family." Maria could see the worry on Claire's face.

"If you wouldn't mind. Let me ask my husband," Claire disappeared into the kitchen and returned a moment later. "Yes, if you wouldn't mind, I will go and stay with my parents. Perhaps I will be gone one week, possibly two at the most."

"That's fine; you take as much time as you need. Let me grab the keys to Pierre's auto, and I will drive you," Maria suggested.

"Thank you. Give me a moment to go and pack a few things. I will meet you back here in the lobby in just a few minutes," she replied over her shoulder as she hurried off to get packed.

* * *

Pierre had been busy, first selling the Town's assets to raise money, and now that he had the funds, he was busy spending it. The town hadn't paid its bills in quite some time and needed to pay a sizable sum to the electric providers and sanitation. The latter was so irate about the amounts owed that they insisted the town pay a 250,000-euro bond to continue service. Pierre had to travel to Saint Germaine and then to Bordeaux to plead his case. In the end, Sanitation authorities accepted his apologies and his invitation for a weekend in Saint Charles as his guests.

On the train ride back to Saint Germaine and his car, Pierre lamented, *The things I must do to get our garbage picked up and keep the streets clean.*

Once off the train in Saint Germaine, Pierre decided to take some time off from his mayoral duties and put in some time at the Tree Trunk. He hadn't yet met Gabrielle, and he felt like being social.

Pierre walked into the Tree Trunk just as the evening service was getting underway. "Good evening. May I have a table for one?" Pierre said, catching Michelle off guard.

"Pierre, good to see you. Where have you been?" Michelle asked while giving her uncle a big hug and a kiss on the cheek.

"I have been working hard trying to keep the town solvent and creditors away. How has business been, and how is the new sommelier working out?" he asked while raising his eyebrows.

"Just great, business is great, and she's great. No complaints except as usual we could use more help," Michelle admitted, cutting her chatter short as several guests came through the door.

Michelle smiled, greeted the party, and took them to an empty table. While she was busy, Pierre surveyed the dining room. He was surprised to see more full tables than empty; even the veranda had full tables. "Wonderful, and dinner service started just 30 minutes ago. I think I'll go change. They'll need some help before too long," Pierre thought as he exited out to the inn's lobby and then through the library to his apartment.

Pierre shaved, showered, and opened his closet door. There, wrapped in plastic, fresh from the cleaners, was his maroon tuxedo. He smiled, thinking *Should I tempt fate? Why not?* He grabbed the tuxedo from the closet, laid it out on his bed, looked around for his cufflinks, and got dressed.

Pierre entered the dining room from the kitchen, first saying hello to Daniel and Paul, who was filling in for Claire as the second chef. He entered the dining room, pushing the doors back and hesitating as he caught the eye of Gabrielle. Her hesitation was noticeable, as was the surprise on her face. *Impossible,* she thought, then quickly recovered, blocking what she had just seen from her mind.

Pierre's face was frozen as well, but he quickly recovered and walked toward his podium, smiling and waving at those he recognized, shaking a few hands, working the crowd like a true politician.

Michelle walked up to Pierre, "So, Captain, do you want to take the helm?"

Pierre was lost in his memories and, for a second, had no idea what Michelle was talking about. "What, oh, yes, I'll take the front. Where are you going to go, the kitchen?" he asked.

"No, I make a terrible waitress and an even worse chef," she admitted, knowing full well that if anyone wanted to make the evening a disaster, just assign her to the kitchen. "I'll relieve Mother from the front desk, and she can help in the dining room. Oh, and by the way, you look very handsome in your tuxedo."

"Thank you. I appreciate the compliment. Gives me a bit of confidence. Well, go get Maria; I think we'll be busy this evening," Pierre replied as he surveyed the dining room to locate an empty table for guests who were just coming through the door. He felt happy to be back at his podium, but couldn't help this eerie feeling, tingling, that went up his spine as he caught a quick glance at Gabrielle. He wondered to himself, *could it be the same woman*? as he produced an almost genuine smile for the newly arrived party.

He graciously led the guests to a clean table and politely pulled out the chair for the woman. He motioned Thomas over and introduced him as their waiter before calling Gabrielle and introducing her as the sommelier. Pierre wished them an enjoyable dining experience and excused himself.

Gabrielle lingered at the table, offering a drink before dinner. As Gabrielle went to the bar to fix the drink order, she ran into Pierre again, and not by accident.

"Tell me, I am not looking at who I think I'm looking at," he said, staring into her eyes, not giving her any room for a story.

She stuttered, shuffled about, obviously uncomfortable, still in a state of shock, not knowing what to say. She became defensive and agitated, "What do you want from me? Do you want me to lie? What do you want me to say? I'm an orphan, raised in a convent?"

"I know who you are and where you've been. I want nothing, nothing but the best for my brother and the best for my family. Promise me that. Promise me you'll never hurt a member of my family," Pierre said sternly.

"I am different. I am no longer involved in that life. I respect your brother and your family. No harm will come to them, not from me. I want to live, and I don't want to have to run and hide. Let me be. It's over; I left that life behind long ago. Now, please let me get back to work."

She shook vodka over ice and poured the chilled beverage into two romantic-looking martini glasses. She added two green olives to each and a twist of lemon. She placed the two glasses on her tray. "Excuse me," was her only remark to Pierre as she went around him to deliver the drinks.

Pierre watched her go. He was lost in his memories. Memories that he'd like to forget as well. *What are the odds? Almost twenty years ago*, he thought, "*What are the odds?*"

The two managed to avoid each other for most of the night but occasionally exchanged glances, both trying to alleviate their tension. Gabrielle kept telling herself to focus, while Pierre kept telling himself to forget. By the end of the night, both were exhausted, The Tree Trunk having a hectic night.

Daniel came out of the kitchen, a glass of cognac in hand, looking like he just spent five hours in front of a stove cooking for 200 of his closest friends. "That was some night. We must have had three seatings, did we not?" he said to no one in particular and made his way to the bar where he refilled his cognac.

Gabrielle saw him in the bar and went up to him, giving him a tap on the bottom, "Well done. The kitchen certainly earned its money this evening. You were incredible. I am very proud of you. Tonight, when we get back to your place, I will do something special for you."

Daniel smiled and felt flush, imagining what she meant. He looked about and saw that there were only four or five full tables left. "Good," he thought. "Something special. Good!" He ran back to the kitchen and started cleaning furiously.

"What's got into you?" Paul asked as Daniel began tearing the kitchen apart.

"I need to go. I do not want to be here all night," he said while piling up pans for the busboys to wash.

"What about prepping for tomorrow?" Paul asked, "We need to make the dough, marinate some meat, and thaw chickens. Don't you want to check supplies so we can order first thing in the morning?" Paul said, not believing Daniel would let this work go, especially with tomorrow being Saturday, the busiest night of the week.

Daniel stopped, almost as if he had been hit by lightning. "You are right. I must prepare. I cannot let my emotions carry me away from what I must do. This is my kitchen. I am the head chef. I am responsible. Excuse me."

Daniel walked out of the kitchen and over to where Gabrielle was cleaning a table. "Gabrielle, I know you are tired. So am I, but I must stay late and prepare for tomorrow. It will be busy, and I want to be ready. Here are my keys. Go to my apartment, and I will come as soon as I am able. But first, I have to take care of my kitchen."

"Of course. Please, do what you have to. I will wait for you," she replied, admiring the righteousness of the man and loving how honest and straightforward their relationship was.

Daniel kissed her, "I will be some time, but the more time I spend this evening, the more time I will have in the morning. "

Gabrielle smiled as Daniel walked back to his kitchen, thinking of the myriad of tasks needing to be completed before he could say he was ready for tomorrow.

Chapter 40

S aturday was busy, as everyone anticipated. The underlying belief of the family was that The Tree Trunk was finally coming of age. It was now time to start the revolution. Daniel was slowly introducing ideas he picked up from his journey down the west coast of the United States. He roasted whole chilies and stuffed them with various meat and vegetable fillings. He created lighter sauces incorporating cumin, cinnamon, and turmeric. There was sweetness and heat to many of his dishes that patrons found intriguing, satisfying, but just couldn't place the flavors.

He was adept at using citrus juice as a curing agent, creating a new take on bouillabaisse, the popular fish stew from Provence. Daniel's traditional cassoulet was reinvented using capon, spicy local beef sausage, Rudy's smoked pork, and whole roasted chilies. It was just what the locals wanted after working the fields all week -- a large bowl of hearty, spicy cassoulet along with a bottle of robust, flavorful red wine.

Gabrielle did an admirable job presenting the wines that were held in the cellar or were offered to The Tree Trunk for distribution. But she was more ambitious than sitting around waiting for someone to call, pedaling their bottles. She wanted to build a wine cellar that would be the envy of any respectable establishment. She wanted to find the region's hidden treasures, wines that, when paired with the right food, would be comparable to a dining experience of the highest caliber.

She wanted to chase down the leads, meet the vintners, and understand their philosophies and what they were trying to produce. The cellar was clean and organized, and she had room for many more bottles. She was ready, but, unfortunately, she still did not know many of the people in the region.

Daniel knew of the various families but did not know them well enough to provide introductions.

She asked Maria for assistance. "Maria, may I have a word with you?" Gabrielle asked, standing in the doorway of the inn's small office.

"Yes, of course. Come in. Good morning. How is everything?" Maria replied, looking up from the long column of figures Michelle had prepared to help her better understand the origins of The Tree Trunk's profitability.

"Everything is well. I really like it here, and I like what I am doing. Not once have I regretted coming to Saint Charles," Gabrielle answered.

"Wonderful. Everyone has nothing but good to say about your contribution. I know Daniel seems more ambitious and serious now that you are here and, of course, together. I think we may still have to fine-tune some personnel decisions, but rest assured, we all want you to stay. Doing exactly what you are doing," Maria said happily, thinking Gabrielle, as sommelier, is one decision the family got right.

"Thank you. That's what I would like to talk to you about. I can do better. I know I can. There are many bottles of great wine out there, produced by locals, just waiting to be discovered. Bottles are sitting in cellars, forgotten, or overlooked, and some are stored away by people just too busy trying to make a living to do anything about it. Some of the wine might still be in casks with vintners not bothering to bottle it since no one has shown an interest in it," she lamented, hoping she was getting through to Maria and hoping she would be sympathetic.

"What would you like to do?" Maria asked, giving her all the room she needed to explain herself.

Gabrielle sat down and leaned forward, her eagerness apparent. "I would like to pay visits. I want to visit and let vintners know we want to hear about their production endeavors. We would like to try their products. Most importantly, I'd like to find out what they are producing. What families are producing blends, and who is bottling single varietals? I want to investigate to see if someone is doing something truly unique and having interesting results. I want to go out and meet the families. I want to show that, indeed, we are interested. I want to show them that we, The Tree Trunk, can be their outlet to the world."

Maria was swept up by Gabrielle's motivation, "I think that is a great idea, and it's, what's that concept I used to hear all the time, proactive. You want to be proactive."

"Yes, that's absolutely correct. I don't want to wait. I want to go out there and see what I can find," Gabrielle agreed, happy Maria appeared as enthused as she was.

"I think it will be a welcome surprise to many locals to have someone come to them, asking about their wines. I know many families have vines and have been harvesting grapes, crushing, and producing vintages for years. But they don't talk about it. It's not that they are shy; the families are very proud of their accomplishments. It's just part of their life; it's just that it's not news. It's ordinary to produce wine. It's part of their family's heritage," she said calmly to Gabrielle.

"I understand completely. I must change their mindset. I have to convince them that their time and effort can and will amount to something," Gabrielle stated, then continued, "but I fear many will feel I'm intruding, that it's none of my business."

Maria grinned, "Over the years, I have met a good number of the local people, and I am sure they would all be friendly, but the person to take you around, the person who can really open doors, is Pierre. Pierre not only knows everybody, but he also knows something about everybody. I have never known another person with such incredible people skills," Maria stated, curious about Gabrielle's attitude. The look on her face changed when Pierre's name was mentioned. "Are you alright?" she asked a suddenly sedate Gabrielle.

"Yes, of course. I was just hoping the two of us could do this. I just thought it'd be an opportunity for us to talk, get to know one another," she said demurely, not doing a very good job of hiding her change in mood. Gabrielle didn't relish the idea of driving around the countryside with Pierre. He was a reminder of a past that she had worked hard to leave behind. Now that she had been successful, she didn't need any reminders.

"There will be many opportunities for us to chat," Maria added, complemented by Gabrielle's suggestion. "There are too many families, too many kilometers apart, to visit them all in one day, even in one week. You and Pierre should draw up a schedule, a road map of sorts, to do this efficiently. Perhaps, I'll come along on one or two trips. I haven't seen some of the families in quite some time, and some I hardly know at all," Maria said, thinking a drive out to the country would be entertaining and a pleasant diversion from the everyday routine.

Maria also thought about the retail store that she proposed to Peter Fawcett. This would give them a great opportunity to spread the word. "I think I'll get Michelle to work on a flyer we can give to everyone explaining the concept."

Gabrielle sat quietly for a moment. "I don't see Pierre around much except when he is busy being Maitre'd. How can I get in touch with him?" she asked Maria, again not relishing the thought of having to spend days and days and days with the man, especially cooped up in a small auto.

"He'll be Maitre'd until Claire returns. But meanwhile, given the bistro is closed today, Pierre can probably be found in his office at Town Hall," Maria informed Gabrielle.

"Oh, there you are. Am I interrupting anything?" Daniel ducked his head into the office, purportedly looking for Gabrielle. Daniel was wearing large, knee-high boots, a heavy smock over his shoulders, along with a large canvas bag. He was carrying a long shovel that had a rake on its opposite end.

"Hello, Daniel. No, we were just finishing up," Gabrielle said with a smile and rising from her chair.

"Please don't let me disturb you. I am going to the forest for mushrooms and, maybe if I am lucky, a truffle or two. I must replenish my farm. I just wanted to let you know." Daniel spoke to Gabrielle, then to Maria, "Good morning, Maria. Will we have a family meeting tonight and, if so, what time?"

"Yes, let's have a meeting at 6 p.m. Would you like to prepare dinner?" Maria countered.

"I can or Rudy can, whichever you prefer. I enjoy Rudy's tarts. I will make the salad. Let's get Rudy to make tarts. Maybe we can come up with some new interesting taste combinations," Daniel said, smiling. "I will see what ingredients we have left over in the kitchen."

Maria smiled, "Excellent. Thank you, Daniel. So, you are off now to the forest? When will you return?"

"I am not sure, but I will watch the sun, and when it begins to set, I will head back," he said, and then adjusted the coat over his shoulder.

He turned to Gabrielle, and after giving her a short kiss, said, "I will see you later when I return."

"Ciao, for now," Gabrielle offered.

After Daniel left, Maria continued with Gabrielle, "Well, there's your solution. You should attend the family meeting tonight. I will bring it up with Pierre, and we can all provide some ideas. Also, I would like to discuss the retail store. We were selling bread at one point and starting to build a reputation. We always wondered how we could expand our offerings. Peter Fawcett had the idea of cheese and wine. Having a local Farmer's Market, with items all sourced locally, would be a great way for people to get their products known and earn some revenue. So instead of expanding to be a bakery or a general store, we can just be a local store. Wouldn't it have great appeal to tourists?" she asked.

"Yes, I agree. I think it would enhance the appeal of Saint Charles; if the products were of the best quality and fresh, then it would be a reason to come to Saint Charles." Gabrielle agreed, then added, "But who will work the store, ensure the shelves have products, and make sure suppliers are compensated?"

Maria looked at Gabrielle, "Michelle wanted to take charge of the retail. I am worried, though. She has the mind for it, but she is very tough with people. She does not like to be pushed around. She needs to learn how to be clever with people, get them to relax. I think she is a bit too confrontational," she admitted.

"I would be glad to help. As part of my job, we had to undergo sensitivity training. We were taught how to diffuse situations. I can help her understand what people are saying and how to recognize certain situations," Gabrielle volunteered.

"Tonight, at the meeting, let it be known, you'd like to be involved," Maria suggested. She thought Gabrielle would be an excellent role model for Michelle. Even though Michelle had years of education, Maria observed, she still needed to improve her people skills. *Frankly*, she thought, in certain situations, *Michelle's social skills were...clumsy.*

* * *

Everyone turned up for the family meeting except for Claire and Daniel, who, Maria surmised, must still be out foraging in the woods. There were still a few hours till nightfall, so she wasn't worried.

The talk started with a discussion of the retail store. Everyone agreed that it was a good idea to go in the direction of cheese and wine or at least wine.

Rudy said it best, "Whatever we decide to carry, it would be a good idea if the item was already wrapped for consumption and had an extended shelf life. That way, people could take the amounts they needed, without any intervention by us. We wouldn't have to worry too much if a product was still good or not. I think wine fits that criteria, but cheese, I am not sure. I think we might need some refrigeration, and I think a lot of local cheese is made in large quantities. I think it is better suited to be sold by weight, so many euros per kilogram or whatever, which then means selling becomes a labor-intensive activity."

Gabrielle added, "The best shops in Paris sell cheese by cutting a portion from a large block or round. This way, you can try it before you buy and buy the exact amount. I agree the space you have is probably not set up to sell cheese this way, but I think it is the best way and what people are accustomed to. If you sell pre-packaged cheese, then it is like an American or British food store. You don't know what you are selling, and after a certain date, you must throw it away. Let me help. You don't need a sommelier for lunch service. Let me help with the store in the daytime and assume Sommelier duties in the evening. We'll start slow and eventually figure out the best way to do this."

Rudy replied, "Fair enough. This is new ground for all of us. I agree to start slow, and to figure it out as we go along is probably the best course of action." He then continued, "But that's only half the problem; the other half is how do we get the word around? How do we account for and pay for inventory? Or do we?"

"Well, we can't go to our friends and ask for five kilos of their best cheese without paying?" Pierre stated before suggesting what he thought was the best way to go. "I think if we are starting slow, which I think is the intelligent thing to do, we go ahead and purchase the products at a shopkeeper's price and then mark up the price accordingly. Isn't a sixty percent mark-up a typical retail mark-up? Anyway, we mark up in such a manner that we make our money back and cover our expenses quickly. We then sell what is left and, unfortunately, if we must dispose of some amount, we do so. But by then, it doesn't matter; we've already made our money back."

Gabrielle quickly cut in, "But we don't want to be a cheat. We don't want to buy at ridiculously low prices and then sell at exorbitant prices. I want to be partners with locals, not a thief, and what will people think when they come to visit? Are we just another tourist rip-off? There are plenty of those places in Bordeaux, Toulouse, and Lyon. We want people to see us as a place that offers good quality products at a reasonable price. We want it to be a treat to come to Saint Charles, but we also want people to see us as a pleasant place to go, get a meal, have a picnic, and spend the night, all at a reasonable price. We should appeal to the average man and woman and not to an elite-only demographic."

By the time Gabrielle had finished, everyone could see the passion in her eyes. Her emotion was easily detectable. Her face turning a rosy color, she sat on the edge of her chair and caught her breath.

Maria slowly, carefully added, "I agree wholeheartedly with your thoughts, and I am overwhelmed by your enthusiasm." She turned to Rudy, "I am glad she is on our side."

Gabrielle continued, having caught her breath, her demeanor much calmer now, "My apologies to everyone. I did not mean to be so bold as to explicitly say 'we.' I will admit, I do feel like I am part of the team, but I know I am not family. Please forgive me."

Rudy added, "No issues. No apologies are necessary. I feel you are part of us. Family, the Team, those are just labels. You are with us, and I will say with confidence, we are better with you as part of us. So, use 'we,' 'I,' 'us,' whatever best describes what you are feeling," Rudy spoke warmly and without hesitation.

"Yes, indeed. I agree," Pierre added. "The dining room has never felt so professional as it has since you arrived, and that is not just me talking. Everybody has noticed." Pierre spoke while looking about to see that people were listening. He checked to see if he had his matches, an unlighted cigarette twirling between his fingers.

"Thank you. Being noticed and appreciated makes me try harder. I really appreciate how you have welcomed me. I made a big move to come here to be with Daniel. I did not know what to expect. What I have found has exceeded my fondest dreams. This is really a fantasy for me, a fantasy come true. Thank you, sincerely, thank you," Gabrielle replied, addressing all who were there.

Maria smiled, "As Daniel would say, the pieces are coming together. By the way, has anyone heard from our wandering chef?"

"No, but I hope he returns soon," Gabrielle mentioned, a bit of concern in her voice.

"He will. He'll show up sooner or later." Maria went on with the meeting. "Our sommelier, Gabrielle, would like to be proactive and meet members of the wine-making community. She is actively seeking bottles for us to stock. I think it is what The Tree Trunk needs: a cellar stocked with a good selection of superb, drinkable wines. I suggested the best person to make introductions is Pierre."

Maria continued as Pierre suddenly became interested in what she was saying, "And Michelle, if you'd like to go along and tell people about our store, well, I think that would be a great idea, an efficient use of time."

"I think it's better if I stay behind and assume Maître'd duties. Noon service has become somewhat busy, and besides, Gabrielle has a good grasp as to what we are doing or attempting to do," Michelle countered. She wasn't that interested in winemaking and thought the discussions would be boring. She also didn't relish the idea of spending the day crammed into the back seat of Pierre's Citroen.

"Pierre, what do you think?" Maria asked.

"I am all for it," was Pierre's reply. Looking at Gabrielle, he added, "Just let me know when you want to go."

"The sooner, the better. Can we start tomorrow?" Gabrielle asked.

Pierre seemed buoyant, "Why not? I'll go down to my office later this evening and make a few calls. I am sure everyone will be pleased to hear that the sommelier from The Tree Trunk would like to drop by and discuss wine. You know they'll go down to their cellars and pull out the very best. Yes, they will be out to impress," Pierre contemplated out loud, then turned to Maria, "This will be fun; I look forward to this."

Chapter 41

I t was early Tuesday morning. Pierre and Gabrielle climbed into his bright yellow Citroen on their way to visit the families Pierre had contacted the night before. Pierre was quite excited. He was correct in his assumption that a visit from The Tree Trunk's sommelier would be welcomed, and all the families he contacted had hinted they had something special to share.

Pierre's car started on the first try, which he took as a good omen. He adjusted a few items, the seats, mirrors, and turned on the radio, knowing full well it hadn't worked in years, but thinking, *well, there was always the chance.*

The last thing he did was set the suspension to comfort, thinking Gabrielle was a city girl; she would appreciate a plush ride.

Gabrielle sat with tears in her eyes, emotionally distraught. Daniel had not come home the night before. She didn't know where he was or what had happened to him and being like most people with a missing loved one, her imagination got the best of her. She envisioned him lying at the bottom of a ditch somewhere, his legs broken, an arm missing, rats and vermin eating his flesh and, with his last breath, calling to her for help. She openly wept, frustrated by her inability to do anything.

Maria sent them off, insisting they go, hoping a diversion would help Gabrielle get through her distress. She knew Daniel could be anywhere, doing anything, completely unaware of the time, the day, and of the worry he was causing. In her heart, she knew he was okay.

The first family Pierre wanted to visit was the Villagrosa family. Pierre thought it was important for Gabrielle to put a face with the name and to pay respects to the family that provided every bottle of red wine currently sold by The Tree Trunk.

They arrived and were greeted immediately by Giorgio and his eldest son, Antonio. Like many families around Saint Charles, there were numerous other sons and daughters, but they were out working the fields or involved in other farm work.

Giorgio was in a good mood and very happy that The Tree Trunk was serving his wine. He had Antonio bring around a case of wine from his cellar and offered it as a gift. He said this was his very best and, if they liked it, he had ten more cases he'd be willing to sell. Giorgio referred to this bottle as his "Fruits de la Terre."

Gabrielle asked, "I'm curious, Giorgio, why would you be willing to sell wine from your own collection? Wouldn't you want to keep your very best?"

Giorgio replied, "I still drink a glass now and then, as does my wife, but my children and their families have not developed a taste for it. We all know what good wine is, but we find the challenge and fun is in making the wine, not the drinking. We get a great deal of satisfaction knowing that we, a family of dirt farmers no less, can produce a very good bottle. It pleases us to no end when we visit the Tree Trunk and see table after table of happy patrons, sitting there, enjoying the evening with our bottles on their tables, my wine filling their glasses. That makes me, my wife, and my children feel very good."

Pierre was humbled, "Thank you, Giorgio. Thank you for all the great wine, for this present, and for being a great friend to my family and me."

Giorgio smiled, "Our families will continue to be friends. I appreciate your visit today and the chance to meet your sommelier. Please, Gabrielle, if you have any needs or requests, do not hesitate to contact us. We will do what we can."

Gabrielle smiled, her beautiful face beaming, "That is very gracious of you, Giorgio. I look forward to your next visit to the Tree Trunk, and please let me know when you take your recent vintage out of the oak. I will enjoy watching, even partaking, if you feel I can be of any help."

"That is generous of you. We would welcome another set of hands. Would you be interested in helping with the harvest? We always seem to have a problem getting the grapes off the vines in time. In fact, this last harvest, we left a good many clusters unpicked. We just didn't have the help we needed," Giorgio reminisced.

"Certainly. I would be happy to. I have a vehicle and would not at all have a problem arriving out here at sunrise," Gabrielle advised Giorgio.

"Good, you seem to understand how a harvest works. I'll be in touch sometime in late August to let you know how the grapes look. We pick as early as September and as late as November," Giorgio said as he and his son shook their visitor's hands, concluding the meeting.

As Giorgio and Antonio walked back to their barn, Pierre and Gabrielle loaded the case of wine into the small backseat of the Citroen and drove off to the next destination.

The pair visited another family. Before too long, it was time to return to the inn. Gabrielle wanted to get back. She still had no idea what had happened to Daniel, if he had returned, was found dead, or what?

Pierre insisted they make one last stop before returning. "You have to meet Francois Renaud. He is quite a character and always has something up his sleeve. He has crafted some truly remarkable wines, including both white and red. He has a lot of land but only farms a small portion. Apparently, his ancestors left him very well off, and he only works if he finds it interesting."

They drove for what seemed like hours down narrow country lanes, some still not paved and some paved so long ago that the asphalt had crumbled away, making the road seem like just a gravel path.

"Where is this place you are taking me?" Gabrielle asked, sounding concerned and for a good reason. She had no idea where she was, and it had been some time since she had seen any evidence of civilization.

Finally, they arrived at a narrow dirt lane, marked only by a small opening in the crumbling stone wall that ran parallel to the road. "Ah, here we are," Pierre said as he swung the wheel, turning down the lane.

They bumped along for quite a distance. Gabrielle could see fields on both sides of the dirt road. Some of the fields looked as if they were abandoned; others had rows and rows of something very green, neatly planted. Some of the areas had animals grazing. She had to look twice, but as they drove, she swore she saw buffalo.

Finally, they arrived at a house with a few other buildings. All the buildings were made of stone but looked very contemporary in design and construction.

Next to the barn was a pen with horses. She was amazed. Everything looked very modern and well cared for, and the animals looked healthy; it was not what she was expecting way out here in such a remote location.

Though everything looked well-kept and neat, there were no signs of life other than the horses and a few chickens wandering about.

Pierre parked and led Gabrielle around to the opposite side of one of the buildings. He pushed open a large wooden door. Inside, the building was full of wooden casks, large, taller than a man. The casks were sitting sideways and were lined up neatly, one after the other. The building was large enough for three columns of the large casks and many, many rows. Given the musty, yeasty, fruity smell, Gabrielle knew the casks were probably made of oak and filled with wine.

There was open space between the wall and the first row of casks. Two men were seated there, facing each other, sitting on short stools, a small table between them. An assortment of farm tools, horseshoes, and empty wine bottles were scattered about. On the table was a chessboard. Both men were deeply engrossed in the game, smoking cigars, glasses of wine by their sides, and a half dozen empty bottles sitting on the floor between them.

One of the men moved a chess piece, "Ha, ha, I have you now. Check." He then looked up, noticing the visitors for the first time. Daniel Villeneuve smiled and said, "Oh, we must hurry. My ride is here." He then took a large drink of his wine. "Francois…"

"What, wait. Check? Give me a minute; let me get out of this first." Francois Renaud scratched his chin and sat quietly, puffing his cigar, taking more than one drink from his glass.

Then Francois, without turning and looking at his visitors, announced, "Glasses are on the sideboard there; grab a bottle, make yourself comfortable. I'll be with you in a minute."

Gabrielle looked at the two men, relieved the mystery of Daniel's disappearance had finally been solved, and spoke loudly, "Daniel is this where you've been?"

Daniel Villeneuve puffed his cigar. "Yes, here, I've been here. I guess we should be getting back. We have a family meeting at 6 p.m."

Pierre laughed, "That was yesterday."

Daniel looked surprised. "Yesterday? Really? No? Did I miss it?"

Pierre answered, "Well, I didn't see you there. Do you know what time it is?"

"No, not really, should I?" Daniel replied, then looking at Francois, "How long have we been playing?"

Francois looked about at all the empty bottles littering the floor, "By the looks of it, since the beginning of time. What does it matter?"

"Hello, Francois…" Pierre spoke, "I'd like you to meet…"

Francois cut him off, "Can't a man get a little silence to concentrate? There is entirely too much chatter."

There was silence as Francois finally moved one of his chess pieces, "There, that will teach you. Try to check me when I'm not looking."

Daniel smiled, "Is that a trick? You are always looking. I cannot place you in check when you are not looking, don't be silly." He then turned his head to face Gabrielle, giving her a wink.

Francois looked at Daniel, puffed his cigar, and shook his head, finally turning around, "Hello Pierre, good to see you. Who's your lovely friend?"

Daniel sat quietly and smiled.

Pierre then answered his question, "This is our new sommelier. Her name is Gabrielle. She has a very educated palate. I brought her here to meet you and, of course, to sample your wines."

"Is that correct, all this way to taste my wines? I am flattered, humbled," Francois said, standing up and bowing deeply towards Gabrielle.

Francois turned to Daniel, "I concede. The game is yours." He finished his glass in one large gulp.

Daniel smiled, a large cloud of cigar smoke surrounding him, "A wise decision, indeed, a wise decision."

Francois turned back to Gabrielle, "I occasionally crush, press, age, and eventually bottle. I say occasionally because if I feel the harvest is not up to standards, I feed it to the pigs or sell it if there is an interested buyer. The last time I made wine was two years ago. You're looking at it. It's been nineteen months in new oak. I think I'll bottle in another four, maybe five months."

"That sounds remarkable, two years in new oak. The wine should be complex, exciting, but it could be overly tannic," Gabrielle commented.

"Yes, it should, and it could," Francois said, conceding the point. "You seem to know something about winemaking." He moved closer, looking her in the eye, challenging her. So, you think you have a discerning palate? Let's get your opinion on my latest efforts. My good friend Giorgio calls his best 'Le Fruit de la Terre,' I call mine 'Le Fruit de Mon Travail. "

Francois led everybody down a narrow corridor between the large casks. He stopped about midway down and climbed up over the side of one of the casks. Straddling the cask like a giant horse and using an oversized corkscrew, he popped open a cork the size of a man's fist and dipped in a glass tube. When he removed it, it was filled with a dark, cherry-red liquid.

"Let me have your glasses," Francois asked.

They all held up their glasses, and as Francois filled them, the air took on a lovely, flowery, strawberry aroma, almost like cotton candy, accented with a spicy, vanilla, and leather scent. It made every mouth water.

Gabrielle held the glass up to the light, twirling it slightly and commenting, "Very nice consistency, and the bouquet is delicious." She finally drank an ample amount, swirled it around in her mouth, allowing it to settle on her tongue, and eventually swallowed the tasty elixir.

"Oh, my word. I have tasted wines from the best Chateaus in France, California, Australia, and Argentina. Nothing I have ever tasted, nothing compares to this. It is incredible," Gabrielle gushed, almost out of breath from the one taste of wine.

She took another sip, finishing the modest amount Francois poured. "Sir, you have made a perfect wine." She looked around. "Does every barrel contain the same?"

Francois nodded, "I'll let you answer your own question. Pick a barrel, any barrel."

Daniel followed Gabrielle as she moved down the rows of casks, finally arriving at the far end. She stopped and pointed at one of the casks. "This one."

Using a giant mallet, Francois hammered the large cork back into the barrel they had tasted. He moved to the cask Gabrielle had pointed to, and using the same technique, extracted a sample, portioning it among the glasses.

Gabrielle held it up to the light, recognizing the deep color and the long legs on the side of the glass. She took a large sip, filling her mouth and swishing it around, her cheeks expanding out and in. She let the wine settle on her tongue. Her eyes closed, she let out a slight, satisfying moan, and then swallowed.

"Yes, there is consistency," she observed. "The only thing I have to say is it's drinking beautifully. Why wait, why not bottle now?"

Francois thought a minute. "Well, I might be persuaded. I'll tell you what. Each cask is approximately eight cases. I have thirty casks. I will bottle one cask, eight cases. I will call it 'Chateau Renaud, Early Bottling.' You tell me what people think. If there is interest, I will bottle. Give me a couple of days to arrange for bottling. You'll have eight cases by the weekend."

"That is outstanding. Thank you. But I do not expect you to provide this service for free. Will you please invoice the Tree Trunk? Whatever amount you think is reasonable. We will pay it," she said.

Daniel added, "Yes, absolutely we will." Then he wondered about all the excitement. *Weren't they drinking similarly since he first arrived?*

Pierre and Gabrielle walked to the car, wondering how the three of them would fit in Pierre's little Citroen, when they noticed Daniel was not with them. Gabrielle looked quickly about and then ran back to the building to find Daniel and Francois playing chess. Francois was in the process of lighting Daniel's fresh cigar.

Gabrielle walked up to Daniel, "Daniel, would you like to come home with us?"

"I have one more game to play, and then we are even. That's where we like to leave it." Daniel answered Gabrielle's inquiry while still studying the board, a new game in progress.

"Ok, but isn't it quite a distance to travel? How will you get back? I'd come to get you, but I have no idea where we are or how we got here," she replied.

"I can walk. That's how I got here. It is not too far when you go through the forest. Maybe I will wait till sunrise. That way, I can pick up mushrooms and truffles on the way back. By the way, let me give you what I picked up today; I mean yesterday." Daniel looked about for his basket. Finding it, he carefully emptied the contents on the floor. "If you can place these items in the cellar, I'll plant them when I get back."

There were mushrooms of all types, small but healthy-looking, and then there were three small white lumps, unremarkable looking, about the size of large marbles, but not as round.

"What are these?" Gabrielle asked, having a good idea what they were but wanting Daniel's verification.

He answered in typical Daniel style, "Those are very rare white truffles. They are difficult to find and much more pungent, more delicious, than the black. They are small. I thought I'd plant them and see what happens," he said as if finding white truffles was just a matter of looking in the right spot. He placed everything carefully in another sack provided by Francois.

"You found a white truffle?" Gabrielle was astonished.

"No, three," Daniel corrected.

* * *

Daniel returned home early the next day in time to shower, take a quick inventory, get an order to suppliers, and start prepping his kitchen for noon service.

Gabrielle was astonished. "Daniel, when was the last time you slept?"

"It does not matter. I am here, and I have a job to do. Did you miss me? I missed you," he admitted while cutting large pieces of beef from a hindquarter. "I will make beef stew today, to be served for dinner tonight. Would you care for a steak?"

"No, I will eat later. Thank you. Pierre has more people he thinks I should meet. I told him I'd like a break today, and then tomorrow we can go visit," Gabrielle informed Daniel.

"Yes, that is what you must do. You should try and meet as many people as possible. What did you think of Francois?" Daniel asked, not waiting for an answer. "The man is a genius. He can look at the soil and tell you exactly what to plant. He can look at fruit on the vine and tell you if the fruit will make good wine. He is a man in touch with the world around him. He can converse with anybody about anything. He is a man I admire considerably." Daniel talked and just kept talking as he moved about, not really noticing if Gabrielle was listening; he just talked, perhaps to keep his mind off fatigue. He was obviously wired, his energy supplied by adrenaline.

Gabrielle observed him closely. She was concerned by his condition and behavior. "I don't know how you will make it through the day. Why do you do this to yourself?"

"Do what?"

"You know what I mean," she shot back at him.

"No, I don't know what you mean. I went foraging. I did not expect to find anything, but I went anyway. It is how I understand the forest. I must do this every so often else I will lose touch," Daniel replied.

"But you weren't foraging. You were sitting in Françoise's storeroom, drinking wine for two days and smoking cigars. You didn't even know what day it was," she replied, growing perturbed at his cavalier attitude.

Daniel chuckled, "Were you worried? That is good. It shows there is something there. But you don't need to worry; I will always return. I enjoy a good cigar, a challenging game of chess, and of course, superb wine. Francois he can make wine. There should be no doubt in anybody's mind. Now, please excuse me, I must prepare. We can talk later tonight if you still would like."

Daniel leaned over to kiss Gabrielle, but she turned her head at just the right moment, leaving Daniel to place the kiss on her cheek.

He gave her an odd look, shrugged his shoulders, and went back to work.

Gabrielle watched as he returned to setting up his kitchen. She felt insulted when Daniel began whistling as if to demonstrate he had no worries.

Chapter 42

The French Culinary Society arrived slightly after 3 p.m. on their first visit to Saint Charles. Maria was at the front desk and in fine spirits as the party of five entered the Inn's lobby. Andre immediately greeted them and asked if there was any luggage other than the small bags everyone appeared to be carrying.

Claude was obviously in charge and replied no, thanking Andre for his consideration.

Maria saw the reservation was under Louisa's name, and a small note left by Michelle mentioned they were her relatives. "Welcome to the Inn at Saint Charles. I hope you enjoy your stay. I have five rooms reserved for two nights. Is that correct?" Maria asked politely.

"Yes. That is correct," Claude answered with a polite smile.

"Monsieur Duggart, I have given you what we refer to as the penthouse suite on the fourth floor, and the others will be right below you on the third floor. I imagine you are weary after a day of traveling. Your rooms are available now. Would you enjoy champagne? I will have Andre bring you to your rooms and follow along with champagne. Please accept this as a gift and our way of saying welcome to our home."

"Well, thank you. There are five of us, though," Claude wanted clarification as to who was getting the champagne.

"Yes, I understand. But it is your first time here. Out of the many places you could have stayed, you made the effort to stay here with us. I feel that deserves champagne. It's our way of thanking you for joining us. We do hope you enjoy your visit to Saint Charles," Maria said to Claude and the rest of his party.

Claude was charmed by Maria's sincerity and immediately let his guard down, turning to his associates and smiling, "Well, who are we to refuse a bottle of champagne?"

A polite chuckle and a few murmurs of agreement came from the four others. Maria smiled and gave the keys to Andre, "Rooms 7, 8, 9, and 10. Monsieur Duggart, the tall gentleman, is in the penthouse."

Claude immediately turned to Maria, "Please call me Claude. I am Louisa's uncle, and with whom am I speaking?"

Maria chuckled at Claude's formality, "I am Maria Villeneuve. I am the proprietor."

"Thank you. Maria, you are very charming. Thank you for your generosity. On another matter, we would like to dine this evening at the bistro. I believe it's called The Tree Trunk."

"Wonderful. We would love to have you. May I make a reservation for you?" Maria replied.

"Yes, please." Claude turned to his fellow travelers, "Does 8 p.m. sound reasonable?"

After receiving consensus from his party, Claude turned back to Maria, "Would a table for five at 8 p.m. be available?"

"I'm sure there is. Would you like to dine outdoors on the veranda?" she asked.

"If the weather permits, I think that would be lovely," Claude replied.

"Fine, I have you down for 8 p.m., party of five on the veranda. You should come a few minutes early and enjoy a glass of wine or a cocktail in our courtyard. It's lovely in the early evenings," Maria said as she wrote down a note reminding herself to inform Michelle of the reservation.

Andre sent everybody to the third floor and followed along, opening the doors for each guest and making a quick inspection of each room. He checked the baths, opened the curtains, and made sure the trash bins were empty.

He brought Claude up to the penthouse. He opened the door before standing aside and allowing Claude to enter. Claude took three steps into the room and looked about. He gasped, astonished, "This is my room?"

Andre replied crisply, "Yes, sir. If you'll excuse me, I'll return with champagne."

"Please, yes, I mean, thank you." Claude could only mumble as he was completely taken back by the warmth, the charm, and the elegance of the penthouse.

He walked into the bath and came upon a large clawfoot bathtub. Antique leaded windows let the afternoon sun in, warming the room. Claude felt giddy. He confided to himself. *This is truly mystical. I am going to take a hot bath and sip my champagne while sitting in the tub. How decadent.*

Andre reappeared, knocking on the door, before entering with a bottle of champagne sitting in an ice bucket, a white napkin surrounding the bucket to catch the condensation, and one glass. "Shall I open it, sir?" Andre asked.

"Yes, please," Claude instructed as he reached for his wallet, pulling out a fifty euro note.

Andre expertly popped the cork and poured a glass, then placed the bottle back into the bucket, covering it with the napkin. "Sir, my name is Andre, and I will be on duty all evening if I can be of any service."

Claude rushed over to catch him before he left, nonchalantly handing him the fifty euro note. "Thank you, Andre. I dearly appreciate the service. You've been very gracious."

Andre looked down at the note, "Sir, this is fifty euros, I cannot take…."

Claude cut him off, "Nonsense, you earned it. Please. I would be insulted if you didn't take it."

Andre smiled and bowed slightly, "Thank you, sir."

Claude replied, "Thank you."

As Andre left and closed the door behind him, Claude grabbed his glass and bucket of champagne and headed to the bath.

* * *

Dinner traffic was moderate as expected, the usual for a Thursday night. Claude and the other four committee members met at the lobby entrance to the Tree Trunk at 7:30 p.m. and surveyed the scene in front of them. It looked at first glance as a well-choreographed ballet without actual dancers, just Pierre and Gabrielle, Paul and Thomas moving about, successfully making the evening as enjoyable as possible for their patrons.

The committee felt the hum of efficiency and saw the smiles on people's faces, enjoying where they were and what they were doing. They liked what they saw and what they felt.

Pierre approached the party of five and checked off the name on his register. He still had his remarkable memory, but he found if he wrote something down, he had evidence. People would argue against his memory but not if he wrote it down.

He asked whether the party would enjoy something to drink while waiting for their 8 p.m. reservation and led them to the courtyard. Gabrielle joined them and introduced herself. She took their drink orders and offered them crostini from Rudy's oven to enjoy before dinner.

Before long, the party was seated. The group had the Veranda to themselves except for a party of two who were already on dessert and coffee and waiting for their bill to be tabulated.

Daniel, being relatively close to Louisa and having his suspicions about the group, put on a fresh chef's jacket and went to introduce himself to the five guests.

Wanting to make a good impression, he presented himself as a worldly, sophisticated master chef, which, of course, backfired.

Daniel started off rather awkwardly, "Good evening." Then when half the people were replying with good evening, Daniel resumed his talking. "My name is Chef Daniel, you may call me, you may call me...." Not knowing what to say, he repeated himself, "Chef Daniel."

Claude looked at him with an odd look, "Well, that seems appropriate."

Daniel was embarrassed but managed to dig a deeper hole for himself, "Yes, of course, very appropriate, why would you call me anything else..." and stood there looking at the people as they looked back.

Finally, Gabrielle, sensing something was wrong, came to the table and very patiently, in firm control, said, "Daniel, why don't you tell our guests what they have to look forward to?"

"Yes, of course. For casual dining, a tart, steak and potato, or a roasted young chicken from our wood-burning oven. The wood imparts a rustic, smoky flavor that accents the flavors of our wines. It is simple yet quite marvelous. You will taste food, as nature intended. You have my word on that."

Claude raised his eyebrows, "That sounds wonderful. I am a firm believer in letting the flavor of the food come out, not the preparation."

"If you are interested in classic cuisine, we are preparing classic bistro dishes but with a little something added, something that will make them, we believe, bolder, more appealing, more memorable. Your palate will thank you. Again, I ask that you trust me on this," Daniel said, performing a slight bow towards the table.

"Lastly, may I offer, many of the dishes mentioned will be served plated, but we also suggest our patrons think about family-style. For example, we serve a large roasted capon, family-style, and carved at the table."

Claude was amused, "That sounds absolutely marvelous. A meal should be shared. Great food should be shared; what better way than passing a serving bowl or platter? "

He then looked at his dining partners; "This is a bistro offering good, hearty, country food, served the country way, family-style. "

Then, looking at Daniel, "Sir, your rank just went up a notch in my book."

Claude looked at his friends, "Let's eat family style this evening; tomorrow, we'll dine formally."

The group agreed, with each ordering separate appetizers. For an entrée, Beef Bourguignon was ordered for the whole table.

Daniel smiled, "A wonderful selection. Gabrielle will suggest a wine that will make your evening memorable. I am sure of it. Now, excuse me while I return to the kitchen. I will instruct your waiter to bring freshly baked bread and accompaniments. Thank you again for joining us this evening."

Daniel bowed, but this time it was a deep, sweeping bow. If it weren't for quick hands by one of the busboys, Daniel would have knocked over a nearby outdoor heater.

The appetizers served, Gabrielle suggested a bottle of Francois Renaud's Early Bottling Red Blend. She decanted it at the table, knowing that the potent wine's bouquet would drift over the table. Leaving it for just a few minutes, she poured a small taste into Claude's glass.

Claude looked at the contents of his glass, "Ladies and gentlemen, if the wine in this glass tastes as good as its bouquet, then I suggest we have found…" he paused for effect, then continued, "perfection."

He placed his nose in the glass, inhaling a satisfying breath of wine. Then, taking half the serving into his mouth, he gently pushed it around, letting it linger before he swallowed. He turned to Gabrielle, "Please pour for my friends."

Gabrielle poured a full glass for everyone. Before they could take a sip, Claude raised his glass. "Please, a toast, to the Tree Trunk, to Francois Renaud and his Early Bottling, and to perfection; I declare all three to be interchangeable."

The whole table raised their glasses and simply said, "Salute."

Back in the kitchen, Paul was furious with Daniel. "How are we going to serve five people Beef Bourguignon, family style? Tell me how?"

Daniel replied calmly, "We get a large serving dish, we fill it with stew, and we place it on a cart, and we roll it to the table. Then we serve them. As a waiter, I would expect you to know this."

"Yes, ok, but where do we find a large serving dish? And who has the time to stand there and serve? Hello, tell me, this smart man?" Paul countered Daniel's overly simplistic solution.

"You need not talk to me like that. It is not becoming a gentleman, and please remember I am the Head Chef. Even if you do not respect me, you must respect my title. No matter what," Daniel instructed Paul.

Realizing, perhaps, he was a little harsh, Paul said what he needed to say. "My apologies, Daniel. Of course, I respect you. I know this is your kitchen, but you have put me in a very difficult situation. What do I tell them?"

"Here are my keys. Go to my apartment. In the downstairs closet, there is a large, antique porcelain pot with flowers on it. Go now, quickly," Daniel said to Paul, handing him his keys.

Paul quickly ran off and returned minutes later, a look of agony on his face. "Daniel, this is a chamber pot. We're not going to use this, are we? Where did you get this from?"

"I found it out in the woods, next to an abandoned cottage. The top was chipped, but I found the piece and repaired it. It looks new, no?" Daniel said proudly.

"It smells," Paul replied.

"Give it to the busboys. Have them clean it. Scrub it with bleach if necessary. But tell them to do it quickly. Stop whatever they are doing," Daniel insisted.

"Scrubbing it with toilet cleaner would be more appropriate," Paul added, walking the pot over to the sink and running it under hot water. "God, it smells."

Paul left it on the sink and went to fetch the busboys. Both were on the floor and came back into the kitchen, dropping off trays of dirty dishes. One asked out loud, "What smells. Did someone get sick?"

Michelle walked into the kitchen a moment later. She had a spare moment and was looking for a snack or dinner of some sort. She entered the kitchen, asking, "Daniel, what's that smell? Do we have a toilet overflowing somewhere?"

"I do not know," He replied with his back to Michelle, trying to focus on the half a dozen pans on his stove.

The busboy came over carrying the large pot. "Here is your pot, Daniel."

Michelle looked at the pot, "Daniel, what are you doing with a chamber pot in the kitchen?"

"It is not a chamber pot. It is an antique serving vessel. We are using it to serve beef bourguignon family style." Daniel informed Michelle of his plans.

Michelle stood there, as if frozen, finally saying something, "You are using a chamber pot to serve food? Beef Bourguignon?" She looked carefully at the pot, "Well, it's a pretty pot." She then shook her head quickly a few times, as if she were dreaming and trying to wake up. "I think I will go back to the front desk. I was never here. Ok, guys? I was never here." With that, Michelle turned around and went out the same door she came in without saying another word.

Paul cleaned the pot and assembled a cart with dishes, a silver ladle, and two warm loaves of fantasy bread. He arranged the centerpiece, the large flowery chamber pot with a lid, filled to the brim with beef bourguignon. Daniel added a candle and lit it as Paul wheeled it out to the table, announcing as he arrived, as he thought he should, "Beef Bourguignon." He then proceeded to ladle a portion into each bowl, accompanied by slices of the still-warm fantasy bread.

It would be an understatement to say the five devoured the hearty stew, made interesting by Daniel's choice of herbs, spices, and roasted peppers. The five finished their portions before Paul could fetch and open a second bottle of wine.

As Paul poured from the second bottle of Renaud's delicious Early Bottling, Claude spoke, "I have not been so utterly satisfied by the food, the selection of wine or the service in I don't know how long. Frankly, I can't remember a time when I felt so satisfied. Please waiter, my compliments to the Chef, compliments to the entire staff. Now, may I get another small helping if you please?"

The entire table murmured in agreement with Claude's compliment, and then in unison, all handed their bowls over to Paul for another helping.

As Paul served, he purposely allowed the spoon to hit the bottom of the pot, hoping the clang of silver against porcelain would give everyone a hint the pot was nearly empty. He surveyed the table, topped off a few of the wine glasses, and excused himself as he wheeled the cart back to the kitchen.

Once inside the kitchen, Paul exhaled a long deep exhalation, as if finally reaching safety. He leaned against the cart, "I am glad that is over. I was afraid someone would recognize the pot."

Thomas went by carrying a tray of food, "You were afraid someone would say, 'Hey, I've used that pot to….'"

Daniel interrupted, "Thomas, enough. You do not have to describe everything in detail. It is a nice serving pot. If anyone asks, it belonged to my grandmother. "

One of the busboys then spoke, "And she used it every time it was too cold to go outside."

Both busboys laughed, as did Thomas, and even Claire had a smirk on her face. Daniel appreciated the joke and laughingly replied, "Ok, you are a guy that is wise. For that, before you leave tonight, I want you to clean the public bathrooms. You are too smart for your own good."

The committee finished their meal and adjourned for the evening. The party, feeling very satiated, slowly and casually made their way to the Inn's elevator. The five stood by the lift, waiting for it to descend, when one member asked another, "Did you notice anything unusual about the large serving vessel they used? It reminded me of…" The woman didn't get a chance to finish her thought as the lift finally made it down to the lobby.

* * *

The committee spent the day touring around the region, traveling almost to Bordeaux but electing to cut their ride short in favor of taking an afternoon hike. Claire's brothers had laid out trails, and for the older hikers comprising the five committee members, the trails were just challenging enough.

The troop returned to the Inn with plenty of light left and plenty of time to enjoy afternoon tea. Claude enjoyed another hot bath before the evening's dinner reservation.

Dinner that evening was flawless, with Rudy providing delicious tarts of fennel and anchovy, gruyere and roasted onion, and roasted pepper, mushroom, and sage with local mozzarella and a touch of hard, grated parmesan. The tarts were brought to the table and served, with each patron receiving a piece of each tart.

Gabrielle was her usual pleasant self and insisted the table try a bottle of Villagrosa's remarkable Le Fruits de le Terre. She freely admitted, "Once I open this wine and take my first sip, I cannot stop. I cannot say no, only yes."

Hearing Gabrielle, a very beautiful and composed woman, admit that this one bottle of wine causes her only to say yes, had the whole table grinning, their imaginations running wild. Finally, one of the gentlemen asked, "Would this wine be available at the front desk? I am sure my wife would enjoy such an experience."

As his fellow members looked at him oddly, he clarified, "Enjoying the wine, I mean."

Gabrielle politely laughed, "I would be happy to make a bottle available to you." By the time she had finished pouring, she had five requests for Villagrosa's Fruits del le Terre.

The diners applauded the first course and were pleasantly surprised by the second-- Daniel's take on Onion Soup, Moroccan style. The Spanish Sherry blended perfectly with his blend of North African spices. Every sip of the soup caused a bursting of flavor, which was subtly and slowly quenched by a mixture of pungent Gruyere and mozzarella cheese.

The main courses were also perfect in execution. Simple dishes of young chicken were enhanced by roasting the bird with cloves, garlic, and honey. Then the bird was carved, and the meat drizzled with a buttery pepper sauce with a bit of cumin and cinnamon. Depending on your point of reference, it tasted of the Middle East or Mexico, or North Africa, but all agreed it was hearty and the perfect host to Villagrosa's fruity and tannic wine.

Daniel created an updated version of Pork aux Pruneaux, using tart plums instead of prunes. He used pork tenderloin and added fresh lemon juice, a bit of lime juice, and a sweet late harvest white wine for its sugar. To counter the sweetness, he added a few roasted chili peppers. The peppers added heat but also imparted a beautiful coloring to the plate. Claude was mystified by the flavors but enamored with the combination of sweet acidity, tartness, roast pork, and Villagrosa's wine.

For dessert, Rudy made apricot tarts with goat cheese, honey, and cinnamon. The pastries were brought to the table just seconds out of the oven and served with fresh cream laced with a hint of vanilla. Gabrielle brought cognac for the whole table, which feigned only fleeting resistance.

The five members of the committee sipped their cognac and sat back in their seats, gazing up at the clear black night to see a full moon and shining stars. A female member said softly, mesmerized by the sky overhead, "I don't think, in my whole life, I have ever felt so, so...."

Another member finished her thought, "Satisfied. I was just thinking the same thing. I sincerely want for nothing, except...."

And still, another finished his sentence, "Except to come for dinner tomorrow."

The whole table burst into laughter. Claude laughed heartedly then had the final say. "Ladies and gentlemen, I must say we have experienced something truly extraordinary. Though I am impressed, my professional responsibilities require me to maintain. I remind everyone here; we have two more visits before we are able to form an opinion. Let's adjourn for the evening. We need to wake early for the long drive back to Paris. Please, don't forget your wine at the front desk. I will settle the bill and all other charges. Good night and see you in the morning."

Claude finished his cognac in one large drink. He then said to no one in particular, *That's very good. I think I will have another sent to my room.*

Chapter 43

M aria held the weekly family meeting as usual on Monday evening. The first item on the agenda was Louisa Duggart's relatives and Daniel's spontaneous idea to feed the group family style, using a chamber pot as a serving dish.

Daniel was adamant, "Who can tell what is the purpose of the pot? If I told you it was part of my grandmother's tea set, you wouldn't know."

Michelle replied, "Daniel, I knew what it was as soon as I smelled it, I mean saw it." She grinned, having a little fun with Daniel.

"That is not funny, and I am not laughing." Daniel was indignant. "I try to do something that is unique, that entertains people, and I get this. From now on, I will not think. I will just be a robot. I will only do as programmed." He then adjusted his seat, looking very stiff and disinterested, thinking, *This is how a robot would look.*

Rudy tried being diplomatic, defending Daniel's decision as best he could. "I think the issue is this. If we are going to offer family-style, we should be prepared for it. I honestly think we were lucky. We got away with it. Next time, we might not be so fortunate. "

"Do upper-echelon establishments offer family dining?" Pierre asked. "I personally have never heard of the concept until the other day when I saw a large chamber pot full of stew going out to a table." He grinned, looking around to see if anyone caught the humor in his last statement.

Gabrielle tried her best to remain neutral while relating her experiences with family dining. "It is popular in less formal, casual establishments and is very popular in the States. When you visit an Asian establishment, meals are always served family-style. Asian cuisine is very popular among Americans. Many of my co-workers like to eat Asian during layovers in Los Angeles, but they will only go if there are four or more people; otherwise, food is wasted."

Maria tried to keep everyone together to make a decision, "We have agreed to restrict Sundays to families only. Why don't we provide family dining to our patrons on Sundays, and of course, upon request?"

"I agree." Rudy countered, "I agree; it's something we should think about and determine if we want to go in that direction. Sundays would be the logical choice to try it out. We have eighteen tables inside and eight outside. How many chamber pots do we think we'll need?" Rudy couldn't help himself and received a kick under the table from his annoyed wife.

Daniel spoke, "You may laugh now, but you will not laugh later. I will be laughing then, and those that laughed, those, everybody will be, will be? I don't know. I have lost my thought."

Gabrielle smiled warmly at Daniel and squeezed his hand, "Everybody will be glad you thought of it."

"Correct. Thank you, Gabrielle," Daniel answered, leaning over to kiss her on the cheek. "I am glad you are a member of my family. I am glad you are my member."

Michelle looked at Gabrielle, who was in the middle of a grimace and spoke, "Sometimes, it's just not worth it. I think I'd just let that one go."

Gabrielle looked back at Michelle and said the words *thank you* without speaking.

Once again, Maria tried to keep the ball rolling, "I will look in the food service catalog and see what is available for serving dishes. We should also get a dozen or so serving bowls for accompaniments and maybe a dozen or so large platters. I am just not sure what we will need. "

Maria then changed the subject, "Did anyone get a good glimpse of Duggart and his group? Is there still the notion that we are being reviewed?"

Pierre spoke first. "I'm suspicious, but at first glance, they seem too relaxed. So, my gut says to be cautious, but my eyes tell me false alarm."

"Daniel, do you have anything to add?" Maria asked.

"Perhaps, but first, is everyone finished with their jokes?" he asked, unusually defensive, even by Daniel's standards.

Maria stepped in, "Daniel, we were only poking fun at you. You know we have nothing but the highest regard and utmost respect for you. Please, we did not mean to insult or belittle you. Please, don't take it that way."

Rudy added, "Daniel, you are my mentor, role model and my uncle. You did something unusual, and it worked. From what I heard, we scored points with those guys. You should be proud of that. Don't get depressed over a little joking by the family. The bottom line: you tried it, and you pulled it off. A lesser man, such as myself, would have folded."

Pierre added, "That's right, Daniel, at the end of the day, we all have to admit, the night was successful if that makes sense?"

"Thank you. Yes, perhaps my ego was black and blue. I don't know why serving in that manner occurred to me, but the group seemed very tense, very uncomfortable. I wanted to do something to bring them together, so I suggested family dining," Daniel admitted.

"I think it worked because the next day, when they came for dinner, they were friendlier and much more relaxed. That is what you did for them," Pierre said, giving a boost to Daniel's suffering self-image.

"It was not just me; everyone helped. That is why we are successful because when we all succeed, when everyone must get to where they are going, everyone crosses the road," Daniel said, smiling but leaving everyone puzzled over what message he was actually attempting to convey.

"Daniel, you have it sort of backward and upside down," Michelle replied.

"What? You think no one helped? You think it was just me who crossed the road? Well, thank you, but no. I think I have it straightforward, not backward." Daniel stubbornly stood his ground.

"Daniel, what is your take on the Duggart party?" Maria, sounding fatigued, tried to get something useful out of the conversation.

"I think they are nice people. Do I think they are here to cause us harm? No. Are they going to review us? I would say no. I agree. They were relaxed, cordial, and looked like they were enjoying themselves. That is not the behavior of reviewers; in my opinion," Daniel stated.

"Well, I thought Claude was certainly pleasant. I hardly spoke to the others. They liked our food, and they seemed to like us." Maria shrugged her shoulders and smiled, "We treated them well, as we do everybody. So, whatever will be, will be."

"That is what I've heard," Daniel added.

* * *

Pierre and Gabrielle continued to visit families in the rural area surrounding the Tree Trunk. Gabrielle was astounded by the quality of the wines. She was correct in her assumption that many families made great wines but didn't bother to bottle because no one had expressed an interest. On more than one occasion, Pierre and Gabrielle were given glasses and served pitchers of the tastiest wine imaginable. This prompted Gabrielle to inquire if it were possible to buy a full cask, not having any idea how to move it to the Tree Trunk or, once there, where it would be stored.

Returning from a successful outing to the countryside, Gabrielle spoke to Pierre. "Pierre, I just want to thank you for allowing me to be part of the family. I know our past is not something either one of us wants to bring up. I want to thank you for being a gentleman and giving me a chance. I sincerely mean that."

Pierre was taken aback by her words and had to pull over. He sat quietly for a moment and then spoke. "We all tend to do something foolish in our youth. The quality of a person should be measured not by the mistakes, but by the corrections; by what a person accomplishes once they realize they're on the wrong path." He looked down at his hands, not knowing what to do with them. He continued with his thought, "The past is gone. What you have accomplished since you arrived has been miraculous. You have made us better. You have shown us how to be professional, and that, more than anything, has made us successful and taken us to the next level. I have only my gratitude to give to you."

The two looked at each other for a moment, just inches apart. To Pierre, she was as beautiful as ever, and her scent, her scent was the scent of a woman, delicious and sensual. To Gabrielle, he was handsome and masculine; she felt her heart pound, she wondered if she could refuse.

The tension, the electricity between the two, grew intense. Without saying a word, Pierre turned back to the road, started his car, and drove on. He opened the window, letting the cool breeze flood the cabin. He spoke again to Gabrielle, "Maybe if we have a good year at the bistro, I'll go out and buy myself a sports car. German or maybe even something Italian."

Gabrielle laughed, the tension gone, relieved that nothing had come between them. "You would look very exciting in a little red two-seater."

Pierre liked what she said. Looking at her and smiling big and broadly, he gave her a wink.

* * *

The weeks went by, and Duggart brought his committee back to Saint

Charles on two different occasions. Each time Daniel had a new trick up his sleeve. He offered cured sardines in grapefruit, a beef filet stuffed with chanterelles, and foie gras. Daniel reprised his braised pig cheeks for the final meal and served a pig brain consommé, this time with shavings of his rare white truffles picked fresh from his cellar garden as a first course.

Gabrielle was able to offer something new each time the committee sat for dinner. She offered Villagrosa's Pinot Noir with lighter meat dishes and Tremont's Bordeaux Blend with heartier dishes. She provided a lovely, sweet late-harvest white from Paul Stephenson with plates of pate' and foie gras. Francois Renaud finally got around to bottling his wine, allowing Gabrielle to pair his hearty, fruity and tannic red with wood-fired oven-roasted meats.

The five committee members raved about the food and the wines and always requested a bottle or two to take back to Paris.

The committee, in the midst of a review, was allowed to share the bottles but forbidden to identify or reveal the origins of these fantastic, well-regarded wines. By the time the committee went into isolation to compose their opinions and ratings, a substantial buzz was circulating through the culinary community as to the source of these magnificent wines.

* * *

The French Culinary Society finally came out of isolation but would not release their ratings and opinions until the official release night, set as September 1.

Louisa was excited. Her uncle would not reveal their opinion of The Tree Trunk. All he would say was, "Everyone enjoyed their experiences there immensely."

Coming from her uncle, she felt it was like the pope saying, 'You've been good.'

Louisa called Michelle to make sure she was planning on watching the show. "Hello, Michelle, Louisa here. How are you, babe?" Louisa said in her quick, shoot-from-the-hip style.

"Hello, Louisa. How have you been?" Michelle answered, still not entirely comfortable talking with Louisa. She kept her guard up.

"Very good, business as usual. But I just wanted to touch base with you. Will you be watching the French Culinary Society Annual Awards on the first?" Louisa inquired.

"I wasn't planning on it," Michelle replied.

"Oh, but you must. You absolutely must. I'll be in the audience. I'll wave to you." Louisa wanted her so badly to watch, but couldn't tell her why, and it was killing her.

"That's funny. Well, the only television we have is the one in the bar, and I'm not sure it works. I don't ever remember it being on," Michelle said, adding, "Maybe I can get Pierre to drive down to Saint Germaine and pick up a new flat screen. I understand they are priced very reasonably."

"Well, whatever you do, you need to watch it. Promise me you will. Daniel and Pierre should too. Everyone should watch it. It's loads of fun, so entertaining. Oops, there's another call. Must run. Ciao, see you on TV," Louisa said excitedly and terminated the call, leaving Michelle a little confused.

Why was it so important that we watch? Just so we can see her on TV. I don't get it? Michelle stood holding the phone, wondering what Louisa was up to.

Later that day, Michelle related her conversation with Louisa to Pierre.

"Well, she is egotistical. "Pierre observed, "I think that is in the realm of her behavior to call people, letting them know she can be seen on TV."

Michelle was not convinced. "I think there's something peculiar. I mean her uncle, three visits, now we must watch this show. Something just doesn't pass the smell test."

"The smell test? What test is that?" Pierre asked for clarification.

"Figure of speech. Don't sweat it," Michelle replied.

"Sweat, smell test? Where is this conversation going?" Pierre said, pretending to be confused and not doing a very good job of hiding his amusement.

"Uncle, please," Michelle replied, annoyed at being her uncle's source of humor.

"Well, ok, if it allows you to pass the smell test, I'll drive over to Saint Germaine and pick up a flat screen. I hear they all work with the internet these days," Pierre said, thinking he wouldn't mind watching the show.

"Good, thank you," Michelle answered abruptly, still wondering what's up with Louisa but now understanding how Daniel could get so upset.

* * *

The first of September was a Monday night. The bistro was closed, allowing the entire family and staff to gather around the flat screen. Pierre had bought the largest screen available. The screen was so large there was no place to set it up except in the main dining room.

With much fanfare, the show began. Music played as the cameras took in a large stage with a single podium slightly off to the side. The music stopped, and the audience broke into applause. Suddenly, from behind the curtain in the center of the stage, Claude Duggart appeared. Wearing a tuxedo with a white dinner jacket, he smiled, bowed to the audience, and calmly walked over to the podium, like he'd done many times before.

Pierre was first to remark, "Michelle, wasn't it you who used to say trust your gut? I should have trusted mine."

Maria, in a pseudo-state of shock from watching the elderly, affable gentleman she knew as Claude walk confidently across the stage, remarked, "Well, he certainly looks dashing in his tuxedo."

"Well, what can they say? We did everything right. If they criticize us, then you know this is all phony." Rudy added.

Michelle, always the sarcastic one, said, "Well, they could say here is an establishment that had the audacity to serve its main course in a chamber pot."

"Please, don't remind me," Rudy countered, a bit deflated.

Claude began speaking with an air of authority as if he alone determined the outcome. "Ladies and gentlemen, welcome to The French Culinary Society Award Show. My name is Claude Duggart." Claude paused and waited for the applause to subside.

"Tonight, you will witness many surprises. You will see joy as individual hard work pays off. You will see heartbreak, as others' lack of attention to detail causes them to return to square one."

Daniel, missing half of Claude's opening remarks while fetching another glass of cognac and not really paying attention anyway, glanced at the large flat screen as he walked by, declaring, "I know this guy. I have seen him someplace recently."

Claude continued after another round of applause, "Finally, you, the audience, will witness what has never happened before in history, as we pay tribute to an establishment, a group of people, that have accomplished what we all hope one day to accomplish. That is, to combine a wonderful, perfect culinary experience with the fond memories of friends and family being together. Let's begin."

To everyone at the Tree Trunk, the show seemed to go on and on. Awards were given, ratings were removed, and tears flowed. After a while, Michelle, Pierre, Rudy, and all the others became immune to the endless demonstrations of extreme emotion.

Michelle wondered out loud, "Why was it so important to Louisa that we watch this?"

Rudy added, "Really, this is starting to get very tedious."

"Starting? My mind began to wander when Claude said Good Evening," Pierre fumed.

Daniel, on his third or fourth cognac, accompanied by approximately the same amount of tarts, said between mouthfuls, "I agree. When is this over?"

Finally, Claude came to the podium. The lights dimmed, the curtains pulled back, displaying a large screen. Shown on the screen was a recently taken picture of the main entrance to the Tree Trunk. The sign mounted on the wall, just to the left of the door, was clearly visible: 'Welcome to The Tree Trunk Bistro.'

"Ladies and gentlemen, I know it has been a long, emotionally draining evening, but I must share with you something special," Claude stated.

"Uninvited, and of course, unbeknownst to the staff, the committee visited a lovely little village called Saint Charles en Liberte and an establishment with an unusual name, 'The Tree Trunk Bistro.'"

Michelle suddenly woke from semi-sleep, "He's talking about us. That's us, look!"

Everyone suddenly perked up. Pierre was flabbergasted, "My word, thank God I was wearing my maroon tux, though, I do like his dinner jacket."

Claire looked at Rudy, "See, I told you. You never know. You should always look your best."

"You are right; you never know," Rudy admitted.

Claire tousled Rudy's hair, "You need a haircut. You still do."

Claude continued, "The Committee visited on three occasions, as is our custom when reviewing an establishment. We felt it uncanny, the consistency of service, the ease with which the staff provided for us, their guests, and the sincerity they displayed when serving us. They made the entire committee feel special, as if the evening was entirely ours."

"But this, after all, is about our culinary experience. The committee was profoundly impressed with what we were served. The flavors were unique yet played off the fresh, natural flavors of the ingredients. The use of exotic spices and aromatics was intriguing and added depth, compelling us to taste again and again. A chef would be hard-pressed to better match the food and flavorings, even if the ingredients stood up and offered you instructions," Claude admitted.

"That's what you must do. You must develop a rapport with your ingredients. Let them tell you what to add or what not to add. It is that simple," Daniel said, asking, "Would anyone care for a cognac?"

Maria spoke up, "I need a stiff drink, please, Daniel. I'll take a double."

Pierre added, "I'll take the same."

Michelle stood up and stretched while yawning, "I have a feeling this is going to be some night. I hate to let everyone drink alone. I'll give you a hand."

Daniel and Michelle walked off to the bar to fetch cognacs while everyone sat mesmerized by Claude's speech.

"Nevertheless, the food was exquisite, the flavors wonderful, the presentations simple, elegant, and to the point. Daniel Villeneuve, the Head Chef, must be commended for his bold and imaginative remaking of traditional bistro fare. Everything from the fantasy bread to the lovely, flavorful dessert tarts made the committee yearn for more. Again, my compliments to the chef."

Claude did not let up. "The wines served were expertly selected by the most gracious and well-spoken sommelier I have ever encountered. Gabrielle accurately selected and described what she was pouring, allowing us to place our full trust in her judgment. If I were a soldier and she were my general, I would follow her anywhere without hesitation."

Speaking of wine, the wines themselves were impeccable, delicious, and, as I have mentioned, perfectly matched our various courses. Villagrosa, Renaud, Stephenson, and Fawcett are names that every lover of fine wine should become familiar with; I believe they soon will.

"Lastly, I must mention one of the warmest, genuinely kind hosts we have ever had the pleasure of meeting. A woman who exemplifies France and its ideals, Madame Maria Villeneuve. Madame, if you are listening, and I hope you are, promise me, nothing at the Tree Trunk will ever change, including you. I say this for all on the committee. We have all fallen madly in love with you and your wonderful establishment. Thank you for being you," Claude said, pulling a handkerchief from his pocket to dry his eyes.

Claude straightened up, and, once again, his voice took on a serious, all-business tone. "The Society has been in existence for over 200 years and during that time has never awarded more than three stars. "

A murmur went out over the crowd, anticipating that something unusual was about to happen.

Claude paused and then continued. "Members of the committee, then and now, simply could not justify it, believing four or five stars implied perfection, an unattainable goal better left to a philosopher's imagination." Claude slowed his cadence, adding drama to his speech and forcing people to hang on to each and every word.

He looked out at the audience and, with sincerity and confidence, spoke straight into the cameras. "For the first time in our history, we believe we have found perfection. On behalf of the French Culinary Society, the Committee honors the Tree Trunk Bistro, by unanimous vote, awarding it five stars."

The audience went wild, cheering, jumping to their feet, and applauding. Claude finally calmed the audience and simply said, "Congratulations to all the award winners. Thank you for your continued patronage. Good Night." He then walked off the stage, as calmly as he had walked on hours before.

It was very quiet at the Tree Trunk. Everyone who sat watching the presentation in the main dining room was stunned, shocked, and unable to comprehend what had just occurred. Michelle stood up as if in a dream, walked over, and turned off the device. She calmly turned to Pierre, "Nice picture. Was it expensive?"

Pierre sat with a blank look on his face. "What? No, I don't want any coffee."

Maria, also expressionless and in a daze, said to no one in particular, "It doesn't matter. We're closed tomorrow."

Gabrielle looked dumbstruck. "Shall we go look for more wine? We'll need more wine."

Daniel, half asleep, came out of his cognac-induced stupor, "What? Is it over? Did I miss it? What happened?"

Pierre spoke, calmly and slowly, not moving his head, staring into the fireplace, "Yes, you missed it."

"What happened?" Daniel asked.

"We won." Pierre answered.

Daniel asked again, "Won what?"

"Five stars," Pierre said, still staring into the fire.

Daniel, not realizing what five stars implied, stood and shouted, "What? Those pigs. We should have received better. I think we need to protest this decision. I am a little more than just a bit perturbed. Yes, I am a whole lot more than just a bit perturbed."

Rudy exhaled and lamented, "I think we are in for trouble, lots of trouble."

Daniel, still oblivious to reality, shouted, "No, we are not in trouble. They are."

Pierre, slowly coming around, agreed, "No, Rudy is right, we have trouble coming our way, big trouble. Our world is about to change."

Michelle ran to answer the phone. She could be heard through the open doors to the Inn's lobby. "Good evening. Why, yes, hello? Yes, it is. Yes, sir. Yes, sir, I am not sure. It's a very large party. Yes, sir. I am not sure. Yes, sir. Please give me a moment while I check."

Michelle came walking slowly, tentatively back to the dining room, announcing, "It's the social secretary to the President. He wants to know if the President can host a dinner for foreign dignitaries here at the Tree Trunk in two weeks. He wants to know when we could get him a menu and if there's a place to land a helicopter."

Maria asked, "A dinner? For how many?"

Michelle replied, "He said at least 125, but possibly 150."

In the background, Daniel could be heard asking, "President of what, helicopters?"

The End

www.ingramcontent.com/pod-product-compliance
Lightning Source LLC
Chambersburg PA
CBHW050122030726
47505CB00007B/1995